When **Lauren Canan** began writing, stories of romance and unbridled passion flowed through her fingers onto the page. Today she is a multi-award-winning author, including the prestigious Romance Writers of America Golden Heart® Award. She lives in Texas with her own real-life hero, two crazy dogs and a mouthy parrot named Bird. Find her on Facebook or visit her website, laurencanan.com.

Four-time RITA® Award nominee **Joanne Rock** has penned over seventy stories for Mills & Boon. An optimist by nature and a perpetual seeker of silver linings, Joanne finds romance fits her life outlook perfectly—love is worth fighting for. A Golden Heart® Award recipient, she has won numerous awards for her stories. Learn more about Joanne's imaginative muse by visiting her website, joannerock.com, or following @joannerock6 on Twitter.

Also by Lauren Canan

Also by Joanne Rock

Discover more at millsandboon.co.uk

STRANGER
IN HIS BED

LAUREN CANAN

This book is dedicated to Terry:
the one who keeps me going. I couldn't write
without your inspiration and encouragement.

And to Kathy Douglass,
the best critique partner you could ever hope for.
Thank you for all you've done for me!

And many thanks to my editor,
Charles Griemsman. Bless you for your brilliant
guidance and for having the patience of a saint.

One

"I think she's awake."

As her vision cleared, the most beautiful pair of eyes she'd ever seen came into focus. They were a vibrant brown with so many flecks of gold they appeared to gleam. Framed by dark lashes, they were strong, compelling, and she couldn't look away. She didn't want to look away. It was as though they offered a lifeline and she desperately held on.

Her gaze widened to take in the rest of this man's face. The sharp angles and high cheekbones. The full, sensuous lips, drawn into a straight line, surrounded by a dark bearded shadow. His thick, tobacco-brown hair gleamed golden where the fluorescent lights touched it.

A second man in a white lab coat stepped into her field of vision on the opposite side of the bed.

"I'm Dr. Meadows, your neurologist." He spoke softly, clearly. Something she was grateful for.

The glaring white lights overhead burned with the same intensity as the sun. The pounding in her head became more pronounced, almost overwhelming, throbbing in time with her heartbeat.

"You were involved in an automobile accident two days ago. You had some injuries. Most were minor, but you did sustain a fairly bad concussion."

The doctor withdrew a pencil-sized flashlight from the pocket of his lab coat and pointed the light quickly into one eye, then the other. She couldn't help flinching as the beam touched her eyes. He returned the light to his pocket and flipped open a chart. After sifting through an array of pastel-colored pages, he made a notation on one of them before closing the folder.

"Can you tell me your name?"

"I'm… My name is…" She drew a blank. *How can I not know my own name? How is it possible?* Confusion added to her pain. "I don't know," she whispered almost to herself. A feeling of panic slowly crept in.

"Do you know who that man is?" The doctor nodded toward the stranger.

Once again she took in his features, the solemn face that was so full of character, the deep jaw and those eyes, so mesmerizing. But nothing about him was at all familiar.

"No." She slowly rolled her head against the pillow. "Should I?"

"I'm Wade," the man said, his deep voice conveying strength. "Wade Masters. I'm your husband."

Husband? She was married? The stunned disbelief must have shown in her eyes, because Wade Masters's expression turned into a frown of serious contemplation, and his eyes snapped across to the doctor. No. That couldn't be right. Could it? She raised a hand to her forehead. Frantically she searched her mind for any memory of a wedding. Of him. Of them. Of their life together.

Nothing.

"I don't know you." She heard the emotional quiver in her own voice. "I'm not married. How can you say that?"

Alarm set in, adding to the pounding in her head. This was all wrong. They had the wrong person. They thought she was someone else. She had to get up. She had to leave. She had to go home. Grabbing the railing at the side of the bed, she tried to pull herself into a sitting position. Hands immediately pushed her gently back down onto the pillow. "No. Please. I need to go home. I need to call..." *Who? Who was she going to call?* She couldn't think. Her head hurt. Everything hurt, and she had no memory of the person she was or the life she had known.

She heard the doctor call for a nurse. "Try to relax, Mrs. Masters," he said. "You're going to be fine. Your home is waiting when you regain your strength. You took a pretty hard knock on the head. Try not to worry if you can't remember people or names, including your own. With this type of injury, retrograde amnesia is not at all uncommon. I'm confident everything will come back to you in time."

"When?" She felt a tear slip down the side of her face. "When will it come back?"

"Unfortunately, we have no way of knowing how any one individual will react. Occasionally a memory may come to you as a kind of flashback. Then you may start to remember everything all at once, or it may come back in small fragments, like random pieces of a jigsaw puzzle. It could return tomorrow or months from now."

Months? No. She had to remember. There was something important she had to do. People were counting on her. She sensed a need to hurry. But the more she tried to recall the circumstances, the harder the hammer slammed into her head.

"Your tests have come back and everything is looking very good." The neurologist continued flipping through forms in her chart. "The cerebral swelling is all but gone. Your heart sounds good. Blood pressure is within a normal range. If no other concerns surface, we can talk about sending you home tomorrow." He looked from the chart directly to her.

A nurse bustled in. She injected medication into the intravenous tubing. "This should take effect in just a few minutes. I'll be back to check on you, sweetie." She nodded at the two men and left the room as quickly as she'd come in.

As I mentioned to your husband," the doctor said, "there is a good chance being in familiar surroundings will stimulate the return of your memory."

Her husband. She returned her gaze to the tall man with broad shoulders who stood to her left, watching her in silent consideration. He was dressed in a dark business suit, his blue-and-gold-striped tie loosened at the neck, the top button of his white dress shirt undone. Her gaze fell on his hands, which were resting on the metal bar of the bed. They looked strong and capable. A gold wedding band gleamed on the third finger of his left hand.

She swallowed back the fear that something was terribly wrong.

"We will get through this. You're going to be okay." The man leaned down, bringing his face closer to hers. His hand covered her own, and the warmth felt good. His voice was as deep and seductive as his eyes were mesmerizing. "If there is anything you need…"

"Please tell me who I am."

"Your name is Victoria. Victoria Masters."

The man stood up straight, appearing relaxed and self-assured, and slipped his hands into the pockets of his trousers. She realized her initial impression that he was attractive had been an understatement.

He was *devastatingly* attractive.

She could smell his rich, enticing cologne. His white shirt set off his tan skin. The sharp lines of his face and the straight, proud nose were indicative of good breeding. His hair with its slight wave hung just past his collar and shadowed his forehead. The golden intensity of his eyes and the lack of a smile on those full, sensuous lips brought it all together: Wade Masters was the personification of danger. Not dangerous like a criminal, but dangerous like a man who was capable of stirring a woman's passion with little to no effort. And he knew it. It was part of that confidence he emitted.

And he was here to take her home.

With his gaze trained on her, she felt a heated blush rush up her neck and over her face. The barest hint of a smile touched his lips as though he knew what she was thinking. She looked away, swallowing hard.

The doctor interrupted her thoughts. "Right now, I don't want you to worry about memory recall. Try to relax and give it some time."

She felt the drug the nurse had given start to take effect and her eyelids grew heavy. She fought to keep them open, wanting to know more about the man who claimed to be her husband.

Dr. Meadows turned toward him. "I want to see her in two weeks. Have someone contact my office and set up an appointment. If she develops any dizziness, vomiting or severe headaches, bring her back to the ER immediately." He looked at his patient. "Bed rest for a day, then you can move around, but go slowly. No hundred-meter hurdles for at least a week." He winked at her, then smiled.

"Okay." She couldn't help but return his smile.

"You folks have a good day." He handed Wade his card. "If you should have any questions, don't hesitate to call."

"Thank you, Dr. Meadows," she said as the good doctor disappeared out the door and down the hall. Her gaze returned to the other man. She felt a wave of anxiety shimmy down her spine. She was alone with this person, this man who claimed to be her husband. She still didn't recognize anything about him. There was nothing in his voice or the way he moved that was remotely familiar. For all his sex appeal, he seemed cold, unfeeling. Would she have married a man like that? Apparently so. Surely there was something about him or about their situation that would register?

There were so many questions she wanted to ask. She felt as though she was standing on the edge of a precipice, about to plunge down into the dark depths of the unknown. Could she do this? Evidently there was only one way to find out.

He had not made any other move to touch her. No hug. No kiss—even on the cheek. In fact, she'd received more compassion from the doctor and nurse than from the man who said he was her husband. Maybe he was just holding back because he knew she had no recollection of him? If that was the case, she appreciated his thoughtfulness. If not, they obviously had a major problem within their marriage and one she could do nothing about until her memory returned. She hoped, yet again, that would happen soon. In the meantime, she had to speculate about what would be asked of her. What would her husband expect?

The pain in her head and body began to fade, and before she could ask another question, she returned to the comfort of oblivion.

Wade Masters stood motionless as he watched Victoria fall back to sleep. She'd been monitored closely for the swelling in her brain and tested often to ensure no veins in her head ruptured from the building pressure. Today, when he'd received the call that she seemed to be regaining consciousness, he'd come to the hospital immediately. This, after having to cut short a business trip to London when he'd first heard of the accident.

He hadn't been prepared for the news of her amnesia. Or the fear he'd seen in her eyes, the way her gaze had held his as though his strength was the only thing holding her together. She'd looked at him with desperation and a silent cry for help, and he'd not been able to stop himself from wanting to make everything better. It had to be tough to wake up in a hospital and not remember your own name or what happened to put you there.

He was equally surprised the snobbishness she normally wore like a shield was gone. She tended to walk a fine line between arrogant and outright rude. But instead of demanding answers from the doctor, she'd asked questions with true concern and a hint of anguish in her voice. Still, she might not have the strength to be demanding. Perhaps it was all the pain and medication. Whatever the cause, something had changed. It was more than the cracked ribs and head injury. He had come here anticipating the worst, expecting he would have to deal with her demanding behavior. Instead, he encountered a woman who was frightened and wasn't afraid to let that anxiety show.

And the way she appeared now, without a half ton of

makeup covering her face and her hair in disarray, she looked amenable and, in a strange way, actually more attractive than usual. Despite the bruising from the accident, she was a very beautiful woman.

But she was fastidious about the way she looked. The hospital staff had better keep any mirrors well away from her until she healed or be prepared to bear her wrath and interminable temper. They all had better relish this peaceful time. The true Victoria would be back soon enough.

It was too bad, because she had so much to offer. If only she would get a grip, stop being so superficial and entitled, and set goals for her future.

With one last glance at the woman sleeping in the bed, he grabbed his briefcase from the chair and walked out into the corridor. As he approached the row of elevators, his mind was spinning. He had to get a handle on how to deal with this. Maybe Dave Renner, his attorney, could shed some light on what the hell he should do now. The documents to end this sham marriage had been prepared and were awaiting Victoria's signature. They had both agreed to a settlement offer. In a matter of days he would have been free of her and all the baggage that came with her, including the outrageously snooty and often flamboyant behavior.

He would have been free of this woman who was his wife in name only.

His jaw clenched in frustration. He knew there was no easy answer. In fact, there was only one answer. Take her home when she was released and care for her until she completely recovered. He shook his head at the unbelievable twist of fate.

Wade was glad Victoria would eventually be okay. He certainly wished her no ill will. He'd had his secretary clear his calendar for the next few weeks so he could remain close until she was better. Anything she needed would be provided. But he couldn't help but speculate if she would keep the amnesia thing going even if her memory returned. Her ability to maintain a lie was one of her best attributes. It was why he'd chosen her.

He pressed the elevator call button, still grinding his teeth. Their arrangement had been intended to benefit them both, giving her a much-sought entry into Dallas's inner circles and providing him with the facade of being a settled family man, which worked to his advantage in business negotiations. It had also been intended to eliminate unwanted emotions and potential complications found in a real marriage, something he had neither the time nor the patience to deal with. Those complications had been replaced by new ones, but at least it had provided him the freedom to come and go as he deemed necessary, and of late *go* seemed the option that worked best. The less time he spent in her company, the better.

Eight months after signing the agreement that bound him to her as her husband, she'd begun to be seen with various men out in public, often making the gossip columns, effectively negating the very purpose for which he'd needed her, causing all the carefully staged efforts to blow up in his face. After she'd ignored repeated requests for discretion, her actions had continued, albeit on a lesser scale, but enough that he was still not happy, especially when it had begun to negatively affect his business dealings and made him appear the fool, which he would not permit. Victoria had scoffed and asked him if he really expected her to live like a nun. He'd assured her that was not his intention. What he did demand was discretion. He'd reminded her of her desire for social esteem and warned she was about to lose all she'd set out to achieve. She'd ignored him, deciding to call his bluff.

Other measures had to be taken. He had thought she was intelligent enough to know he would not allow this to go on, and she had pushed him as far as he would tolerate. The bottom line: she was an employee paid to act the part of his wife, and had been compensated very well for that effort. In addition, if she had lived up to the terms, she would have received a million-dollar settlement at the end of a year. Now less than a week away from being free of her, she'd had this accident.

He drew in a breath and blew it out as the doors to the elevator opened. He was stuck with an impetuous, ill-tempered wife in name only, who would most likely milk this amnesia thing for all it was worth. He fought to control his temper.

He needed to call his brothers Cole and Chance, who resided in Calico Springs on the Masters family compound. He hadn't spoken to either of them since his flight had landed. He supposed he should call Victoria's mother, too, to tell her she'd be out of the hospital soon. But all Corrine was really worried about was herself and ensuring her rank at the top of the social food chain lasted a while longer. And really, wasn't that all that mattered? He scoffed at the woman's preposterous behavior. If one of his brothers had been injured, he would not have stayed home and requested a daily update. He would be there at the hospital, not waiting for a phone call. His brothers would do the same. They showed up for each other. He almost felt sorry for Victoria. After being raised by that woman, it was no wonder she acted the way she did.

Bracing himself, he speed-dialed Corrine's number and headed for the side entrance door of the hospital, where his car and driver waited.

Two

As the doctor had promised, a nurse arrived at her room with a wheelchair the next afternoon. Victoria had requested that the flowers she'd received be given to other patients who might not have family. She didn't recognize the names on any of the cards anyway. Her clothing had been discarded when she had been first brought into the ER. Her husband had arranged for some loungewear to be delivered.

They headed toward the front entrance, the nurse pushing the wheelchair, Wade following. As they cleared the automatic glass doors to the outside, she embraced the warm afternoon air and the sounds of normal life all around her. It was summer, the trees were green and plants in full bloom, the colors so bold it was hard to take it all in.

What had she been doing before the accident? Where had she been going when she was hit? She turned her gaze from the flowers to focus on where they were headed now. Directly in front of her was a champagne-colored stretch limo waiting in the circular drive.

"Oh, my gosh," she uttered in complete surprise when two men stepped out. A driver and a *bodyguard*? One came around the car to open the rear passenger door for her. She looked up at her husband. "Is this yours?"

"It is."

"Seriously? I don't think I've ever been in a limo before. Maybe at a funeral…"

Wade smiled. "Actually, you have ridden in a limousine many times, but, since you don't remember, let's hope you enjoy this ride like it's your first. And we will certainly steer clear of any cemeteries."

He placed his hand under her arm and gently helped her stand and take three steps to the limo. Once inside, she leaned back against the rich leather seat and inhaled the new-car scent. Closing the door, Wade walked to the other side and got in next to her. Seconds later, they were off.

The scent of his cologne, distinctly masculine with hints of spices and sandalwood, blended with the rich smell of the leather upholstery. It was a heady aroma.

"Do you need the temperature adjusted?" he asked. "Are you comfortable?"

"I'm fine. It feels strange to be outside again. Good. But strange."

He nodded as though he understood.

"We're near Dallas, aren't we?"

"Yes. You remember Dallas?"

She pointed at the window to his left. "I recognize the skyline."

He nodded.

"How long have we known each other? Where did we meet?"

He seemed to hesitate, looking out the window before turning to face her. "We met at a party. Several years ago."

She again let her eyes fall on this man who was positively dripping in sex appeal. It seemed too much to accept he was her husband. He fell into the category of something too good to be true. And didn't that usually turn out to be right? But she would run with it while it lasted. Until her memory returned, there was little else she could do.

"Let me guess," she said with a smile. "You saw me from across the room and couldn't take your eyes off me. It was love at first sight, right?"

He appeared amused. Amused was good. Better than the deadpan stare that was all she'd seen so far.

"You made...an unforgettable impression. As you are now."

That shot the nurse had given her this morning must have been the cause of her runaway mouth. She wanted to giggle for no apparent reason. But maybe that was normal in her circumstances? She took a deep breath and tried for sincerity.

"How long have we been married?"

"Almost eight months."

"Practically newlyweds. Maybe that's why I can't remember you."

"Possibly, but not likely."

She had to agree. Short of an injury like hers, how could she ever forget loving and being loved by a man like Wade Masters? "What do you do? Like, for a living?"

"I have a business. Actually, it's a family business."

"Let me guess." She gave a tiny snort. "You make pizza, and this is the delivery van?"

Again those eyebrows shot up, and the tiny smile returned.

"Close. Avionics, electronics, ranching, Masco Laboratories... I'm sure there must be a Domino's Pizza in there somewhere." The gleam was back in his eyes as he tilted his head. "Are you hungry?"

"Yes. No. Depends on what you've got."

Again he turned toward her, giving her a look of surprise. She hadn't meant it the way he might have taken it, but she couldn't stop the blush that crawled up her neck. She was hungry, all right. Hungry for knowledge; starving for memories, good or bad. And if he didn't curb that sexy hint of a smile, she would be well on her way to hungry for him. Who was this guy? How in the hell had she met and married a man like Wade Masters? It didn't feel right. But at the moment it didn't feel all that wrong.

"There will be a wide selection when we arrive at the house. You can eat at your leisure." His voice rolled over her, deep and solemn as he readjusted in his seat. "I'm certain we can meet any needs you might have."

"Anything?"

He smiled a wide, unpretentious smile. "I'm fairly certain we can keep you well satisfied."

What needs would she have? More important, what needs would *he* have, and what expectations would he have of her? She could see him pulling her into his arms and carrying her to a large bed in a master suite for a night of... *Oh, God.* Moaning softly, she closed her eyes and rubbed her forehead. What was it about this guy that made her thoughts run straight to the gutter? One quick sideways glance and she saw him smirking. Did he read minds? At least he had a sense of humor. While she couldn't explain it, she couldn't see herself marrying someone who didn't. That was the most important thing. It was what got you through everything else in life.

Gathering herself, she raised her chin and straightened her shoulders. "Do I have any brothers or sisters?" *A safe topic.*

"No. As far as I know, only your mother and father." He pulled a cell from his inner suit pocket, glanced at the screen, then put it back. "I have spoken to Corinne daily since the accident. I'm sure she would like to hear your voice. You might want to give her a call."

"Corinne? Is that my mother's name?"

"It is."

"Sounds like some sort of bleach."

Wade ran a hand over his mouth and jaw as though he didn't know what to make of that one.

A mother. And a father. Add two more people to the list of folks she just didn't remember.

A memory suddenly surged through her mind accompanied by dull pain. She was standing just outside the front door of a redbrick house, a blonde woman hugging her. They were both crying. But it didn't feel like it was her mother.

This memory loss was absolutely the worst thing she'd ever been through. At least that she could remember. The other injuries from the collision took a back seat by comparison.

The rest of the drive passed in quiet contemplation. Who was Wade Masters? Where were they going? She didn't sense anything sinister about him except maybe a wicked sense of humor. In spite of him being well above normal in the looks department, he was well mannered and courteous, not snobbish, at least not that she'd picked up on. Granted, she'd seen him only two times—that she could recall—but, while he was apparently wealthy, he

didn't give the impression he held himself in higher esteem than anyone else. Neither did he seem like a happily married man. She would have expected him to hold
her, kiss her or give reassurances. *Something.* But he remained aloof. Polite to a fault, but distant.

Eventually the limo turned into a driveway, coming
to a stop in front of tall black wrought-iron gates. They
opened immediately and the car proceeded up the hill
and to the right where a circular drive dipped under a
high portico. She had a strong suspicion it was the larg-
est house she'd ever seen. A mansion complete with tur-
rets that made it look more like a castle than a house.

"Is this where you live?" The sheer colossal size of it
required confirmation.

He nodded as the driver opened his door. "This is
where *we* live."

She leaned toward the window and glanced up at the
top of one of the towers, then back to her husband. "I
guess the ghosts don't come out until night."

He looked at her with surprise. One eyebrow lifted
higher than the other, and then he once again pursed his
lips as though hiding a smile. "I guarantee it. And if you
become frightened, I'll be close by."

She didn't think she was a negative person, but if the
good doctor hoped coming to live in this place was going
to stir any memories, he was sadly mistaken. She might
not remember a ride in a limo, but no way would she forget living in a castle.

Yet apparently that was exactly what she'd done.

Her door opened, and a man held out his hand to help
her out of the car and into a waiting wheelchair. "Welcome home, madam," the man said and attempted a
smile. Two other men, clearly security, waited on either
side of the front door.

The ground floor of the mansion, at least what she could see en route to the elevator, was amazing. Pure elegance even a visiting royal would appreciate. They wheeled through the marble and glass foyer, then slipped by the huge living room to the right and a dining room that could easily seat four dozen people on the left. Beyond was the kitchen. She smiled and waved at the staff who had come out to welcome her home. They looked at each other in surprise. One hesitantly waved back. Before she could ponder that odd reaction, she, Wade and the attendant who pushed her wheelchair were inside of a small elevator, and for the first time, she caught a glimpse of herself in the mirrored walls.

There were few words that could describe the reflected image. *Horrible* was one. *Appalling* was another. It was so not her. Her hair hung in long, limp tendrils. Her face was still pretty banged up, although the bruises were fading to a relatively nondescript yellow. Her left eye was bloodshot, and she could see a slight, almost healed cut on her bottom lip. The swelling was going down. She patted her face. Overall, she looked like she'd been in one whale of a fight and had not been on the winning side.

There was a soft *ding*, and the doors opened onto a wide corridor, the floor inlaid with beautiful white and gold-embossed marble tiles. The attendant wheeled the chair to the right and followed the hallway almost to the end, finally turning into a large bedroom. It was done in pastels, primarily in varying shades of green. Very nice. Very soothing. Very bland.

"Does this suite suit your needs?" Wade asked from the open doorway.

"Yes. It's great," she replied. "It's…big." The spacious room had a separate sitting area on the far end, with comfy-looking chairs surrounding a fireplace. French doors opened onto a huge terrace. There was even a bar with a small fridge. A luxurious bed with silk wrappings completed the effect.

"Do...you...stay in here as well?"

He watched her almost as though he was measuring the question, and she thought she saw a spark of devious temptation flash in his eyes. "No. My suite is next door."

A feeling of relief rolled through her. At the same time, it struck her as odd that a newly wedded couple would have separate bedrooms. More than likely he was letting her have her own room, thus giving her space and time to readjust rather than push her to move directly into the master suite. And she was grateful. She wasn't ready to share a bed with a strange man despite her attraction. And regardless of any marriage certificate that might say otherwise, he *was* a stranger.

Standing up from the wheelchair, she walked around the room, looking at the paintings and art objects decorating the space. Most of the paintings were by renowned artists, some of which she recognized. There were pictures of flower gardens and old ivy-covered stone walls and gates.

"Either you or your designer has very good taste."

"You know art?"

She shrugged. "I recognize Monet and Barber. And I guess I know what I like."

"Do you?"

She pivoted around to face him. Her heart skipped a beat at the look of sensuous suggestion on his face, in his voice. She had the distinct impression he wasn't talking about fine art. Was he flirting with her? Establishing his claim? Or had her imagination overtaken her common sense? Still...he was her husband. Maybe he was reminding her of that fact.

Not sure how to respond, she turned to look at the painting hanging over the mantel. A little girl with long reddish-blond curls stood in the corner of her room, presumably being punished for something she'd done. Her dog, a little brown terrier, stood guard against anyone who would come near his child. A name flashed through her mind. *Murphy.* She turned to Wade. "Is... Murphy here?"

A sharp frown met her question. "Who?"

"Murphy."

The gracious warmth of his welcome instantly turned to icy cold foreboding. "There is no one named Murphy in this house."

His clipped reply indicated she'd struck a nerve. But why? Who was Murphy? Why did she remember that name when there was no face to go with it?

"I have work I need to take care of. Henry, our chef, put a menu next to the phone. I have taken the liberty of arranging your first meal based on the foods you generally like. If it isn't acceptable to you, feel free to order something else. Call the number on the bottom of the menu once you've made your selection."

"That was very thoughtful. Thank you."

"Your mother's phone number is on your bedside table in case you don't remember it." With a sharp nod, he left the room, closing the door behind him.

What was that all about? She had no idea why simply asking about a name would cause such a change in behavior. His sudden hostility caused regret to surge through her. Apparently there was someone named Murphy who stood between them. It wasn't a good feeling. How could she remember that name and not remember her own husband? A numbing chill slid over her. Was another man the reason Wade had acted so distant?

A soft knock on her door brought her out of her worried contemplation.

"Yes? Come in."

The door opened to a stout young woman in a nondescript black dress and shoes.

"Excuse me? Mrs. Masters? I'm not sure if you will remember me. I am Rowena. Roe. Mr. Masters asked me to assist you with anything you need."

"Oh. That's very thoughtful. Thank you, but I'm fine."

The maid hesitated before saying, "I hope you feel better very soon." Then she backed out of the door.

"Roe?"

"Yes, ma'am?"

"I think… Could I change my mind? Would you mind helping me draw a bath?"

"Yes, of course, ma'am. I'd be happy to." She hurried past Victoria and disappeared into the bathroom.

Victoria ventured into the huge closet while Roe started the bath. It was lined with clothing for every occasion. Many garments still had the price tag attached; others were still in the designer's bag. Shoes filled one wall, and in the built-in bureau, there was lingerie in every style and color.

She was a clothes hog. It looked like she'd bought more clothing than she would need in a year. Maybe two.

"Your bath is ready, Mrs. Masters."

"Thank you." She smiled at Roe. "You're very kind."

That earned her a surprised, wide-eyed stare from the housekeeper. "Thank you, ma'am."

Grabbing a robe, she ventured toward the elegant powder room, then on to the beautiful marbled bathroom. The oversize jetted tub couldn't have been more appealing if it had been edged in twenty-four-carat gold. Across the room, a glass shower large enough to hold five looked equally tempting. But right now, she wanted to soak away the hospital smell. The dull ache in her head persisted, but hopefully the warm water would take care of it. Soon she was lying back, eyes closed, as the hot jets of water massaged away the soreness from her bruised body. She grabbed the liquid soap she'd selected from a wide array of bath salts, soaps and shampoos in a cabinet. Soon she was inhaling the wonderful exotic scent and enjoying the sense of cleanliness it offered.

When her fingers began to get pruny, she knew it was time to get out. After toweling dry, she slipped on the fluffy white robe. She found both a comb and a brush, plus a new toothbrush and some toothpaste in one of the drawers. Standing in front of the large mirror, she combed the tangles from her long dark hair.

As she looked at her reflection, a feeling of unease passed through her. Something was off. It was probably just the bruises and cut lip. She turned her face to the side. Maybe some swelling remained. "Stop it!" she muttered to her reflection. She had enough to worry about without adding to it.

"Are you all right, Mrs. Masters?" Roe called from the bedroom.

Excellent question. Placing the comb back in the drawer, Victoria headed to the bedroom. With the succulent smell of the food being wheeled into the room, she let the internal quandary go for now.

As good as the food looked and tasted, she did little more than sample a couple of the dishes. Her appetite had disappeared along with any positive hopes that coming here—coming *home*—would rekindle her memory. So far, all it had served to do was add more unknowns to the growing list. She felt tired and melancholy. Her husband's earlier reaction to her inquiry about the name stirred apprehension. Everything she thought she would find here was still missing. In fact, she had an overwhelming sensation that she didn't belong here. In this house. She couldn't explain it, but the feeling was strong.

After the food cart had been removed, she found a clean nightgown, pulled back the covers and sat down on the bed. She really should call her mother. Even though she didn't remember her.

Finding the number written on a sticky note, she placed the call.

"Hello?" a woman answered.

"Hi, Mom. Mother." *What did she call her?* "It's me, Victoria." There was an obvious pause on the other end.

"Oh, my dear. You don't sound at all like yourself. Are you still in the hospital?"

"No. No, I'm at home."

Another pause. "Are you telling me that man dumped you off at his house and left? That might be a cause of action for abandonment or mental distress. You really should speak with Burt as soon as possible."

What was she talking about? "Uh... Wade has been with me the entire time. He's still here."

"Oh. Well, we will just have to think of something else. Sooner or later Wade Masters will screw up and he'll pay for it dearly, if you get my drift. If you can find a private moment, it wouldn't hurt to call Burt anyway. Maybe he can think of another angle."

An angle? For what? "Who's Burt?"

"Why, your attorney. How could you not remember *him*? Do you really have amnesia? Wade said you couldn't remember anything. You're making me nervous, Victoria. You need to get over this memory thing before you say or do something that Wade will use to boot you out the door. Call Burt's office. He needs the information on the driver who hit you, his insurance and such. Look, sweetheart, I really must go. We'll talk again soon."

"Uh...okay." And before Victoria could make sense of any part of the conversation, the line went dead. How odd. Not once had her mother inquired as to how she was feeling. And all that about calling an attorney. What was that? She had no info about the accident and had assumed Wade would take care of it.

She hung up and eased into bed. It felt good to lie down. The silk sheets were amazing, the mattress and pillows so soft, especially compared to the bed at the hospital. Her vision again fell on the painting above the mantel. What was it about the painting that called to her? Surely Wade would know. But was it somehow related to what had caused his hostile reaction earlier?

She still had the dull throbbing in her head, though it wasn't bad enough to get up and take one of the pills Dr. Meadows had prescribed. She didn't know if it was caused by the accident, being in this strange unwelcoming monstrosity of a house, or Wade's show of anger and the anxiety she'd felt at his reaction. But neither the bath nor putting some food in her stomach had eased the pain totally. Maybe when she woke up everything would be back to normal.

Whatever *normal* was.

Three

Wadding another piece of printer paper into a tight ball, Wade tossed it against the far wall with the idea of bouncing it into the trash can below. There were significantly more small white balls on the floor than in the basket. He didn't care.

She could bloody well remember the name of one of her lovers but not her husband? That was a hell of a thing to admit. His irrational irritation continued to mount as he sat at his desk, trying to drum up sufficient enthusiasm to concentrate on the work in front of him.

Of course, she wasn't really his wife in the biblical sense. And considering their history, he really shouldn't be surprised or affected either way. But she had drawn him in with the sweet, innocent act, then waylaid him when he wasn't expecting it. One minute she seemed so innocuous...so...*not* Victoria. Those lilac-blue eyes—which had never seemed so blue—radiated such warmth, need and an almost childlike innocence. She'd silently implored him to help her. Then in the blink of an eye she was dredging up memories of some man. It was Victoria at her best. He snatched another sheet of paper from the printer tray. If ex-lovers were what it took to help her memory return, they definitely had a problem. He didn't know all their names, and he didn't care. But they were not going to visit her here. Just the thought of it had him again gritting his teeth. Another ball sailed through the air. Another miss.

He ran a hand over his mouth, sat back in the chair and took a deep breath. This entire situation had begun as one of those *Why didn't I think of this before?* ridiculously brilliant ideas. Or so it had seemed at the time. Victoria's father had given her a taste of high society before he lost everything by making foolish moves in commodities trading. Even when she had been poor as a church mouse, she had continued to maintain the facade of wealth and privilege, which was exactly what Wade had needed: a beautiful woman who knew how to dress and function skillfully at social gatherings, and who epitomized a billionaire's wife. In that regard, Victoria was exceptional. She could even do *happy* if he pressed her on it. What she couldn't do was *discretion*. He'd soon discovered Victoria didn't know the meaning of the word.

Wade had long ago stopped longing for a wife, someone he could love, trust and raise a family with. Twice he'd fallen for a woman who had seemed so sincere, so earnest, only to learn it was all a ploy to gain money. After the last time, he'd called an end to it all. Bitter and discouraged, he refused to again put his heart on the chopping block.

Now, because of the accident, it was as though Victoria had a complete change of personality. And apparently that change had a far-reaching effect, because he'd sure been snagged and reeled in. It seemed that, in the blink of an eye, she'd gone from a wife-in-name-only with a cardboard persona to a three-dimensional woman he found extremely hard to resist. He knew an illogical desire to be near her, to be with her and protect her. His mind raced to curb visions of him holding her close through the night. It was crazy. A mere three weeks ago, the last time he'd been in Dallas, he couldn't stand the sight of her.

How could he never have noticed how slender she was, how tiny her waist? How perfectly her breasts suited the other contours of her body? When she'd walked around her suite, her hips swayed enticingly, something he should have noted long ago. Had her lips always been so full and luscious? He'd never been physically attracted to her in the past. Yet the thought of her lying in his bed gave him insane ideas of forgetting all about the parameters of their previous relationship and making love to her with such wild abandon it would cause her to forget the names of her lovers and cry out his name instead. Such notions had never entered his mind in the almost five years he'd known her. Why now? Hell, maybe he was the one who needed to see a doctor. He crinkled another sheet of paper in his hand before it joined the others on the floor.

He had to get a grip. Such thoughts were completely ridiculous—outrageous and totally inappropriate under the circumstances. She'd just come from the hospital. Still, when their eyes had met in the private hospital room, for the first time he'd seen honest emotion there, something he hadn't thought the woman capable of. And against all reason, his body had responded. Then today, in the limo, he'd encountered her sense of humor. Who knew hidden away under all the glamour and glibness Victoria Wellington Masters actually had a sense of humor?

He couldn't explain why he suddenly wanted to be

close to her. He couldn't rationalize it, but he had to accept the reality of it. That was half the battle. A man couldn't fight something until he acknowledged its existence. So, okay. Fine. He now found something about her appealing. Quite a few things, in fact. Heaven help him. But he would not give in to this insanity or be suckered into her little games. Despite the way his body reacted every time they came close enough for him to inhale her scent, in spite of his eyes being drawn to her full, enticing lips and the delicate features of her face, he would bide his time, keep those lunatic feelings to himself until she was fully healed, at which time she would be escorted out the door. And all this would be nothing but a bizarre memory.

He wouldn't ask her to leave, certainly not until she'd fully recovered, even at the cost of his sanity. But he damn sure wouldn't lay himself open to becoming involved with Victoria. His face was already hitting the front page of the tabloids, the kind that exploited the secrets of the rich and famous. Headlines like Does Her Husband Know About the Other Men? or Who's Been Sleeping in Victoria's Bed—Lately? were a dime a dozen. Victoria had sworn she was dating only one man. She had been making an earnest attempt to keep their affair under wraps. Perhaps the tabloids were pulling from old photos. Though it was hard, maybe he should give her the benefit of the doubt.

She kept an apartment in North Dallas. He didn't know the location but imagined it would be easy enough to find. If returning to familiar surroundings would help her memory, they would definitely make a trip there. Add it to the top of the list. She'd never stayed in this house more than it was necessary to keep up appearances. She'd never shared his bed. There had never been anything about her that had tempted him to want to get closer. Until the damn accident. The sooner she regained her memory and signed those divorce papers, the better.

Pushing the work aside, Wade grabbed the phone, dialing his attorney's private line before settling back in the black leather chair.

"Wade." The voice on the other end held surprise. "What's going on?"

"I think we may have a problem."

An hour later, Wade hung up. He'd been right. There was no way a document signed by a person with confirmed amnesia would hold up in court. He had no choice but to wait it out and hope her mind righted itself quickly. Hell, that was a scary thought. At least she wouldn't be going out in public anytime soon, so his main worry was leashed for the time being.

Wade booted the computer and waited for his mail server to appear. He might as well try and get something done. When her memory returned, he intended to be waiting, documents in hand.

Victoria tossed and turned and plumped her pillow, and still sleep refused to return. The clock on the nightstand said 2:40 a.m., some twenty minutes later than the last time she'd looked. She sat up, knowing she wouldn't be going back to sleep anytime soon. More than likely it was due to the strange surroundings—even though they shouldn't be strange to her.

Throwing back the covers, she swung her feet over the edge of the mattress and stood up. Opening the French doors leading onto the terrace, she stepped out into the warm night air. She immediately heard the sound of water spilling over rocks. Soft, diffused light filtered through the trees and highlighted a water feature. Leaning over the railing, she spotted the huge waterfall and a rock-lined stream that wound through trees and out of sight. What castle would be complete without a waterfall? And what had Wade done with the moat?

The soft floral scent of roses mixed with lavender reached her on the light evening breeze. She would have to go down and explore in the daylight. But she didn't see any chairs or other places to sit in the manicured garden below. Wade needed to get a bench so they or their visitors could sit outside and enjoy the beauty.

A fast knock on the door to her suite pulled her attention away from the calming scene. She headed back inside and was halfway across the bedroom when the door opened. Wade stood in the doorway, his dark hair tousled as though he'd been running his hand through it. He wore sweats and a baggy top that revealed signs of moisture, as if he'd been working out. His mouth was drawn into a tight line, underscoring the fatigue that showed in his eyes. Behind him, two of his security staff stood poised and ready for anything that might go wrong.

Upon seeing her, Wade visibly relaxed.

"Were you just outside?"

"Yes. I woke up and couldn't go back to sleep, so I stepped out onto the terrace." She frowned. "Was I not supposed to?"

"No, it's fine," Wade assured her, rubbing the back of his neck. "All the outside doors and windows have silent alarms that are activated overnight. In future, please call security and let them know your intent so they don't see it as a break-in. Just hit pound six on the landline phone."

"Oh…okay." She glanced past Wade's broad shoulders at the two men. "I'm sorry. I didn't know or, if I knew, I didn't remember."

They smiled and nodded. "That's not a problem, ma'am."

When her gaze returned to Wade, that look of surprise was back on his face.

"You seem to be feeling better," Wade pointed out as the two security men left.

So do you, she thought. At least as far as his attitude went. "I am. I just wish my mind would catch up with the rest of me."

"I'm confident it will in time."

"I was looking at your garden." She pointed toward the French doors. "Below the balcony? It's beautiful. The sound of the water falling over the rocks is so relaxing. But I didn't see a bench or any place to sit."

Wade readjusted his stance. "A bench? No one ever goes back to that area."

"Maybe it's because there's no place for them to sit."

He looked dumbfounded. "I suppose that's possible."

She shrugged. "Why have the flowers and the water-fall if no one ever sees them?"

He stared at her like he'd never seen her before. As though she was an apparition and he didn't quite know what to do about it.

"Yes. I...see your point."

But he was frowning.

The character lines framing his mouth were tantalizing. She'd bet he had an awesome smile—so far, she'd caught only slight glimpses of it. She would love to run her hands over those indentations and kiss his full lips. He would be a great kisser. She didn't know if it was a memory or female intuition, but she knew it all the way to her core. A vortex of heat suddenly surrounded her, making her breath shallow and her heart rate speed up considerably.

"Well, um, I'm sorry I triggered the alarm. I'll do my best to remember to call the next time." She needed him to leave so she could turn on a fan.

"Not a problem." For countless seconds he stood in the same place, just watching her, as if his feet wouldn't obey his command to leave. Then his brain must have repaired the connection, because he blinked, shook his head slightly and turned toward the door. "Have a good evening."

"Wow," Victoria muttered to the empty room when he was gone. She had no idea where she'd found him, but at the moment, despite his earlier anger, she was very glad she had. He still didn't act like a husband in love with his wife. Maybe it was a case of him not knowing what he should or shouldn't do regarding her injuries. Surely, as they became reacquainted, that would change.

The morning light sifted into the room through the sheers drawn across the floor-to-ceiling window. Slowly Victoria stretched, yawned and sat up. Tired of robes and hospital gowns, she wanted her jeans and a comfortable shirt. In the closet she found some designer stretch jeans. No T-shirts, but an ample selection of blouses to choose from. Unfortunately, all the shoes and boots appeared to have four-or five-inch heels. *Ugh*. She wasn't up to that and, really, she shouldn't have to wear such things in her own house. She'd just go barefoot. The decision felt right. After securing her long hair in a ponytail, she ventured into the hall and paused, trying to decide which way to go.

The garden. She'd see if she could find it. She elected to take the stairs instead of the elevator. The grand circular stairway ended in the foyer. Maintaining her sense of direction, she turned and walked toward the back of the house. Surely there was a back door.

And there was. It opened at her touch, and she stepped outside into the morning light. Just ahead of her was a huge pool with a hot tub. It was surrounded by natural stone, banana trees and other exotic plants, which gave it a tropical feel. To the left was the huge waterfall, with more tropical ferns and plants growing at its base. Following her instincts, she rounded a corner of the mansion, and there it was: a floral garden set into an alcove.

It was even better from here than from the terrace. Peeking into the water that formed a stream at the base of the falls, she spotted beautiful gold, red and white fish. She didn't know how she knew, but these were koi. She knelt down on the thick grass and watched them with delight. Between the concentrated scents of various flowers and the roar of the waterfall, she felt more relaxed than she had since leaving the hospital. Stretching out on the luscious lawn under the rays of the morning sun, she closed her eyes.

No one had seen her leave. She'd all but disappeared. What was Victoria doing, and where was she doing it? While the housekeeping staff searched inside the house, Wade followed a hunch that led him outside. As he rounded the back corner, he immediately spotted her. Lying on her back in the grass with one arm thrown over her eyes, she appeared completely relaxed. It was a sight he'd never imagined seeing. Victoria was not one to embrace nature in any size, shape or form. Apparently that had changed. At least temporarily. He noted she wore no shoes. Perhaps a call to Dr. Meadows was warranted?

Wade approached slowly, not wanting to startle her, but needing to know she was all right.

"Victoria?"

"Hi," she responded but didn't move. "This is so great."

"We do have chairs."

"Not out here. Only around the pool. You don't have a bench, remember?"

She had him there. "No. No bench."

Using her arms, she pushed herself into a sitting position. "I think over there, under that tree, would be the perfect place to put one." Intending to scramble to her feet, she winced and grabbed her left side, the site of the bruised ribs. Pushing on, she got to her feet and walked over to the place she'd suggested. "About here. You can see the waterfall and most of the flower beds from this location. It's shielded by water ferns and banana trees. It's quiet, private and beautiful. What do you think?"

Wade wasn't sure what to think. Her behavior was anything but normal for Victoria. "Yes. I agree. It looks like a perfect place."

He watched as she once again lowered herself to the ground. "Come and join me." She patted the grass next to her.

Hesitantly, he ambled over and looked around for an alternative place to sit.

"Sitting on the grass won't hurt you."

"It won't help either," he muttered, then lowered himself to the lawn. He couldn't remember the last time he'd sat on the ground. She was right: it wasn't bad. He was surrounded by the smell of rich earth and flowering plants. Images sprang to his mind of the ranch where he and his brothers had grown up. The rolling hills, the unbelievable palette of color in the fall, trail riding for days, campfires at night. It was long ago, but those memories he would keep forever. Their mother had insisted her brood be raised in the country, believing a child needed to feel a bond to the land. His father had reluctantly agreed, so their sons had grown up on a ranch, learning about cattle and beef prices and what it took to operate a spread of enormous size.

He had always envisioned raising a family on the Masters ranch. He pictured his wife loving it there as much as he did and their kids spending their days on horse-back exploring the countryside. In his early years, he'd hoped to find someone who shared his heart as well as his dreams. Finally, he'd given up and made himself settle on a wife that shared nothing except what was required in the contract. A facade for all to see.

"Victoria, do you remember any part of your past? Childhood? Adolescence?"

"Intermittently. I have mental glimpses of people and things. Like I recognized the Dallas skyline. I don't know how I knew it was Dallas. I just knew." She was quiet for a few moments. "I think I used to work with my hands." She held them up in front of her face. "They feel…empty." She sighed.

This was the first he'd heard of such a thing.

"And I'm pretty sure I used to like being outside."

"*That* I can assure you was not the case. At all."

"No?" She frowned and seemed to let the thought roll around in her mind. "I've been getting these feelings that just seem…right." She glanced at Wade. "I can't explain it better. I wish I could. But being here, outside, feels right."

Wade didn't have an answer to that, so he didn't try. "Sit up and let me see your face," he said.

The bruising was almost gone and the cut on her lower lip had pretty much healed. "Better," he stated and was gratified to see her smile. "How do you feel, generally?"

"Good," she said and looked up into his eyes.

Less than a foot separated them and the temptation to lean toward her and put his lips against hers was over-whelming. *What was wrong with him?* This was Victoria. How out of place was any temptation to touch her? She raised one hand and placed it against his cheek and he shuddered at the sensation.

"You have such a handsome face," she whispered.

Her gaze lowered to his mouth. Wade could feel himself harden at both her touch and the implication of her words.

Pure lust shot through his body as his mind fought to hold on. As hard as it was to believe, he wanted her.

"Your lips are very..."

Wade's tentative hold on his self-control grew thinner. His hands cupped her face, and he eased her toward him. For an infinitesimal moment his face remained a breath away, his lips open, ready to taste her. He wanted to kiss her. Hell, he wanted to do more than that. His subconscious mind screamed *no!* Just behind her moist lips, perfect white teeth guarded the nectar he knew he would find there. He could feel her soft breath on his face, saw her eyes close as if in preparation for his kiss. Heaven help him. Slowly he placed his lips against hers, and the grip on his desire slipped away.

He pulled back and for a few seconds fought to hold on to the control he desperately needed. The raw hunger for this woman rose in his gut. This was insanity. He could not—*would* not—be attracted to Victoria. He damn sure wouldn't have an affair with her. She would use it against him eventually, somehow. Yet all he wanted to do was make love to her right there. Near the flowers she apparently loved. Right in front of God and everybody.

Anger at his own weakness overcame the temptation. He rolled to his feet. She was watching him, a look of confusion in her eyes. He took a deep breath and tried for normal.

"Have you contacted your mother?" he asked after clearing his throat.

She frowned. "Yeah," she whispered, then took a deep breath. "It was awkward. I didn't know how to address her."

Victoria claiming she didn't remember that vile

woman could be a good thing. Still, he knew when the memories came back, more than likely her mother would be among them.

"Wade, why did you—"

He cut her off. "It was a mistake. I shouldn't have kissed you."

"I was going to ask why you stopped." Victoria lay back on the soft grass. "Please don't go."

Pheromones shot through his body, and it took most of his strength to refrain from going back to her. His body was hard, tense. He needed a release. Dammit, he needed Victoria.

"I have a meeting." And if he didn't get away from her soon, he would never make it to that meeting.

"That's too bad. I think you need to relax occasionally. And I think you would enjoy daydreaming in this beautiful garden."

"Daydreaming doesn't allow much time for business."

She looked at him, a smile warming her face. It was the first time he'd seen her without anxiety and pain marring her delicate features. Or the mask of disgruntlement she normally wore. It was the first time a freshly scrubbed and exceedingly beautiful Victoria had actually smiled at him rather than smirked.

"That's too bad. Really."

There was absolutely no way Victoria would normally sit outside on the grass under the shade of a tree. Let alone smile about it. He would definitely take it up with Dr. Meadows when they went in for her appointment.

"I'd better get back inside. The meeting is in about half an hour."

She wiggled to a more comfortable spot on the ground. "Here? At the house?"

"Yeah."

"What's it about?"

He couldn't help looking at her to see if she was joking. Victoria had never shown any interest in any aspect of the business, not that he would have let her be privy to much of the information. As long as the contractual installments that kept her here were paid on time, she couldn't care less how the money was earned. It was odd that she'd asked. But what about this entire situation *wasn't* odd?

"We've just received all the clearances for the resort we're preparing to build in the Caribbean. I'm meeting with the architect and the designer to finalize the plans for the cottages."

"That sounds like fun."

"Fun?" He scratched the side of his face. "I never really looked at it as fun."

"Might as well like it if it's something you have to do." She shrugged. "Thank you for coming to look for me."

In the five years he'd known her, he had never heard the words *thank you* leave her mouth. He was pretty sure he'd never heard Victoria say those words to anyone. Her mind-set was one of privilege. She expected people to wait on her, and in her mind that didn't require any thanks. He could get used to this new Victoria.

He brushed off his slacks and bid her good day, heading back to the door. He couldn't help but wonder what else would be revealed on her journey to wellness and how much longer this new Victoria would be around.

Four

Dinner that evening was held in the dining room. The forty-eight-seat table kind of put it in perspective: her husband had yet to discover the world of casual. But the food, when it was served, was delicious. She closed her eyes, savoring the taste of the fresh Maine lobster. "My gosh. This is so good," she said, not waiting until she'd chewed and swallowed.

"I'm glad you find it to your liking." There was an unmistakable glint in his eyes.

She nodded her head. "How'd your meeting go?"

"Okay. It was just a formality to finalize plans for the resort. John provided an artistic take on the landscaping, and Mac reiterated the completion dates."

"Landscaping?" A picture flashed in her mind. A woman sitting in a windowsill, behind her a glorious sunset as she smelled a rose, a soft smile on her lips. Victoria's head throbbed with the memory.

"Yeah." Wade took another bite of his lobster. "The final idea seems off to me, but I couldn't say what is missing or what, if anything, needs to change."

She nodded, taking a sip from her water glass, hoping the throbbing in her head would go away on its own.

"Would you have any interest in seeing the sketches? Maybe you can spot something we missed. You seemed to enjoy yourself at the waterfall today and had good ideas about putting in some seating."

Her gaze shot to his face. "Me? You want me to look at them? Seriously?"

"Yeah." He shrugged. "Why not? Unless you don't want—"

"Yes. I'd really like that." He was reaching out to her for the first time. He was offering her a glimpse of his world. It was a small step toward rebuilding their relationship, maybe even a few steps in the direction of trust.

They ate in silence for a while. Victoria looked around the massive dining room, at the wainscoting, the three crystal chandeliers above the table and the forty-six empty chairs. It was so formal.

"Do you...*we* always eat in here?"

"In the past, you've preferred it." His answer was dry, like he didn't necessarily share her taste for it.

"Isn't there a kitchen?"

He raised one eyebrow, indicating her question was absurd. "I believe we have one, yes. That would be where the dinner was prepared."

"I mean, does it have a table?" she pressed. "Something smaller than this? Or a bar? You know, with stools? A place where just a couple of people can sit and eat. A place not so formal."

Wade looked perplexed. It was as though the idea had never occurred to him or he'd never expected her to make such a request. And now that she'd said it, she wasn't at all sure why she wanted somewhere unpretentious. After being married to Wade for eight months, she should be used to this type of formality.

"I believe we do."

She refocused on her plate. "Have you ever had all these chairs filled? Like, at the same time?"

"On occasion."

"That's a lot of pizza."

He stopped with his fork halfway to his mouth. His lips pursed at the unexpected humor. Clearly, he remembered their previous joking about his family business being a pizza joint.

"It is. And we serve only the best. But no jalapeños," he said in a serious tone.

"Agreed. Or anchovies."

"Or anchovies." He finished taking his bite of food.

"How long have you lived here?"

He patted the linen napkin against his mouth. "It's actually the family home. My grandfather started the business and did well enough that he had the core building erected before he died. My father later added the west and east wings. It works well for meetings that last several days and provides enough space for guests to stay without going to a hotel. The business associates visiting from other countries especially seem to prefer to stay here."

"When they're not here...it's a big house for just two people. Do you ever get lonely? Do I?"

He shrugged. "You've always seemed to manage. I've been staying here off and on most of my adult life. I guess I've never really thought about it. I have other houses, an apartment in New York, a villa outside of Rome, a flat in London. I stay in whatever area my business requires."

"So...you're here now because of me?"

"Primarily."

Why did that realization make her a bit sad? What important things had he had to cancel because of her?

She glanced at him as he returned his focus to his plate. He was so incredibly male. A tuft of hair hung over his forehead. Combined with the tanned face and dark features and the way he sometimes looked at her, he clearly gave off the impression there was a bad boy inside just waiting for a chance to come out. It was a total contrast to the proper, ever so polite Mr. Masters persona he strove to make people see. It was a look that said he could eat her up and still stick around for dessert. She'd had the same thoughts this morning when he'd kissed her in the garden. That kiss may have been soft and tentative, but it would have quickly grown to hunger he couldn't hide or easily control. She had to wonder if he ever let go of the rigid restraints he maintained and let raw passion determine his actions. Let the beast inside free. She took another sip of her water, determined to keep her imagination at bay.

"What about your family? Any brothers or sisters? Parents?"

"Both parents deceased. I have three brothers. All younger. Cole is also involved with the business, just a different facet of the corporation. Chance is recently retired from the military and runs the ranch in Calico Springs. Seth lives in Los Angeles. We all try to get together a couple of times a year or whenever possible. Haven't seen Seth in a couple of years. We stay in touch by phone or Skype."

"You all grew up here? In this house?"

He shook his head. "No. Actually, we lived on the ranch." He hesitated as if wondering whether or not to say any more.

"Please go on."

"My…mother came from a ranching family. She learned early on to respect the land, and she was determined her sons would grow up in the same environment. Apparently Dad finally agreed, so, just before Chance was born, he built a house on some land his family owned. We attended the local schools and grew up checking out the wide-open spaces on the back of a horse. Seth is a half brother and was born and raised in LA."

Wade rested his elbows on the table and linked his fingers. His gaze was directed at the far wall, but Victoria sensed in his mind he was a long way from here.

"Mom and Dad both believed a person should work for what they had and were determined for all of us kids to know the value of a dollar. Since we were living in Mom's playground, those lessons were learned by mending fences, feeding the livestock, taking on the general responsibilities of ranch life. Later, after college, Dad introduced each of us one by one to the world of business. One day led to another and here we are."

"You've never gone back? To the ranch?"

"I did for a while. But it's been close to a year."

"I think you should go," Victoria encouraged. "I think you should take a week—or more—and revisit your memories. See if you can still saddle a horse."

Wade laughed and the glitter of amusement shone in his eyes. "Maybe I will."

"What…" She cleared her throat. "What did I do while you were away or working?"

Wade laid his fork down on the plate and seemed to give her question some thought. "I don't think you did… anything."

"That's crazy." She frowned, placing her fork across

the gold-rimmed plate. "I had to do something. I mean, no one can just sit around and breathe day after day."

Wade shrugged. "You went shopping. Went to the hairdresser. Visited your friends. I really don't know."

Now it was Victoria's turn to look shocked. "I didn't work? Didn't help a charity? Arrange garage sales? Dig holes? *Nothing?*"

"Victoria, we didn't really see a lot of each other. On average, I spend more than half the year traveling. When I'm not out of the country, I'm in meetings or working in my office in the city, where I also keep an apartment. Occasionally we do attend a social gathering together, but even then, you have your acquaintances, and I have mine."

She was speechless. She couldn't imagine living the life he described. It sounded horrible. For a married couple, it just didn't make any sense. Somehow she knew within herself she was not the type to hide away day after day in this big house. And Wade had to take some downtime and enjoy life occasionally. No one could live as he'd described for years on end without paying for it physically, if not emotionally. Everybody needed time to relax. To laugh. To dream.

As she watched him eat his dinner, she realized she wasn't seeing a man who was happy and content with the world in which he lived. She was seeing a man who marched to the drum his current life demanded. He was staying well away from any friends or relationships that would take his time away from his business, including his own wife. The question was *why*. He was polite to a fault, handsome, rich…and very much alone. Why had he married her? It was like the dog that finally caught the car it had chased for years. Now that he had it, he wasn't quite sure what to do with it.

It was just sad. Period. All of it. How he rarely returned to his childhood home and had little to no personal contact with his brothers except, she assumed, in emergencies. Flying around from one country to another and never realizing a true home... Maybe she could plan something to get his family together.

She took one last bite of her dinner, laying the fork on her empty plate. "This was excellent. I didn't realize I was so hungry."

An older man came into the room and politely inquired if either one would care for dessert. Victoria placed her hand over her stomach and declined. "I'm stuffed."

"None for me either, Jacob. Dinner was good, thank you."

The man nodded, took the plates and left the room.

"Do you feel up to looking at those design renderings?"

"Sure." Her headache still had a dull throb, but it was slightly better than earlier today. She refused to let it keep her from sharing this time with Wade.

Together they walked down a long corridor. His hand was resting on the back of her waist. It felt odd, but not unpleasant, to be guided through the colossal home by this man. He stopped in front of double doors and opened one side for her. Like everything else in this house, his office was huge. Wade went directly to a side table and picked up a plastic tube containing the drawings. He removed them from their carrier and spread the sheets out on his desk. She walked over and stared at the first composite drawing. Wade was right. Something about the balance was off. As to the color, there wasn't any.

"Are the cabanas going to be white?"

"Yeah," Wade said, stepping closer until she could feel the heat from his body against her back. "More of a cream. The idea is to use them as a kind of palette for all the colors found on the island. The tropical plants contribute color at ground level, and I believe someone said there are over three hundred bird species, including parrots and macaws."

She realized she was once again shrouded in a warm vapor of sensation that was getting hotter by the second. She shook off the beginnings of arousal his closeness was causing, fighting to ignore the sexual response her body was determined to set in motion. She looked at the next few drawings, forcing her mind to stay on them. The cottages were primarily adobe-style with small variations around the entrances obviously intended to make each unique. But even with different doorways and variations in landscaping, they looked the same.

"What do you think?" His tall, muscled body pressed against her as he gazed at the sketches over her shoulder.

"These are very nice."

"Nice," he repeated. "Victoria, tell me what you think." His warm breath caressed her ear, his voice— that deep, rich baritone—causing shivers to run across her skin. Anxiously she reminded herself to breathe.

Shaking her head, she pivoted around from the drawings and found herself wedged between Wade and the table. The top of her head almost touched his chin, requiring her to look up into his face. His gaze found hers and for countless seconds neither moved.

She gave a slight shrug. "Who am I to be giving advice on multimillion-dollar vacation complexes?" It was almost a whisper, but it was the best she could do. "I don't even remember my own name." His mouth was so close, so tempting. He had a sexy five-o'clock shadow that only served to reinforce her earlier reaction to his masculinity. The feeling of warmth spread through her body like a wildfire fanned by the wind, causing her breasts to swell and her breath to become shallow. She couldn't help but stare at his lips: so masculine, so tempting.

He slowly lowered his head, bringing his lips only inches from hers. A little warning bell sounded in her head, reminding her that she was about to start something she wasn't sure if she was ready for. And if she crossed that line, there was no going back. While he was her husband, she still didn't know him. She didn't know what their relationship had been like before the accident. She clenched her hands into fists, determined not to place them against his chest, stand on her tiptoes and press her lips to his. With more strength than she thought she had, she turned back to the sketches.

She glanced down at the desk and took a deep breath in an attempt to fight off the growing desire to be in his arms.

She cleared her throat. "If you want the cottages to meld with the island, I would think you would paint some of them a rich sandy brown reflecting the color of the beach. Others could be a pale peach or light orange— pick up the colors in a tropical sunset and maybe a dark turquoise representing the water. The flowering plants will still be striking against a colored wall as long as the blooms aren't the same color as the walls. Also, each cabana has a private courtyard." She pointed to the area. "To me that screams *hammock with a coconut cocktail.* If you can find any hammocks made locally, consider adding one or two to each cottage. Comparatively, I don't think it's a big expense and the visitors might really enjoy it. I know I would. I think."

She felt his hand slip across her back and cup the side of her waist as he leaned closer to the drawings.

"And here—" she pulled out another large sheet and

placed it next to the one on top, determined to keep herself from melting at his touch, his masculine scent "—they have palm trees centered in front of each cottage. They look...planned. Plant them in small groups at either end of the house and change the positioning with each cottage. Make them look random, like they're part of the natural element there. I would think the very last thing you would want in a posh resort in the Caribbean is cookie-cutter anything."

She could feel his gaze on her face. When she looked around, she was caught by the intensity of those brown eyes. A heated blush encompassed her face. "I'm...sorry. I shouldn't have said anything. Don't pay any attention to me."

"That's all I seem to want to do," Wade said softly, his voice gravelly as he tipped his head and lowered his lips to hers. "Pay very close attention to you," he said against her mouth.

She couldn't have moved if she'd wanted to, and she didn't. Her total focus was on Wade and the look on his face that held her captive. His full lips drew her in, and she clutched his shirt with both hands, wanting more, holding on for dear life. A small whimper left her throat when he pressed his lips against hers. Then he drew back before kissing her again, harder, determined. His mouth opened over hers, and his tongue pushed inside, exploring, filling her. His hands rose to cup her face. She could feel his breathing becoming fast, could sense his intense emotion taking her own body to a new level.

Too soon he lifted his head, breaking the contact as he looked deeply into her eyes. She sensed he was going to kiss her again, but instead a frown covered his handsome features, and he drew back as if weighing the wisdom of his actions. As he continued to hold her face in his hands, his eyes lingered on her lips.

Something in his eyes made her sense that he regretted getting this close to her. Although she didn't have a clue why, that suspicion was confirmed when he took a step back and turned away. His mouth set in a straight line. She swallowed hard, feeling awkward and exposed.

She wasn't sure what to say, so she said nothing. With one last glance at her husband, she hurried to the door.

"Victoria…"

Gathering herself, she stopped just inside of the door. "I think cream cottages will be very nice, just the way your designer has it," she said without turning around. "They are lovely just as they are."

With that, she made for the elevator.

"Wait. Victoria," Wade called.

She kept walking. Still feeling the moist throbbing low in her belly, she fought the temptation to go back and do something really stupid.

She had to be realistic. The sky was the limit on what had happened between them before the accident. For all she knew, they were in the final stages of a heated divorce. Come to think of it, that would certainly explain why he'd made no move to touch her before, why he was so distant and, at times, gave her the distinct impression he didn't even like her. She wished he would just come out with it and tell her what had come between them.

Not that it would necessarily make her any readier to share his bed if theirs was a true and happy marriage. Although, after what she'd experienced five minutes ago and this morning, he wouldn't have to try very hard to convince her. At least she would know where she stood in his life. If he wanted a separation, a divorce, she was doing well enough physically that she could move on.

She didn't have to stay here. Surely she had some type of skills that would earn a position somewhere?

She stepped into the elevator and sensed the same awkwardness as she'd felt the day she arrived. The renewed frustration of having no memories plus her body's strong reaction to Wade before he turned away increased the volume on her headache. By the time she reached her room, it was full-blown. She hurried to find the bottle of pills.

It was time she and Wade talked. Really talked. If she was a burden, if there was no love between them, she needed to leave. Before she fell in love with her husband.

Wade stared at the door Victoria had closed behind her. What in the hell was he thinking? Never had he entertained the idea of kissing Victoria. Before the accident, if it had so much as crossed his mind, the very idea would have been ridiculous. She was undeniably attractive, yes. But he'd never been even remotely attracted to her. She met the requirements as far as being the perfect wife for a billionaire: beautiful, poised, charming when the situation demanded. Victoria had no compunction about her role as his pretend wife. Nowhere was it written or assumed they had to genuinely like one another. They rarely saw each other. Any attraction would have been one-sided on her part and, as far as he knew, that was not the case either. Yet since she'd awoken from the accident, he had been inexplicably drawn to her. He would watch her lips as she talked almost to the point of not listening to what she was saying. Her eyes were the shade of the irises his mother used to grow in her garden. Blue with a hint of lavender, amethyst. They were fascinating. How had he never noticed her eyes before?

As he turned, his gaze fell to the drawings on his

desk. Her suggestions were remarkable, and he would definitely pass on her comments to the designer. But it only added to the growing list of suspicions he had about her behavior. Something about her was off. There had to be a catch, something about her he wasn't seeing. This whole new persona had to be fabricated. *Had* to be. There was no other viable explanation for it. In the years they had known each other, but especially in the months since she'd agreed to the sham marriage, this was the first time she'd ever shown any interest in what he did. The fact that she'd made suggestions—good suggestions at that—blew his mind.

If she really was faking the amnesia—whatever her game plan—she was doing a number on his psyche. The closer he got to her, the closer he wanted to be. By the time she'd finally begun talking about the drawings, he was as hard as a steel girder. *Damn.* In those moments when he'd looked into those eyes, he was past caring *why* he was suddenly attracted to her. Hell, what did it matter? He wanted to taste her. He wanted to be inside her. Hell, he wanted a lot more than that. Desperately, he wanted Victoria to stay the way she was right now, memory or no memory.

Never in his previous relationships had he experienced the desire he now felt for Victoria. The cloud of suspicion for most women that had come after Cynthia, his fiancée of two years ago, was slowly evaporating, something he hadn't thought possible. His throat tightened as long-repressed memories of their final moments tore at his mind. Cynthia had even gone as far as to claim she was pregnant. All in a staged effort to ensure that a marriage between them would come to pass. Then weeks before the wedding her father had stepped forward, admitting his daughter's scheme. The devastation he'd felt at Cynthia's betrayal still brought back the anger.

Victoria had always viewed others as inherently inferior. Her quest for permanent acceptance within the circles of the rich had hardened her. She'd become ruthless in her determination to regain her family's previous status and had turned into the cold, cynical person she was today. Or at least the person she was before the accident.

Some of the questions she asked intrigued him. She had appeared completely surprised when he'd told her that she didn't hold down a job. Working at anything was unthinkable to the Victoria of the past. He knew she was a clotheshorse, always dressing to perfection. Sometimes she even set a fashion trend with one of her styling ideas. But the way she looked at those sketches...her approach was almost professional.

Her actions were becoming more unusual by the day. Could a knock on the head cause a person's basic character to completely change? It was almost as though she had a dual personality thing going on. He definitely needed to speak with Dr. Meadows, but since it wasn't an emergency, it could probably wait until her scheduled appointment. Until then, all he could do was to wait and watch. If she was acting, sooner or later she would slip up. It was inevitable. Like a kid, he had his fingers crossed in hopes that the wicked witch wouldn't return. Yet, at the same time, he needed some answers.

He'd racked his brain to try to figure it out. If this was a hoax, what was the payoff? It would have to be about money. With Victoria, it was always about money. But he hadn't come up with one solid idea of what she might be up to. Yet.

Five

Prior to going to bed, Victoria stood in her bedroom, staring at the picture that hung over the mantel. She still didn't see anything in the painting that reminded her of anyone. It was 80 percent background, and the only subjects were the child and her dog. The artist, Charles Burton Barber, had signed the painting in the lower right-hand corner. So why did it bring the name Murphy to mind? There was no reasonable explanation. She took in a breath and blew it out in yet another sigh of frustration. Memories were churning in the back of her mind; she could almost feel them spinning around and around, searching for a way to come out. How could she open the door and let them?

A soft knock on the door broke her concentration.

"Come in," she said, wondering who could be knocking on her door so late.

The door opened, and Wade stood on the threshold.

"I just wanted to make sure you were okay. You left rather suddenly." He tipped his head in question, and his gaze held hers.

"I'm fine." She shrugged. "Thank you for letting me look at the drawings. The resort will be incredible."

He paused for a long moment as though considering saying something else. Then he nodded. "I hope so. And your insights will be passed on. I think you were right on." He bumped the door frame with his left fist. "All right, then." He gave an affirmative nod. "Have a good night."

"You as well."

Victoria gave up searching her mind for answers and got ready for bed. Lying on the soft mattress in the darkened room, she couldn't stop herself from reliving the earlier moments in his office. The warmth of his body against her back. The way his lips moved over his strong white teeth when he spoke. She hoped he would kiss her again. Long and slow and deep. Damn this memory thing. Only a few more days and she would see Dr. Meadows again. And she wouldn't be short on questions.

Everything was moving in slow motion. Multiple shades of red splattered on the glass in front of her. She couldn't see out. She couldn't tell who was behind the pane. She tried to sweep the colors away, but that served only to swirl and mix them into an insipid, lifeless gray. Shards of glass flew about her head, lingered in the air above her before turning and heading straight down, each one piercing her skin with the precision cut of a razor.

She heard a scream. Over and over, someone was screaming. Was she the only one who heard it? She had to go for help. She had to find someone to help, but she couldn't move. Then she was again looking in the glass that had transformed into a mirror. She watched the blood run down her face as the sound of a siren filled the space around her. Everything was distorted. The world was spinning upside down. The face in the mirror was talking, but she couldn't understand the words. Over and over she heard a man's voice telling her he would free her from this place. He kept telling her to hang on. But she was so tired. The pain in her head was unbearable. Better to give in to the darkness. But she had to breathe. She had to fight for the next breath. If she gathered enough air in her lungs, she could scream and someone would hear her. But the blackness was stronger than she was. Like a wave coming to shore, it rolled over her, soothing her, giving her peace. She had to hang on. *No! Please no!*

She felt the warmth of strong arms around her. The darkness began to recede. She buried her face in the muscled shoulder of the man who held her as she cried, the sobs uncontrollable, as was the trembling that tore through her body. She held on to him, needing his strength, afraid he would leave her alone again.

"Victoria." The reality of Wade's deep voice broke into the nightmare. "It's all right. Come on, hon, wake up. You're having a bad dream. You're safe."

His soothing words and the warmth of his body as he held her began to diminish the fright of the nightmare. Blinking open her eyes, she saw the increasingly familiar surroundings of her suite. She was in her bed, with Wade holding her safe and protected. She should feel embarrassed that she'd apparently awakened him from his own sleep, but the warmth and safety she felt as he held her close overruled any idea of pushing him away or putting up a front of bogus bravery. The dream had held her in its horrifying grip until Wade had forced it away and brought her back to reality. She took a deep, shaky breath to calm the last of the tremors.

"It was so awful," she whispered, her cheek against his naked chest. "I couldn't move. I couldn't breathe."

His arms tightened around her, then one hand began to soothingly rub circles over her back. "I heard you cry out."

Her mind wouldn't let her recall everything, but she remembered the vivid colors of red everywhere. She had been in so much pain. Was it the accident? Was that what had happened to her?

She sat up then, moving away from his chest as reality fully set in. Her gaze roamed the handsome features of his face. With tenderness, he wiped away her tears.

"Wade, I—"

Her remaining words were reduced to an unfinished thought when Wade leaned down and his lips found hers. Briefly. A feather-soft meeting. He drew back, watching her, and she thought she saw a battle going on in his eyes. She reached up to touch his face, tracing the character lines that only added to his potent allure. With a deep moan, he kissed her again, this time more forcefully, moistening her lips with his tongue, demanding entrance to the deeper secrets of her mouth, and Victoria didn't think of resisting. His hand grasped the back of her head, holding her to him as his tongue pushed inside, hungry, seeking.

It was an explosion of sensation. He tasted of coffee, a hint of vanilla and a whole lot of hot-blooded male. His mouth covered hers enticingly, drawing back before returning with even more vigor. His lips were simultaneously soft and firm, enveloping her own, yet she could sense the passion he held tightly in check. His natural masculine scent surrounded her, stimulating her own need with every breath, making her hunger for more. In that moment, she wanted only to lose herself in his arms.

She felt weightless, then the softness of a cloud touched her back. Her body grew hot, the heat centering at the apex of her legs. Every thought in her head floated somewhere in an abyss.

Absently, she realized her head was against a pillow, his hands cupping her face while his lips and tongue continued to stir the passion pooling hot and deep in her belly.

His body was over her, his erection hard and almost painful as it pressed against her belly. She squirmed in a frantic effort to move so he would be at her opening, where she desperately needed him to be. For a minute in time, he helped her, repositioning himself against her core, the barrier of her panties the only thing keeping them apart.

Suddenly, with a groan, he pulled back and sat up, leaving her confused and wanting. Breathing hard, he watched her in the soft, indirect glow from the lights in the garden below. The muscles on his jaw moved in rapid succession, and regret covered his features.

He stood from the bed and ran a hand through his hair.

"Damn. I'm sorry, Victoria." His voice was husky.

Before she could answer, Wade turned and walked out the door.

Victoria fell back against the pillows. What just happened? She inhaled a deep breath and blew it out in an effort to slow her racing heart. At least she knew without any doubt that passion was still very much alive in their marriage. Maybe she could get him to talk about what happened that had apparently put a wall between them. Or, if he was merely concerned about hurting her, she would make sure the doctor assured him she was fine. Because she was.

She pulled the covers up to her neck. The room suddenly seemed cold. In fact, she'd felt the chill as soon as he'd withdrawn his arms.

Why had he apologized? Was it because he'd almost made love to her? Or because he'd stopped? One thing stood out in her mind: he wanted her. For now, that was enough. For maybe the first time since the accident, she had hope. Memory or no memory, maybe they could work it out.

What in the hell had he been thinking? *Goddammit.* He didn't give a hot damn about her lovers or any other aspect of her personal business, as long as it didn't affect his own. So what in the hell was he thinking when he'd kissed her? Even worse, he'd kissed a woman who didn't even remember who he was. She was barely out of the hospital after sustaining a major concussion. She needed to be able to trust him, at least until her memories came back. And he'd pounced on her like some love-starved jackass. He'd taken advantage of her having a nightmare. How pathetic was that?

Entering his own suite, Wade closed the door behind him, ambled across the room and fell onto the bed. This was not good. He didn't know what had changed between them, had no idea why suddenly Victoria had become so appealing. But she had. He'd felt the change growing since she'd batted those baby blues at him in the hospital. He'd shaken it off as just human compassion for another who was hurt, frightened, and needed his help.

That rationale had been blown to hell when she'd invited him to sit on the ground under a tree. *Him.* The Wizard of Wall Street. Wade Masters, revered financial genius, sitting on the ground under a damn tree. And—worse still—he'd liked it. It took him back to his childhood, to the memories of growing up on the ranch with his brothers. The tricks they would play on each other. The camaraderie.

He had not wanted to stop kissing Victoria, even though he knew it was the wrong thing to be doing. He was playing into her hands like a blind fool, and until he could figure out what she was after or prove she was lying about the amnesia, he had better pull himself together. Every second spent in her company was a step deeper into her web of deceit. The only hope he had was to get her out of this house and permanently eliminate the temptation to take their relationship to the next level.

His attorney had cautioned Wade about doing anything she could claim would be placing her in danger, meaning she had to be healthy and fully capable of taking care of herself before he asked her to leave. If Dr. Meadows gave her the all clear in spite of the memory loss, some time spent on the family ranch might be just the ticket. Despite her urging him to revisit the ranch and her little sit-in-the-grass party, he knew damned well Victoria didn't like nature or anything remotely outdoorsy, regardless of how much she was pretending otherwise. She had a distaste for animals, and zero appreciation for anything country. He still hadn't figured out why she was pretending to enjoy things totally out of character. She had to be scheming. The big question remained: *What was she after?*

Maybe the answer would be revealed after she'd washed and groomed a dozen horses and mucked out a few stalls. Taking her to the ranch seemed like the perfect plan. Push enough country living in her direction, while he relaxed in his favorite place in the world. Something would give, and it wouldn't be on his end.

Whatever had happened to Victoria in that wreck, he would not let it affect him. He couldn't afford to. He'd leave all of her peculiarities to a psychiatrist to try to figure out. From now on, he would stick to his office and keep the damn door closed. Or, better yet, leave. It was a little over a week until her doctor's appointment, and he had more than enough staff to see to her needs. There was some business he honestly needed to address in New York. Without further consideration, he picked up the internal phone and dialed the house manager.

"Curtis? Yeah, I need to fly to New York for a couple of days as soon as it can be arranged."

"Yes, sir. The plane is fueled and ready. I'll contact the pilot. I can have a car sent around to the front… Give me two hours on everything?"

"Perfect. Thanks. Oh, Curtis? Something else."

"Yes, sir?"

"Victoria… Take her shopping. She's been complaining about not having comfortable shoes. Take her to a few of the better clothing boutiques. Tell her I said to get whatever she wants."

"Yes, sir."

He'd known if he ever let emotions enter his life, his neat and orderly existence would go to hell in a handbasket. But…was it emotion that caused him to want to be close to Victoria? Taste her lips? Feel the warmth of her breath on his face? Hear her whispered sighs as he held her close? Emotion meant he had to feel something for her.

Feel something for *Victoria*? *Oh, hell no!* It was animal instinct. Purely sexual. Even that was a stretch of the imagination. This was Victoria he was thinking about.

This was the third time in as many days she'd suckered him into whatever game she was playing. Regardless of whether it was on purpose or not, despite how much he'd enjoyed kissing her, it damn sure would not happen again.

The next morning at breakfast Victoria was advised by a man who introduced himself as Curtis Shepherd, the house manager, that Wade had been forced to return to New York for some urgent business. Wade had asked him to pass on his apologies and assure her he would be back in time for the appointment with her doctor. A nagging suspicion had her wondering if Wade really did have urgent business. Or had he left to avoid her? The idea made her uneasy and a little sad. Was it possible Wade had not seen their passion the previous night as a positive thing? A step toward rebuilding their marriage? She hadn't had the opportunity to talk with him about their marriage. The subject of why it might be in trouble wasn't a conversation she'd wanted to bring up. But it was making her crazy. She had to know. When he got back, they were going to discuss it.

Curtis also told her Wade wanted her to go shopping for shoes and anything else she needed. Curtis was to accompany her, driving to the stores she used to frequent. It was nice of Wade, but the only thing she needed was a good pair of sneakers, and that hardly seemed to be worth the man's time.

Finishing her breakfast, she decided she would go on a mission of discovery. Between the house and the estate grounds, there was so much to see. It seemed like the perfect opportunity to refamiliarize herself with this gigantic house.

Her first stop was the kitchen. The chef and his two assistants were busy turning out what would no doubt be another spectacular dinner. Surprised by her presence, they were immediately uneasy. She had to assume it was because she'd come into their area of the house. Finally, after she gave them plenty of compliments and ready smiles, they began to loosen up and seemed only too happy to explain what they were preparing, their words conveying such pride in their work.

An idea began to form. Maybe one of the chefs would know of a smaller, more intimate area they could eat, instead of that huge, formal dining room. She turned to the one who was most proficient in English, even though his thick French accent still made him difficult to understand. He gleefully took her to a diminutive alcove between the hall to Wade's office and the elevator. The area was just big enough to fit a table and a couple of chairs. Maybe a plant for ambience? A floor-to-ceiling bay window filled the far wall, framing a water fountain just outside. The only piece of furniture there was a sofa. It was perfect. As soon as she could have a small table and two chairs delivered, she wanted all future meals to be served here.

Eventually, she found herself back at the elevator. Returning to her room, she placed a call to Curtis and gave him her request. A small table and two chairs would be delivered tomorrow along with one ficus tree. Curtis suggested the area where she wanted to place the new furniture might need repainting, and they'd want to remove the sofa. Victoria gave the go-ahead, excited to see how it would all come together. She especially wondered how Wade would like it.

Curtis also politely reminded her of the shopping spree. She didn't know if it would be a *spree*, but she would go and get a new pair of shoes. They made arrangements to leave at two that afternoon.

When the time came, Curtis and two security guards met her at the car. Two hours later, Curtis pulled the car back into the circle drive. Victoria got out with two bags, both containing everyday casual shoes.

Her spirits lifted, she dumped the two boxes inside her closet, slipped on a bikini and headed for the pool.

The flight back to Dallas seemed endless. Never before had Wade felt like pacing during a flight. He knew Victoria was the cause. He was actually looking forward to seeing her again. That was a first. He was probably setting a new world's record for foolishness.

"We are in the flight pattern for landing, Mr. Masters," the pilot spoke from the cockpit. "ETA about five minutes."

Good. For the first time in…maybe forever, Wade looked forward to returning home. After a perfect landing and a quick switch to the waiting car, he was on the last leg of his journey. It was well past midnight. He was tired and irritated. His stay had lasted longer than expected. The meetings hadn't gone well, primarily because he'd not been prepared. He'd left half the documents on his desk back in Dallas and couldn't keep from constantly wondering what Victoria was doing. For the first time that he could remember, he vehemently did not want to conduct business. And then it had been a long flight home, made even longer by his internal agitation.

The next day was Victoria's appointment with Dr. Meadows. Wade had refrained from calling him about Victoria's bizarre behavior, and he wasn't sure why. Maybe it was that some of her new quirks he rather liked. In all honesty, he didn't want her to revert back to the woman she'd once been. It wasn't fair to her, granted.

She deserved to have her memories and her life back. But still…

"We're here, Mr. Masters," the driver said before stepping out and opening the door for Wade. "I'll have your things cleaned and the luggage stored. Have a good evening, sir."

Wade made the appropriate reply and headed to a small side entrance of the house that not everyone knew about. To a stranger, it would not appear as an entry at all, since the door was hidden behind an evergreen. He'd taken this path so many times he could do it blindfolded. From the driveway, there was a series of stepping stones through the landscaping to the carefully hidden door.

The first stepping stone felt strange under his foot. The second one even more so. It was as though the flagstone had been removed, which was ridiculous. The third stride almost took him down. He recognized his problem: he was standing in pure mud. *Where in the hell were the paving stones?* On the fourth step, the mud encased his foot up to the ankle and had him fighting for his balance. Struggling, he finally managed to take another step forward, but his shoe remained behind. He groped the air for something to hold on to seconds before he fell to his knees. His briefcase was claimed by the darkness as he determinedly fought his way to the side door, finally reaching the concrete entrance by crawling on all fours like a dog.

Standing on the small cement step, he looked back in the direction he'd just come. From this angle, Wade could see that someone had indeed removed the stepping stones and apparently decided quicksand was more to their liking. But who? Who would do this? Victoria's face flashed in his mind like an image on a big screen.

Nahhh. Why would she do something like this? Landscape design wasn't her thing.

Wade entered the security code, pulled open the door and stepped inside. Reaching down, he removed his one remaining shoe and both muddy socks. His slacks were in no better shape, so he ditched those, too. With grim determination to keep a tight rein on his temper, he set out for the elevator. He'd not gone far when he tripped over a large obstacle directly in his path. Wade felt himself go down in what seemed like slow motion, his feet tangled in God knew what. The sound of wood and metal hitting the floor echoed down the empty hall. *What the hell?* What was a chair doing in the hallway?

Clambering to his feet, he didn't notice the table until his head hit the bottom of it, setting off another series of bangs and crashes as it fell onto its side. Levering himself carefully to his feet, he righted the table and once again turned toward the elevator. He never saw the potted tree that stood more than double his height until he and it were waltzing in the dark. He finally fell against a wall that prevented him from losing his balance yet again.

Suddenly the lights came on, and he was able to view the obstacle course he'd just come through. Two wrought-iron chairs with wooden seats, a matching table and a damn tree. He noticed traces of white covered his hands and the sleeves of his suit jacket. The pungent smell of fresh paint reached his nose. The chef stood in the kitchen opening, his eyes as big as saucers. No doubt the noise had echoed all the way through the kitchen and into the employees' section of the house.

"Get this tree out of the middle of the damn hallway," Wade barked at the man, who scurried to do his bidding. With a scowl, Wade limped to the elevator.

When the elevator doors opened to the second floor, he cut a beeline directly for Victoria's door. And this time he didn't pause to knock.

And there she was, sitting up in bed reading a book, a look of pure innocence on her beautiful face. She looked up, obviously surprised by his late-night visit. Then her eyes quickly went wide as she took in his appearance.

"Wade?" Frowning, she threw off the covers and hurried toward him. "What happened? Where are your pants? You're...covered in mud. How did you tear your shirt?" Reaching up, she pulled a small, six-inch-long twig from his collar. "What's on your suit? It looks like white paint all over the back of your jacket... Oh dear."

"*Oh dear?* Did we do a little shopping while I was gone?" His jaw worked overtime. "A little rearranging?"

"Yes." She had the decency to grimace. "I bought two pairs of shoes and...the little dining room was supposed to be a surprise."

"Let me assure you, in that you succeeded."

"We didn't have a small table for meals, so I bought one, along with two chairs to go with it. Remember? We talked about it that night during dinner. And you were right. I found a perfect area for just the two of us to eat, but no furniture." She bit her bottom lip. "Curtis thought it might need repainting. So I told them to just put the furniture in the hallway. And the ficus."

"The what?"

"The...the tree. It's a ficus tree. The painters needed room...to work." She narrowed her eyes and frowned. "Actually, I don't really understand how you could have missed seeing the tree. It's about twelve feet tall and almost as wide."

"I know. Believe me. But I can't see trees—or furniture—in the dark."

"In the dark? Was something wrong with the lights?"

"No."

"I don't understand."

He took a deep breath, determined to keep it civil. "It was dark because I didn't turn on any lights. I didn't think I needed to. It should have been a simple walk to the elevator, one that I've made countless times."

"Surely you're not blaming *me* because you didn't bother to turn on any lights?" She looked incredulous. "And the hallway would have been clear if you'd come back when you were supposed to. You weren't scheduled to be back until tomorrow."

She was right, but he refused to allow her to turn the tables on him. "Did you remove the paver stones between the driveway and the house?" He heard the growl in his words.

She nodded. "I had help, but yes, I did. I needed them moved in order to plant a garden."

"A garden."

"For fresh vegetables. I didn't want to dig up the lawn," she explained as though those were the only two options she had. "All I saw was bark chips and some stepping stones that led nowhere, which seemed rather pointless to me."

"They led to a door. It's intentionally hidden."

"Then why do you have stepping stones leading to it? Isn't that a dead giveaway?"

Wade ran a hand over his lower face, remembering all too clearly why Victoria had her own place in the city. "Tomorrow perhaps you can help me understand the need for a vegetable garden? It isn't like we have no food in the house," he barked. He could hear the frustration in his own voice and tried to rein it in.

He took a deep breath and turned to leave, not willing to stand there one moment longer covered in mud, half naked at one o'clock in the morning and debating the need for a vegetable garden. The top of his head was still tender from the encounter with the table. All he wanted at the moment was a hot shower. There was no doubt she had set this up. She was pushing him to lose his temper. She had to be. He just didn't know why. A move to the ranch was looking better and better. She'd be well-advised to watch out. Paybacks were hell.

Six

The door closed behind Wade. Victoria looked at the twig she still held in her hand. She was honestly sorry he'd experienced a problem coming into the house. A problem of her making. But he really wasn't supposed to have gotten home until tomorrow. Or technically today. She'd intended to have everything set up and ready to surprise him at dinner tonight. Well, she'd surprised him, all right. Just not in the way she'd intended.

She returned to her bed and set the book aside. Turning off the bedside light, she lay back on her pillow and stared into the darkness. One thought ran in circles through her mind: after this long, she was still the stranger here. Regardless of how hard she tried, she still managed to cause havoc, either by setting off alarms or making well-intended changes to this house. Everything was so formal it was difficult to breathe. How she'd ever spent eight months in this house doing nothing, especially with Wade gone most of the time, was something she couldn't imagine. She could relate to the old adage about the bird in a gilded cage. And nothing she did seemed to make any difference for the better. And how could it ever? She lived in a perfect house with a perfect man. She consumed perfect food and slept in a perfectly soft bed. She didn't like perfect. She certainly wasn't perfect and was pretty sure the real world wasn't either.

She'd been counting the hours until Wade returned, imagining his smile when she showed him the changes she'd made. Instead, everything had blown up in her face. By the look of him, Wade was really mad. She supposed he had a right to be. But he must know she hadn't intended to sabotage him. Actually, she'd intended just the opposite.

She slid off the bed and padded to her door, then continued to Wade's suite. A moment of hesitation had her almost turning and running back to her room, but she held firm. Reaching out, she knocked on his door. No answer. She knocked again, this time a little harder.

Suddenly the door was wrenched open, and Wade stood in the doorway, one towel slung low over his hips while he blotted the moisture from his head with another, grimacing when it touched the top of his head.

Before she could open her mouth, he stepped back into the room and disappeared around the corner, leaving her to choose to come in or to turn around and leave. Taking a deep breath, she stepped forward into the lion's den.

"I just wanted to apologize," she called out, hoping he could hear her. "It never entered my mind that…well, that you would come home early. Or at night. Or that you wouldn't turn on the lights. Or that there was an entrance there, and you would use it." She huffed out a sigh. "You could have called and told me, and none of this would have happened."

Wade stepped back around the corner, still wearing the towel. His thick dark hair was damp from his shower, softly curling about his head as though it refused to be tamed. His broad shoulders filled her vision. The sleek muscles of his chest and arms moved under tanned skin with oiled precision as he brought his hands up to rest on his waist. "This is how you apologize?" His eyebrows rose, a spark of challenge in his eyes. "Saying the debacle downstairs was my fault?"

"No. I'm to blame for what happened. Ultimately. I'm just pointing out you could have avoided it."

"You'll have to pardon my disagreement, but calling home to announce my arrival so a tree can be moved out of the way from the center of the hallway is not normally on my list of things to do."

"Which is why you should have turned on the lights."

Wade opened his mouth as if about to argue, but no words came out. Instead, he closed his eyes, shook his head and uttered a sigh.

"I'm sorry you got paint on your suit coat. I hope the dry cleaners can get it out. Where are the pants?"

Wade's mouth was set in a straight line. His eyes narrowed to golden-brown beams as he caught her gaze. He stepped toward her and the urge to retreat was strong. Wade was a powerful man, in more ways than one. She was surrounded by an incredible scent of hot clean male, and there was little between them but her flimsy nightgown and a towel barely hanging on his hips.

Rather than frightening her away, his gaze held her in place.

Stopping a mere foot away, he said, "I don't think

this is about lights or the tree or whether or not I should have called."

Victoria frowned. "I don't understand."

"Don't you?" He reached out one arm, his hand cupping her face, his thumb rubbing gently over her cheek. With little effort, he drew her to him.

His thumb traced the line of her lips and his gaze lowered to watch the movement. Her heart was doing cartwheels, and her breath stalled in her throat.

Wade closed what little distance remained between them and lowered his lips to within a breath of hers. "I think maybe you were trying to get my attention. Rest assured, it worked."

"No, that's not at all—"

"The next time, just tell me what you need, and I'll make sure you get it. It's more direct and involves a lot less drama. In fact, it's not too late." He nodded his head toward the large bed.

His mouth covered hers, devouring her lips, seeking the deep recesses of her mouth. His hand cupped the back of her head, ensuring she didn't move away. She had no desire to do anything other than respond to the heat he was causing throughout her body and the moisture pooling between her legs. His mouth was hot, his tongue exploring the cavern of her mouth. His arms encircled her, and he pulled her tight against him, causing his granite erection to press against her stomach. With a little moan, her hands found his bare shoulders, and she answered his need. She was quite sure she'd never been kissed in such a manner or by a man like Wade Masters. He was amazing. He knew exactly what she wanted and proceeded to give her more. How could she have forgotten moments like this?

"You make it very hard to remember you're injured,"

Wade whispered against her lips, his voice rough. Then his mouth covered hers in one last, lingering kiss before he raised his head and took a step back. "Go. Go back to your room while you can. I'm trying damn hard not to pick you up and..." He took a shaky breath. "Go, Victoria. Now."

Victoria backed to the outer door, turned and all but ran down the hall to her suite. God, how she'd wanted to stay in his arms. She trudged to her bed and climbed in, pulling the covers around her. Visibly shaken, she knew she was walking a razor-thin line between making love to her husband and denying them both until she could remember him and what transpired between them before the accident. The way she felt right now, she wished she'd just said *no* to his demand she leave and stayed exactly where she was—where she wanted to be—in his arms. In his bed.

As far as she could tell so far, he was the man she'd always dreamed of. Not his wealth. Not his power. Just Wade. The man. Purely the man. What had she done to make him want to keep his distance? And how would they overcome it?

Dr. Meadows closed the door behind him and extended his hand first to Victoria, then to Wade. He set a small laptop on the counter and powered it up. "So, how have you been, Mrs. Masters?"

"Good." Victoria smiled at the good doctor. "My ribs are still a little tender, but not bad."

"Headaches?"

"Yes. Some. But they are manageable for the most part. And they don't happen very often."

"And the memory? Any improvement?"

"Not really. Maybe a quick flash of an image or a name here and there."

"Are you able to retain those images?"

She nodded. "Yes. But I don't understand any of them. I don't recognize them."

"She is experiencing some changes in her personality." Wade spoke up.

"Like what?"

"Basic likes and dislikes. Opinions. Her interests seem to have shifted." Wade stood in the corner, his hands thrust deep in the pockets of his slacks. "She likes going barefoot. She enjoys sitting on the ground. Outside. Under a tree. Before the accident, she wouldn't be caught dead doing that."

"It's pleasant. You should do more of it," Victoria countered.

"She doesn't want to go shopping. I had to leave instructions for my houseman to take her shopping and I was told, even then, she didn't want to go."

Wade turned a frustrated glance to Dr. Meadows. "And she planted a garden. She had one of the employees remove paving stones and landscaping and plugged the space full of tomato plants. Do you understand what I'm saying, Doctor?" Wade rubbed the back of his head. "We don't need tomatoes!"

Dr. Meadows stifled a grin and looked down, rubbing his forehead.

"Mr. Masters, while I can appreciate what you're saying, sometimes amnesia can cause a person to temporarily change their core values, their likes and dislikes. It doesn't happen very often. But I must say, in all honesty, if my wife staunchly refused to go shopping, I would consider myself a very lucky man."

He trained his sights on Victoria. "Do you have any memories associated with what you like or don't like?"

Victoria looked at her husband, then shook her head.

"No. As I explained to Wade, some things just feel right. I can't offer a reason other than that."

"While it's not a common occurrence, it is possible with a traumatic head injury such as you sustained. We can't rule anything out." He turned to face Wade. "I would suggest just being supportive of your wife's new interests, as long as she sticks to growing tomatoes and doesn't start robbing banks."

She couldn't stop the small snort of laughter. She dared a look at her husband and received a stern glare. Apparently Wade didn't share in the humor.

"I would like to see you again in about three weeks, just as a precautionary follow-up. We'll do another MRI and see how things are looking on the inside, but I don't anticipate anything negative. You seem healthy otherwise and I see no reason that you can't return to your full activities. It might even help with memory recall."

"Great." She hopped down from the table. "Thanks, Dr. Meadows. I'll be here on the eighteenth for the MRI." She turned at the door and watched as Wade shook the good doctor's hand before accompanying him down the long hall and out the front door. When they stepped out of the building, she felt the summer sun on her shoulders. She glanced at her husband. He appeared deep in thought.

"Wade?" she said. "I know my cell was destroyed in the accident, but why do I have no friends? I mean, not one person has called or come to see me since I've been home. I talk to Mother on occasion, but she doesn't seem to have the time or the desire to discuss it. She says I'm being silly to worry about it. Keeps telling me to stick to the business at hand...whatever that means. Getting my memory back, I suppose."

"Of course." He didn't sound convinced. "I'm afraid I can't answer your question, Victoria. I don't think you had very many that you considered close friends. Perhaps they will come around in time. Unfortunately, I don't have names or numbers to give you."

That seemed strange. Surely her husband would know the name of her best friend? Theirs was truly an odd lifestyle. Or so it seemed. But she had no concrete foundation to base her suspicions on. Perhaps it was just the way life was.

When they arrived back at the mansion, Victoria headed upstairs, and Wade made his way to his home office. He closed the door and sank down in the leather chair behind the desk. Reaching for the phone, he dialed the number to the ranch. It was answered on the second ring.

"Triple M Ranch," a woman cheerfully answered.

"This is Wade. Is Chance around?"

"No, sir. He has gone to a cattle auction in Oklahoma. He won't be back for a couple weeks. But Holly is here. Or at least at her vet clinic."

"I'm bringing my wife out for a short stay. Could you have someone freshen the Pine House cabin?"

"It will be wonderful to see you again, sir. We will have the house and vehicles ready to go. Do you have a general idea of when you'll be arriving?"

"Toward the end of next week."

"Excellent. I'll let Holly know you're coming, and we'll see you then."

He sighed and ended the call. Every day they were together he felt drawn to Victoria more and more. But Wade had to give her some leeway while she healed, not press her on the return of her memories. But the time was drawing near. He knew sooner or later she would revert to the Victoria he knew, and giving any thought to

consummating their marriage would be setting himself
up for a hellacious time when she regained her memory.
Sharing a bed at the ranch wasn't going to help to put
distance between them. In fact, it was going to be damn
hard to keep from making love to her. Victoria saw him
as her husband. Not a cardboard replica of a man whom
she married on paper only. She didn't know that part,
and he was hesitant to tell her. Would it shock her memory into returning? Or would it just shock her, period?
Maybe the news would have no effect. Yeah. Probably
not. He knew this Victoria well enough to know that
if it didn't bring back her memory, it would most certainly disturb her.

He exhaled a deep breath. He was ready to put his
plan into action. He'd use the horses, the campfires, the
hiking and anything else he could find to send Victoria running back to Dallas after admitting her memories had returned. It had been hard enough staying away
from her the times they had been together. He would shut
his mouth, keep his distance and stay alert to any further changes in her demeanor. If Victoria had honestly
changed and discovered a love of the outdoors, she would
get her fill at the ranch. If she was pulling some type of
con, the ranch would have her confessing in no time.
High-society types like her did not normally fit in with
cowboys, cattle drives and longhorn steers.

A glance at his watch said it was past two o'clock.
Wade took the elevator to the second floor and knocked
on Victoria's door. After several minutes he knocked
again. This time the door was thrown open. "Hi."

"Uh…hi." Wade swallowed hard. Victoria was standing before him clad in only the briefest neon-yellow bikini. Her dark brown hair was pulled back into a knot. "I
was about to head down to the pool and get some sun."

"I wanted to see if you'd care to have lunch."

"Sure. Let me throw on a T-shirt and pants—or is a dress needed? Are we going out?"

"Casual will be fine. I'll wait. Go ahead." Wade strolled into the room while Victoria raced for the closet. Uncharacteristically, her suite was as neat as a pin.

He expected the wait time to be at least ten minutes, but before he could sit down, Victoria was back, dressed and ready to go. She'd even put on a pair of shoes.

They made their way downstairs. When Victoria turned to go into the dining room, Wade took her arm and directed her toward the kitchen.

"Where are we going? I thought you said we were going to eat here."

"We are."

Victoria couldn't hold back the surprise when they turned left and stopped in the entrance to the alcove. The table and chairs she'd bought had been placed in the center of the cozy space, and the table was set with dinnerware for two. The tree was to one side of the window. The water feature outside had been turned on, its droplets glowing like crystals in the afternoon sun.

The full smile on her face was breathtaking.

Wade cleared his throat and seated her at the little table. Victoria simply could not keep the smile off her face. "Thank you, Wade. I mean that."

He shrugged. "You did all the work. You selected the table and chairs."

"Actually, Curtis did. We picked them out together from a catalog, and he placed the order. Even the tree."

"Bless him for that," Wade said, straight-faced but slightly sarcastic. "Well, whoever was responsible for getting them here did good. And this is hands down better than eating in the formal dining room." He sat back in his chair. "And I'm going to enjoy the view as well as the meal."

He looked directly at Victoria, and she lowered her head, refusing to meet his glance. Not the normal response for Victoria, who sought out any and all attention whenever she could find it.

"But the next time you redecorate, remember to put up some signs warning of construction."

She nodded her agreement. "And turn on some lights for through traffic."

Jacob chose that moment to approach the table. "Are we ready to dine, sir?"

Wade nodded. "I believe we are."

The old butler disappeared for a few minutes and returned holding two large flat boxes. He set both in the center of the table. "Here we have a meat lover's with pepperoni and sausage." He moved it to the side and opened the other box. "Here we have a sampling of meats and vegetables. I believe this is a Supreme. No jalapeños or anchovies."

Victoria burst into laughter.

"Thanks, Jacob," Wade said, grinning.

"You are most welcome." He turned to Victoria. "I'll be right back with your salads. Uh…dig in."

Surreal. She'd even had a positive effect on the staff.

She grabbed one slice of each pizza and placed them on her plate. Picking up the pepperoni and sausage slice, she took a sizable bite and rolled her eyes, muttering, "Oh man! That is *so* good."

Wade helped himself as he continued to watch his wife enjoy her meal. In the past, she'd rarely shown such enthusiasm, even for a filet mignon prepared by a world-renowned chef accompanied by a rare wine that cost thousands per bottle. Who knew she would have been content with a pizza from Domino's and a Diet Dr Pepper?

"Do you have any plans in the coming weeks?"

"Me? Plans?" She took a sip of her beverage. "I'll have to check my social calendar," she said, then grinned. "What did you have in mind?"

"I thought you might like a small vacation."

"Really? Where?"

"Let it be a surprise."

After lunch, Wade excused himself and returned to his office, saying he needed to make some phone calls. Victoria walked with him partway; when he turned left down another corridor, she got onto the elevator. But instead of selecting the second floor, she leaned on the hold button. She didn't want to go back to her room; she wanted to be outside. The late-afternoon sun was still shining, and the memory of the tranquil blue-green water of the pool was a heady invitation. Without further thought, she stepped back out of the elevator and headed to the pool.

Towels were kept in a cabinet, along with sunscreen and sunglasses and a few other items. She grabbed one of the towels and walked to the edge of the enormous pool. It was shaped like a lagoon and was surrounded with tropical plants. The waterfall at the far end was too tempting. She quickly shed her blouse and jeans to reveal the yellow bikini underneath. Without testing the water, she dropped the towel on top of her clothes on a chair, moved to an area where the water was deeper and dived in. So cool and refreshing! She loved to swim. She loved the water. Both were things she hadn't considered yet. Maybe some of her memory was coming back.

She turned onto her back, partially floating, partially paddling the water with her hands, each stroke taking her closer to the falls. The giant boulders flanking each side had natural indentations where ivy and other cascading plants grew. The falls fell from a height of fifteen feet or more above the water and were just as wide.

She dived under the falls, came up on the other side and found herself at the opening of a huge cavern. The water gradually grew more shallow until she was walking up a wide set of stairs leading into an aboveground cave. The space would easily hold a dozen people. It had heavy wooden beams across the top and a skylight set into the center. There were reclining chairs, a sofa, a table for four and a small bar. It even had a large flat-screen television. The cave was made entirely of rock. The cream-colored floor was smooth alabaster laced with the brown color of the cave walls. Lit from beneath, it cast a soft glow over the space, giving it a feeling of solitude where the busy world could not break in. A fire pit lay ready and waiting, extending up from the center of the wide steps. She could hear soft music being piped in over the sound of the falling water.

It was amazing. Without any thought of *should she or shouldn't she?* Victoria climbed the four steps and stepped onto the translucent stone panels, which melded perfectly into the softly glowing floor. The bar top was made of the same smooth material and was the highlight of that area. She roamed around, amazed that from the outside, the hill covered in tropical plants and flowers was in fact a cover-up for a cavern complete with furniture and a big screen.

"What are you doing in here?" Wade's voice cut into the tranquility.

She spun around to face him. "I... Nothing. I was just looking around. This is incredible." She felt the blood drain from her face as she perceived this to be yet another area of this colossal house that was off-limits. Wade wasn't smiling.

He climbed the steps without seeming to move at all, dressed in a pair of trunks that left very little to the imagination. Heat pooled in her lower abdomen, and her mouth became dry. The closer he got, the better she could see his expression. He didn't look angry so much as amazed. "More to the point, how did you get in here?"

"Through the falls. I don't know of another way in. Is there one?"

"What are you even doing in the pool?"

"Swimming. What, am I not allowed in here either? Is there a silent alarm here, too?" She could hear the frustration in her voice. She had reached her limit of being told where she could go and couldn't go, what she could and couldn't do.

"Victoria." He gripped her upper arms and gave her a small shake. "Dammit. You don't know how to swim!"

Seven

"Apparently I do," she replied. "Actually, I love the water. I think. And this grotto behind the falls is awesome. I've never seen anything like it—that I can remember. I didn't hurt or damage anything."

"It never occurred to me that you would. I was merely concerned for your safety." Still looking at her as though he didn't believe a word she said, he finally nodded his head and released her arms but refused to let her out of his sight. "I need a drink. What would you like?" he asked over his shoulder as he turned and walked to the bar. "I used to keep this pretty well stocked, but there hasn't been anyone using these facilities in a couple of years."

"Not even you when you are at home?"

"No time. What will you have?"

"I haven't got a clue."

"Okay, well, you used to like rosé, so let us find out." He walked over to a large wine rack and selected a bottle.

"This is Château d'Esclans 'Garrus' Rosé from Provence, France, 2010. They produce only six barrels per year. I was lucky." His fluent, near perfect French was seductive.

"How many languages do you speak?"

"Six. A seventh if you want to count just getting by. Why do you ask?"

Victoria shrugged. "Just curious. You speak French beautifully. It sounds sexy. I can't help but wonder if I speak other languages. Probably not."

She walked over to Wade and watched as he easily removed the cork and grabbed two wineglasses from the glass shelving behind them.

"I think we need a toast," Victoria said after he had poured each of them a glass of the sparkling rosé. "To your project in Belize. May it be amazing."

"I'd prefer a different toast. Here's to my wife not drowning today."

She laughed and touched her glass to his. "I'll definitely drink to that." She took her first sip. "Oh, my gosh, this is delicious!" she said as she swallowed another. "Oh, my gosh, Wade."

"Glad you still like it. It's what I usually prefer when I'm out here near the pool."

"Wade, I really do know how to swim." She was determined to make him believe her. "I enjoy doing so. Either you misunderstood me, or—"

"Or you lied to me before." He looked at her straight on, but she met his eyes without flinching.

"Why would I do that?"

"I don't have the slightest idea, but it happens. Quite often, actually." He sat down on the edge of the couch and turned to face her. "How did you know you could swim?"

"I don't know. I enjoyed the pool while you were in

New York and wanted to come back. It's amazing." She took another sip of her wine. Was that why they weren't together? Did she get caught in a lie? Her instincts were screaming *no!*

"You do know that if you'd been wrong and couldn't swim, you would have been in trouble with no one around to help you."

She shrugged. "Maybe. But as soon as I got in the water, it felt okay."

Wade ran a hand across his lower face. "Victoria, I don't want you coming out here unless you have someone with you. Someone who knows how to swim."

"*I* know how to swim," she countered.

"Maybe. Maybe not."

Victoria set her glass on an end table. "How do you think I got here?"

"Probably because you can swim a little, but a percentage of that could have been luck."

Victoria knew what he was saying, and she felt her heart speed up because he apparently cared. "I appreciate the sentiments. I do. But I assure you nothing about me swimming to this grotto was luck. Why do you think I can't swim?"

"Because you've always been very nervous around the water. You told me you never learned to swim and didn't care to try. You avoided pool parties at all costs. You lived off Dramamine the few times I got you on board the yacht."

"We have a yacht?"

"The point is I don't want you taking unnecessary chances."

"I…" She didn't know what to say. She wouldn't have said such a thing to him, would she? Either he mistook something she said, or she had lied to Wade. According to Wade, lying was a common practice for her before her accident. That thought made her very uncomfortable.

"I'm going back to the house." Before he could try to stop her, she ran down the steps, dived into the deeper water under the falls and kept swimming. By the time Wade caught up with her, she was out of the pool and grabbing a towel.

"Victoria, wait," Wade called behind her. His request was ignored. She wanted to go back to the house. She needed to be alone. She had to have time to sort this out. What had happened between them? She didn't feel as though she was one who would lie to her husband, especially about something as trivial as knowing how to swim.

She scooted through the back door and headed down the hall toward the elevator and pushed the call button.

"Victoria, I need you to listen to me."

"Why? So you can accuse me of telling more lies?" She shook her head and glared at him. "You have the winning hand and refuse to give me a chance. Something is wrong between us. I felt it the day we came home from the hospital. If you won't tell me what happened, then I can do nothing to fix it." She pushed the button again. "If this is the way our marriage was, I don't care to continue. Two people who are married are supposed to love each other. I feel no love coming from you, Wade. Only brief glimpses of sympathy."

The door opened, and she stepped into the elevator. Unfortunately, Wade followed her inside.

"I won't stay in a house where I'm not wanted, and clearly that's the case. Give me a couple of days to make some arrangements, and I'll be out of your hair."

"Victoria, you can't leave."

She glared. "Do not tell me what I can and cannot do.

Except for my memory, I'm perfectly healthy. Your obligation to bring me here until I healed is over. You won't have to look at me again or listen to any more lies."

She was mad, hurt, frustrated; all the emotions that had been building over the past two weeks had reached the surface. Nothing was ever going to change. To remain in a loveless marriage that had no hope of getting better was pointless. She didn't need her memory to know that.

"Victoria—"

She held up a hand indicating whatever he had to say she didn't want to hear. The elevator doors opened, and she quickly stepped into the hallway and beat a path for her room.

For the first time, she locked her door behind her. Wade knocked and was rewarded with a clear "Go away."

After a few more attempts, he must have left. Turning to the shower, she dropped her bathing suit and stepped under the spray. Where would she go? There must be women's shelters somewhere nearby. Maybe Roe could give her some ideas in the morning. She hated to involve Wade's staff, but she didn't know the answers. Maybe she could find the apartment Wade had mentioned she kept in Dallas? Unless he owned it. Oh, God, if only her memory would come back.

It had been almost a month. Surely Victoria should be getting her memory back by now. Wade was a man, and he knew she wanted him. She needed his body as badly as he needed hers. But she was holding out because she didn't know anything about their past. He'd considered many times not telling her the whole truth and just saying they had been about to divorce. Then they could work their way through their issues and become a couple. But no. When her memory came back, she would sure as hell know about their past, about the contract. And what actions would she bring in a lawsuit then? Why should he want them to be a couple? He'd never especially cared for her before the accident. He'd never been attracted to her the way he apparently was now. And when her memory returned, there was every likelihood she would revert to the snobbish woman she'd always been. This entire situation was driving him crazy.

What if he told her the truth? What if he told her about the contract? Would that appease her? Would Victoria then understand what kind of marriage this was and accept it? It might even serve to bring back some of her memories. Certainly he wanted her fully healthy. But telling Victoria the truth of their relationship could cause more consternation than she needed at this time in her recovery. Still, did he have an option? He was tired of the half-truths. Tired of kissing her, feeling her body respond to him and having to step away. He knew the time was coming when he wouldn't be able to stop. Each time he held her, it became more difficult to let go. At least if she knew the truth, she could make the decision knowing all the facts surrounding their relationship. Right now she thought he had stopped loving her. How convoluted was that? He'd only in recent weeks begun to see her in a light that could lead him to *start* loving her.

Dinner that evening was uncomfortable, and that was an understatement. Even so, the menu was amazing. The main course was filet mignon with white truffle risotto and Italian kimchi-style escarole with anchovies and Calabrian chilies. A dark red rosé accompanied the meal. It no doubt was delicious, but the food stuck in his throat. The coziness he'd previously felt in the new dining room was now oppressive. And it seemed that neither one of them had an appetite.

After a long, uncomfortable silence, he decided to address the elephant in the room. "Victoria, people get married for many different reasons. It's not always solely because of love."

"Are you saying ours was like a marriage of convenience? Or...or...did I get pregnant?"

"No, you didn't get pregnant. I wish you would just let it go. What was in the past is in the past. Can we not go forward?"

"Forward to where? How can I go forward if I don't know where I've been?"

For a long minute neither moved.

"Come on." He stood up. "Walk with me."

He guided her back toward the elevator. When the doors opened, he accompanied her inside and pushed the button for the second floor. Rather than taking her to her room, they went farther down the hall to his. When they were inside, he indicated for her to sit. She chose one of the chairs near the fireplace. He pulled up a chair and sat down facing her.

He rubbed the back of his neck. "I agree that keeping the past from you isn't fair. You have the right to know. Then you can make your own decision whether you want to stay or go. But I won't try to stop you."

"Why at times do I get the feeling you hate me?"

He ground his teeth.

"I don't hate you, Victoria."

"Try again. It's like sometimes you want to hold me and make love to me. I feel your desire. I know it. I can tell. Then you push me away, or you walk away like it would be a bad thing. I... I don't know what I did that was so bad. You claimed that I often lied to you. About what? How am I ever going to make amends if you don't tell me what it is? I need to know, Wade. Like, about the water. Why would I lie about something so simple? What could possibly be my motivation?"

She gazed into his eyes. The golden flecks in his brown eyes seemed to glow in the ambient lighting. His masterful lips were held in a straight line, but she couldn't tear her eyes away.

He released a deep breath. "It's complicated, Victoria. Until your memory returns, I don't know how much you will understand."

"That's unfair." She looked at him. "You're holding something against me that I can't apologize for. I can't make it right because I don't know what it is that I did. I want to know about us." She stared into his face, not willing to look away or offer him the same option. "I want to know the truth. Since the day I woke up in the hospital after the wreck, I've never seen anything more in your eyes than sympathy and, on occasion, the glimmer of arousal, which you effectively snub out. You can give compassion to a homeless person. You can hire a woman if you need sexual release. I want to know why I'm here. Are we honestly even married?"

Wade hesitated to the point she didn't think he was going to answer. "Yes. We are married."

To her horror, tears sprang into her eyes and fell down her cheeks. "Did I have an affair? Is that it? Was that why you got so angry the first day I was here? Because I asked about Murphy? I can tell you I wasn't thinking of any particular man when I asked about that name."

Wade merely looked at her.

"That's it, isn't it? There was another man." She felt sick. How could there have been anyone else in her life when she had Wade?

"No. Yes. I honestly don't know." He gritted his teeth,

his jaw muscles working overtime. "It might be rumor. You are the only one who can answer that, and you can't until your memory returns."

"Oh, that's a great answer. I've lain in bed and tried to imagine what I did that would alienate my husband so completely, but I have no clue. If it's in my head, it won't come out."

"Victoria..."

Her voice was broken. "You're my husband. I love you. But I can't go on like this."

He closed the bedroom door as he watched her closely in the ambient light.

She took a deep breath. "What came between us?"

For several minutes she didn't think he was going to answer. Then he turned toward her, sat back down in the chair and clasped his hands together between his knees.

"Some people say I'm a workaholic. They're probably right. I'm used to traveling, setting priorities and making things happen. I spend more time en route than I do here or anywhere in the United States. Therefore, I'm not good husband material. I realized years ago that CEOs of other companies tended to work better with those who were married, who had a stable home and a family environment. I don't know why, but there it is. Business tends to go better if I give the impression I'm an established family man."

He paused to look at her as if trying to tell if he was making any sense. "There were past relationships. They went badly. I'd rather not go into the details, but marriage to a loving bride was not going to happen for me. Let's just say I have...trust issues."

He rubbed the back of his neck. "And you? You wanted to be in the inner circles of the elite rich. After your father lost all of his money...well, you were devastated. So, we made a bargain. A written contract. You would become my wife on paper only for a period of one year. If we both were in agreement at the end of the year, if we both met the contractual stipulations, we had the option of renewing it. If you bailed out before the year was over, you would forfeit a million dollars. There are other stipulations. Either of us, for instance, could see others as long as we were discreet and it didn't go public. There were other things involved in the agreement, but that's basically it.

"If I made love to you, I'd feel like I was taking advantage of you. It wouldn't be fair until you knew about the agreement. I couldn't do that." He shook his head. "I've tried to leave you alone, but since you came home from the hospital, there's something…something I can't ignore. My apologies for almost letting it get out of hand."

Victoria was in shock. She didn't know what to say. Of all the things she had imagined, it was as far as you could get from this. A contract. His statement explained so much. He didn't love her. He didn't have to love her. He needed only to be cordial and ensure she was made comfortable until the end of the agreement. During that time he would continue to travel, immerse himself in his business matters and leave her in this place alone. A searing pain pierced her heart.

"So…we're really married."

"On paper only."

"And you don't or never did love me?" It hurt to ask the question, but she had to know.

The answer was a long time coming. "No."

The tears welled in her eyes and fell down her cheeks. She felt humiliated. Hurt. A fool.

"I should definitely go." She sniffed and grabbed a tissue from the table by the bed. "If there is a suitcase I can borrow, I would appreciate it until I get settled."

"Go? Victoria, I don't want you to go."

"No, I guess you don't. How would you ever be the settled family man if I left?" She sucked in a deep breath. "Come on, save yourself a million, and just lend me the suitcase. I can't live like this. I don't know anyone who could. Of course, I don't know many people right now." She tried to insert a bit of humor, but it failed miserably. She kept wiping her face, but the tears kept coming. "I must have been out of my mind to ever agree to such a thing." She walked to the door, but Wade beat her to it. Still wiping the tears that ran nonstop, she stood in front of the closed door and waited with more patience than she felt for him to open it. "I'm sorry about the amnesia thing. It must have really put a crimp in your plans."

"Victoria."

"No, Wade. No more. I don't need details. You've told me everything I need to know. I just want a suitcase and a taxi that can take me…somewhere."

He stood looking down at her for the longest time.

"I would like to leave now." He opened the door and she walked through. Somehow Victoria made it to her room and to the bed before the dam burst. She cried hard, tears of hopelessness and deep sorrow. Tears that came from her heart. What a fool she'd made of herself. She thought back on all the worry about not fitting in with Wade, his world, his lifestyle. At least now she knew why. She had to wonder if she ever had fit in. She glanced down at the silver ring on her left hand. With its assorted stones, it was gaudy and too big. She slid it off her finger and put it in a drawer. It was so not her and it didn't represent the caring admiration a real husband was supposed to have for his wife. As she closed the drawer, more tears welled in her eyes. This was a nightmare. A lurid dream from which she couldn't seem to awaken.

* * *

What in hell was he thinking? He had finally admitted the nature of their relationship, and she'd taken it a lot harder than he would have expected. He couldn't believe the truth had rolled out of his mouth. When he'd heard the words, it sounded unbelievable even to himself. It sounded cold and calculating, which of course it was. Victoria's reaction tonight was far from her smile of elation when he'd first presented the idea. She'd gone after it tooth and nail. Couldn't wait to sign on the dotted line. Couldn't wait to move into the mansion. And certainly couldn't wait to begin living the high life.

Wade felt bad about it. He couldn't think he'd done the wrong thing in telling her. She deserved to know. It was a situation of damned if he did, damned if he didn't. But he hadn't expected her to immediately want to leave. He didn't want her to leave, especially since there was no place safe she could go. She would require a bodyguard. She probably didn't remember that and he had a feeling this new Victoria would not be thrilled by that fact. Sadly, that was what his life had come down to when he wasn't at the ranch. He had a feeling that convincing her of this would be next to impossible, which would only lead to more anger and frustration.

But fearing for her safety from kidnapping was not the only reason he wanted her to stay. She had changed. She intrigued him. If their situation were different, he would have already invited this new version of Victoria out, and by now would have had her in his bed. The problem with that train of thought was he didn't want it to be a onetime thing. He wanted more from Victoria than a couple of nights in bed. He wanted to continue getting to know her. She was smart, beautiful and sexy as hell. And she wasn't trying to be any of those things, which made her even sexier. She had an air of innocence about her. Fresh and vivacious, she touched him on more levels than anyone he'd ever known. While he'd not spent time analyzing his feelings, he knew what he felt for Victoria was different from anything he'd experienced with any other woman. It was exciting and new. It was also frightening in that when her memory returned, it was possible she would revert to the way she used to be. She'd become as different as night and day from her old self, and while he wanted her to regain her memory, he desperately hoped her personality wouldn't revert to the way she had been. He'd always envied his brothers for finding the perfect women, while at the same time telling himself he had the perfect life. No complications. Just doing what he loved and what he was very good at: finance. Corporate mergers. Contracts.

He actually had never given any thought to truly settling down and having a family. Until recently. What Victoria would do when her memory returned and how much she and her mother would try to milk him for were suddenly number one on the I Don't Give a Shit list. But that thought twisted into the fact that he desperately didn't want her to become her old self again. He was walking a tightrope between desire and reality and it was making him crazy.

A little voice reminded him of all the lies and the fact that Victoria couldn't be trusted. All the men she had supposedly been with over the past few months alone. Then there was the question of whether it was all a setup. Something staged to make him jealous or for some other nefarious act to provide her with more money. *That* he honestly didn't know.

He paced the floor, needing to find a resolution. Maybe after she'd had a chance to calm down, they could talk. Maybe after he'd had a chance to think, he would see the current situation a lot differently. Right now he felt as though he'd just found her, and tomorrow, if he left it up to her, she would be gone. He would not permit it. Muttering under his breath, he walked to the shower. How had he managed to get himself into such a damnable situation?

Deep down where no one could see, he'd started having illusions of becoming the family man that up until now had just been an irritating thought. Since the accident, Victoria had brought to light how lonely life really was. Oh, there was plenty of socializing, parties on the yacht, dinners at the finest restaurants around the world. If he needed to, he could always find a date with women who knew how to play the game.

But there was no comparing them to Victoria. For the first time, he was beginning to glimpse his solitary, structured life through her eyes. It *was* an empty, often lonely existence. It was a life without nurturing, consisting of accomplishments no one cared about, other than those who would benefit monetarily. Over the past weeks, he had fought against these ridiculous sentiments, but he couldn't deny the way he felt when he and Victoria were together: alive and looking forward to the next day. There was no posturing, no expectations other than to just be himself. At times it felt as though an enormous weight had been lifted. Still, Wade held on to caution.

Because when her memory returned, the old Victoria would be back. He knew it in his heart.

Eight

A knock on the door broke the silence of the night. Victoria turned from the window where she'd been staring out at the garden below. Unable to sleep, she'd paced at first, then started packing a few clothes to take with her when she left. She wouldn't take much because Wade had probably bought most of it for her. When she was done, she'd soaked in the tub, which helped a little to settle her nerves. Then she'd put on a nightgown and gone to the balcony.

She looked at the clock. It was three in the morning. There could be only one person knocking at her door at this time of night.

Finally, the door opened. Wade stood on the threshold, tall and muscled, wearing only a pair of sweats.

"I just wanted to check on you." He ran a hand through his hair; it appeared as though it wasn't the first time he'd done so tonight. "I know I upset you, and that wasn't my intention."

Victoria shrugged. "It is what it is. At least now I understand a lot of things that didn't make any sense before. I'm fine. At least I will be as soon as I can find my own place."

"Victoria, I don't want you to go. It's not safe for you to be out in the world without your memory intact. I don't want you to leave, period."

"Wade...you've shown me kindness by bringing me here and caring for me when I had no place else to go. I can now repay you by breaking that contract. You shouldn't have to be out any more money because of me."

"I don't give a damn about the money." He took in a deep breath and blew it out. "I'm worried about you. We've known each other for almost five years as casual acquaintances. Until the accident, I never really knew you at all. The relationship we have now is different than before. We've gotten to know each other this time. I like having you here. I want to know you better. I'd hoped you might still want to stay here and get to know me after learning the truth of our relationship."

She looked up at him. Was he seriously asking her to stay? "Would a clothing-store mannequin not work as well for you? No feelings, no emotions to have to deal with, just give her a name and there you go. She won't break any rules and I can guarantee she won't be calling out other men's names when you are in her presence. She might have a hard time signing a new contract, but what the hell. You can sign it yourself."

She moved to close the door, but Wade blocked it.

"Victoria."

She loved him. In the short time they'd had together that she could remember, she had fallen in love with this incredibly complex man. But her heart was breaking. All this time, she'd been afraid she'd done something wrong, and he'd let her go on thinking it. She could now add anger to the feelings of frustration and guilt.

"What exactly do you want from me now? I don't have anything else to give."

"Let's see where this goes, Victoria. You might find you want nothing to do with me—"

"Ya think?"

"—but I would like to give it a chance. We have almost two months until the contract is up."

"Oh, okay, let's put it on a timer. See if you can fall in love with your wife in two months. Got a stopwatch?" Her sarcasm was not lost on Wade.

"Dammit, Victoria." Wade closed the door behind him, grasped her shoulders and gently pushed her against the nearby wall. "That's not what I meant. I didn't expect to have these feelings for you when this whole thing started. And I didn't expect you to feel anything for me. You didn't, you know...when we made up the contract. You just wanted money and prestige. I'm sorry for not telling you before now, but it was a two-way street."

It had never occurred to her that she'd wanted the contract as much as he did. Since being discharged from the hospital, they'd both begun to respond to the magnetic pull between them until they were unable to deny the intensity of love growing there. Those emotions trumped a contract as far as she was concerned. She nodded her head.

No matter what else happened in her life, she knew that in his arms was where she wanted to be. Not for money or prestige. Just to be held close and wanted like any woman who was in love with her husband.

He lowered his face to hers so that they were inches apart. Gently he wiped the tears from her eyes. "I want to explore the possibility that we have something special. I want you to be more than a token wife. I want you to give us a chance."

She didn't think she could cry any more, but in that she was wrong. Tears of happiness welled in her eyes. "No more withholding the truth. No more remote politeness. Oh, I'm so tired of being treated like a guest in my own home. Or rather, in your home."

"*Our* home."

"I don't want your money. Promise me that contract will be torn to shreds either way."

"We can discuss it later." One large hand came to rest on her shoulder. "Much later." He placed two fingers under her chin and tilted her head to meet his gaze. "Stay, Victoria. Stay here with me."

The dam broke, and Wade kissed her hard. He drew her to him, and as soon as she responded to him, the kiss deepened. He'd kissed her before since returning from the hospital, but this was different. There was no hesitation, no uncertainty. No right or wrong. It was as though she was his, and he intended to show her exactly what that meant. All barriers were down.

He scooped her into his arms and walked out the door and down the hall to his suite. He threw back the covers and gently placed her on the bed. The soft lighting shone on the muscles of his arms, his broad chest and tight abs. He stepped out of his pants and followed her down, kissing her in long, lingering exchanges.

"You're my wife, Victoria. And you're going to be in every way that matters," he said roughly as he pushed away the straps of her nightgown. "In my bed is where you need to be. If you don't want me, tell me now."

For several long moments she held his gaze. In the ambient light she could see his eyes as they roamed over her face. Then she raised her head and placed her lips on his. He pressed her down on the mattress, and her arms went around his neck.

"I don't think I've ever wanted anything more in my life," she whispered. With that, he kissed her again, more deeply, like he couldn't get enough of her.

He held her tightly, as though forgetting his strength, but it only served to make her heart beat faster with excitement. She'd wondered what it would be like to make love to him without all the restraints he had kept in place when he'd kissed her before. She was about to find out. She wanted to melt into him. She opened to the demands of his lips and tongue.

Without lifting his head, he shifted her to the center of the bed, working his knee between her legs to part them. His body pressed her down into the pliable softness of the mattress. He brushed her hair back away from her face and kissed down her neck, nipping at her collarbone, licking her ear before moving to her breasts. He eased her nightgown all the way off, and his hands covered the velvet softness of her breasts, causing the nipples to go taut. Her back arched up in a natural response, and she moaned.

"What do you want, Victoria?"

She let go of his shoulder and found his hands with hers, causing him to press her nipples more firmly. She heard him chuckle softly.

"Is this what you need?"

He bent his head and sucked a rosy tip into his mouth. She couldn't forestall a moan as he suckled the nipple, hard. She grabbed his hair, holding him to her. Then he changed to the other breast, giving it the same attention. Growling, he returned to her lips and kissed her long and deep.

Wade left her mouth and began a trail of kisses down her abdomen, to the sweet spot between her legs.

"Open for me?" His voice was low, guttural. Victoria complied. His large hands spread her knees farther apart, and he put his mouth and tongue to work.

"Oh…" she cried out in rapture, never having felt anything like this in her life. Surely she would know if she had. How could she forget this glorious feeling? Finding her special spot, Wade alternately teased it with his tongue and suckled. Suddenly everything went still. Seconds later she exploded, her body quivering in a delight that was indescribable. Wade laid his head on her stomach and held her until the tremors had passed. Victoria was limp, satiated. But Wade wasn't finished.

He spread her legs wide again. Then he began to taste every inch of her again. Her nipples were erect, and he sucked them hard, using his tongue to circle and lick the rosy buds.

She felt his shaft press against her core and violent shivers raced down her spine, centering between her legs. Her hands raked at the smooth muscles of his back, silently asking for more. She heard a soft moan and realized it came from her own throat. Wade returned to her mouth, drinking deep, lapping at her tongue. Victoria couldn't get enough of him, her body's natural instincts responding to his every move.

Her fingers corded through the thickness of his hair. She pushed against him, knowing he was the only one who could quench the fire that blazed out of control deep within her.

"I can't hold off any longer." His baritone voice was rough and laced with passion. "I need to be in you." His powerful body was trembling with need.

"Yes," she murmured against his lips. The male scent of him surrounded her. His lips were so hungry, kissing her over and over while his erection pressed against her center. His hand moved down her body to her core, testing her wetness, making sure she was ready for him. Then using his hand to guide his shaft, he pushed inside. Victoria drew in a sharp, deep breath and tensed. Wade came to an immediate stop, realizing he'd met resistance.

His heart was beating hard against the wall of his chest as he held himself still.

"Victoria…"

His upper body trembled as he fought to lift himself from her and bring all activity to a halt.

"Wade, what's wrong?"

He pushed against her inner core again, and again she cried out in discomfort.

"You're a virgin." He shook his head, unable to believe it. It was impossible.

His head swam. How was it possible that Victoria had never been with a man? Her various dalliances had made the headlines. But still, there was no getting around the reality of the situation, surreal as it was.

"Hon, if you've never been with a man, this may hurt."

"I don't care." She pressed her lips to his, hungry for whatever he could give to make the need stop.

"God, Victoria," he murmured against her lips. "Are you sure you want this?"

"Yes," she whispered. "I love you, Wade."

He cupped her face and stared into her eyes. Then lowering his head, he sought her lips before moving to her neck. Taking tender bites along the sensitive cord, he whispered into her ear, "Are you ready for me, Victoria?"

She nodded, breathing fast. Pushing deep inside, he felt the barrier give, and it was done. He held perfectly still, waiting for a signal from Victoria that she wanted to continue.

She began to bestow kisses on his neck and throat, taking small bites, her hands raking his broad shoulders as she silently gave him her answer. He couldn't hold himself back any longer and began to move. With each push, each movement, the pressure once again began to build. Only now the pressure was different. Heat was building to a scorching level.

He couldn't get close enough, couldn't get deep enough as she returned his kisses.

"Oh, Wade," she called out.

He stopped as the perspiration broke out on his face. "Are you all right?" he said against her mouth, then rained kisses over her neck and ear.

Victoria managed to nod her head. "Don't stop."

Then he began to move once again. He grasped her hip with one hand, raising her to him, and the world tilted on its axis. Wade could sense the moment was near; the heat was reaching an all-time high.

"Come for me, babe," Wade growled in her ear, and she cried out. Wade soon joined her, reaching an outrageously intense climax of his own. She held him tight, kissing the moist skin of his face and neck.

Wade dropped onto the mattress next to her, pulling her close, still breathing hard. He gently turned her face to his and kissed her again. Time seemed to stop and the world outside disappeared.

The scent of sex and luscious female enveloped him as Wade lay next to her, his leg over hers, his arm around her. Together they fell asleep.

Sometime later, Wade awakened her with soft kisses. "Sweetheart, you're moaning in your sleep. Let's get you in a warm bath. It will help you feel better."

She nodded her head, her body still boneless from the lovemaking.

Wade had already drawn a bath. He gently lowered

her into the tub and followed her in, situating himself behind her. He adjusted the jets of water, and she relaxed
against him. He loved the silkiness of her skin, loved the
feeling of her hair against his neck. Loved the feel of her.

Later in the night, Wade came to her again. He woke
her with kisses down her shoulder and back until she
turned to him, and his lips once again covered hers. This
time was better than the first. She was hungry for him
and met him touch for touch, breath for breath. The ending was a blazing trail to the stars, and cuddled together,
they drifted back to sleep.

Wade began the next morning by offering to give her
a tour of his downtown Dallas offices. His building was
twenty stories high, all dark glass and concrete. She met
so many nice people. His office, like everything else in
his world, was extreme, taking up almost half of the top
floor. The walls and massive executive desk were ma-
hogany, and the floor-to-ceiling windows offered a panoramic view of the rapidly expanding city. Attached to his
office was a room almost as large for the administrative
staff and yet another with a conference table that would
probably seat twenty people. He had a language center
with employees who handled overseas calls. A personal
bathroom and spa. The list of amenities went on.

"You could almost live here," she laughed.

"Sometimes I do." He had no smile on his face when
he said it. "Ready to go?"

Wade approached where she sat. She couldn't help but
feel a new hope. A huge weight had been lifted. And the
promise of a new future had begun.

She nodded and, with Wade beside her, walked to
the elevators and went down to the lobby and out into
the sunshine.

"What would you think about taking a vacation?" he asked once they were seated in the limo. "You seem to like nature and the great outdoors."

"Sounds tempting."

"I know of a place that's just what the doctor ordered. Pun intended, but he did say you should be fine if we relocated for a while."

"I'm more than okay with that. Where is it you had in mind?"

Wade shook his head. "Wait and see. We won't be leaving the country. I'm not fully convinced you're up to that. But it's a place I hope you'll like."

"Okay." She smiled and shrugged. Why not? It had to be better than the big house in the city. And after his confession last night, she was beginning to get used to the idea of trusting her husband. "When do we leave?"

"In the morning. Dress casual. Jeans would be great."

Jeans. She could handle jeans.

It seemed that Wade was full of surprises. The next morning it was a short drive to a small airport where the Masters family's planes were housed. They drove to the end of a hangar where a dark blue helicopter with Masters International painted in silver letters on the side waited, the rotor blades already churning.

"Are you kidding me?"

"Come on," he said, smiling, no doubt at how her jaw had dropped.

Reluctantly she accepted Wade's hand and got out of the car. The wind from the helicopter blades whipped her hair around her face. She held fast to his hand as they approached the chopper. He opened the door, indicating she should slide into the back seat. Then he closed her door before going to the other side and climbing in beside her. The first thing he did was hand her a set of ear-

phones with a microphone attached. Putting on a headset
of his own, he told her to buckle up and closed his door.

"Ready?"

"No." She glanced around the cozy interior. "And don't
try to convince me I've done this before."

"You're a natural." He pursed his lips, a wicked glint
showing in his eyes.

"At what?"

Wade laughed and gave the pilot a thumbs-up. The
man opened the throttle, increasing the speed of the main
rotor. The sound of the engine grew louder as the blades
spun faster and faster. It was exhilarating and scary at
the same time. After a few seconds, the chopper lifted
off the helipad, momentarily plunging forward before rising, and they were on their way. Victoria couldn't help
but marvel at the sight out her window as they climbed
high above the city skyline and headed east. Roads became ant trails, and cars the ants. She felt as light as a
bird, and any initial fear quickly turned to exhilaration.

After circling the downtown Dallas area, they headed
north. The city gave way to beautiful suburban homes
and finally to the sprawling ranch lands of North Texas.

After about an hour Wade announced, "We're here."
They began descending into a clearing amid a heavily
forested area. The trees began to separate, showing green
pastureland and several structures. The circular landing
pad came into view some distance from what appeared
to be a barn. On a small plateau, an area surrounded by
white pipe fencing stretched almost out of sight. Both
horses and cattle grazed in the abundant grass within
the boundaries.

The pilot gently set the chopper down in the center of
the remote helipad and killed the motor. Wade opened
his door and got out first, then helped Victoria to the

ground. Taking her hand, he guided her to a well-worn path that led into the trees, up a small rise to a huge log home faced with glass walls.

"How beautiful," she said as she pulled him to a stop to take in the beauty all around her. "This is where you grew up?"

He nodded. "Dad built this house when I was about six. Before that we lived three miles to the south in a smaller house. When Chance was born, it quickly became obvious larger digs were needed. It was a good place to grow up."

"Chance is your brother?"

"Yeah. He's the youngest. He and his wife, Holly, live here on the ranch. Chance manages, while Holly has a veterinarian practice across the road from the main house."

Victoria could hear the wistfulness in his voice and knew she wasn't imagining it. To Wade, this place was home. It was where he and his brothers had learned about life. Where Wade had grown into the man he had become today. This ranch was a part of his heart that could never be chipped away or taken from him. The fact that he wanted to share it with her made her almost giddy with happiness.

As they stepped onto the large front porch, the door was pulled open and a small whirlwind of a woman with blond hair raced toward Wade, not pausing until, with a jump, she was in his arms, welcoming him with a huge hug. They both laughed as Wade spun around.

"I couldn't believe it when they told me you were coming," she said with excitement. "It's so good to see you again!"

Wade set her on the deck, grinning broadly. "Holly, I want you to meet my wife. This is Victoria."

Her beautiful face still full of smiles, she didn't hesitate to welcome Victoria to both the ranch and to the family. "Wade Masters! You sure took your time bringing her out here. Oh, my gosh!" She laughed and, stepping over, gave Victoria a hug. "It's nice to meet you," she said with honest enthusiasm. She glanced back at Wade. "She's beautiful." She nudged his shoulder with her own. "You did *good*, dude."

"Victoria, this is Holly." Wade made the introductions. "Like I told you, her husband, Chance, manages the operation here. Holly grew up on the ranch. Her father was the previous manager. And this *brat* has been a thorn in my side for…twenty-three years?"

"Twenty-four next month," she corrected, a bit of pride in her voice. "Y'all come on in and make yourselves at home." She pushed open the heavy door and stepped aside, indicating they should precede her. "No one's been here since last August when Wade stopped by for a few days. I had Ms. Hughes give the house a good once-over to address the dust, freshen the linens. There's food in the pantry, steaks in the freezer, wine in the cellar… I think that's it. But if you need anything else, you know to call the office."

"Thanks, Holly. I appreciate it." Wade looked around and seemed to relax.

"No worries." Holly turned toward the door, stopping just inside. "Chance should be back on Wednesday. I hope you both will still be here then."

"That is the plan unless I get a call. You know how that goes."

"Good deal. I gotta scoot. Later!"

"She's a special person," Victoria commented when Holly had gone.

Wade nodded. "Honestly, I had some concerns about

her when Chance first enlisted in the military. She loved him even back then as a teenager. Saying goodbye was hard on all of us, but especially Holly. But she's tough. Chance ended up a Navy SEAL. I didn't think anything or anyone could inspire him to give up that life. Holly did it. I don't think she really ever asked him to leave the navy, she just made Chance realize how much she loved him and what he was giving up here."

Victoria nodded her understanding. Obviously Holly thought of Wade as an older brother, which said a lot about Wade. She had a feeling this was going to be an eye-opening visit in a number of ways.

She took in her surroundings. It was a magnificent home. Large but cozy, with walls of split log and drywall, a thirty-foot-high ceiling and a huge stone fireplace with a hand-carved mantel. Massive overhead beams ran the length of the ceiling and the tall glass panes gave a view of the valley that was to die for. The kitchen featured a large island with hickory cabinets and granite counter-tops. A polished hardwood floor finished off the design scheme. "This house is fantastic. I love it. Thank you for bringing me here."

"There are four bedrooms and a master suite upstairs. Our luggage will be taken there if you have no objections."

They would be sharing a room? She grinned. "No problem here."

Wade leaned over and kissed her. "Someone will bring our luggage in a little while. Are you hungry?"

"No. Not at all." They'd had a light breakfast before they left. "I want to see your ranch."

That earned her a raised eyebrow, tipped head and curious look from her husband. He shrugged. "Say no more. The ranch we will see. At least part of it."

Wade led the way outside to a storage unit also made of logs and mortar at the rear of the house. He opened the double doors, revealing several four-wheelers parked inside.

"The best way to see anything on a ranch this size is an ATV." He turned toward her. "Ever ridden one before?"

All she could do was shrug. "Not that I remember. But I'm willing to give it a shot."

"Let's not take a chance. How about you ride with me for your first outing?"

Wade swung his leg over a red ATV. Revving up the engine, he nodded to her to climb on behind him and handed her a helmet. Her arms went around his waist, and she felt the tight abdominal muscles beneath her fingers.

With two revs and a squeal from Victoria, they were off. She couldn't hold back another scream as they topped a rise and plunged down the other side.

"Slow down!" she called out, laughing. She was holding on to him so tight she probably fractured one of his ribs, but Wade didn't seem to mind. He was a big, incredibly fit man, and her arms barely reached entirely around his waist.

He nodded his head, indicating he'd heard her request to slow up. But instead, he gave it some gas, and they shot forward. They hit rises that took them off the ground, skirted holes in the turf and drove full speed up and over mounds of dirt, with Victoria screaming and laughing the whole way.

The first stop was the main barn. Victoria quickly got off the four-wheeler, swearing she would never get back on the thing. "You're a maniac!" Wade actually laughed out loud.

Most of the stalls were full, and the horses inside them

looked amazing. She hurried to one, a beautiful black-and-white paint.

"Wade." She looked back to make sure he was behind her. "She's beautiful. I've never seen anything like her. Well, that I can remember."

He stepped up beside her. "She's a Tobiano paint Tennessee Walker. As you can see, she's basically white with black patches on the body and legs. Some have dark brown, bay or chestnut patches. Most paints are Overo, which is a black or brown body with white patches. Some, like her, have a two-toned mane and tail and a dark face with a star and a snip or a wide blaze."

"She's amazing."

"My grandfather was concerned about this breed slowly being integrated with horses of solid color. If no one stepped up, we could have lost the DNA that produces these amazing markings. Thankfully several ranchers joined in, and they turned it around. Dad started a small herd years ago. I think today we maintain about thirty for our own use, including breeding stock."

With her long multicolored mane and tail and intricate patchwork of black against the white body, the horse was breathtakingly beautiful.

"Over here is a roan or, specifically, an Appaloosa." Wade moved down to the next stall. "They are also known for their odd markings. Most common is dark brown legs, mane, tail and lower body. Then they have a white blanket on their rear with tiny brown spots inside. This pattern is typical, but some are white with small brown or black spots covering the body, neck and legs."

"Sounds like you're describing a dalmatian."

Wade smiled. "That's what many look like. Often they have bold, clearly defined stripes on their hooves. Their temperament, endurance and versatility make them very popular. The Appaloosa and the Quarter Horse, more than any other breeds, helped make the West what it is."

They continued down the long aisle, Wade answering questions, and Victoria bubbling with excitement as stall after stall housed a horse that was beautiful and unique.

She felt as though she was staying at a Western resort. As they walked together down the center of a barn that had to house a hundred horses, Victoria couldn't take it all in. Every breath contained the scent of freshly baled hay, cedar shavings and leather.

"Most of the horses on the ranch are Quarter Horses," he explained. "You might see an Arabian or two and, of course, the Walkers. We breed and train the Quarter Horses and sell them to other ranches for work or recreation." She watched as Wade looked around the huge structure with wonder in his eyes just like hers.

From the massive barn, they ventured to the foal paddock, where the newborns were just finding their legs.

"We keep the mothers and their babies in this area for the first few weeks, just to make certain everything is okay. Then they are turned out into the general pasture until the foals are six months old and it's time to wean them."

"They are so adorable." The foals followed their mothers as they grazed. "It looks like they're all legs."

Wade chuckled, a sound she loved. "At this age, that's just about what they are. But they'll grow fast."

"When do you start to train them?"

"Already started. As soon as they are born, they are fitted with a halter and taught it's okay to feel pressure against their heads. By the time they enter this pasture, most can be led around. At six months, groundwork starts. They are trained to become used to someone handling them, brushing them, giving them baths. But they don't feel a saddle until they are about two. At three they carry their first rider, and an entirely new training begins."

Victoria didn't know how long they stood watching the foals—their antics were so fascinating. Finally, Wade called it a day.

"It's getting late. You must be hungry. Let's head back. We can saddle up a couple of horses tomorrow, if you like, and I'll show you more of the ranch."

"Sounds like a plan." She smiled and walked side by side with Wade out of the barn.

Nine

Wade was amazed. So far, Victoria hadn't made any negative comments since they'd first gotten in the chopper and headed to the ranch. He figured, when she realized the cabin was remote, she would find a bone to pick with that, but she hadn't said a word. She had even seemed to really enjoy looking at the horses. He just couldn't figure it out. None of this was typical Victoria behavior. Inside he was glad. Especially after what they'd shared. But at the same time, he remained cautious. None of it made any sense. It was the same twist-tie emotion he'd had since bringing her home from the hospital. He expected the worst but relished the feeling of delight when her behavior was nothing like what he'd anticipated.

Tomorrow they would head up to Stockman's Ridge. The only way to get there was on horseback. There were some really scenic views, but it was a tough ride. They should get back before the sun disappeared to attend the campfire. They'd sit on a log, eating red beans and sausage cooked over an open fire with some corn bread. As a kid it had been one of his favorite meals. No French chef, no expensive wine. And the only music was if one of the ranch hands brought his guitar.

If Victoria survived tomorrow, he was going to give up watching for inconsistencies in her behavior and just accept that she had amnesia and wasn't faking it. He had to accept it. Short of having her muck stalls, there was not a lot else he could do to bring out her true colors. If it turned out she really did love the ranch and the horses, he would enjoy every minute he was with her until her memory did truly return. If she changed at that time, he would face and deal with it then.

He certainly had never expected, with all the men she'd paraded around, that she would be a virgin. He'd almost lost it that night. No, Victoria wasn't at all what he expected when he brought her home from the hospital. And he thanked his lucky stars for that. If she truly did love the outdoors as much as he did, it was a match made in heaven. And that he was hard-pressed to believe. He must always remain aware that this was, in fact, Victoria. Her memory could come back at any time and bring with it the return of her old self as she was before the accident. A tinge of sadness touched his heart. Would there ever be a time he could believe she was who she presented herself to be?

When they returned to Pine House, a member of the household staff told them their bags had been left in the upstairs hallway outside the master bedroom. She ran up the stairs, curious to see what it looked like. The room was very spacious, with a large bed in the center draped in silk and printed with images of deer and the forest. Across from the door a balcony beckoned. Pushing the heavy drapes aside, she pulled open the French doors. Below her was the barn, with pastures and trees surrounding it as far as she could see. In the distance she spotted a river with bright blue water. The whole setting was breathtaking. How could Wade not want to live here?

Dinner that night was around a campfire. About twenty of the ranch hands joined them, digging into the red beans, sausage and corn bread. She took her plate, fork and napkin and found a seat on a huge overturned tree trunk. Wade soon joined her. The ranch hands ran the conversation, and Victoria was content to sit, eat and listen. Talk about some tall tales. Most were hilarious stories, and many involved Wade and his brothers as kids. She laughed and ate until she felt she would pop.

She glanced at Wade, who sat back with his hat pulled low over his face, listening to the stories, occasionally denying he had any part in the mischief being described. This would cause the guys to all boo good-naturedly. There was nothing arrogant or snobbish about Wade. He'd known many of them most of his life, and it appeared they liked him just like they would one of their own. *He should be here*, she thought. This was his home.

She realized she was looking at a completely different man from the one who lived in Dallas. Rather than having a forced smile on his face, this Wade sat back, totally contented and happy. He seemed to speak more freely and had an overall laid-back demeanor.

As the group began to break up, Wade and Victoria walked back to the house. "Did you want anything to keep by the bed in case you get thirsty tonight? Water? Tea? The housekeeper has the night off."

"No, thank you. I'm fine."

"Which side do you want?" Wade asked as they entered the suite.

"It doesn't matter to me. You pick."

She grabbed her nightgown and headed for the shower. Soon she was standing under the water, the warm spray enveloping her. The thought of sleeping with Wade that evening had her heart pumping. Wanting to be with him was turning into a craving so deep it almost hurt.

After a quick shower, she brushed her teeth and applied facial cream before brushing out her long hair. The flesh-colored silk nightgown clung to her curves, from her breasts to her hips. She opened the door and gazed out into the suite. It was dark. She could just make out the bed and the large figure on the far side of it.

She quietly padded to the free side of the bed, lifted the covers and climbed in. The mattress was indented from his weight, causing her to roll in that direction. Turning away, she wiggled until she could catch a hold of her side of the mattress and scoot herself over. This was a heck of a thing. If she let go, she would slide back against Wade.

"You can't possibly sleep holding on to the side of the mattress." Wade's deep voice carried a bit of humor. "Chance and Cole each have their own home. I'm the only one who sleeps in here, and I usually sleep in the middle."

"Great." She grabbed one of the extra pillows and tucked it between them. It helped a little. Turning her back to him, she plumped the pillow under her head and tried to get comfortable. It was chilly in the room; the temperature really dropped here at night. She reached down toward her feet and grabbed the extra cover. Spreading it over her, she once again plumped her pillow and tried to find a comfortable position.

Silence filled the room. Victoria closed her eyes. It felt really odd to be sharing a bed with her husband with a pillow crammed in between them.

"Wade?" she whispered. "Are you asleep?"

"No."

"It feels funny."

"What feels funny?"

"Sleeping in the same bed with my husband and having a pillow stuffed between us."

"I didn't put it there," he muttered. With a brief movement, he pulled it from between them and sent it flying across the room. "Problem solved."

"I was trying not to smush you."

"Sweetheart, you couldn't *smush* me if you tried. Don't worry about the bed. If you end up on top of me by the morning, there will be no complaints from this side."

"I know this should feel normal, but—"

Wade rolled onto his other side to face her. He propped himself up by the elbow and leaned in toward her ear. "One night is all it will take to feel normal."

Victoria was quiet. One night of what? One night of sleeping in the same bed? One night of feeling his warmth next to her? One night of making love?

Any of the three would work.

"You're right." Whatever he meant.

"Roll over, away from me," he said in a deep, rich voice. She did as asked, and his arm came around her, just below her breasts. "Okay?"

"Yes."

"Good. If you get too hot during the night, be sure to wake me up." He kissed her on the neck. "Mmm. You smell good."

She lay with her head on the pillow and Wade's arm around her. Her back was warmed by his tight abs and powerful chest. She could feel his erection against her bottom and fought not to shift against it. She could hear her heart beating in her ears and struggled to breathe normally.

She couldn't say how long she lay in that position, but it grew hot. Who was she kidding? Wade was a man in every sense of the word, and he knew how to please a woman. She knew it in every cell in her body. And he knew exactly what he was doing to her.

"Wade, are you asleep?"

"What's wrong, sweetheart?" he asked in an innocent voice.

"It's hot."

She heard him chuckle before he turned her over to face him. His lips covered hers, and his hands got busy making it a lot hotter.

After a quick shower, she dressed in jeans, a cool blouse and her new sneakers, then hurried down the stairs.

"Ready to do a little exploring?"

"Absolutely."

Victoria glanced around as she stepped off the bottom stair. Wade was standing next to the kitchen bar, a shirt held in one hand, a letter in the other. Whatever its contents, it had captured his attention and the way he was dressed captured hers. He was wearing jeans—tight, worn, ripped jeans that hugged his body like a second skin. Above the leather belt, a tight six-pack led upward to a broad chest and wide shoulders. The muscles underneath his skin moved like well-oiled steel cables. She'd never seen him dressed in anything but a suit or jogging pants. But in jeans, he was…amazing. It didn't take a pair of tight jeans for her to know that, but they served as a great reminder.

"The sugar and cream are on the table. Do you want something to eat?"

He reached out for his cup of coffee, taking a sip, then

setting it on the bar without taking his eyes off the letter. Did the man not know the effect he had on women? On this woman, at least? It was like someone put all the world's sexier-than-hell ingredients in a pan and stirred. The final product stood nonchalantly in front of her. And his innocent manner just made it worse. Or better, as it were.

When she didn't answer the question, he looked up. "Victoria?"

"What? Oh. Uh. No. Not hungry." She turned away as she felt the blush spread over her face.

"You don't look like you had a good night."

"I had a very good night." She smiled at him. "I require very little sleep."

"Good thing," he said and winked.

"Do you have something I can take along to drink on the trail? Maybe a lemonade?"

She realized she was staring at him again. She couldn't help it. He frowned, no doubt sensing something was up. She turned toward the fridge and her hand accidently brushed against some glasses on the counter. Scrambling, she managed to catch them before they fell and shattered. He tilted his head and those golden-brown eyes glittered wickedly as though he'd just realized the effect he was having on her.

"You up for a horseback ride?"

"Uh, yeah. Sure."

"Have you ever ridden horses before?"

Victoria just shrugged.

"Right. Well, we're going to find out. Did you find a lemonade?"

"A what?"

"You were looking for a lemonade…"

"Oh, right. I found a Diet Coke. That will do."

"Then let's go." He swung his shirt around his shoulders and pushed his muscled arms into the long sleeves. Then he proceeded to fasten the front, button by button. For Victoria, it was torture.

They returned to the massive barn, where two horses stood saddled and ready. Wade pointed to the Tobiano paint she'd loved when she'd seen it the day before. Following instinct, she took the reins and approached the mare from the animal's left side. Using the portable steps made it easy to reach the stirrups, and soon she was in the saddle and ready to go. She shot a grin of accomplishment at Wade, who nodded his head with approval. He mounted a nice chestnut gelding and they were off.

It didn't take very long to get the feel of the paint mare. The Tennessee Walker was well trained and had a smooth gait. After an hour Victoria felt as though she'd been riding all her life.

They followed the river that snaked through the Masterses' property for miles, through stands of pine and over occasional hills with views that were picture-book quality. Wade seemed completely at home in the saddle. Even to someone who was not used to horses, it was clear he'd been riding pretty much his entire life. This ranch was his home. The wind that blew through the trees called to him. The crisp morning air fed his spirit. Here, he was in his element. Victoria liked who she was with now.

"Are you getting hungry?" Wade asked from beside her. "It's almost one o'clock."

"I could eat." She nodded. "But I don't think we'll find a restaurant out here."

"You might be surprised." He grinned.

Sure enough, the trail they'd been following took a sharp curve to the right and went steadily uphill, away from the river. When they reached the top, Victoria immediately spotted a quilt spread out over the grass and a picnic basket placed in the center. It was an area that bordered a steep cliff, and a view of the whole valley was before her.

Quickly dismounting, she tied the mare by her halter rope to a nearby tree and hurried to the blanket. "Oh, my gosh, Wade! The view is breathtaking."

Wade dismounted and joined her. "This was one of my favorite places to come as a kid. Just over this hill—" he nodded to his right "—the river catches up with it, and there are some good places to fish."

She looked at him and smiled.

"So how are you doing with the horse?" he asked.

"Good, I think. She is amazing. So easy to ride." Victoria looked out over the terrain. "I just can't believe the beauty of this place. You need to have a painting done and hang it in your house."

"My mother was the artist of the family. She did landscapes, portraits. You'll see the paintings displayed in most of the buildings on the property. I don't know if she ever got up here. I don't remember seeing one depicting this view."

"That's a shame."

"Do you paint, Victoria?"

"I don't know. I must have done some before the accident, because right now I'm itching to have a charcoal pencil and a sketch pad. But whether it's just being caught in the moment of this beautiful place or if I really can paint, I couldn't tell you."

"We should go into town and get you some paints and a couple of canvases."

She shook her head. "That's too much trouble. But some paper and pencils would be great." The idea of getting some of the beautiful places she'd seen this morning on canvas intrigued her, but better to take small steps. Her phone had been destroyed in the accident. Pictures would have been great.

After they had finished their meal and a shared bottle of wine on the bluff overlooking the valley, they mounted their horses and continued down the trail, again finding the river. Through tree-covered hillsides and grassy pastures flanking the river, they made their way farther north.

"Oh, Wade. Look. It's an old house." To her right, set back in the trees, was a very old cabin made of logs complete with a chimney rising over the wooden roof.

"It's an old trappers' cabin," Wade said. "Men would set up camp here while they hunted for fresh game in the hills. We've got a couple of those dotting the property here and there."

"I want to see," Victoria said as she scrambled off her horse.

The old door was barely on its hinges, but she pushed it open enough to see inside. It had a dirt floor and two small bed frames, along with a crumbling rock fireplace. It was rustic, to say the least.

"How old do you think this is?" she asked Wade.

"Don't really know. It was probably built before my grandfather bought the land, so that would make it about a hundred and fifty years old." He dismounted. "When we were kids, we used to roam all over this area. Take enough supplies to last us three or four days. One time we came upon an old homestead. There was a cottage and what was left of a picket fence, and a barn next to it. We found an old high-top shoe and a silver comb inside the house. I think Holly still has them. If you're a history buff, you've come to the right place."

Wade walked over to her and put his arm around her

shoulders. She turned to face him, and he covered her lips with his own for a kiss that was entirely too brief. "I could go on doing this forever," he said. "But we'd better head back if we want to arrive before dark."

"Okay," she agreed, standing on her tiptoes to give him another kiss. "I wish I had a phone. I would love to have a picture of this cabin."

"We will have to get you a new one. Until then, you're welcome to use mine," he said as he handed her his cell. "No reason we can't come back again."

She happily snapped off a few photos before returning his phone. Wade handed her the reins of her horse. "There's ninety-two thousand acres to roam through. Next time, we might go a different direction and find something even more to your liking."

Victoria grinned. She didn't know if she'd ever been horseback riding in her life. But it would definitely be a part of her future.

Ten

The next morning Wade climbed the steps to the back door of Pine House cabin. He saw Victoria through the window, sitting at the kitchen bar sipping a cup of coffee.

"Morning," he said as he stepped in the door.

"Good morning," she replied as he placed a large sack and its contents on the table.

"This is yours," he said, watching her.

"For me?"

In the bag was a sketch pad, drawing pencils, a small set of oil paints and two canvases. There were also brushes and a small easel that could be set up on a tabletop.

"Oh, my gosh. I hope you didn't waste your time and money."

"We'll find out," he grinned.

"Thank you, Wade." She ran into his arms and gave him a tight squeeze.

She grabbed the sketch pad and selected a pencil and

soon was hard at the task of drawing the little cabin they'd seen yesterday. He left her to take care of some business calls.

Early in the afternoon, Wade returned to the kitchen. As soon as he walked into the room, his eyes grew wide in amazement. Sketches, beautiful sketches, covered every available surface. There were several of the old cabin, the river valley, one of a mother cow grazing while her baby enjoyed its lunch. There were close-ups of pinecones hanging from the branches of a tree, all detailed, all remarkable. Some were taped to the cabinet doors, others covered the countertop, even the stovetop and chairs. Victoria was at the kitchen table hard at work on yet another one. The detail in the drawings was amazing.

"Victoria?"

His voice seemed to bring her out of whatever trance she was in.

"Hi." She gave him a grin.

He walked over, kissed her, then picked up a sheet of the sketch paper, frowning as he looked closely at the drawing. "How long have you been an artist?"

She sat back and looked around her. "I didn't know I could draw." She shrugged.

"I'm assuming it just felt right," he said, using her own words. "We don't have to go anywhere today. If you like, why don't you try out the paints and do the old cabin on canvas?"

"I would love to. Are you sure you wouldn't mind?"

"Not a bit."

Wade was stunned by the artistry that had flowed from her hands. How had he never picked up on the fact that Victoria was an accomplished artist? This was no small thing. The drawings were professional and brilliant. He wanted to ask where she'd studied but knew she wouldn't remember. While their time together had always been limited, how could he never have picked up on her amazing talent?

She didn't waste any time opening the small box of colors and setting the canvas on the easel. She chose from among a dozen brushes of various sizes and shapes and got to work.

"I'm going to head over to the loafing shed and take a look at some new heifers. I'll be back in about an hour and we'll have lunch."

"Okay," she responded, already pressing some colors onto the palette. By the time he stepped outside, Victoria was already absorbed in what she was doing.

Early that evening, Wade stood just inside the back door, looking over her shoulder at the painting in progress. He whistled, low and long. "That is spectacular, Victoria. I never knew you had such talent."

"Thank you. I can't say if it's good or not, but it feels good to have a brush in my hand. Are you ready for lunch?" she asked, wiping her hands on a dish towel she'd found beneath one of the cabinets.

"Lunch has come and gone, darling. It's after seven. I came back around three, and you were really into your painting, so I just left you alone. I came back to see if you wanted dinner. You really should eat something. A starving artist isn't necessarily a good thing."

"Okay. You're right. Let me clean up my mess and we can go."

It was a short walk to where the ranch hands congregated every night around the campfire. Tonight chili was the main course. As before, Victoria got her serving and sat next to Wade on the tree stump. Tonight there were guitars, and soon music filled the air around them. It was a cool evening with a light breeze out of the south. Victoria seemed contented watching fireflies light the night. There was a full moon overhead.

"I'm so glad you brought me here. I have a feeling I haven't felt this relaxed in a very long time. I hope... I hope it's not the last time we come here."

"We'll come back, sweetheart. I promise. But we need to get back to Dallas. There is a meeting that Cole and I both need to attend next week concerning a merger we've both been involved in. I was notified this morning that the other parties are ready to sit down and hash this thing out. Apparently things have progressed since I was last in Japan."

"That's always the excuse," a man chimed in behind them.

Wade immediately grinned and stood up as the man came into view. He was as tall as Wade and had the same muscular physique, the same stance.

"How're you doing, bro? How was the flight in?"

"Good. I wanted to say hello and meet your bride. Holly told me you finally brought Victoria to the ranch."

"Victoria." Wade looked down to where she sat. "This is my younger brother, Chance. You met his wife, Holly, the day we arrived. Chance, this is Victoria."

She immediately rose. "It's very nice to meet you."

"And you as well." Chance shook her hand. "Wade treating you right?"

"So far. Can't complain."

"Ha! Give it time," Chance teased. "I'm glad you brought her out to the ranch. We all thought you'd made her up."

"Nope, she's as real as they come."

"Welcome to the family, Victoria. Glad to have you with us."

"Thank you."

Wade accompanied Chance as he made the rounds, saying hello to the ranch hands around the fire. The brothers had that certain something that made them stand out in a crowd. Both were strong, powerful men in their own right.

"I talked with Cole just a few minutes ago," Chance told Wade. "They are on a flight back from London. He said you were here and asked me to remind you that you both have an appointment with a Mr. Takahashi on Monday."

"I know," Wade replied. "We're going to have to get back to Dallas tomorrow. How did the meeting in London go?"

"Very well, according to Cole. Synecom will soon be a part of Masters International. They will merge with the pharmaceutical division by the end of the year. Loudon Deeming, the president and CEO, is reportedly excited to have his company involved with ours."

"Excellent."

"Oh," Chance added. "One other thing. Cole said the date for the probate of Dad's will has been set. Seth is expected to fly down. I'm glad he'll be here."

"Me, too," Wade agreed. "He's a good man. Seth is our half brother," he explained to Victoria. "He lives in California."

"Well, take care you two. Have a good trip home." Chance looked at Victoria. "Again, it was really nice to meet you."

"You as well."

Bidding the ranch hands a good night, Chance disappeared into the darkness as he headed to his truck. No doubt Holly was awaiting his return.

Wade hated like hell to leave Victoria alone when he

had to conduct business, especially since she still didn't have her memory back. But at least now, with her art, she would have plenty to keep her occupied. That thought had run through his mind more than once today. And maybe it would even be therapeutic and help her heal. For the first time, Wade really hoped things could work out between them.

When they got back to Dallas, he was going to find a specialist, someone trained in memory recall. Surely there was some way to give her back her full life. It was only then that they would be able to have a full life together. After the time he'd spent in her company since the accident, he couldn't believe he'd ever thought she could be hateful or deceitful. He didn't have an answer as to why she had changed over the days since the accident. But he was not willing to let her go back to the way she was. Whatever he had to do to accomplish that end, he would do it.

"Are you about ready to go?" Wade asked, holding his hand out to her.

"Sure," she replied and stood up, taking his hand.

They tossed their paper bowls and plastic silverware into the trash and headed to the log home on the hill. He put his arm around her shoulders, her arm went around his back and together they walked toward Pine House.

After a second day of horseback riding, they cooled off from the afternoon sun near a small waterfall. It was nothing like the one at his home in Dallas, but it had a beauty all its own. At the bottom of the falls was a natural pool, again about half the size of his pool in Dallas. But this one was created by the elements eons ago. They swam and splashed and laughed, then dried off on one of the big boulders adjacent to the pool.

"How about we head back and give you time to pack for our trip home and get ready for tonight?" Wade asked. "Our reservations are at seven. That means we should leave here by five or five thirty if we go in the chopper. I would highly recommend that means of travel. It's beautiful at night."

"Reservations?"

"Yeah. When we get back to Dallas, I thought we would stop and eat at a restaurant I know. Really great food. After we eat, I thought you might enjoy going to an art exhibit on our way home."

"I'd love to!" She sat up, leaned over and kissed him. "You're too good to me," she whispered against his lips. "I don't deserve you."

"Woman, you've got that reversed."

His lips covered hers as he rolled her over to show her just how glad he was to share this moment with her. But by later in the day, he'd grown impatient. Twenty minutes after five, he stood at the bottom of the staircase, waiting. But fifteen minutes later when Victoria finally did come down the stairs, the slight frustration of having to wait disappeared in a puff of smoke. She had changed into a black dress that softly glimmered as she walked, hugging her every curve. It came down to about six inches above her knees.

It was draped low in the back, making a perfect frame for her hair, which was pulled back, letting soft curls cascade from the crown of her head. She had added makeup, but it was so subtle it served only to enhance her delicate features. As if they needed enhancing. Her lips were a deep, sultry red. Quite honestly, he had never seen her so beautiful. He swallowed hard.

"You look ravishing," he said in greeting. The dress, along with the combination of the heady scent of perfume and Victoria's own erotic aroma, nearly brought him to his knees. "Where... How did you get the dress?"

"Every girl always needs that little black dress just in case."

He kissed her neck, cupping her face and trying hard not to scoop her off her feet and carry her to the closest bedroom. Or the kitchen table. Or the sofa in the den.

"I want to take you right now," he said against her lips before deepening the kiss. "I haven't a clue how I'm ever going to get through this evening."

She laughed. "We'd better go. That's a subject for later."

"And it will be addressed. Or undressed as the case may be."

They ate at a restaurant located some fifty stories up. The glass-dome enclosure slowly revolved, giving them a panoramic view of the lights of downtown Dallas.

Dinner was delicious. Wade watched Victoria with a glint in his eyes. She guessed he was thinking about the end of the evening when they returned home. And a little bird told her it was going to be quite a night. He was so male, so strong, so handsome. Behind closed doors he knew how to make love like no other. She looked forward to getting home.

Dinner finished, they took the glass elevator down to street level and entered a waiting limo to head to the art exhibit. Victoria was thrilled at the prospect of seeing a gallery show for the first time since her accident. Wade picked up on her nervous energy and folded his large hand over hers. She smiled at him through the darkness, so grateful that he would take the time to do this for her.

When they got to the gallery, Wade confirmed his reservations for the evening with an attendant in the front lobby. "Good evening, Mr. Masters," the woman said. "It's so nice to have you both with us this evening. Take your time and enjoy. I'll be here if you have any questions."

"This isn't a public showing?" Victoria asked once they were out of hearing distance. She noticed that the people in attendance were exquisitely dressed.

"Nah. We're doing this privately. You couldn't enjoy it nearly as much with people crowding around the paintings. Have a glass of champagne." He took one for each of them from the tray of a passing waiter. "Go at your own speed, and look to your heart's content. A friend of mine owns the gallery. These are paintings from various artists that have been sold but have yet to be shipped."

Most of the paintings near the front were abstract. On the wall underneath each canvas was a typed label with the name of the piece, the date it was created and sometimes but not always the name of the artist who painted it. Victoria stood there, fascinated by the brushstrokes and colors. They slowly walked through the space, and the paintings became less abstract. There were pictures of bridges, geese flying over a tranquil lake, clouds over a green field with the rain imminent. It all stirred something deep within Victoria.

As she turned to leave, one painting in particular caught her eye. It was a snapshot view of a farm with a small white house. A storm was coming, the sky already dark. The lady of the house was outside with her clothes basket, trying to bring in the wash from the line, with sheets blowing in every direction and bolts of lightning in the not-too-distant background. Victoria stepped over to the painting. Again there was no artist name, just the year it was painted and the title of the painting: *Storm Is Coming.* She couldn't stop her hand from reaching out to the painting, but she stopped short of touching it as she continued studying the detail. A shiver ran up her spine. She'd seen it before. She was sure of it.

"You like that one?" Wade asked from behind her.

She turned to face him. "Wade, I know this painting. I mean, I've seen it before."

"Maybe the fact you remember it means your memory is coming back."

"Oh, I hope so."

He nodded. "The artist's style reminds me of yours."

She looked even more closely but only found initials in the lower right-hand corner of the canvas: *L.D.*

"Can we find out who the artist is?" she asked Wade.

"Let me make an inquiry. I'll be right back."

Victoria wandered on through the gallery, taking in the statues and other creations of art. By the time Wade returned, Victoria was in heaven yet a bit unsettled by the whole experience. All this beauty had her in its grip. The amount of talent represented here was overwhelming. And the style of the paintings was somehow familiar.

"The painting you asked about is by a relatively new artist. Laurel Dawson. She lives outside the Dallas metroplex to the south. This painting has been sold, but they have our name should she return with any more paintings."

She couldn't thank Wade enough.

Once back at the helipad, they quickly boarded the chopper and began the ride home. The helicopter took a slow path around Dallas. Wade had been right. The lights were amazing. He leaned over and took her in his arms.

All in all, it had been a remarkable evening. A fairy-tale night. But even in the arms of the man she loved, sailing through the darkness in a flying chariot, she still carried that tiny feeling of trepidation that all was not right. Wade picked up on it.

"What's the matter, Victoria?"

"Nothing." She shrugged and touched his cheek. "This trip has all been so great. I think I'm just sad that it's over. I already miss the ranch."

"We'll go back again. The Governor's Ball is coming up next month. It's an event you usually look forward to. I had completely forgotten about it, but my assistant just sent a reminder. This is a charity we sponsor each year. You need to have your dress fittings, and I've got some work I must see to before then. But I had your art supplies sent ahead to the house. You should have plenty to keep you busy."

"The Governor's Ball?" she asked. "Wade, I can't go to something like that."

"Why not?" He frowned.

"I won't know anyone. I won't remember anything, what to do, how to react… I can't go to something so important. I haven't even been out of the house to speak of."

"Victoria, it's just an annual event for charity. The people there won't know if you remember them or not. It just isn't a big deal."

"It sounds like a very big deal."

"The designer will come to refit your dress. And we will attend together. Don't worry."

"I would imagine there's quite a bit of work waiting for you, especially knowing how much time I caused you to miss."

Wade lowered the mic and kissed her on the end of her nose. "I haven't had any time off since… I can't remember. The company is at a point where it pretty much runs itself day-to-day. I have to step in for mergers and certain other corporate dealings, but Cole is there to handle things almost every day. Once he gets back from London and we take care of a few matters, including our conference call Monday morning, I should have more time to spend with you."

"It must be a big deal if you're both needed on the call."

"When you're dealing with foreign dignitaries, it helps to have backup." He lowered her mouthpiece for the mic and leaned over and stole a kiss. He held her eyes with his as he replaced both microphones. "It won't take long, I promise. I should be back by late afternoon."

"Take as long as you need. Your business comes first. I'll sleep in, paint and enjoy the pool while you're gone."

"Be careful of the pool—" he began, and Victoria cut him off.

"I will, and we've had this discussion."

"I'll agree to you sleeping in, getting some rest." He raised his microphone and pulled her headset away from her ear. "'Cause you're gonna need it," he said against her ear, his voice low and sexy. He replaced the microphone and sat back satisfied as a fat pampered cat.

The chopper landed on the Masterses' private airfield, and the pilot killed the motor. A car was waiting to take them to the mansion. The sounds in the city were so different from the ranch. There, while they'd eaten their dinner, in the distance the coyotes howled at the moon, cows mooed and birds sang their song.

It was a short ride from the landing pad to the mansion. Once they reached the house, Victoria excused herself to take a quick shower and change her clothes. When she stepped under the gentle spray in the shower enclosure, she regulated the heat and shampooed her hair. With her eyes closed, she didn't see Wade step into the shower. His big hands, loaded with soap, proceeded to lather every inch of her body. Her heartbeat tripled at knowing he was here with her. He paid special attention to her breasts, which swelled under his touch. Then his hands moved lower, gently rubbing the sensitive area between her legs. He knelt before her, his mouth finding and enjoying the little nub of her womanhood.

Just as Victoria lost the strength to stand, he stood and grabbed her hips, lifting her to him. Her back was against the cool wall of the shower, the water coming down all around her. She gasped as Wade settled her onto his erection. With one push, he was all the way inside her. Her legs came around his hips, her arms around his neck as he began to move.

"I can't hold it back for long, Victoria. I have no willpower where you're concerned."

She could only nod her head in understanding.

He began to move faster and faster, pumping into her until they both were frantic for release. Wade pulled out, picked her up and carried her to the bedroom, drying her with a soft blanket before helping her onto the bed. He reached into the nightstand drawer for a silver packet and quickly got it open and slipped the condom into place. Then he was inside her again, working his magic and bringing them both to the edge of ecstasy. Victoria let out a cry and felt the electric current run down her spine as her body detonated. She held on to Wade with all the strength she had left. Wade followed seconds later. She glowed in the aftermath, listening to his heart beating in a rhythm as fast as her own, surrounded by the warmth and the scent of this man she loved.

After holding her and allowing time for them both to catch their breath, he reached over to the night table and picked up a small black velvet case. He held it out to her. Victoria sat up, not fully understanding. When he opened the lid, there was the most exquisite diamond ring in the world. Wade took it out of the box and took her left hand.

"I realized, belatedly, my wife isn't wearing her wedding ring. Could it be because the other was given as merely a token to wear out in public and not with the feelings that are supposed to come with it?"

"I took it off after you told me about our marriage. It's in the drawer in the side table."

He shook his head as though it amazed him. "Will you please accept this until you can pick out your own wedding band to go with it?" he asked as he slipped it on her finger.

It was beyond breathtaking, with an enormous diamond surrounded by clusters of smaller ones. It fit perfectly. "Wade. You didn't have to do this. Especially since...well, since we are kind of only just married on paper."

"Then marry me for real, Victoria." His voice was deep and soft; his eyes indicated his sincerity. "Be mine in every way a man and a woman can be joined."

There were no words. She scrambled up on her knees to get closer, fell against him and found his lips with hers. "I love you, Wade Masters."

The next few days were the paradigm of perfection, with Victoria alternately painting and enjoying the pool while Wade went to his office. The nights were pure magic. They talked about anything and everything. Wade told her some of what he contended with at his business, talked about his family and his childhood. Victoria hung on each and every word and hoped someday she could regain her memory and share herself with Wade in the same way.

Today, they were having lunch together at the house. It

was one of the rare occasions that Wade could get away from work to be here with her during the day. They sat in the nook Victoria had designed for them, eating sandwiches and discussing her latest canvas.

"Mr. Masters," Curtis interrupted, approaching them with a tentative air. "Excuse me, sir, but your assistant is on line four."

"Excuse me, Victoria. I'd better take this."

"No, you go ahead. She probably misses you, since you're so seldom away from the office."

Wade stood from the table, kissed her on the head and disappeared. After only a few minutes, he was back.

"Everything okay?"

He nodded, sitting back down and taking up his fork and knife.

"My assistant was just updating me on the second conference call with the Japanese dignitaries next week. She has all the requested information gathered and in order. She wanted to know if there was anything else I would need."

Victoria nodded her head in understanding.

"I know," Wade said, setting his cutlery on the table and reaching for her hand. "Reality always finds a way of rearing its ugly head just about the time I start to relax and enjoy myself. It's just one of the drawbacks of being CEO of Masters International. At least I won't be coming home to an empty house. I thank you for that, Victoria."

"I love you, Wade."

"All right, that's it—I quit. I'll have my notice on… somebody's desk this afternoon."

She giggled. "I don't think you can do that. Think of all the people that are counting on you. You can't let them down."

"Seriously, thank you for understanding."

Victoria smiled. "So, what does Cinderella do at the Governor's Ball?"

"Stand in a receiving line that goes on for miles, pretend you're having a wonderful time, ensure the governor and his wife are having a wonderful time. Enjoy the desserts and dance with your husband until your feet scream *no more!* And as soon as we can get an opening, we're out of there."

Victoria laughed.

"Actually, you attended last year and didn't stop talking about it for weeks. Before the accident, you were looking forward to it this year, too, as I recall. Most of the people you encounter there are nice enough, and the music is provided by a special touring section of the Dallas Symphony Orchestra.

"But the main thing will be for you to have an enjoyable evening, make some new friends, say hello to the old ones you can't remember and know that I'll be right there with you."

"It's scary meeting the outside world without knowing anyone. It's one thing to not have my close friends—if I have any—drop by. But this...this is a big deal. It's important to you. What if I mess up?"

"You won't mess up, Victoria. The attendees will be glad to see you after news of your accident. Just try to relax and have a good time."

"Okay, then. If you're sure you're okay with what might happen, I'll do my best and let my Prince Charming escort me to the ball."

Eleven

In the days that followed, she saw less and less of Wade. But as insane as her schedule became as she prepared for the ball, she could only imagine what his must be like. At least it would only be for a few more days. Then they could return to the ranch for a while.

The dress designer and his staff had arrived for the final fitting of her gown and set up in one of the guest bedrooms. When they removed the protective cover, Victoria gasped in amazement. It was the most beautiful thing she'd ever seen. The black-sequined silk clung to her body, falling all the way to the floor, a plunging neckline and scooped back adding to the dramatic effect. Though she couldn't remember, it was more than likely the most daring dress she'd ever worn.

"Oh, madam, you have lost weight over the past few months since your original fitting," said the designer. "Still, we have time. We will take it in, and it will be perfect and ready for you before the ball."

Something about the fitting brought it all home. She was going to attend one of the most important functions in Wade's year. She wouldn't be able to remember names or faces. She would be a laughingstock and bring embarrassment to the entire family.

When Wade arrived home that evening, he immediately sensed something was wrong and asked what was the matter.

She sat in a chair staring out the bedroom window. "Nothing. I'm glad you're home."

"Honey." He tossed his jacket on the nearest chair. "Don't be concerned about the gala. It's really not a big deal. There will be over three hundred people in attendance, but you'll be the most exquisite woman there. Just stick close to my side. No one will notice if you remember them from a year ago. In fact, most of the attendees won't know I'm married, so there will be plenty of congratulations. If asked, just say we decided against a big wedding."

She nodded. What else could she do?

The next morning a package was delivered from a local art gallery. Victoria fretted for a while as to whether to open it or wait for Wade. In the end she gave in to her curiosity and pulled the brown paper away from the gold-edged frame. It was a simple painting of a Siamese cat perched on the edge of a small table, completely absorbed in watching the antics of a butterfly in metallic blues and golds, with one paw raised in alert concentration and fascination. The combination of mute tones and shadows and the bright effervescent colors of the eyes of the cat and the butterfly combined to make a painting of near photographic quality.

She leaned in closer and gazed at the delicate brushstrokes. Despite the overall beauty of the painting, Victoria saw flaws. The fur of the cat could have been made to appear thicker, fluffier. The eyes were the color typical of that breed of cat, but they also should have reflected the color of the objects surrounding it.

Suddenly Victoria realized she was viewing the canvas with a professional eye for detail. Her hand closed as though she was holding a paintbrush, ready to finish an incomplete work of art, to add the tiny minute strokes and bring the painting to its full completion.

Wade's heavy hands came to rest on her shoulders, breaking her out of the spell. "I like it," he said, leaning over to kiss the side of her face.

"It's not finished." She frowned.

"What? Victoria, you bought this painting a few days before the accident. You called and told me about a small gallery you'd discovered and an up-and-coming artist you'd met there. You said you had arranged to have the painting delivered when the show was taken down, which is now."

"That must be why it looks recognizable." She shrugged, a slight headache taking hold. "I couldn't understand where I might have seen it before, yet it looked incredibly familiar. Maybe it's a sign of my memory returning."

"Maybe it is. We'll have it hung in the library. Seems fitting for that room. It's a beautiful painting," he added.

"I guess so." Again she leaned forward intently, gazing at the details. "But it needs to be finished before it's hung."

Wade shrugged and looked at his wife. "It looks finished to me. Are you hungry? Victoria?"

"I guess."

"Maybe your memory is returning. Familiar is a good thing."

She nodded her head.

"Come on, sweetheart," he prompted, taking her hand. "I'm starved. Don't worry about the painting. Apparently you selected it before the accident. It will all come back eventually."

She sighed, nodding. "I hope you're right."

It was now just two days until the Governor's Ball. Her gown hung in what used to be her bedroom, and her shoes had been placed on the floor beneath it. The makeup artist was scheduled to arrive four hours before they were due to leave, just after the hairdresser and manicurist finished their jobs. Everything was all set.

But Victoria's nerves were tied in knots. Wade had continually assured her it wasn't a big deal, but Victoria knew better. It was the event of the year, with a list of attending dignitaries as long as her arm. She wouldn't know anyone there. Even those she'd met last year she wouldn't recognize. That had to be the reason for her trepidation.

Wade's brothers and their wives would be in attendance. Holly had been calling every day to try to alleviate Victoria's fears, assuring her no one would notice if she forgot a name or two. Or three. Victoria wasn't convinced. But Wade was depending on her to go with him, and there was no way she would let him down.

Wade was due back from his office in a few hours, and Victoria wanted to do something nice for him. She ventured down to the kitchen area and asked the chef to prepare Wade's favorite meal to be served around seven. Every moment they had together became more and more special. She was truly in love with her husband. Head over heels.

Despite his massive wealth, she still liked him best

when he was on the ranch, dressed in his worn, tight-fitting jeans, with a laid-back look on his face that said all was right with the world. And the ranch was so beautiful. She was so grateful he'd shared that part of his life.

The candles were lit and burning in the center of the small table. Jacob had brought his amazing insight to bear, apparently guessing this was to be a special night. He'd covered the table with linens and arranged a small bouquet of flowers.

She'd dressed in a daring black creation with a mesh fabric between the areas of lace that covered only the briefest parts of her anatomy. Its plunging neckline and low back finished the overall effect. Her hair was pulled back with a silver comb.

Wade arrived home a little before six thirty. His eyes lit up the instant he saw her. Then he frowned, a question forming in his eyes.

"Did I miss an invitation? Are we having guests?"

"Nope. Just the two of us."

"Mmm. Brings all sorts of possibilities to mind. You look delicious, by the way."

"Thank you," she replied. "So do you."

He grinned. That gorgeous, sexy grin that made her want to make love to him where they stood. Wade loosened his tie and shed his jacket, tossing it over a chair. "Hope you don't mind. I'm going to take a shower." He leaned over and kissed her.

Smiling, Victoria followed him up the stairs. "The sea bass will be ready in about half an hour."

"That may be too soon."

"Too soon?"

He entered his suite and walked to the phone, dialing the kitchen. "Yeah, Jacob? Put a hold on that dinner until you hear from me." He looked over at Victoria. "At least an hour. Maybe two," he said into the receiver. Hanging up, he unbuttoned his silk shirt. Next went the belt, socks and shoes. She couldn't help but notice a slight, almost devious smile cross his face.

Without preamble he approached her, spun her around and unzipped her dress. He gave it a slight push and it fell off her shoulders and onto the floor. Soon she stood before him in only her lacy bikini underwear and black heels.

"Wade, I don't understand…"

With one hand he removed the silver comb that was holding her hair back, letting it fall around her shoulders. When she turned back to him, she shook her head and her hair fanned out, just covering her breasts.

"There is only one thing I'm starving for tonight."

"And what would that be?"

"You." He dropped his pants, took off his shirt and led her to the bathroom. "Can I interest you in joining me?"

Victoria grinned. "Maybe."

"Maybe? Maybe *yes*?"

"Yes."

His lips met hers, and the kiss was deep and hungry. She could never get enough of the taste of him, of how his lips were so soft yet firm. He had his nightly stubble, which made him even sexier.

Suddenly she was in his arms, and they were standing under the shower. Without breaking their kiss, his tongue going deeper into her mouth, Wade reached down to her hip and slowly slid the silken panties down her legs.

Stepping out of her shoes, she grabbed the scented soap, worked it into suds and began washing his broad chest, down over the six-pack abs and lower to his erection. This time it was Wade's turn as she knelt before him. After rinsing off the soap, she slid her lips over his engorged penis, clutching its length with her hand.

"Victoria," he moaned.

"I want to touch you," she said, backing away momentarily. "Tell me how to do it better."

His hands cupped the back of her head, gently guiding her back to his length. "You're doing just fine." He inhaled a ragged breath. "Oh, God, Victoria!"

For a few minutes she enjoyed the feel and taste of him. Her hand slid up and down the velvety skin of his shaft while her mouth and tongue licked and teased the sensitive tip.

"Victoria, that's enough," he said in a rough voice. He lifted her to her feet. "If you continue, this will be over far too soon."

He turned her around and, after lathering her hair, proceeded to wash her breasts, then run his hands down over her waist and belly. He palmed her mound before spreading her folds, making her weak with joy. She lost all the strength in her legs yet, needing more of what he was giving, managed to stay on her feet. He reached out and gripped her arms to steady her, then turned her toward him. Grasping her hips, he lifted her up and onto his erection. Pausing to line up with her core, he pushed inside. Her head lay back against the shower wall, so engaged in what he was doing she couldn't think of anything but Wade. He placed his open palm against her neck, his thumb under her jaw, and he began to move. His movements became faster and faster until, with a cry, Victoria fell apart and Wade followed, calling out her name.

She had a few seconds to catch her breath before he covered her with a warmed towel, scooped her up and carried her into the bedroom. After drying them both, he threw back the covers and laid her down.

He opened his lips to hers, and her arms went around his neck. He moved from her lips to her neck, taking small nips and bestowing kisses down to her breasts. Where Wade touched, her body came alive. With his hands he kneaded the firm skin of her breasts, taking the swollen tips into his mouth, sucking hard, first one, then the other.

Victoria arched her back in response.

"Wade," she whimpered.

"What, sweetheart?" he said. "Tell me what you need, Victoria."

As an answer, she reached down and found his swollen shaft. The tip had a droplet of moisture, and she took pleasure in rubbing it over his erection before guiding him toward her opening.

He smiled in the darkness. "Not yet, sweetheart." He began to kiss his way farther down the feminine curves of her body.

Taking his time, he continued to trail kisses down over her stomach and on to that special place between her legs. Pushing her legs wide apart, he dived in, tasting of her essence, using his tongue to drive her wild. Victoria sucked the air deep into her lungs as she was consumed with sensation. A pressure began to build within her. For a moment the world stopped turning and everything went still. Then she felt completely out of control as electric currents shot down her spine in a pulse-pounding climax. Wade stayed with her until she quieted, then pushed off the bed, quickly slid a condom into place and returned. She was exhausted, but his mouth and hands transformed fatigue into need. Soon she was ready for him again. He slid into her, filling her.

He began to move, this time taking it slow, loving her

in the only way he knew how. With each stroke, the intensity grew.

"Are you up for trying something new?" he asked against her ear, his deep voice causing chills to run across her overheated skin.

"Yes," she answered breathlessly. With Wade, she'd try anything.

He pulled out and rolled her onto her stomach. Grasping her hips, he pulled her up and toward him. Holding her hips, he gently worked his swollen shaft into her from the back. She grabbed the silken sheets with her hands.

"Okay?"

She nodded. "Yes."

Slowly he began to move. Victoria couldn't hold back the moan of delight. His hand came between them, and he gently massaged the intensely sensitive nub between her folds. Wade was a master at sex, raw sex. Between his thrusts and what his hand was doing, in seconds she cried out, her inner core tightening against him in climax. That was all it took to push him over the edge. Wade ensured her climax went on and on, milking it to the very end, pushing inside her over and over again until finally he collapsed to her side.

He brushed her long hair away from her face. "Now, what were you planning for dinner?" he asked, breathing hard.

She smiled. "I think we just had dessert."

"No, Victoria. That was only the first course."

He felt her kiss his sweaty chest and neck. The heat they had created felt like a vapor, covering them both in the warm aftermath of sex.

He couldn't believe how much she had come to mean to him. How much he wanted her memory to return so that they could have a full, rich relationship. It bothered him how heavily the amnesia weighed on her. Her apprehension about attending the ball was only one of the ways it played out.

He gently rolled her onto her side so he could spoon her to sleep, with one arm tucked under her head and the other around her side and under her breasts. His erection was already coming back to life against her bottom. She smelled of patchouli and spices from the soap and a delicious scent that was all her own.

After the gala was over and behind them, he wanted to give her a wedding, the wedding of her dreams. Let her go as big or small as she wanted. And a honeymoon; wherever on this earth she wanted to go, he would take her.

How this remarkable romance had come to pass, he didn't quite know. It was definitely against the odds that she would wake up from an accident and be someone he wanted to spend the rest of his life with. Because of her sincerity and gentle nature, her love of adventure and her ability to tug at his heart, he was quite sure he was falling in love with Victoria, and this time around it was for real.

Twelve

Victoria sleepily turned over, smiling as she heard Wade's snoring. She loved to lie awake and listen to him as he slept, to feel the warmth of his body and kiss him when he didn't know she was doing it. And she couldn't help but notice that the beautiful diamond on her left hand glittered even in the subdued lighting of the room.

She glanced at the clock; it was just past midnight. The thought of some milk and a snack suddenly stirred her appetite. Grinning, she slipped into her nightgown and robe and left their bedroom, descending the stairs. Soon she was standing in the immense kitchen. Before she could open the refrigerator, she heard a sound at the side entrance. She turned in time to see someone push open the door and step inside. As soon as she approached the doorway, she spotted a woman turned away from her, shaking out an umbrella from the light mist that was falling outside.

A twinge of fear raced down her spine. "Uh...hello? How can I help you?"

The woman slowly turned to face her.

And all the breath left Victoria's lungs as she looked into her own face.

Who was this woman and what did she want? Before Victoria could ask, she felt a searing pain in her head.

"I see you've been having quite the time in my absence," the woman said. Her eyes narrowed as she looked at Victoria from head to foot. "Just what in the hell do you think you're doing?"

"I...don't understand. I don't... Who are you?" The white walls and alabaster floor began to tilt. She felt a severe headache coming on like she hadn't experienced in months; the pounding in her temples was excruciating.

"You were supposed to be out of here by now," the woman raged, stepping still closer to Victoria. "Instead, you convince my husband to take you on a damn joyride. How nice for you. But it's over. It's done. I want you out of my house. *Now.*"

"*Your* house?" She raised a hand to her throbbing head. Visions began to whirl in her mind. Random pictures of her art studio. Of Murphy, her rescue dog. And of this woman threatening to blackmail her if she didn't play along with her scheme.

"Don't even go there, you little bitch. Why wouldn't you answer my calls?" She was screaming now, becoming more enraged by the second. "Just what in hell did you think you were going to accomplish? Oh...maybe you thought Wade would fall in love and forgive our little game plan." She snorted in disgust. "Sorry to break the news, honey, but Wade Masters will never love anything or anyone. He's a cold, calculating bastard. But that's my problem, not yours. Where is he, by the way?"

"He's...upstairs." *In the bed where we just made love.*

"Here?" she screeched. "Wade is here? You've got to get out. You must leave immediately. My car is still outside. Take it, and get out of here before he comes downstairs. I'll meet you at the studio tomorrow. *Go!*"

Victoria was in serious pain. She couldn't stop the memories from slamming into her mind. Absently, she reached for the top of the cabinet and held on as the room continued to spin.

"What's wrong with you? Didn't you understand what I just said?" The woman walked over to where Victoria stood clutching the cabinet. "Leave now. Get out!"

"What in the hell is going on?" Wade stepped into the room.

It took the woman almost a full minute to regain her composure. "Why don't you ask her," she snarled. "I've been on a short vacation, and this woman apparently decided to take my place while I was gone."

"That's not true." Her mind was whirling as the memories came flooding back. She remembered. She remembered everything.

Laurel. Her name was Laurel. Not Victoria.

Victoria Masters had come into her art studio in Waxahachie and bought a painting. She had introduced herself as Laurel's aunt. The resemblance was uncanny.

Over a cup of coffee that day, Victoria had explained that, decades ago, her much older sister had landed on tough times and had a child in poverty and died giving birth. Victoria had recently found a small box of old pictures at her mother's house and asked who they were photos of. One in particular was of a newborn baby. Her mother had finally admitted the child was Victoria's niece. Laurel was that child. Hence the family resemblance—they were practically twins.

Laurel had been raised in a series of foster homes, so this seemed nothing short of a miracle. She didn't know she had any family let alone an aunt. Yet Victoria had tracked her down. To have a real family was more than she'd ever dreamed of. Laurel was delighted to meet Victoria. She could barely sleep that night in the hopes of seeing her again.

Victoria had come back two days later, this time saying she needed a huge favor. She needed to leave the country for a few months and offered Laurel a large sum of money to take her place during that time. To stay in her home and pretend to be Victoria. She assured her that her husband was in Europe, and no one would ever find out. With the right hairstyle and makeup, no one would question who Laurel really was.

Laurel couldn't imagine pretending to be someone else. Trying to fool anyone like that would be ridiculous, and immoral. Laurel had refused. She wouldn't know how to be another person. But Victoria would not accept her answer. She had been prepared for Laurel to decline before she walked in the door.

Victoria had pushed back, demanding Laurel do as she wanted. But Laurel again turned her down, refusing the money. That had been when Victoria turned from nice to vicious, threatening her, saying she would ruin her in the art world if she didn't agree and assured her she had the clout to do so.

Art was all Laurel had. It had been her dream most of her life. If she lost that…she hated to think what she would do or where she would go. The art community was close-knit. Especially among those commanding top prices and whose paintings were world-renowned. She knew she had what it took to make her childhood dream come true and was beginning to show here and there in galleries. And now this person threatened to ruin it all if Laurel didn't pretend to be her for three months. Victoria had thrown out several names of the more prestigious art dealers in the area, claiming to know each personally. Victoria was a very good client and they would have no trouble turning away a wannabe if she asked. Laurel had felt her dreams begin to fade. This was surreal.

Victoria had assured her she was married to a billionaire who stayed out of the country 90 percent of the time. Laurel would live in his mansion and basically do as she wanted for those three months. Shopping sprees, museums—she could even build her own temporary art studio and paint to her heart's content. "Do it," she had insisted. "What do you have to lose except your livelihood? It's three short months."

Laurel had asked, "Why? What's the reason you need me to do this? What's so important?"

Victoria had snarled at her. "It's none of your damn business. Just do as you're told. I assure you the less you know, the better."

"Is it because you're pregnant?" Laurel had quietly asked. Great pains had been taken to conceal Victoria's condition, but her efforts were not good enough. She looked to be about six or seven months along.

"That's none of your business!" she'd retorted. "Now, take this key and write down the passwords. A car is waiting to take you to the house."

"Now?"

"Right now."

Laurel had had no choice but to agree, although how she was going to manage to carry out the ridiculous scheme, she didn't know. She had worked too long and too hard, kept her dream alive through too much to take a chance that this woman could bring it all to a screeching halt. If that happened, she would have nothing.

She had called her best friend, Beth Hamilton, and told her she'd been invited to stay at a friend's house for a few months, promising she would be in touch. Victoria had arranged for a limo to pick her up and Laurel had left the studio in Victoria's chauffeur-driven Lexus, keys and pass codes in hand, when an eighteen-wheeler ran a red light and plowed into them. By the time she reached the hospital, the real Victoria was on her way to Paris.

Now Victoria was back and telling lies, blaming all of this on Laurel. Wade looked beside himself, staring at the two nearly identical women in the same room. "Will one of you tell me what in the hell is going on?"

"She's an intruder. Can't you see what has happened?" Victoria snipped. "I told you, I've been away. I returned home this evening and found this woman in *my* house."

He glared at Victoria, then at Laurel until she wanted to curl up and die.

"Wade, it isn't what it looks like," Laurel began to explain. Her head pounded as she reeled with all of the memories suddenly released in her mind. "She approached me and asked if I would pose as her while she was out of the country."

His eyes shot fire. "You agreed to that?"

Tears welled in Victoria's eyes. "Not at first. But eventually, yes," she whispered. "I did, but it wasn't like she's making it sound."

"What in the hell is your name, anyway?" he demanded.

"Laurel. Laurel Dawson."

"You're a very good actress, Laurel Dawson. I assume the amnesia was all a ruse as well?"

"No, Wade..."

"It doesn't matter now, darling. I'm back. Just let it go," Victoria stated.

Wade glared at the other woman. "Where have you been for all these months, Victoria?"

She breezed over to Wade. "I've been in Paris. Remember, I told you. We were going to meet last week at the Café Le Bruin. But you never showed up."

"Why fly all the way to Paris when I thought it was you here with me?" Obviously Wade hadn't gone to meet Victoria there, since he thought she was at home, recovering from her accident. And in his bed.

"Victoria came to my studio," Laurel began, knowing Wade was listening but doubting every word. "She said she was my aunt and wanted to take advantage of our resemblance and asked me to take her place. I refused."

"Right," Victoria interjected. "We can see how well that went. What a lie. Honestly, Wade, I don't have a clue what she's talking about. And while our appearance might be similar, I certainly don't have a niece my own age. You know Mother and Father. Do you really think that's possible?"

"You were pregnant," Laurel stated. "You went to Paris to have your baby."

That got Wade's attention. He directed his hard gaze back at Victoria, and now Victoria was seething. She began screaming and cursing, going so far as to approach Laurel with her hand raised as though to slap her. Wade intervened, and the two began a heated battle, one Laurel wanted to neither partake in nor listen to.

"I want both of you out of this house! Now!"

The tears streamed down her cheeks as Laurel backed from the room and ran up the stairs to change her clothes.

She closed the bedroom door behind her and fell onto a chair. It was all back. The accident. The memories of

Victoria approaching her in the studio. The threats. Her hands were shaking so badly she could hardly button her blouse.

It had all been a lie. Everything she and Wade had between them was based on a lie. The reality was unbearable. She wanted to break down and pray this was just a nightmare, that she could just wake up and all would be back to normal. But she couldn't. It wasn't a nightmare; it was reality. She had to leave. She had to get out of the house before Wade came looking for her. She'd seen the pure rage in his eyes, the fury that he'd been played for a fool, and she never wanted to see that again. Nothing she could say would excuse her actions. Nor would he believe her word over that of his wife. She couldn't face him. She knew it was cowardly, but she didn't want to see the hate for her in his eyes. She could never live with that.

She quickly changed into jeans and a shirt and headed for the door. Before she walked out, she looked down at the beautiful diamond ring on her left hand. With tears blurring her vision so she was unable to focus on the brilliant diamond, she removed the ring from her finger and placed it on the nightstand. Unable to avoid one last look at the bed, where only moments before she'd lain in Wade's arms and pledged her love, she turned and ran from the room.

Once at the front door, she asked the security to summon a taxi. As soon as it arrived, she climbed in, unsure where she was going or what she was going to do. In a matter of minutes, her world had been turned upside down. And the love of her life was gone forever. As they cleared the front gates, she looked back at the mansion on the hill. Inside was the only man she would ever love. He thought she was part of Victoria's scheme to bilk him out of money by covering for her while the real Victoria disappeared to Europe to have another man's child.

Wade now would never believe she'd had amnesia or that she was forced by Victoria to live at his house. She couldn't blame Wade. He was the innocent in all of this. If what he'd told Laurel was the truth, he had fallen in love with the woman he thought her to be. He had fallen in love with his wife, which was as it should be. But now Victoria was back, and Laurel had to return to her own home and her own identity and begin again. The fairy tale was over. The magical kingdom had closed the door with her on the outside. Cinderella would return to her small world knowing she would never see her prince again.

The pain tore at her heart, threatened to overwhelm her. The tears fell like the rain outside the cab window.

She looked back one more time, but the mansion was already out of sight.

Wade Masters was beyond furious. He had been deceived by someone he trusted, someone he thought he loved. Sucker punches didn't get much worse than that. He couldn't believe it. He walked to the bar and poured himself a glass of whiskey and threw it down his throat. All this time... All this time he had played right into Victoria's hands. Unbelievable. He would never have thought she'd find a twin to help her carry out her deception. He honestly didn't know if he would ever get over this. Victoria he could deal with. She was on her way out the door as soon as she could scrape some clothes together. It was the other Victoria—Laurel—who had held his heart in her hands and crushed it.

He couldn't put all the pieces together. Yet. From what he'd gained from that quick conversation in the kitchen, the accident had started all of this. But by then, Victoria had already been on her way to the airport for the trip to Paris to have some man's baby, for God's sake. He doubted she was even sure who the father was. He expected a scam like that from Victoria, which was why he'd been about to divorce her before the accident.

But it was Laurel Dawson who'd been involved in the accident. It was Laurel, not Victoria, who woke up in the hospital not knowing who she was. Not knowing who he was. Or so she'd claimed. Victoria's plan had been diabolical. Since Wade had planned to spend the summer in London, had it not been for the accident, he would never have known. The hospital had called him because they thought his wife had been in a serious car accident. Her ID had been found in the wreckage. He'd immediately flown in from London. Flown in, come to the hospital and held a strange woman's hand while she fought to survive.

He'd known Victoria was capable of a lot of underhanded things, but this had to be her finest hour. What blew his mind was that, were it not for the accident, she would've succeeded. She would've installed a woman in his house to take her place while she did whatever she felt she had to do in Paris, and he would never have been the wiser because he was away, too.

He poured another two fingers of whiskey into his glass and drank it in one gulp. The rage was greater than anything he had ever felt. Ironically he didn't know whom to be angrier with: Victoria for setting the whole thing up; himself for walking right into it; or the woman named Laurel, who'd agreed to make the whole thing happen. That was the part that hurt the most. That was the part that wrenched his gut and left him open and bleeding.

As he began to calm down, he remembered parts of the conversation from earlier. How Laurel had tried to explain that the true story wasn't anything like the way Victoria made it sound. *That* he could believe. But what was the truth? Victoria had made a plan, Laurel had helped with it and like a total fool he'd walked right into the middle of it. Over the months they'd been together, she hadn't impressed him as one who would lie and connive with no regard for the feelings of others.

Wade sat in the darkness of his home office and had another drink of the amber liquid. Victoria had returned, intending to step back into her role as his wife, with him none the wiser. She had only a month remaining of the contract that would have made her a very wealthy woman. She was just insolent enough to think she could get away with it and still receive the amount Wade was to pay her. But Wade had given her two hours to pack her bags and clear out. He'd ship what she couldn't carry with her. And he'd let his attorney take over from there. There would be no payment. She'd be damn lucky if he decided not to sue.

From a quick online search, he'd discovered that Laurel had been a free spirit, used to cutoff jeans and baggy shirts and probably going barefoot. An up-and-coming artist with great possibilities. In one picture, her dark hair was caught in a long messy braid falling over her shoulder as she smiled her beautiful smile at the camera.

But it didn't matter. Hell, it didn't matter at all. Victoria had been caught. Laurel Dawson had been forced to come clean regarding her role in the scheme, and he had learned a very valuable lesson: don't trust anyone. Ever.

Wade had seen the hurt and remorse in her eyes for only a few seconds before Laurel had run past him and out the door into the night. How could she have betrayed him like that?

The rain continued to fall outside, lending its sweet

smell to the foul odor of deception he sensed throughout the house. And as if on cue, Victoria walked past him just then with absolute audacity, as though she was the one wronged in all of this.

"Get all your things and get out," Wade couldn't resist saying. "And don't forget the painting in the library. I want no reminder of your presence in this house. Needless to say, you just relinquished any claim to any money you might otherwise have had."

"We'll see about that when my attorneys get finished reviewing this mess. And that's not my painting in your library. It came from the little bitch. She painted it. I bought it two days before she convinced me that her plan would work and encouraged me to go to Paris, assuring me everything would be fine."

Wade knew that was a lie. But he didn't see any reason to drag it out further by arguing. "It doesn't make any difference. You lost at any rate. But I would like to know one thing. How did you find her? How did you find someone that looks so much like you?"

Victoria's body slumped forward as though she had maintained an air of false indignity as long as she could. "My older sister had a baby out of wedlock and had to give her up. My curiosity got the better of me, and I tracked her down. As soon as I saw her... Wade, I made a mistake, and I had to go to Paris to make it right. I might have been wrong in not coming clean with you up front, but, after all the verbal attacks and warnings to keep my affairs discreet, I didn't really know how you would react to a pregnancy."

"What happened to the baby?"

"I left her with friends in Paris. I will be joining them as soon as things are arranged over here. I plan to start adoption proceedings when I bring her back. For what it's worth, this was not an attempt to purposely defy or shame you in any way."

"You just wanted the million dollars."

"Yes."

"Victoria, you are a piece of work." She'd been only a month out from their contract ending. But by then her baby would have been born and clearly he wanted no part of that. It was between Victoria and the father of the child. Bad timing on her part, to say the least.

He took three seconds to let his eyes roam across the face of this despicable woman before he turned and walked out of the room.

Victoria would soon be forever gone from this house, never to return. He wouldn't listen to one syllable of her whining or her lies. And Laurel was gone as well.

Which was fine with him, too.

Thirteen

"It's almost five o'clock," Beth Hamilton called from the back of the small shop. "I think we can start to clean up for the day."

Beth's store in the small town of Waxahachie was a combination art gallery and learning center for the neighborhood. Some twenty students from finger-painting five-year-olds to the more versatile teenagers and young adults filled the art studio on a daily basis and after school for their group and one-on-one instruction in painting with watercolors and acrylics. A couple of the older kids and adults had begun using oils, and it reminded Laurel of her own excitement when she'd first worked with that medium many years ago.

It didn't take Laurel long to clean the already cleaned work spaces and tidy up in preparation for the next day.

"How are you coming on your painting?" Beth asked as she came into the back studio. "Are you gonna let me see this one?"

Laurel shrugged. "I don't know why you make such a big deal of my paintings. They are just landscapes, nothing new about them."

Beth walked over to an easel standing in the corner. Carefully removing the drop cloth, she stood back and contemplated the canvas before her.

"This is amazing. Even better than the last few, and that's saying something." She replaced the cover on the canvas. "You know, Mrs. Bridgeman is going to have a hissy fit if you don't let her put your collection in one of her gallery exhibits."

"I don't have a collection," Laurel corrected. "And these are not for a showing."

"Seriously, Laurel. You know you are an exceptional artist. I wish you would let her show them just one time and see what happens." Beth shook her head. "I can't imagine where you come up with the landscapes that you do. I'm pretty sure the places don't exist anywhere on this planet."

Laurel smiled but said nothing. The images to which Beth referred were not in Laurel's imagination. They were in her memory, indelibly permanent, but for her eyes only. They were the special places she'd gone with Wade. The pine forest, the still pool, the small waterfall, the pastures with the cattle and calves and the horses whose spirit shone in their eyes. These memories were her life now. She would never see them again. But, somehow, with each brushstroke she felt close to Wade: his deep voice, his warm breath against her skin, his brooding laughter. It was all she had. She didn't want to share them with anyone, let alone put them on public display. That would be wrong. It would be sharing personal, precious moments with the world. They were her memories. They were all she had left of the man she'd loved and still loved.

It had taken over a month before she could pick up the ruins of her life and trudge forward again. She'd stayed with Beth for a while, withdrawn and silent. Beth had picked up on something not right and hadn't pushed her for any answers. Gradually, Laurel had begun to try to rejoin the world of the living. At first, she'd refused to go out with their other friends, preferring to stay at home, quietly remembering, silently crying with a broken heart she knew would never heal. But eventually she'd joined their small group of six old and loyal friends, who didn't push her for information but were just grateful she was taking a few first steps. They knew something horrendous had happened during the months she'd been gone. And clearly they could see that it had broken her soul. Laurel appreciated their friendship and understanding, and it was that understanding that had eventually brought her around.

Her oldest friend, Beth, had done the most. Finally, unable to listen to another night of sobs from her guest room, she had given Laurel a good shake, figuratively, and demanded to know what had happened. To be fair, Laurel told her some of the story. Very little, however. Just that she'd met the wrong man and had become heartbroken through her foolishness. Relieved that Laurel wasn't suffering some debilitating disease, Beth had finally left her alone to work through the shredded emotions. She gave her a place to tuck her tail and hide from the world and provided friendship and encouragement when it was needed.

"Mrs. Bridgeman will not give up," Beth persisted. "She has been a fan of your work since we were in high school, and she will have that showing. Are you staying over tonight?"

"Yeah. I'd like to work here for a while, if that's okay?"

"Of course. Just be sure to grab a bite to eat. There's some fruit and some lunch meat in the fridge. If you lose any more weight... Just eat, okay?"

"Okay."

She heard Beth tidying the front of the small art studio and the clang of the cash register as her friend put the day's take in a bank bag. Then, after a friendly *See ya tomorrow!* there was the tinkle of the bell over the door, and all was quiet.

Laurel walked to the corner of the room where her current work in progress was propped on its easel and took the cover off. It was another one of the old hunters' cabin from a different angle. The use of alternating shadow and light made each tile of the roof stand out. The overall impression was one of gentle decay. The painting was set in the fall, and leaves fell dispassionately down over the entire scene, the reds, golds, greens and browns swirling around the old chimney and accumulating on the ground. Rays of sun broke through the clouds, highlighting the hundred-and-fifty-year-old structure. Maybe that was why she was drawn to it. So many things in her life never lasted. Her mother had died when she was born and, with no other relatives, Laurel had had a firsthand glimpse of the state's foster-care system. Going from family to family, house to house, she had always felt like she was on the brink of losing it all.

But she'd always had art. It was the one thing that got her through the hard times. A small sketch pad and a pencil had become her best friends. Inside the pages of her spiral notebooks were images of the people and places that, when compiled, told her story. Good, bad or indifferent, she'd captured the visuals and the essence that made up her life.

The tolling of midnight from the bell tower of the

small church across the street brought her back into the here and now. Stretching, she flexed her back and dropped the brushes into the cleaning solution. She sat back rubbing her neck and looked at the picture in front of her. Better. Some of the details could be enhanced, but for the most part she was happy with her work. Through the smell of turpentine she could almost sense the tang of fall in the air that surrounded the little cabin. Thanks to Wade, there would be plenty more pictures to paint. It was the only release from her tortured mind. Images of Wade caught unawares by something she'd said or done. Or rubbing the bump on his head with a towel after he'd upended the table in the middle of the hallway. And the incurably adorable look on his face in the moments of discovery of anything he should have already known.

What she could neither paint nor forget was the look on his face the last time they'd ever made eye contact. The waves of fury at having been played for a fool. The look that said *I trusted you. How could you do this to me?* The internal rage that distorted his handsome features into a mosaic of the raw pain of betrayal.

She carefully replaced the protective cover over the canvas, rinsed and dried her brushes, and turned off the light on her way out. Tomorrow was Sunday, the one day of the week she dreaded. No kids came on Sunday. The little bell over the door didn't ring. No shoppers filled the still time. Beth wasn't there, telling her what she had to eat for lunch. It was a day to remember. A day to try to forget. One more day to somehow get through. A sixteen-hour day applying paint to canvas, bringing alive memories both bitter and sweet. It was a day to live inside the vacuum, where pain could only get in if she wasn't strong enough to prevent it. She had to prevail.

If not, the feelings would intrude and yet again shatter the bruised remnants of her heart.

Wade had ensured Victoria made it out of his house and off his property, and he let his security staff and attorneys handle the rest. Clearly, going to Paris or anywhere else to have another man's child broke the stipulations of their contract. But dammed if she hadn't almost gotten away with it. For all Victoria knew, Wade had been in London during the months she was away and Laurel was taking her place. The whole scenario was intended to play out with him none the wiser.

Then an eighteen-wheeler had run a red light.

And when he thought of Laurel, all that surfaced was the look on her face when he'd screamed at both women to get out. Laurel had run from the room, and he'd not spoken to her again since then.

It had been over a month, and Wade still couldn't let go. His instincts told him to walk away from it all. Be glad he was rid of both of them. His heart said he should go to her. She'd been played as much as he had. Laurel was the first and only woman he'd ever loved. He honestly believed she loved him, too. Or had, before he'd lost his temper big-time the night Victoria had come wandering home. Would Laurel still want anything to do with him after he'd lost it and screamed for them both to get out of his house?

He'd found her ring on the nightstand. His heart had lurched when he picked it up. She could have gotten a pretty penny for it. The fact that she left it behind said something. Didn't it?

He ran both hands through his hair. Victoria had admitted that Laurel had refused to take any money. Was she, in fact, the pawn in Victoria's scheme? Had it been her fault the car was hit by a truck? Had she faked amnesia? No. He couldn't believe any of that. No one was that good of an actress. She had loved the ranch, the horses, swimming in the mountain pool. All of the things that meant most to him Laurel loved as well. Deep down, Wade knew he would never find another woman who was so incredibly perfect for him. But could he find her? And if he did, would it be wasted effort? Would she even speak to him again after the hateful way he'd treated her in the end?

He reached over and picked up the house phone and dialed the number to his security division. "Matt? I need you to find someone, if you can. As soon as possible."

Laurel was so angry at Beth she wanted to hit something. There had been plenty of times she'd said *yes* to an exhibit of her paintings, but showing those of Wade and the ranch was a big fat loud *no*. Beth had gone behind her back and done it anyway, arranging it with Mrs. Bridgeman. And it wasn't as if they were going to be shown in a small exhibit hall. Oh no, they were, at this moment, on their way to Dallas. She needed to get to the art gallery and see if she could protect her privacy and prevent this from happening.

Even though it was only three o'clock in the afternoon, she closed the shop early, flipping the sign from Open to Closed, and hurried to her car. It was a good hour's drive from Waxahachie to Dallas if she didn't run into the ever-present road construction. Backing out of the parking space, she put the car in Drive and headed south.

It was almost five when she turned into the parking lot of the art gallery. She noted Beth's car parked next to the building.

"What do you think?" Beth asked when Laurel finally entered. "Great place, huh?"

"Where are they?"

"In the back. Oh, come on, Laurel, don't be mad. This is what you've worked for your entire life."

"Not with these paintings. Beth, you don't understand. I thought you did."

"Come on. There are some from before your accident and a couple since. They gave you two entire walls. I think it looks spectacular."

Laurel rounded the far corner, and there they were. Still lifes, landscapes, portraits. The one of the woman sitting on a stone wall holding a rose against the backdrop of a sunset was still one of her favorites. Then, on another part of the wall, there were the landscapes of the ranch. All served to bring the walls to life.

"How long?" Laurel asked Beth.

"The showing is just for the weekend. Well, Friday, Saturday and Sunday."

There were seven of Laurel's paintings in all. Among the landscapes were smaller, individual canvases focused on smaller things. Like the pinecone hanging from a tree branch, the early-morning dew making it look fresh and crisp.

"That one is adorable." Beth pointed at the calf with its mother. "And I love the mystery men." She turned to Laurel, grabbed her arm and spun her around. In front of her were two portraits.

Laurel's heart dropped to her knees as she stared at the two portraits of Wade Masters. She hadn't noticed when she was painting them, but Wade was every man; the stern, cold, brooding man of wealth and privilege. Used to commanding a boardroom and governing financial aspects of international corporations, he was a powerful man who expected to be treated to lavish parties and approached about supporting governors and top politicians. The second painting was of a man who was carefree, had no worries other than concerns of family and close friends. This was a guy in worn jeans and an open shirt and whose hair was tousled by the wind. One who would jump on a motorcycle and do wheelies in the dirt, who would throw a saddle on a horse and cut cows for fifteen hours straight. One who was content with who he was and the world around him. A man who judged others by their actions and their word. It was this man Laurel had fallen in love with. It was this man she had hurt.

"Laurel, is that him?"

She could only stare, and a trickle of fear ran through her. If Wade found out about this viewing, he would truly and thoroughly hate her. That being said, he already did. What did she have to lose if he found out? They were, after all, her paintings. Maybe she owed it to the world to let people see what a complex, brilliant and loving man Wade Masters was.

"Yeah."

"Which one?"

She looked back and forth between the two paintings. "Both."

Wade had never seen anything like it. A complete section of the Montrella Art Gallery contained pictures of his home. Detailed paintings of the lower falls and swimming holes, the valleys and the pine groves. Insightful, detailed glimpses of his ranch, captured forever. There was one of the old trappers' cabin, next to the spring and Stockman's Ridge with the view of the valley spread out far below.

When he'd first been told that paintings by a new artist were to be included in an exhibit of another artist's work, he'd look at Sylvia Fields, his senior administrative assistant, like she had grown a second head.

"Do I look like an art connoisseur? Why would I care?"

"Because two of the paintings are of you and I'm guessing the landscapes are of your ranch."

Laurel had done this. Her skills, perspective and amazing talent had brought the ranch alive. His mother was considered a great artist, but nothing near this scale. He slowly walked the area, looking at each picture, seeing his valley through her eyes. There was great beauty in each scene, even in the painting of the old hunters' cabin. But it was as he turned the last corner he saw the portraits of himself.

To say he was stunned would be an understatement. There were two paintings. One was the facade he showed to the world; the other revealed the side he kept hidden from all but close friends and family. Laurel had nailed each one perfectly. She had seen through the mask and knew both men intimately.

Only someone who saw the differences in his character, who knew him that well, could have painted his portrait so authentically. She'd painted what she saw. First the cowboy who enjoyed letting his hair down and eating beans around a campfire. Then the hard, cynical businessman he became in Dallas.

"Mr. Masters." The woman he'd asked about speaking to the artist returned, wringing her hands. Never a good sign. "I'm so sorry, but she just left. I couldn't find anyone who knew when she would be back. But I can tell you the paintings are not for sale. There was a misunderstanding between the owner of the art gallery, Mrs. Bridgeman, and the artist. These were not intended to be shown. May I give Ms. Dawson a message or a phone number?"

Wade shook his head. "She knows how to reach me. Consider each and every one of these paintings sold. I don't care what you were told. If Mrs. Bridgeman has a problem with that, she can work it out with my accountant. You will receive a call in a few minutes from Bradley Jarrod, who will arrange for payment and delivery." He glanced once again at the paintings. "I stress, Mrs. Colbert," he said, reading her name tag, "do not let one single painting by this artist leave the building other than under my instructions."

"Of course, sir," she assured him, a light of excitement appearing in her eyes. "In fact, we'll close the section so no one else can see them."

"Good." Wade turned and headed for the door, Crawford and Jenkins flanking him. They drew glances from others as they walked toward the front door, but Wade ignored it. He had more on his mind than dim-witted people who might be staring. Laurel had been here. The gallery attendant had indicated she'd left only moments before he arrived. If she knew he was here, she'd managed to slip by him. It wouldn't happen again.

"Laurel," said Beth over the phone. "Your paintings… they sold. All of them."

"Sold?" It couldn't be. She hadn't intended for them to be shown, let alone sold.

"You and Mrs. Bridgeman can't do that. I told you not to—"

"I think it's okay," Beth broke in. "They were all sold to one man. I wasn't there, but I'm betting it was Wade Masters. That's who's in the portraits, isn't it, Laurel?"

Laurel didn't respond.

"Yeah, I thought so. Anyway, thought I'd give you a heads-up. He asked for you and didn't look happy when he was told you weren't here. He and the two men with him, I'm guessing bodyguards, walked out after he'd arranged to buy the paintings. I'll bet they are headed your way."

"He doesn't know where I live."

"Don't be dumb. If he found the paintings, he can find you. You love him. I'm guessing he loves you, too. If he isn't there in an hour, you can say I was wrong and throw it in my face the rest of my life. But you need to talk with him, Laurel. Whatever happened between you needs to be worked out."

The line went dead.

What had happened at the Masters estate wasn't something that could be worked out or made better. She had ensconced herself in another woman's house, assumed her identity and made love with her husband. In fact, she'd fallen in love with her husband. It was all immoral, possibly even illegal. She knew he was hurt. And angry. Put in his position she would be livid.

She was certain he'd heard about the art showing and had gone there to correct a foolish mistake. He'd probably felt required to purchase the paintings to keep his privacy intact. She knew if Wade found out about the exhibit, he would be angry. She should have demanded the paintings be taken down instead of just saying they were not for sale. She just hadn't expected him to find them so soon.

Regardless of how much he must hate her, Laurel didn't regret a second of their time together. She still loved Wade deeply. It wasn't supposed to have happened this way. She should never have met him, let alone had the chance to fall in love with him. And now he thought

her a woman as conniving and malevolent as his wife.
No doubt he thought she was trying to make money off
the paintings of his beloved ranch. Laurel blinked back
the tears and gritted her teeth to combat the surge of pain
again slashing her heart. Were Wade and Victoria back
together? Was Wade holding her in his arms even now?
Making love to her? Ironically, all Laurel would ever
have of the man she loved were a few precious memories.

She headed into the back room of the paint school,
where her current painting was still under wraps. The feel
of adding paint to a canvas always helped to soothe her
nerves and prevent her mind from wandering to places
she didn't want to go.

But knowing Wade had walked into the art exhibit
in Dallas and seen her paintings brought that last night
back to the forefront of her mind. The sheer horror of
it all. It seemed no matter how hard she tried, she just
couldn't seem to get it right. First agreeing to Victoria's scheme, then allowing an opportunity for Beth and
Mrs. Bridgeman to waylay her paintings and take them
to an exhibition. And Wade had walked into the middle both times.

She selected two brushes and uncovered the canvas.
Turning on the extra lights, she scrutinized the painting. Artificial lighting was different from true sunlight.
She would have to be careful, but she couldn't bear to
go home. She would just wind up back here after pacing
the floor half the night.

"That's very interesting."

Spinning around, she faced Wade.

Even backlit, he could tell she had gone pale. He
watched her closely, afraid she would again disappear.
The painting she'd been working on was going home

with him, and it would remain there until he could figure out what had happened to the brilliant artist whose technique had changed so drastically. He'd fallen in love with the artist who had painted it. And more than anything wanted her back in his life.

"How did you get in here?" she asked, her eyes darting around the room as though looking for a way out. The art room had only one door, and Wade was standing in front of it.

He held up a key. "Thanks to Beth Hamilton." He tossed the key onto the table. "I was wrong, Laurel. That night. When I told you to go. I was speaking through anger and frustration, and I didn't mean to direct it at you."

"Yes, you did. I saw your face." She began to back up and ease around the large table at the center of the room. "You have every right to hate me. I didn't know what I was doing at the time, but if I hadn't been in the wreck, I still would have been at your house. I would still have pretended to be Victoria."

"Because she threatened you if you didn't," he countered and took a step forward. "She came clean about those threats. If the only thing I had in this world was threatened, I would probably give in, too."

"No, you wouldn't. You're strong. You're a fighter. I'm not."

"You're the strongest woman I know. You are the most honest person I've ever met. And I love you, Laurel Dawson."

She bowed her head, giving it a slight shake, and the tears began to roll down her face.

"Look at me, Laurel."

She shook her head. "No."

Then she felt his hand under her chin, slowly raising

her face to his. Her lilac eyes glimmered from unshed tears, making them appear almost iridescent. "I think you love me, too."

She sniffed, unable to confirm what he said for fear it was a ploy.

"So, what are we going to do about this?"

When she didn't respond, he stepped closer to her and placed his other hand against her face. "Victoria is gone, never to return. Our divorce was final last week. I want you to come home with me. I want us to be as we were before that fateful night. Only this time, you know who you are. You have your memories. I fell in love with you a long time ago. I just mistakenly called you by a different name. Marry me, Laurel Marie Dawson."

He lowered his face to her, giving her the option of kissing him. With a small whimper, she placed her hand against his chest, and her lips against his. It was as though time had never interfered; they were back living and loving as they had been before. Her lips were hungry, and he was ready and more than willing to fill that hunger.

"Marry me," he whispered against her lips.

"Yes—"

She barely had the word out before he pulled her hard against him and kissed her deeply, passionately. "I love you so much." Then he was kissing her again, his body reacting as it had always done to this beautiful woman.

"The paintings." She broke the kiss. "I didn't intend for them to be shown. They were only for me. Beth…"

"It's okay, sweetheart," he said. "They are coming home with us. They're beautiful, and I will enjoy looking at them the rest of my life. Someday we may even decide to share them with the world."

Then he took her left hand and pulled the diamond

ring from his pocket and slipped it on her finger. "We will be married tomorrow. I refuse to wait one second longer. Later, if you want a big wedding celebration, you can have whatever you wish. But I don't intend to wait another full day without knowing legally, spiritually, emotionally—in every way that matters—you are mine."

Tears filled her eyes as he again pulled her into his arms, held tight in his embrace. His mouth covered hers, and their love soared.

Epilogue

The wedding was held in a small country church on the ranch. Old and forgotten for years, the building had been refurbished, painted and filled with new pews and the restored altar. White roses and mums with matching white ribbons decorated the interior, spilling out into the trees surrounding the church.

Wade's brothers and their wives were there, along with the ranch hands and a few special friends. It was a family wedding. That was what Laurel wanted, so that was what Wade had provided.

Although they had been officially married for a couple of months, Laurel had wanted a ceremony that could be shared by their closest friends and family. She arrived at the church in a barouche pulled by two white horses, their harness adorned with matching white roses and ribbons. Wade was waiting at the entrance and helped her from the carriage.

After the ceremony, the party lasted for hours, held in the covered pavilion a mile from the main house. Country music filled the air, and the summer night set the stage for a wonderful evening. "Are you ready to sneak out of here?" Wade asked his bride as they danced. "I need to get you home." He pulled her close, and she felt his erection against her belly.

"I'll follow you," she replied, smiling. She wanted to be alone with her husband and knew the night ahead would be magical. It was always so when she was in his arms.

Wade took her hand, and she marveled again at how strong and warm he was as he led her the few steps to the front door. His car was parked right outside.

"I love you, Laurel Masters."

She smiled as he started the car and followed the path to the main ranch area, then on to Pine House. When they got there, he helped her from the car, then picked her up in his arms and carried her up the steps and inside the front door. Not pausing there, he went up the stairs and into the master suite.

Setting her down, he lost no time removing the beautiful silk gown and the diamond-encrusted pin that held her hair, cascading slowly past her shoulders.

Laurel removed his silk shirt and bow tie and pulled at his belt, unzipping his pants. Wade kicked out of his pants, cupped her face with his big hands and brought his mouth down over hers. Laurel was lost. She fell deep into his arms and kissed him back with all the love she felt for this great man.

He turned the lights out and lifted her into the bed.

"I'm going to love you forever," he said against her mouth, his voice deep and rough.

"As I will you," Laurel replied and pulled his head down to hers.

And neither spoke another word for a very long time.

* * * * *

ONE NIGHT SCANDAL

JOANNE ROCK

To Mandy Lawler for all of your
help and guidance.
Thank you!

One

Hannah Ryder scavenged her last scrap of patience as the film director she despised zoomed in on her for a close-up shot. The bright lights were making her sweat right through the thick layers of makeup. Itchy, dry hay poked her bare skin. She lay smothered in the stuff on the floor of an old barn temporarily transformed into a movie set. The scene called for her character to fall through the loft in the middle of hooking up with a cowboy; thankfully, the stunt had been pulled off by someone else paid to do that sort of thing.

Now, Hannah had to perform the sequence following the fall after her cowboy lover had abandoned her. Her face was covered in cosmetics to look like blood and bruises. All of which was fine, if she hadn't been in her third hour of shooting reaction shots while drowning in hay that made her eyes water and her skin burn. Her makeup had to be retouched every twenty minutes to keep it from sliding off, and the flesh-toned bodysuit she wore under the hay didn't protect her in the least. Horses flanked her on either side, their impatient hooves providing a frame for the scene, according to the sadist in charge. What if one of the animals decided he was tired of a sneezing woman writhing on the floor of his barn?

Twice she was sure a spider or some other creepy-crawly had skittered up her bare leg, and a cramp knotted her calf.

She would have walked off the production days ago if she hadn't wrangled a part in this film for a very specific reason. She needed evidence of the director's sexual harassment of women on the set to help avenge what he'd done to Hannah's younger sister a year ago.

The incident had transformed nineteen-year-old Hope from a bright-eyed aspiring writer, with a coveted job as script reader and assistant to director Antonio Ventura, into a quiet shell of her former self. Hope now worked in retail, content to unlock dressing rooms for customers since it was a job that surrounded her with women. Hope didn't write anymore, and she showed no desire to leave the house for any reason but work. She startled at noises and cried when she thought Hannah couldn't hear.

The change broke Hannah's heart, and months of therapy hadn't seemed to help her sister. Hope refused to file charges, insisting she'd destroyed evidence after the fact because of conflicted feelings, and she didn't want to bring a case she couldn't prove. When months of gentle encouragement and outright coercing had proven ineffective, Hannah had taken a new approach. She'd spend time on one of the bastard's sets to see for herself if he was victimizing other females.

So far all she'd learned was that every single person who worked on his film *Winning the West* thought he was a tyrant and a megalomaniac. But she had no evidence that he was locking vulnerable women in closets to forcibly grope them the way he'd done to Hope.

Just the thought of it steeled Hannah to withstand the cramp throbbing in her calf for another minute while the camera closed in on her tears. She'd been Hope's guardian ever since her sister had moved to Los Angeles to be with Hannah. Their parents had never been much help since their high-powered attorney father had walked out on their mother long ago—taking his family fortune with him. As for their mom, she'd done her best to raise Hope and Hannah, but she'd made no secret of the fact that she was "done" once Hope had turned eighteen.

Hannah would never be "done." And she would fight for her sister even if Hope refused to fight for herself.

A horse snorted and tossed his head, a hoof momentarily pinning Hannah's hair to the floor before shifting away again. She couldn't smother her gasp, ruining the take.

But before the director could explode in rage, a tall, broad-shouldered cowboy stepped into view, casting a long shadow onto the floor where Hannah lay.

"Ventura, I need to take my horses," the man demanded, his tone uncompromising as he confronted the despot in charge of the shoot. "Now."

A murmur of collective surprise—quickly stifled—stirred the production team ringing the small barn.

Hannah stretched quietly in the sea of hay, wanting a better look at the cowboy whose arrival had diverted the director's ire away from her. The newcomer blocked the lights, providing a welcome moment of coolness for her itchy skin.

She craned her neck to see around a horse's knee.

And got an eyeful of feminine fantasy material in denim and worn boots. The hard-muscled cowboy stood a head taller than the director, his biceps straining the fabric of a gray cotton T-shirt as he reached to stroke a hand over a horse's nose.

The man's features remained in shadow, thanks to the set of his dark Stetson, but the sharp edge of his jaw and the hint of dark hair curling along the collar of his shirt were enough to make any woman long to see more. For now, Hannah settled on taking in the rest of him, from where his shirt tapered along his back, from his formidable shoulders down to his lean hips.

"You are ruining my shot," Antonio Ventura snapped at the cowboy, his dark eyes narrowing. "Now, thanks to you, I'll need the animals even longer."

The fury brewing under the quiet words made the sweat on Hannah's back turn cold and clammy, worry chilling her.

"Whether you need them or not isn't my concern." The cowboy took the reins of the one closest to him. "They're not professional actors, and they're done for today."

Hannah would have admired anyone unafraid to stand up to a bully like Ventura. But she took a special brand of pleasure in seeing this big, strong guy put the smarmy brute in his place.

"As you can see—" Ventura enunciated each word as if the cowboy was a simpleton "—they are hardly being asked to act. They're standing in the middle of a barn, just the same as they will be when you take them with you. I suggest you consult your boss before you make a choice that will cost you your job."

The dirtbag. How unfair to threaten the man's livelihood. Hannah was already mentally composing a letter to the ranch owner in the cowboy's defense.

"My choice is made." The sexy stranger gathered the other horse's reins in the opposite hand. "And since we're making suggestions, I'm going to advise you to take better care of your actors." The man's gaze fell to where Hannah sprawled in the hay. "Do you need a hand, miss?"

His eyes were blue. Clear sky blue.

Wide-open spaces, Wyoming blue.

Hannah wanted to fall right into them.

Except, she realized, she couldn't afford to thumb her nose at Antonio Ventura before she'd gathered evidence of his criminal behavior. With more than a little regret, she shook her head, a stray piece of hay poking the back of her neck as she moved.

"No. Thank you." She risked a small smile at the horseman, hoping the director was too busy seething to notice.

When she gave her boss a quick glance, he seemed to be pounding out digits on his cell phone as he paced away from the camera equipment.

"You're going to regret this show of stupidity," Ventura threatened between clenched teeth.

Around him, the production team buzzed with new life, sensing they were done shooting for the day as the cowboy guided the animals out of the wide barn door. The night air rushed in.

Hannah watched his retreat, her breath stuck in her chest as she followed his long-legged stride, an easy swagger that made her wish she would have accepted his hand when he'd offered it. What might it have been like to touch him? To keep that blue gaze trained on her a little longer?

Behind her, the wardrobe stylist cleared her throat. "Um... Hannah?"

Swiveling away from the enticing view, Hannah glanced up to find the young woman holding a robe in her hands.

"Sorry. I must have gotten distracted." She grinned conspiratorially as a production assistant shut off the hottest of the set lights nearby. Hannah didn't want anyone to see how stressed this shoot was making her. Her muscles were cramped from the strain and tension of working with her sister's molester as much as from holding the twisted pose for hours.

"Didn't we all?" the stylist, Callie, agreed. Her high, dark ponytail swung in front of her narrow shoulders as she leaned down to wrap the cover-up around Hannah, shielding her in the flesh-tone bodysuit. "I think I forgot to breathe just now."

The woman's vanilla fragrance settled around Hannah as surely as the silk dressing robe. Hannah's itchiness eased immediately from the fresh air, the cooler temperature without the set lights and being free of the hay.

She was stepping into the leather slides that Callie had brought out for her when, from the other side of a rolling cart stuffed full of electronics, a series of shouted curse words blistered her ears. Callie flinched and Hannah's eye started to twitch while they listened to the director yell at whoever was on the other end of the call.

Hannah needed to get away from here. Three hours

of dealing with that man was more than she could take. She had a private cabin on-site at the Creek Spill Ranch, close to where filming took place each day. No need to stay here and listen to Ventura's tirade when her accommodations were within walking distance.

"Callie, I think I'm going to call it a night and head back to my room," she said softly, tying the belt on her robe. It was blousy and pretty enough to pass for a caftan. "I can take off my own makeup."

"I don't blame you," the stylist muttered under her breath, her gaze moving furtively toward their boss. He looked ready to pop the vein in his temple, his face contorting as he shouted about ineptitude in his staff and incompetence in the production company. "Take some makeup wipes," Callie said, passing a small plastic packet before gesturing to Hannah's face. "You don't want anyone to think you've just been in a horrible accident."

Hannah was already peeling out a damp cloth from the pack. "You're a lifesaver." Retrieving her purse from behind one of the barn columns, she headed for the door, leather shoes slapping the bottoms of her sockless feet. "Thanks, Callie. I'll see you in the morning."

Part of her wondered if she should stick around a little longer while Ventura was all worked up and angry in case the bad mood brought his criminal tendencies out. But she was physically exhausted, her spirit weary after the trying day. She needed to de-stress tonight. Conserve some energy for tomorrow.

She'd take a soak in the tub. Maybe try some yoga. The porch of her tiny, secluded cabin had a beautiful view during the day. And at night, she could see stars for miles. But as she hurried across the ranch to indulge herself in some much needed downtime, an image of her sister's tearful face returned to chastise her.

Back home, Hope wouldn't be de-stressing tonight. And she sure as hell wasn't taking any feminine joy from admiring the way a brash cowboy looked in jeans.

Priorities quickly realigning, Hannah double-timed her steps toward the cabin. She'd shower, change and sneak back over to the barn to see what else Antonio the Ass got up to tonight. Because nothing would give her more pleasure than putting him behind bars.

Not even a diversion with the sexy horseman who'd rescued her from the shoot today.

Brock McNeill couldn't get the actress out of his mind.

Two hours after he'd removed his quarter horses from the set of the idiot director who was making life at the Creek Spill Ranch a living hell, Brock was more than a little preoccupied by thoughts of the curvy blonde covered in hay. There was something about her that appealed to him—something far more intriguing than her looks, although she was easy enough on the eyes even with the heavy blue and purple makeup meant to look like bruising.

Now, riding back through a rocky ravine to his place after a late consultation with the vet, he found his thoughts on the woman instead of on his sick filly. As the head of the quarter horse breeding and development program at the Creek Spill Ranch, Brock realized his focus needed to be on his portion of the family business now more than ever. The film shoot required it. But the timing couldn't be worse.

Because the McNeills were bracing for a scandal. A

blackmailer had promised to reveal his stepmother's secrets to the world two days from now. The whole Wyoming branch of the family was on high alert, waiting for the other shoe to drop because they'd decided not to meet the blackmailer's demands.

To make matters worse, Brock's stepmother was still recovering from a suspicious hiking accident that had put her in a coma right around the time the blackmailer had first surfaced. It was a mess.

Brock needed to protect his family. As the youngest of his brothers, born after the twins Carson and Cody, Brock had always been the odd-man out. It had been easy to fly under the radar in a big family, but the time had come to step up and prove himself now that his brothers needed to focus on their own relationships. Plus, his half sisters were particularly vulnerable because the blackmailer was hinting that their mother's marriage to Donovan McNeill was invalid. Brock needed to be there for his father, his stepmother and his half sisters.

So it was flat-out wrong for him to spend his mental energy thinking about the hay-strewn beauty on the floor of his barn. Dating an actress would only draw more attention to his family when they needed to lay low. It was bad enough his sister Scarlett had been in the tabloids recently for dating one of the film's lead actors. Besides, thinking about the woman so much was crazy, considering he'd watched her work for only half an hour or so. He'd shown up at the shoot because the ranch hands tasked with bringing the horses back hadn't returned. Brock didn't appreciate having his generosity with his animals taken advantage of, so he'd gone to set Antonio Ventura straight for himself. And gotten distracted by the woman crying tears that looked all too real.

She'd only been performing, of course. He understood that. But the tears had gone right through him,
the pain in her eyes so damn convincing it had been
tough to look away. What made a woman choose a job
so emotionally demanding? Because—performing or
not—tears like that didn't manufacture themselves. They
came from somewhere deep. Seeing her like that had
felt oddly intimate.

Maybe that's all it was. He'd caught a stranger in a
moment that felt intensely private. Except then she'd
smiled at him. The smallest twitch of her lips when their
eyes met, and there'd been...

Heat.

He would swear from the look in her eyes that he
hadn't been the only one feeling a connection.

Brock decided to circle back to the remote barn Ventura had been shooting in earlier, wanting to see for
himself that the guy had released the actress from work.
Because while Brock had succeeded in freeing his horses
from the director's overheated set, he hadn't gotten the
satisfaction of witnessing the blonde walk away from
the grueling job. He'd rather lift bales of hay all day than
spend an hour sitting in the stuff half-naked the way she
had. Especially the old, super-dry variety the director
had spread all over the floor. Brock guessed a bed of
nails would be more comfortable.

Reining in his horse as he reached the old, small barn
that had outlived its usefulness on the ranch, Brock could
see filming must have stopped since the lights were dim.
A damn good thing, since he would be well within his
rights as a partial owner of the McNeill lands to shut
down filming if the company violated safety protocols,
a clause his brother Carson had the sense to put into the

contract with the production company. And working in a wood barn with hot lights and overheated straw that could catch fire veered into dangerous terrain.

The doors were open, though, inviting bears and other foragers inside. Someone must have forgotten to close up for the night. Swinging down from the mare, he patted her neck before dropping the reins and stepping through the open wood doors.

A dark shadow emerged from behind a support post. A curvy shadow.

Brock recognized the shape of her instantly. No mean feat considering she'd been mostly covered in straw the last time he'd seen her. Apparently, his imagination had done a highly accurate job of filling in the blanks where her body was concerned.

She was dressed in dark leggings and a dark T-shirt. Her platinum hair was tucked under a ball cap with the logo of a West Coast football team. With her face scrubbed clean of makeup, he could see her features better now. The long lashes over her eyes. A few freckles on her nose. Then the stubborn tilt to her chin as she spotted him just inside the barn entrance.

"I sure hope you're off the clock at this hour." Brock summoned a smile, not wanting to startle her when she was alone. "I came back to make sure your director knew enough to call it a day."

She shuffled from one tennis shoe to the other. Was she uneasy?

He took a side step to lean against the barn door, giving her plenty of space to walk out if she chose.

She folded her arms across her chest and stood her ground instead.

"So did I," she claimed, although something vaguely

defensive about the way she said it made him wonder if that was true. "I walked off the set right after you did, but the director was in such a snit, I returned because I wanted to make sure he wasn't—" She took a deep breath and let it back out as if she was forcing herself to relax. "Taking advantage of people with no seniority."

Her careful phrasing seemed...off. She was hiding something, and it didn't take a genius to see she was uncomfortable. Maybe he'd been mistaken about the attraction before. Maybe it had been all one-sided.

"That would make him even more of an ass than I already took him for," Brock said, preparing to leave, in case he was responsible for her feeling uneasy. Straightening from the doorframe, he was about to wish her a good-night when her laugh caught him off guard.

A genuine laugh. Surprise music to his ears.

Some of his tension eased as hers seemed to.

"He is. Most definitely." She took a step closer to him, a smile lighting up her whole face, transforming her from pretty to breathtaking. "I'm Hannah Ryder, by the way."

She extended her hand. Anticipation flared at the thought of touching her.

"Brock. It's a pleasure to meet you." He closed his fingers around hers and squeezed.

His hand lingered for a moment longer than necessary. Just enough to see her notice. Her pupils widened a fraction. She sucked in a quick breath.

Gratified that he hadn't been wrong about their first meeting—that there was something hot lurking just beneath the surface between them—he released her hand. He hadn't mentioned his last name, preferring to avoid the inevitable interest in his well-known, wealthy family.

Brock had been down that road before, not realizing a woman he'd cared about had been after him only for the connections. The McNeill lifestyle. Or, more accurately, other McNeills' lifestyle. Brock preferred hard work to jet-setting, no matter that his hotel magnate grandfather owned five-star resorts all over the world.

Hannah Ryder toyed with the long sleeve of her dark T-shirt, pulling it over one hand, but not before he spotted a silver ring in the shape of an eternity knot. "I didn't get the chance to thank you earlier, but your entrance was very well timed."

There was a slight husky quality to her voice that made the sound as warm and inviting as a whiskey shot. She was about a head shorter than him, maybe a little more. Dressed all in black with her hair tucked under the cap, she looked like she was trying to avoid recognition. Maybe movie people dressed that way all the time when they were off duty. She seemed about as far from his idea of a diva as possible.

"I regret that I didn't intervene sooner, before my horse's hoof landed on your hair." He couldn't act fast enough after that, knowing the animals were too restless to be trusted standing so close to her head. "You barely even winced."

She shrugged, shaking her head. "But it was enough to ruin another shot. Whenever I let my guard down even a little bit, then it's my fault the whole crew gets stuck on the set for an extra hour."

"Is it always like this?" He realized her eyes were gray under the shadow of her cap's brim.

She smelled good, too. Like soap and wildflowers. He caught the hint of fragrance as she played with the shirtsleeve, the fabric rubbing against her skin.

"Not at all. My job is usually pretty fun, but this film is making me see how much the director has to do with setting a production's tone."

Brock wanted to ask her more, but he guessed she must be tired after her long day.

"Well, for what it's worth, I thought you were fantastic today." He wasn't overstating it, or flattering her. She was good. "In fact, it was because I was so caught up in watching your performance that I didn't interrupt filming sooner."

She laughed again, the sound another surprise shot of pure adrenaline.

"So I have no one to blame but myself for my hair getting stepped on? Are you saying that if I'd been a worse actress, you would have come to the rescue sooner?" Her gray eyes twinkled with mischief.

Teasing. Flirtation.

It wasn't a game Brock had played often. Or well. But he damned well recognized it.

He let the new flames crackle through him, stunned that a total stranger could stir that level of heat. What was it about her? Hell, what was it about *him* that he was letting it draw him in?

"I'm saying, Hannah Ryder, that you're not an easy woman to look away from."

He heard the tone of his voice; it was all wrong for the moment. It brought the teasing and flirtation to a halt. The air around them changed. Got warmer.

He saw the confusion in her gaze. The surprise. A whole host of emotions flickered through her expression that he couldn't identify.

But there was one that he knew. Because he felt it, too. Desire.

It pulsed in the charged air like a heartbeat. For a moment, he thought she might take a step toward him. Until, outside the barn, his horse whinnied softly. Breaking the moment and the connection.

"I'd better go." She tucked her chin into her chest and stalked past him. Out of the barn and into the night.

Brock watched her leave, knowing he shouldn't follow. She'd made her decision. He respected that. He needed to check in with his family anyhow, see if their investigator had any updates on the blackmailer.

Taking a deep, cooling breath to ward off the lingering hunger for Hannah, he took his time stepping outside. Only to glimpse her outline in the moonlight.

With her back to him, he could see clearly the image that she'd pulled up on her phone.

A map of the ranch.

Walking directions back to her cabin.

Brock closed his eyes for a long moment, knowing he couldn't let her make the long trek in the dark by herself. He would give his own sisters a hard time about navigating those woods on foot alone at night, and they'd been raised here, fully aware of what to look out for. How much did a West Coast visitor understand about the potential dangers of the Wyoming land?

Steeling himself against the inevitable draw of the woman, Brock stepped closer to make an offer that was going to be hell on his restraint.

"How about I give you a ride home?"

Two

The cowboy's voice smoked through her, heating her insides and sending a shiver of awareness over Hannah's skin.

Did she want a ride?

Her subconscious was going to have way too much fun tormenting her with that image in her dreams tonight. For now, she needed to stop fantasizing about sexy Brock, the rancher who turned her inside out with just a handful of words and a smoldering gaze.

Her legs were still unsteady after whatever it was that had passed between them inside the barn. She'd had meaningful relationships in her past. Men she'd loved. And yet no one had ever given her the sizzling shock to the system that she felt from being around this stranger. Swallowing hard, she braced herself as she turned around to refuse his offer.

"That's okay. I don't mind walking." Her voice was soft and breathless when she needed it to be firm and sure. "I, um, could use the fresh air."

She could also use a new libido. One that wasn't quite so susceptible to tall, muscular cowboys. It must be because of all the stress she was under with her sister. She'd latched on to a pleasurable distraction and now she couldn't quite let go.

Brock folded his arms across his impressive chest. God, his arms were amazing, too. She wanted to skim her hands up the triceps and over his shoulders. Instead, she jammed her restless fingers in the back pockets of her jeans along with her phone.

"You'd probably be fine," he acknowledged. "You must have walked over here in the dark in the first place, although the moon was higher at that hour, making the path a lot easier to follow than it will be now."

She had been thinking the same thing since she didn't remember exactly where she'd broken through the brush to find the barn. Nightfall in this part of Wyoming was nothing like it was in Southern California. Here, there was no ambient light of any kind. Just deep blackness and stars.

"I've got my phone," she argued, although she was beginning to wonder what else might be out there in the wilderness surrounding the ranch lands. She'd heard wolves—or some kind of wild dogs—baying in the distance on the walk over here. "The cabin I'm staying in is just through there."

She pointed vaguely, trying to see any kind of trail.

"I'm not sure calling someone will do you any good if you meet up with a bear. Or an elk. Or some other wild animal that wasn't expecting company at this hour."

She didn't want to be foolish. So, in spite of the out-of-control attraction, she figured the best thing to do would be to accept the ride and get home as fast as possible.

And put this encounter out of her mind.

"Is your truck nearby?" she asked, peering around the barn. During the shoot, there'd been a couple of golf carts and two trucks parked there.

A smile curved that hard mouth of his. Nodding, he relaxed his arms and walked past her, close enough for her to feel the warmth of his body, close enough for his sleeve to brush hers.

"My horse is right this way."

"Horse?" Her belly flipped.

Not because she minded riding a horse. Only because it implied a proximity that...

A shiver stole over her skin. Her nerve endings danced in anticipation of touching him. Something her brain knew was a very, very bad idea.

"I—" Her voice wasn't even there. She licked her lips. Tried again. "I'm not sure—"

"You'll be fine," he assured her, holding a hand out for her while he stood next to a dark horse with a glossy coat. "I'll help you up." He flipped the ring for her foot so it was easier for her to see. "Step into the stirrup and you'll be home in no time."

Her heart pounded a chaotic, fast beat. But stalling wasn't going to get her home any faster. She understood that much. Willing herself to remain calm, she stabbed the toe of her tennis shoe through the foothold.

Brock's hands were quick and efficient as he boosted her up onto the saddle. He didn't linger. But he might as well have been massaging her naked body for how her skin reacted under her clothes. Her thigh tingled. Her waist…

She wanted his hands there again. Before she could gather herself or prepare for more, Brock swung up onto the animal behind her. His chest was against her back. Her hips tucked into the cradle of his lap, his strong thighs bracketing hers.

There was no space. No distance. And it felt so good she couldn't have spoken if she'd tried. The only thing she didn't like about it was that she shouldn't like it so damn much.

But there was no chance to protest now as his arm curled around her waist, his hand bracing her protectively against him while he nudged the animal into motion. Hannah sucked in a gasp at the feel of their bodies moving together. In sync. Rubbing together.

It was the most erotic experience of her life, and she hardly knew the man. Keenly aware of his body, Hannah closed her eyes to try to shut out the feel of him…everywhere. But even that proved dangerous, as her mind vividly supplied even more suggestive details. The scent of him—leather and musky aftershave—drifted around her, the warmth of his body a welcome heat on a summer night that had cooled surprisingly fast after sundown. Searching for a fraction of space, she shifted in the saddle as they galloped through trees. Her movement elicited a sharp intake of breath behind her.

It was the first indication Brock might be feeling some of the wayward attraction, too. She wanted to turn around to face him, to see the expression on his face, but his palm was a firm weight against her belly, his fingers a light graze of warmth along the inside of her hip. The barrier of her leggings didn't begin to dull the intimacy of the sensation.

She didn't know how she'd walk away from him at the end of this ride. For that matter, she didn't know how she'd look him in the eye again after this. It was all so very...

Sensual.

Her heart pounded faster than the horse's hooves. She told herself it was because of the incredible stress she'd been under. The frustrated tension of seeing her sister suffer and not being able to help. The unbearable strain of working with a man she despised in order to find evidence of his misdeeds.

All that anxiety had shoved her to a breaking point, leaving her with zero reserves now, when tempted with the heady pleasure of a generous, honorable man's touch. Brock had strode into her world, putting the bully Ventura in his place, and Hannah had been intrigued. Curious. Attracted.

Now, adding to that attraction, the horseback ride tantalized her with needs she normally shoved to the backburner. These were desires she'd ignored easily enough in the past, only indulging them within committed relationships.

Brock's touch teased her with all the ways she'd gone unfulfilled. Because no man had ever ignited the sort of awareness she felt tonight. As if the slightest increase in pressure from his hands would unleash a tide of passion and desire that would completely sweep her away.

Then, suddenly, her cabin was in sight, the tiny pinprick of light from an upstairs window growing as they neared the small structure. She focused on it like a beacon in a dark sea, telling herself this churn of sensual thought would recede once she arrived there.

When Brock leaned back slightly in the saddle, drawing the horse to a halt, Hannah waited for a break in the seductive spell. But even as Brock swung a leg over the saddle and jumped down to the ground, her nerve endings still danced with awareness. Anticipation.

Glancing at him, she met his gaze for a moment, and that only worsened the heat. He reached up to help her dismount, his hands ready to assist her. And she simply fell into his arms. No thought. No planning. She slid down, her body against his in a way that set her on fire. Then she was reaching for him, wrapping her arms around his neck.

Kissing him.

His lips sealed to hers, his arms banding around her back and waist. She dangled in midair for a moment against him, her breasts pressed to the hard wall of his chest. Flames licked over her skin as their mouths fused, tongues tangling. A mindless need roared through her, a hunger to have more of this. More of him.

When he set her on her feet, he edged back to look at her, his breath coming fast.

She knew it was wise of him to separate them. To break the mesmerizing contact. To give them a moment to think about this. But there in the endless dark, with only the horse and the wind as her witnesses, she couldn't scavenge any reason to deny herself this heat. This connection. This kind of intense pleasure she'd never experienced before. Perhaps it was the inky blackness of the night that made it feel surreal, like a dream she didn't want to wake up from.

All Hannah knew was that her body went to his like a magnet drawn to a more powerful one.

A raw sound rose up in his throat as she found his lips and kissed him again. Brock wrapped his hands around her, this time with more intent and purpose. She could feel the difference in how he flexed his fingers against her, the added pressure tantalizing her all the more.

"Hannah." He breathed her name against her mouth. "Are you sure?"

"Positive." She gripped his biceps, wanting him inside where she could take his clothes off.

Straightening, she withdrew the keycard for the door from the small hip pocket sewn into her leggings. Her fingers were unsteady as she slid it through the reader.

"I don't have protection with me, but my house is just through the woods."

"I have something." An old habit inspired by a college friend's pregnancy. A good thing, because she wasn't willing to wait for him to make a trip to his place.

As she pushed open the door, she knew stepping over the threshold was a point of no return. But she had no reservations about this. It was a moment of pleasure in a year of hell. The only things she felt now were hunger and need, the desire for him so stark she couldn't begin to account for it. Her gaze met his in the dim light cast by two cast-iron sconces that flanked the stone fireplace mantel.

Extending her hand to him, she threaded her fingers through his. "Please. Come in."

Something had happened on that shared horseback ride.

A switch had been thrown. A blaze had started, and there was no putting it out now.

Brock told himself he'd given her every out. Every

option of changing her mind. And she'd refused. He couldn't fight himself and her, too. Not when he'd wanted her from the first moment he'd seen her. Not when the stress of being a McNeill was at an all-time high. He felt like the whole damn world around him was poised to collapse when the blackmailer went public.

How could he refuse a night to forget about that, just for a little while, and lose himself in the promise of what Hannah was offering?

So, stepping into her two-bedroom cabin, he closed and locked the door behind him. Gave himself a moment to try to muster some scrap of restraint, if only to ensure they made it to a bed instead of tearing off their clothes in the middle of the living area.

But Hannah was having none of it. With the same certainty she'd shown when she slid off his horse and into his arms, she came to him now. She wrapped her arms around his neck, pressed herself into him. This time, he didn't hold back, allowing the full impact of those sweetly feminine curves to work their seductive magic.

Purely potent. Totally intoxicating.

The chemistry was intense, the heat so strong he thought they might combust right there. He cupped her cheek, angling her chin higher to taste her more thoroughly. She tipped off his Stetson, winging it to an empty ladder-back chair near the door. Her ball cap had already fallen away, her silky blond waves tickling his arm, teasing along his skin.

He walked her backward, toward the dark hallway where the bedrooms were. He'd helped build this place with his brothers long ago—now it was a guest residence for visitors. Hannah let herself be led, moving with him, pausing near the kitchen bar long enough to pluck a leather handbag from the counter. She brought it with them into the darkened bedroom.

He flicked the switch by the door that lit a small gas fireplace on one wall opposite the bed, the low flames the only light in the room as he toed the door closed behind them. Hannah had already peeled off her shirt, and the sight of her creamy skin, breasts cradled in blue lace, nearly undid him.

Pulse thrumming hard, he reached for her, needing his hands on her. Her skin was incredibly soft as he drew her to him, the scent of her—something sweet and heady like orange blossoms—making him desperate to taste her. He kissed his way down her neck, searching for the source of the scent, taking his time on the journey to lick along her collarbone, nip her shoulder and ear.

She gripped the hem of his T-shirt and hauled it up his back and over his head. The pace was too fast but the hunger too keen to slow down as they undressed each other, tasting and touching as they unveiled themselves. Her creamy skin was rosy in the firelight, her hair turning from platinum to strawberry blond as it fell along her shoulder. He slid a finger beneath one bra strap, tugging it off, tracing the scalloped edge of lace before the fabric fell away.

She arched into him, the taut, pebbled peaks of her breasts almost close enough to taste. Bending to take her in his mouth, he circled the tip of one and then the other, unfastening the hook to free her and cupping the soft weights in his hands. Her moan was a sexy siren's song in his ear.

"Please, please, please," she chanted, one hand on his belt, a fingertip tracing the top edge of the leather.

Grazing his abs. Making him impossibly harder.

Torching all restraint.

She took a condom packet from her purse and put it on the bed. He eyed it before helping her with the belt. Quickly his pants were gone, his boots were gone, boxers gone.

His undressing was faster than hers, since she tangled her feet in the leggings while she watched him disrobe, her attention so damn flattering.

Brock lifted her in his arms, skimming off the scrap of blue lace around her hips before he pulled her down to the white duvet with him. She made soft, sexy sounds of approval in his ear as she speared her fingers into his hair and drew him down to kiss her. Shadows flickered across the bed beside them in the firelight, the need for her—for this—ratcheting higher.

He'd never bedded a woman so fast. Never imagined a night like this where desire smoked away reason and sensual hunger roared with predatory demand. But Hannah was right there with him, her hands shifting lower to smooth down his chest, back up his arms. All the while she urged him faster, whispering soft commands to touch her. Taste her.

He couldn't get enough of her.

When she placed the condom packet in his hands, he tore it open like a man who'd been deprived for years. He wanted to take his time. See the way she looked when pleasure overtook her.

But this thing—whatever it was between them—was beyond that. It was a fever in the blood, driving hotter and faster with every breath.

Rolling the condom into place, he met her gaze. Her gray eyes watched him, her lips parted as her breath came in fast pants. He captured her mouth, kissing her as he positioned himself between her thighs. Edged his way inside.

He caught her cry of pleasure before she arched her neck and back. Her nails dug into his shoulders, and her body went still at last. When he started to move, he took his time, building the pleasure while she adjusted to him. Her foot pinned his calf for a moment, then slid higher, an ankle hooking around his waist. He gripped her thigh and angled her body. Nearly died of how damn good she felt.

Brock waited, trying like hell to slow down. To temper the need. But then, Hannah breathed in his ear, nipping the lobe and licking his neck just beneath it. Somehow that pushed things higher, and started the banked tension building again. He reached between them to touch her, teasing out the pleasure for her, too.

He could feel that same tension in her. Her head tossed from side to side, the rest of her going still. He kissed her again, taking her lips just as the sweet squeeze of her release gripped him tight.

The spasms went on and on, nudging him over the edge and into oblivion. His shout mingled with her soft cries, a chorus of the most perfect pleasure he'd ever felt.

With a woman he barely knew.

The realization slammed home just as he caught his breath. Just as some form of reason returned. Still, the fact that they didn't know each other well didn't take anything away from whatever they'd just experienced. It had been powerful. Passionate.

Incredibly fulfilling even as it made him want her all over again.

In other words, it was pure insanity.

Brock sank into the mattress beside her, rolling her

to his side so they lay together before he drew half of the duvet over their bare bodies.

"That was the craziest thing I've ever done." Her words were softened by the wonder in her voice. The amazement. A hint of a smile curved her lips. "I don't even know your last name."

A stir of warning prickled along his shoulders. He'd withheld it on purpose, of course. But it didn't matter now. She certainly hadn't been trying to get close to him because he was a McNeill. That much had been established.

Besides, as an actress, she had her own path to fame and fortune.

"McNeill." He glanced over at her, smoothing a long blond wave away from her cheek. "Brock McNeill."

Something shifted in her eyes. A recognition, yes. But not the speculative, almost greedy kind that he'd sometimes seen over the years.

No. He could have sworn Hannah Ryder all but recoiled. There was the slightest flinch. A fractional crinkle of her smooth brow. A stillness.

As if the name meant something to her, and not in a good way.

He wanted to ask her about it. Or at least, to talk to her and make some sense of what just happened. But she was already sliding away from him.

"I'm so sorry." She shook her head. "And embarrassed. But I just remembered I have an early call on set tomorrow." She slipped out from under the duvet, turning to plant her feet on the floor. "I don't know what I was thinking. But I guess that's the whole point. I wasn't really thinking."

Perhaps her reaction didn't have anything to do

with his name. Maybe she was just feeling the bite of morning-after regret—far too soon. That much, he could understand. The attraction had caught them like a tornado, touching down with fevered intensity.

He put a hand on her shoulder. "I'll go in a minute," he assured her. "Is everything okay? Are you all right?"

"I'm fine." She nodded, not making eye contact. "I'm just... This is completely awkward, right?" Hopping to her feet, she found her shirt and slid it over her head, the dark T-shirt covering her to the tops of her thighs. "Would you mind if we talked tomorrow, when I've got my head on straight again?"

Something was off here. Wrong.

He was missing it, but he wasn't sure what he could accomplish by staying any longer when she was clearly agitated. He understood that. And she wasn't the only one feeling rattled by what just happened. He just wished he could be sure that the only thing upsetting her was how fast things had escalated between them, and not something connected to his family name. The McNeills already had enough trouble brewing.

"Of course." Nodding, he scooped his clothes off the floor and started to dress. "I'll come by the set tomorrow and we'll talk then."

She opened her mouth, then snapped it shut again. Nodding, she pulled an afghan off the end of the bed and wrapped it around herself.

"Sure." She hugged the blanket tighter while he finished dressing. "And, um, thank you for the ride home."

He couldn't help a wry chuckle as he stepped into his boots. "I sure as hell hope the ride isn't what you remember most about this night." Leaning close to her, he brushed a kiss over her cheek, wanting nothing more than to remind her that what just happened hadn't been a fluke. But he understood about early wake-up calls. "We'll definitely be talking more tomorrow. Good night, Hannah."

Striding out of the bedroom, he retrieved his hat off the chair and dropped it on his head before stepping into the night. If Hannah was hiding something from him—if she had something against the McNeills—he had every intention of finding out.

Three

Hannah knew she couldn't hide from Brock McNeill, but she was tempted to try the next day when he hadn't made an appearance on the set by midmorning. How could the hottest night of her life have gone so terribly wrong?

The sexy rancher who'd turned her inside out was a *McNeill*.

Seated in a makeup chair under a canvas tent erected near the barn where she'd been shooting earlier, Hannah tried unsuccessfully to read through a script to take her mind off of Brock. She tried to get comfortable. There was a full-length mirror in front of her, and a cup of coffee stuffed in the mesh drink holder of her chair. Dressed in her period costume—a calico dress complete with petticoats and chemise—Hannah scrolled through the script for a space Western on her phone. It didn't take a genius to know she was starting to get typecast as a ditz—a role she'd done well once and should have distanced herself from afterward. She played something similar in *Winning the West*, but she would have taken a role as an extra if it meant getting to work on an Antonio Ventura set. Shoving aside her phone, she wished she could feel outrage about her career. Instead, all she felt was anger at herself for making a selfish decision last night.

How could she have indulged herself that way, putting her own needs before her mission? It had never occurred to her that the casually dressed rancher who personally oversaw his horses could be a member of one of the nation's wealthiest families. Hannah knew all about the connection between Cheyenne's ranching McNeills and the Manhattan branch of the family and their lucrative resort chain. She'd also read up on the ties between the Silicon Valley start-up, Transparent, principally owned by Damon McNeill and his brothers.

Hannah had researched all of them carefully before she accepted the film role on McNeill land because of the secret connection between the Ventura family and the McNeills. A connection they'd all hidden so thoroughly, she wasn't sure how many people even knew about it besides her. Not that Hannah cared about the secrets and scandals of the rich. She'd simply done her homework to find out if the McNeills were potential allies or enemies in her quest for justice for her sister.

And despite all the research she'd completed—even briefly working for the Ventura family's cleaning service—she still couldn't be certain. It could go either way. Certainly, Brock McNeill had shown no liking for Antonio. They'd behaved as though they were strangers when they spoke on the set yesterday—one more reason why Hannah would have never taken Brock for one of the McNeill family.

Restless and uneasy, Hannah shot from the chair to pace the temporary makeup and dressing area. She hadn't gone three steps when Callie raced into the tent, her work apron covered with pins and her usually sleek ponytail twisted into a haphazard knot.

"There you are!" The wardrobe assistant skidded to a stop, one sandal catching on the tassels of a floor mat. Her cheeks were pink with hectic color. "Hannah, you have a visitor on set." She lifted her dark eyebrows and lowered her voice. "The hot cowboy from yesterday."

Tension squeezed Hannah's shoulders even as warmth stirred in her belly. How could she pretend the same ease with him that she had yesterday, knowing his identity? Knowing the McNeills hid a connection to Antonio Ventura, the man she hated beyond reason? Not even Meryl Streep could pull off that kind of acting job.

"He's here?" Hannah asked finally. Stalling.

She peered into the full-length mirror, wondering if her expression revealed her distress.

Callie stepped closer, looking at Hannah's face in the mirror. "He said you were expecting him. What's wrong?"

"Nothing. Just a little nervous, I guess." She forced a smile, needing to get it together before she saw Brock. If only she understood his family's link to the Venturas.

Was there a chance her relationship with Brock could help her learn something useful about Antonio? Something that would aid her efforts to unmask him for the monster he was?

Steeling herself for the performance she needed to give for the sake of her sister, Hannah hoped she could extricate herself from an intimate relationship without alienating Brock altogether. Because while she was willing to leverage a friendship to learn anything she could about Antonio, she drew the line at allowing Brock back into her bed ever again now that she knew he was a McNeill.

The rest of the world might not know the truth about the Ventura and McNeill connection, but Hannah had unearthed the secret from a coworker at the Venturas' cleaning service.

Paige McNeill, Brock's stepmother, had married Brock's father under an assumed name. She was actually the missing Hollywood heiress Eden Harris. Daughter of the actress Barbara Harris and director Emilio Ventura. Stepsister to Antonio Ventura himself.

So until Hannah knew where the McNeills stood on the issue of the family they had never publicly acknowledged, maybe it was best to treat all of them—Brock included—like they were her potential enemies.

Brock knew he should stay away from Hannah Ryder.

Publicly, it made sense to keep the relationship quiet since he didn't need to draw more attention to his family in the days—hours, perhaps—before a scandal broke. And privately, Brock had yet to figure out the expression on Hannah's face when she'd learned of his identity last night, so it wasn't a good idea to get too involved with a woman so clearly rattled by the McNeill name.

Yet here he was on the set of her film before noon the day after they'd met. After they'd parted awkwardly and she'd dominated his thoughts all night.

He paced behind the camera while the set crew

worked to change some components in front of the lens. Lights were rolled out of the open barn doors and new lights were rolled in on handcarts and dollies. Props were switched. Hay was raked and "fluffed" using methods that rendered it unusable for horses—glue, silicon spray and filler were mixed in to make the piles look bigger against the walls. The whole place bustled with activity while the actors and director were on break.

Brock had missed seeing Hannah's scene earlier in the day, but he'd been busy with his family. His brother Carson's new girlfriend—Emma Layton, a stunt woman for *Winning the West*—had shared what might be an important clue about a connection between the McNeills and the Venturas, one the blackmailer could be exploiting. Emma's mother, Jane, had been hinting at the connection in recent phone conversations. Jane Layton had worked as a maid for the Ventura families for years and had been privy to many of the family's private affairs, but Emma also confided that her mother was emotionally unstable.

So could they trust any information gleaned from Jane Layton?

The McNeill family's private investigator couldn't follow up all the blackmail leads fast enough now that the time had almost expired on the threat to expose Paige McNeill's past. Brock's father was scared his wife was going to have a nervous breakdown, since she hadn't yet fully recovered from her time spent in a coma. And Scarlett, Paige's youngest daughter, refused to speak to any of them while she nursed her anger that they'd somehow forsaken Paige by not trying to work something out with the blackmailer.

Now this.

The woman who'd so thoroughly captivated Brock last night was hiding something, and he was determined to find out what. The family suspected the blackmailer might be working on the film or have a close connection to someone who did. Could Hannah Ryder be capable of blackmail? Anger flared at the thought she might have used sex to get closer to him. He was certain the attraction was real, but the possibility of deception rankled.

He was so caught up in those dark thoughts he didn't hear anyone approach him as he held the side door open for a woman pushing a catering cart of fruit, breakfast pastries and coffee.

"Brock."

The sound of Hannah's voice behind him sent a spike of unwanted heat up his spine. He really needed to get his attraction to her under control until he figured out where she stood in this mess with his family.

Pivoting on his boot heel, he faced her.

She was even lovelier than he remembered. Her hair was pinned up on either side, the back falling in curls that struck him as a vaguely historical style—maybe because the curls were so carefully molded. She wore a frontier-woman kind of gown, too. It was cream-colored and dotted with tiny flowers. The bodice shaped her torso in an exaggerated manner that looked sort of painful—cinching her waist and lifting her breasts in a way guaranteed to draw the eye. The full skirt of her dress would have reached the floor if she didn't have the fabric tucked into the waist, probably to keep it clean when she wasn't filming.

Even her black lace-up boots with tiny heels were from another era.

He battled the urge to touch her. To greet her with a kiss, or a whispered word about how beautiful she looked. Instead, he needed to come straight to the point. He was running out of time to help his family. He needed to know why his name had upset this West Coast actress who shouldn't care about his identity one way or the other.

"Hello, Hannah." His nod was as terse as his tone, but it couldn't be helped. "We said we'd talk more today. Can we go somewhere to speak privately?"

"My next scene is supposed to start filming soon." She seemed different. More guarded.

Which was to be expected, he supposed, even if she didn't have anything to do with the blackmail scheme. He ground his teeth against the frustration of the past few weeks. He was a horse breeder and trainer, damn it. Not a sleuth.

"I need to ask you about last night," he pressed, unwilling to let it go. He simply lowered his voice more and drew her into a dark corner of the barn, between the side door and the open front doors. "About the way you reacted when I told you my name."

There it was.

A tiny flinch. A slight flare of her nostrils.

He'd been with a woman who kept secrets before. He recognized the signs, and it was an experience he refused to repeat.

"I don't know what you mean," she lied smoothly enough, but the words didn't erase that moment of honest response he'd seen on her face.

"Yes, you do." He wasn't going to drop it. And he wasn't going to let her off the hook. "My family is going through hell right now, Hannah, and if you know something about that—about the threats leveled against the McNeills—"

"I have no idea what you're talking about." She shook her head, the curls brushing her shoulders, catching on the lace detail of her sleeve. Her face paled. "What threats?"

Behind him, another dolly rumbled past with electronic equipment, but with the shouting and noise made by the crew, he wasn't worried about being overheard.

He plowed ahead. "Someone has been threatening my family. Time is running out for me to figure out who's behind those threats." He stepped closer to her, sensing movement behind him as the set workers adjusted lights overhead. "We're being blackmailed—"

His speech wavered, then halted, as something heavy cracked the back of his skull. He had a flash of awareness that he was falling. A moment to see panic on Hannah's lovely face before...

The world went black.

"Brock!" Hannah watched in horror as the big, strong man beside her crumpled to the ground.

It took her a moment to process what had happened. One of the overhead lights had broken free of the grid, hitting the back of Brock's head. The light lay smashed on the floor behind him, the heavy black housing bent on one side. Already, people were shouting, grips and gaffers scrambling to secure the grid and clear the set.

"Brock?" Hannah sank to her knees beside the fallen rancher, her fingers tentative as she touched his shoulder, fear icing her insides. "Are you all right?"

He was breathing, but he remained stone-still.

Two production assistants were suddenly beside her, leaning over him, informing her not to move him.

Because she was flustered and scared, it took her a moment to process why. He had a head injury. He could have a concussion or much worse. A spinal injury would be...

Oh, God. She laid her hand over his, taking his fingers—careful not to move his arm—and squeezing them gently.

"Call 911!" she shouted, even as one of the wardrobe assistants flashed a thumbs-up sign as she spoke into her phone.

Someone was already taking care of that.

The minutes stretched out endlessly as they waited for an ambulance. In the background, Hannah heard the second director yelling at the production staff while someone swept up broken glass. Hannah debated how to reach Brock's family to let someone know what had happened, but she couldn't seem to let go of his hand.

He'd told her someone was threatening his relatives. Blackmailing them. He'd been upset about it—to the point there was even suspicion of her in his eyes—before that light had hit him. Did he suspect her of blackmail?

The thought chilled her even more.

Had he told his family about them? About his night with her or the way she'd reacted when he mentioned the McNeill name? What if they blamed her for the accident?

None of it should matter now when Brock was hurt. But she couldn't afford to get caught up in a scandal that had nothing to do with her. Brock might suspect her of something, but she knew she wasn't a blackmailer. She only wanted evidence against Antonio Ventura, but she couldn't possibly share her secret agenda with his family. Not even to clear her name, if it came down to that.

In the distance, she heard the wail of a siren. The ambulance was getting closer.

Relieved that help was on the way, she let one of the director's assistants know that she was going to follow the ambulance to the hospital. Because no matter how awkward things had gotten between her and Brock, this was still the man who had kissed her senseless the night before. The man who'd publicly told off Antonio.

She needed to be there for him until someone from his family arrived.

"You're going to be fine," she assured him even though he couldn't hear her. She stroked her free hand over the subtle bristle of his jaw. "The ambulance is almost here."

The siren grew louder. Nearby, the production team cleared a path between the doors and Brock, moving aside equipment.

Hannah told herself she should step back out of the way, too. But before she could, she felt Brock stirring.

Relief rushed through her.

"He's waking up!" she shouted to no one in particular, her eyes remaining on him. "He's coming out of it."

She squeezed his hand tighter, watched as he lifted his head ever so slightly. Then, as if he found it too heavy, he rested his head back on the ground, but blinked his eyes open and stared up at her.

"Are you okay?" she asked him, tilting her head to meet his gaze. "It's probably better if you don't move just yet."

She searched his face, looking for clues to any sign of discomfort or injury. Needing him to be okay.

Brock frowned, a scowl wrinkling his forehead as he studied her. When he spoke, his voice was gravelly and deep, his tone oddly distant.

"Who are you?" he asked, his blue eyes never wavering from her face. "Do I know you?"

Four

Was he serious?

Vaguely, she became aware of movement around her, the EMS crew laying a stretcher next to him before gently shuffling her aside to assess Brock's condition.

Did Brock really not remember her?

She squeezed her temples, trying to figure out what that meant. Because while she'd started this day wishing she could have a chance at a do-over with Brock, she had never wanted him to be hurt.

Tension balled tight in her stomach as the EMS workers took his vitals and asked him questions, gathering information about the blow to his head. Hannah paced circles nearby, willing herself to think. To figure out what it meant that Brock didn't recognize her.

He'd stared at her as if she was a total stranger. As if they hadn't been naked together less than twenty-four hours ago.

Her gaze skittered toward him, her heart rate jumping at the sight of him. She couldn't imagine forgetting their time together. Forgetting him. She watched as he tried to wave off the woman taking his blood pressure. Brock reached for his phone, insisting he would call his own physician.

A good sign, right? Except his movements seemed a bit stilted. And when the other EMS worker asked him what day it was, Brock seemed confused.

Worry twisted inside Hannah. For a moment, she considered walking away, before his memory returned. No one would be the wiser that she'd bailed on him.

Except she wasn't that kind of woman. Besides, she should stay close to Brock in case he knew more about Antonio Ventura. Hannah's mission to help her sister came first.

If Brock had forgotten about his night with Hannah, maybe she didn't need to remind him of how far things had gone between them. She could have her chance at a do-over, only this time, she'd be his friend and not his lover.

There would be no expectation of more. No suspicions about why she'd backed away from a relationship so fast. And if a little voice inside her head warned her that it wasn't going to be easy to pretend she wasn't attracted to him?

She'd simply have to ignore it, along with the man's red-hot appeal.

Brock just lay in a hospital bed, skull throbbing, hypoallergenic pillowcase crinkling as he shifted. Some of the pain he attributed to the knot on the back of his head. But the bigger ache came from not knowing how he landed in Cheyenne Regional Medical Center.

There'd been other times in the past he'd woken up to an EMS worker hovering over him. During his rodeo years, he'd broken enough bones and taken enough blows to the head that ER trips had been regular occurrences.

But in the past, he always remembered the fall.

Today? He didn't have a clue what had happened to him. And it didn't take a medical genius to know something was really wrong, considering all the docs who'd come through his exam room to ask him questions and frown over his chart. Where was his family? Not that he expected his older brothers to come running when he fell off a bull. Or his father either, for that matter. But his half sisters normally showed up for him. Maisie, Madeline and Scarlett had always been good to him.

This time, Maisie and Madeline had both texted him their regrets that they couldn't be there because they needed to be by their mother's side before "the scandal broke." Whatever that meant. Scarlett's response was even more puzzling, since she said Cheyenne was too far to drive, but she hoped he felt better soon.

Where in the hell was his youngest sister if not in Cheyenne? He wanted to look back over his texting history—to see if he could make sense of his world again, but he was having the damnedest time operating the cell phone, which was a different model than he remembered.

He stabbed at the touch screen, wondering where the home button had disappeared to.

The door to his room opened and one of his attending physicians entered—a tall, genial guy with a thick Eastern European accent. Brock slid his phone onto the bedside table, anxious to be released so he could get home and wait for his head to clear. The whole world felt off-kilter, but if there was some kind of scandal brewing that could hurt his family, Brock needed to be with his brothers and sisters, not sitting in a hospital bed.

Brock straightened, sliding his feet to the floor.

"Whoa, Mr. McNeill." Dr. Kreshnik hurried closer, his clipboard clattering to the tile as he reached for Brock's arm to steady him. "You've had head trauma. We don't want you moving too quickly on your own."

"I'm fine," Brock protested, knowing he would feel better at home. "I don't know who decided I needed the ER visit, but I'm definitely ready to be discharged."

"I'm afraid that's not possible, Mr. McNeill." The physician frowned as he retrieved the chart from the floor. "We want to evaluate you further."

"I've been here for five hours." Time might be fuzzy for him, but he'd messaged his sisters from the ambulance so he knew he'd been at the hospital that long. The room spun a bit, but then stopped. He was still wearing his street clothes and they'd already done a CT scan. He could have the results sent to his specialist.

"You're exhibiting signs of amnesia…" The doctor continued speaking, rattling off words like "short-term episode" and "more tests."

But Brock's brain stuck on that word. *Amnesia.*

Was that why he couldn't recall what was going on in his family? Why he didn't remember the accident that brought him in here? But he knew his own name. Could remember his friends. His family.

His head throbbed harder.

While the medical expert spouted something about care plans, a soft knock sounded on the exam room door. One of his sisters, maybe?

"Come in," Brock called, needing an ally to bust him out of the facility.

But the woman who stepped into the room juggling two steaming foam cups wasn't a sister. And he thanked his lucky stars for that.

Her generous curves and platinum waves were the stuff fantasies were made of, although her outfit made her look like she'd just stepped off the prairie. Her long, flower-dotted skirt was something from another era and modest in the extreme. But the shirt she wore with it was another matter altogether, the stiff fabric as tight as a corset, nipping her waist and drawing the eye upward to her breasts.

No amount of head trauma would have kept him from noticing her. From feeling the spark of attraction.

"I can come back," she offered, hesitating just inside the door when she spotted the man in scrubs and a lab coat next to Brock's bed. "Is this a bad time?"

"Come in," Brock insisted, waving her forward even though he had no idea who she was. He had a vague memory of her sitting beside him when he first regained consciousness, an unreadable expression in her beautiful gray eyes. But before that—nothing.

Who was she?

"Ms. Ryder." Dr. Kreshnik nodded at the mystery woman. "Any luck getting in touch with his family?"

"I'm afraid not." She shook her head, the curls bouncing lightly as she moved toward Brock and passed him one of the foam cups. He noticed there was no wedding ring on her finger. "I left a message with the foreman at the Creek Spill Ranch, however, and he promised to contact Brock's brothers personally."

That was the last thing Brock needed. He'd spent a

lifetime flying under the radar of his big family, and with good reason. He had no desire to be in the Mc-Neill spotlight, especially when it sounded like his family was in crisis.

"That won't be necessary," Brock interjected. "I'll sign whatever you need to release me." The sooner he got back home, the sooner his head would stop pounding. The sooner he could figure out what was going on with his family. The fact that none of them was here with him spoke volumes.

Dr. Kreshnik frowned while Brock sipped the coffee—too sweet for his taste, but still good.

"You've had a head injury—" The doctor looked like he was winding up for a long diatribe, his pen stabbing into the top paper on the clipboard he carried.

"And I need to rest, not have more tests." Concussions could affect short-term memory. And he knew concussion protocol by heart. No doubt his head would clear in a few days. "So if you want to write up any medical recommendations you have for me, I'll be on my way. My family needs me at home." Brock turned to the woman while the doctor pivoted on his heel and called for one of the nurses. "Is your vehicle here?"

Her coffee cup froze midway to her lips; she appeared surprised to be a part of the conversation. He noticed a name—Hannah—had been written in gold marker on the front of her take-out beverage.

"Sure. Um. Yes." She lowered her drink, standing straighter. "I borrowed one of the set vehicles to follow the ambulance."

Set vehicles?

He didn't have a clue what that meant, but he remembered she had been beside him when he regained consciousness. Everything else—including what he'd been doing with her—was hazy.

"Great. If you don't mind dropping me off at the Creek Spill, I can meet you downstairs in ten minutes." He knew the hospital couldn't keep him here against his will.

Her gray eyes darted from him to the doctor and back again, but she nodded. She reached inside her handbag for a set of keys and slipped out the door.

There was something peculiar about her that went beyond her odd outfit. Something in those uneasy gray eyes of hers, but maybe it was simply worry for him.

Right now, she was his fastest ticket home so he could figure out what was going on with his family. Besides, she'd be able to provide some answers about the accident that had landed him here.

Assuming, of course, he could trust her.

Short-term retrograde amnesia.

Hannah mulled over the term as she steered the compact car onto the county route on their way back to the Creek Spill Ranch half an hour later. The orderly who had accompanied Brock outside had handed her the discharge papers with instructions for follow-up care, giving Hannah a moment to see the diagnosis while Brock buckled his seat belt for the ride. Now, chewing her lip between answering the questions Brock fired her way, she wondered what exactly the amnesia would mean for him.

Did "short-term" imply the problem was temporary? Or had he lost only his short-term memories? She couldn't even ask Brock since he was clearly still reeling from the injury. He'd asked *her* how the accident happened, why she was dressed like a frontier woman, why a movie scene was being filmed on his land and how long they'd known one another.

She was honest about how they met, and even admitted he'd given her a ride home the night before. She just skated over the part about throwing herself into his arms afterward, seizing the chance to conceal their intimate connection.

But she found it surprising that he'd forgotten her yet knew that his family needed him now. He'd said as much to Dr. Kreshnik, but it hardly seemed possible he would recall the McNeills were being blackmailed if he had amnesia. Then again, maybe he'd put things together from reading texts on his phone. She knew he'd been receiving messages from his siblings. No wonder he'd been able to verify today's date when one of the doctors had asked him about it, even though that very same question had confused him in the ambulance. Brock must have been able to orient himself with the evidence on his screen.

"Honestly, Brock, are you really sure you want me to take you home? I couldn't help but notice those discharge papers." She removed one hand from the steering wheel to point at the paperwork now resting on the console between them. "If the doctor is correct that you have amnesia—"

"I've hit my head before. Bull riding." He stretched his legs in the cramped quarters, one denim-clad knee bumping the dashboard. "I know concussion symptoms and I have a good neurologist in Denver. I'll give his office a call when I get home."

She bit her lip, unsure how much to argue. A concussion could make someone irritable. Act out of character. She'd read that much online when she'd been in the waiting room today, hoping all the while someone from his family would come take her place. No one had. But at least she'd learned a little more about head injuries, and she knew that stress could aggravate his symptoms.

"That's a good idea." She tried being agreeable as she turned off the county route onto the private road that led to Creek Spill. "But I'm not sure a concussion alone can account for how much time you've lost if you don't remember that there's a movie being filmed on your land."

Winning the West had been on-site for almost two weeks, and before that, the location scout had been staying with Brock's older brother, Cody, while she worked out the logistics for the filming.

"I'll look into it once I check on my family." He rapped his knuckles lightly on the inside of the window. Anxious? Impatient? Or maybe just agitated. "And keep going past the main house. My family will be at my father's place. I could tell from my sisters' messages today that something is really wrong at home."

The obvious worry in his voice struck a chord with her. Hannah understood all too well the way fierce family loyalty could drive a person to great lengths and behave in a way they wouldn't normally. Like checking themselves out of a hospital when they needed medical care. Or taking a job working for a man who'd molested a family member.

They had more in common than she'd realized.

"I might know something about that," she admitted, wanting to help him if only to make up for the way she'd omitted details about their relationship. "You mentioned something to me about your family before that light hit you."

She drove past the main house at Creek Spill Ranch, as he'd asked. She hoped he remembered the directions to his father's home since she didn't know where she was headed any longer.

"Tell me," he said simply, turning the focus of those blue eyes on her. "What exactly did I say?"

She shivered with awareness, feeling the impact of his gaze even as she kept her attention on the road ahead. Memories of being with him tantalized her. Taunted her with all she'd never experience again.

"I—" Her voice hitched on a breathless note. She cleared her throat and tried not to think about the way he'd touched her. "That is, you mentioned your family had been going through hell lately. That someone was threatening the McNeills."

"I knew something was wrong when no one came to the hospital." His fingers tightened into a fist, his shoulders tensing. "Threatening how?"

She hated to upset him when he was in this condition. But he had the right to know. "Blackmail."

He bit off a curse and reached to withdraw his phone from his back pocket. "There's got to be some clue about what's going on in here. My sister mentioned a scandal, but I'll be damned if I know what she's talking about." He stabbed at the screen, his movements agitated as he muttered, "This thing must be new."

Did the scandal have anything to do with the secret she knew? Her skin prickled, a guilty feeling pinching her conscience that she might know more about Brock's family than he did. But had he forgotten the truth only because of the amnesia? Or had his family carefully hidden their connection to the Venturas?

The road grew narrower as Hannah drove deeper into

the woods. Lost in more ways than one, Hannah wondered how she'd gotten herself so deeply embroiled in Brock's life so quickly.

"Am I still going the right way?" she asked.

He glanced up just as his phone chimed. "Yes. My father's place is up here on the right. Just around that bend."

When he glanced back down at his screen, he asked her for her phone number in case he needed to contact her later. She gave it to him, wondering if he would be in touch with her again, or if it was just a formality. Moments later, he sucked in a sharp breath.

"What is it?" She slowed down as she guided the car around the corner.

Brock's attention remained on the phone. His voice—when he spoke—sounded hollow. "A Hollywood tabloid just put my stepmother's name in the headlines."

Foreboding squeezed her belly. She took her eyes off the road long enough to see his expression.

The shock in his voice sounded genuine when he spoke again.

"Apparently my father's wife is Hollywood royalty." He peered over at her and Hannah hurried to return her focus to the road, afraid her face might reveal her lack of surprise.

She swallowed hard, pretending a confusion she didn't feel. "What do you mean?"

"If this report can be believed, Paige Samara McNeill is actually Eden Harris, the daughter of Emilio Ventura and B-movie actress Barbara Harris."

Hannah waited the space of a heartbeat. And then another.

"That means your stepmother is my director Antonio's stepsister." She hated even saying the bastard's name. But she needed to ask Brock the question that mattered the most to her. "Did you know about that?"

Brock shook his head. "You mean half sister," he said absently, his gaze on the log cabin home ahead of them with several vehicles parked out front. "If this is true, Paige would be Antonio Ventura's half sister."

"Not in a biological sense. Antonio is Emilio's adopted son." Hannah pulled over, parking behind a pickup. She had researched her sister's tormentor thoroughly, but the fact that Antonio was adopted was common knowledge. Emilio Ventura had already been a famous director in his own right before he married Antonio's mother, and he'd made headlines when he adopted his wife's son.

The son had followed in his father's footsteps, acquiring millions along with the Ventura filmmaking connections once Emilio retired. Then, he'd misused the power and prestige to intimidate Hope, banking on her silence. Or that no one would believe her.

"My father's marriage to Paige was never legal since she wed under a fake name." Brock swiped a hand over his face. Rubbed his temples. "My family—my sisters—must be reeling." He held up his phone long enough for her to see the photo on the screen of a teenage Eden Harris next to a photo of Paige's daughters with Donovan McNeill. The resemblance, especially with the youngest daughter, was unmistakable. "Wyoming doesn't recognize common law marriage. So this makes them all illegitimate."

If Hannah had to guess, she would say that Brock's shock was genuine. That he hadn't known about any connection between the McNeills and the Venturas. But was that because of the amnesia? Or had he truly never known about his stepmother's identity?

Either way, for today, he was clearly stunned.

"I'm so sorry." She reached across the console to lay a hand on his arm, the need to offer comfort too strong to resist even though she knew that touching this man had a powerful effect on her. "Is there anything I can do to help?"

She wished someone from his family would come out to the car to help him inside. Was he steady enough on his feet? But there was no sign of movement in the log cabin home.

Brock's gaze dipped to where she touched him. It shouldn't have set off sparks, especially given the family crisis he was dealing with. Yet, strangely, that's exactly what happened. His blue eyes lifted, locking in on hers.

Her breath caught.

"Are you sure nothing happened last night? After I brought you home?"

Had his memories returned? Was the doctor wrong about the amnesia? Brock had been in the emergency room so briefly.

Visions of their time together spun through her mind so vividly she feared he'd somehow see them in her eyes. But she couldn't afford to get tangled up with a McNeill—especially not now that his connection to the Venturas was public knowledge. What if her unwise affair somehow compromised Hope's position to bring charges against Antonio? Or made other potential victims less inclined to confide in Hannah?

"We just talked." She scavenged a smile as she pulled her hand away from the warmth of his arm. She thumbed the silver ring on her finger, a piece that matched one she'd given to her sister. "That's all."

Her heart thudded from the lie. And the impossible attraction that wouldn't go away.

Brock nodded as he slid the hospital discharge papers off the console. "It just makes me wonder why I sought you out today on the set to tell you about the blackmail." He levered open the door and stepped out onto the lush green grass. "That doesn't seem like something I'd confide to a woman I just met."

She could see his point. But she couldn't think of an answer.

"I don't know." Shrugging, she turned the key in the ignition. "But I hope you feel better soon."

His brusque nod was his only answer before he pivoted on his boot heel and strode up the stone path toward the cabin.

Hannah couldn't help but think about how different their parting had been the night before when she'd been wrapped in nothing but an afghan, and he'd promised they'd talk more soon.

Today, she'd gotten what she wanted—distance from a McNeill. A do-over on the relationship that should have never happened in the first place.

Yet in the process, she'd made him suspicious of her.

And with a blackmailer on the loose, Hannah wondered if she'd just made a huge mistake.

Five

Scarlett McNeill sped north on Pacific Coast Highway, the car radio tuned into the same news she'd heard on a loop, over and over again, since the family scandal broke.

With an effort, she eased her foot off the accelerator as she crept too close to the car in front of her. Her whole body felt brittle with tension, her brain too stunned to think.

"…Eden Harris, daughter of troubled actress Barbara Harris and famed director Emilio Ventura, has been living under an assumed name for over twenty years." The disembodied voice on the radio reported the story using almost the same exact wording Scarlett had heard on two other stations since she'd slid into the driver's seat of her rented vehicle.

She needed to get to Logan's house. Needed his embrace to ground her when her life felt too surreal. Everything she thought she'd known about her mother was a lie. The woman she called "Mom," a seemingly simple woman who'd shunned the spotlight for Scarlett's entire life, had run away from one of Hollywood's most famous households when she'd been seventeen years old. And she'd never breathed a word of it to anyone.

Worse, Scarlett wasn't in Cheyenne with her sisters or her half brothers when the news broke, she was on her own trying to deal with the fallout. Of course, they'd all known a scandal was brewing after Scarlett had been handed the first blackmail letter by a stranger in an LA nightclub earlier in the month. But while Scarlett had been a proponent of trying to work with the blackmailer or the police to prevent the scandal from hitting the tabloids, her father and siblings had decided not to bargain with an extortionist. Scarlett had been angry and indignant on her mother's behalf, all the more so since Paige was recovering from a coma after a hiking accident and wasn't well enough to fight for herself.

Between that fundamental difference of opinion and her brother hiring a private investigator to keep tabs on her on a trip to LA, Scarlett had it with her family. She'd moved up her timetable to relocate to Hollywood and try her hand at acting. She didn't regret it, but right now, the eight hundred miles between her and Cheyenne might as well have been a million.

Thankfully, she'd arrived at Logan's. His driveway was on the left, and she pulled off Pacific Coast Highway in front of the three-bay garage. While she parked, she continued to listen to the radio broadcaster's story. "Ms. Harris, calling herself Paige Samara, married heir to the McNeill Resorts empire Donovan McNeill, and has three daughters with him. No word yet on whether that marriage would still be legal under the circumstances."

Scarlett switched off the ignition, quieting the broadcaster's voice. The sudden silence didn't stop the last words from echoing around and around her head, though.

She'd just barely renewed her relationship with actor Logan King, but he'd seemed sincere about wanting a second chance with her. About caring for her.

Today, she needed to believe in that, in him. Locking the car behind her, she shoved open the side gate that led to the outdoor stairs alongside Logan's beach house. Running down the steps, she followed the sound of the waves crashing on the rocks below until she emerged on the patio behind the house.

"Logan!" she called, not seeing him right away.

His house opened onto the patio, with a wall of glass doors that almost completely retracted so the living room could be open on one side.

Peering into the open space, she saw him emerge from the kitchen. She had a quick glimpse of his dark hair and green eyes, his strong shoulders. He was already reaching for her.

She dropped her purse on the ground and realized she was shaking as she lifted her arms to slide around him.

"Are you okay?" he asked against her hair, kissing the top of her head. "Do you want to go home and be with your family?" He stroked a hand down her spine, warm and comforting. Enticing, in spite of everything. "I planned to fly to Cheyenne later in the week to film my final scenes in *Winning the West*, but I can change my flight so we can travel together."

She breathed in the scent of his aftershave mingled with the salty air blowing off the waves hitting the beach below them. The rhythm of his heartbeat and the steady crash of the surf helped to ease some of the panic in her chest.

Logan had a prominent role in the movie shooting on the McNeill ranch. He had offered her his beach house while he was out of town since she was staying in a hotel suite in Beverly Hills until she found a place of her own. But she was trying to take it slower with Logan this time after the way she'd thrown herself into their relationship when they'd first met.

"That's kind of you." She eased back to look up at him. The sun was starting to set, bathing the sky in shades of pink and purple. "I haven't been able to think that far ahead. I'm just so…stunned."

He drew her over to one of the love seats that looked out toward the water and tugged her down onto a cushion beside him.

"I will worry about you if you're here by yourself." He held her shoulders as he looked into her eyes. "I know you were upset with your brother that he had a private investigator keeping tabs on you. But if your family is worried that the blackmailer might target you again, then I'm damned well concerned, too."

Her dark hair blew across her cheek as the wind picked up. She peeled a strand away from her lips, touched that Logan would think about her safety.

"The last blackmail note was delivered to Cheyenne, so there is more reason to believe the person threatening the McNeills is now in Wyoming, not LA." She had kept in contact with her sisters throughout the day, aware of how events were unfolding. She might be upset with her family, but she wasn't abandoning them either. "The instructions for depositing funds into an offshore account were sent by email this afternoon, although my family ignored them since they refused to deal with the blackmailer." And now, they would all be paying a different kind of price. "According to the PI firm, the email originated at an internet service provider based in Cheyenne."

Scarlett had given up apartment hunting before noon, unable to concentrate with the texts coming from her sisters.

"How's your mother doing?" Logan asked. "Has she said anything about the scandal?"

"No. I know she's still recovering from her accident, but I can't believe she hasn't said what she thinks about this story, or if it's true." Scarlett's feelings about her mother had been all over the map since learning the news. "I go back and forth between feeling betrayed and wondering if she has a really good reason for hiding the truth about her past."

"I've seen the photos the media have been posting since the story broke. The family resemblance between you and Eden Harris is strong."

"I know." She couldn't deny it. Of her mother's three daughters, Scarlett had always resembled their mother the most, a point of frustration for her since Maisie and Madeline were more traditionally beautiful. But even Scarlett had to admit the old photos of Eden Harris revealed a lovely girl. A different kind of beauty, perhaps. One more suited to the era she'd been raised in.

A random thought occurred to her, one of many racing through her brain as she stared out at the sunset over the water. "I've been worried about getting a break in Hollywood, and as it turns out, my maternal grandfather was once one of the most powerful figures in the film industry."

"And your mother's adopted brother is my director." Logan had no affection for the man in charge of *Winning the West*. He had said more than once he couldn't wait to be done working for Antonio Ventura.

"Do you think Antonio is loathsome enough to blackmail his own sister?" Scarlett knew Antonio had confiscated Logan's cell phone on a shoot in the Congo Republic earlier in the year, in a misguided attempt to help his cast "bond." So she knew he was already regarded as a difficult director.

"I wouldn't put anything past the guy," Logan muttered darkly, slumping back in the seat. "But he sure doesn't need the money. It seems unlikely he'd risk committing a serious crime for a payday when he rakes in an obscene amount for each film he directs."

Scarlett couldn't begin to imagine who was doing this to her family. She leaned back in the love seat, closer to Logan.

"You're right. And to make matters worse back home, my brother Brock went to the hospital with a concussion today. He got hit by a light fixture during a set change." Scarlett remembered the strange text from him this afternoon, asking her to pick him up at the hospital.

Almost like he'd forgotten she was in Los Angeles.

With his arm draped along the back of the love seat, Logan toyed with a lock of her hair, winding it around his finger where it lay on her shoulder.

His touch was one beautiful thing in a day from hell, and she let the joy of that touch surround her. Heat her skin.

"Your family is struggling with a lot right now," he told her gently. "Are you sure you don't want me to take you to Cheyenne? We could get a private flight and leave tonight."

She appreciated that he was looking out for her. That he cared. Her breath caught for a moment as she glanced toward him. He was incredibly good looking. And those green eyes were only for her.

Her heartbeat quickened.

"I've got a better idea." She wanted to kiss him. Was that wrong of her on a day when everything was falling apart? Maybe that's what love was supposed to be, though.

Something good you could count on even when everything else went wrong.

"You do?" He wound the curl tighter around his finger, tugging gently.

"My mother is still recovering from a coma and clearly doesn't want to talk about her past. But her father—Emilio Ventura—is right here in town." Scarlett was the only one of her mother's daughters who lived close enough to confront the man. "I'll go see him."

"Scarlett." Logan relinquished the lock of hair, already shaking his head. "The Ventura compound will be crawling with paparazzi."

"I'll go incognito." She wanted to be an actress, after all. She'd act her way in there.

"If he's anything like his son, I'm not sure you want to go alone." Logan's voice had a warning note, but she'd just broken away from her overprotective brothers.

She was making her own decisions now.

"I'll find out for myself if my mother is really the missing Hollywood heiress, Eden Harris." Even as she said it, she knew it had to be true. The photos didn't lie. "More importantly, I'll find out why she felt the need to run away from her family and go into hiding for over twenty years." It was the first time all day she'd felt like she had a sense of purpose. A role to play in the family drama exploding all over the news. "If something—or someone—hurt her, I will find out."

An hour into the family meeting, Brock knew he'd made a mistake joining the rest of the McNeills at his father's house. He sat in the recliner closest to the door and wondered when he could make his exit. He didn't want to abandon his dad, stepmother or his siblings, but the ache in his head had shifted from physical pain to a gnawing fear that this injury wasn't like others he'd experienced.

Closing his eyes, he tried to shut out the discussion with the New York–based public relations consultant flown in the day before at Brock's grandfather's request. That was Brock's first indication that something was seriously amiss. It was one thing to forget the seductive actress, Hannah, since by her admission they'd only just met. But to have forgotten that his stubborn father had mended his estrangement with Brock's grandfather, Malcolm McNeill, after a rift that had spanned most of Brock's life?

He couldn't begin to remember how that had occurred. Yet all his siblings behaved like having Malcolm—and Malcolm's girlfriend, Rose—under the same roof as Donovan was no big deal. The extended family filled the living area to capacity, with Maisie and Madeline seated at the kitchen bar so they could be a part of the conversation.

Brock pinched the bridge of his nose, willing his thoughts to realign, his brain to make some kind of order out of the chaos of information floating around him. Strangely, despite the family drama and the very real news that his father's twenty-six-year marriage couldn't be legally recognized anymore if Paige was really Eden Harris, Brock's thoughts returned most often to Hannah.

Was that because being with Hannah was less frustrating since they had very little history together, and therefore, less for him to forget? Or did he think of her more because she made a strong impact on him? She had been beside him when no one else could be today. She'd driven him home. Wished him well.

Maybe that had been all that happened between them on the surface. But he'd felt a whole other layer of things sparking when she'd touched him. She'd meant it to be consoling. Compassionate.

Yet her hand on his arm had stirred a far more elemental response. And he couldn't shake the idea that her gray eyes hid secrets he needed to unlock.

"Donovan, they *need* to know." A soft, feminine voice from the edge of the living room suddenly distinguished itself in the rumble of conversation, quieting the McNeill family instantly.

Brock's stepmother stood framed in the hallway arch, dressed in a blue floral nightgown with a matching cotton robe, her feet bare and her long brown hair unbound. His father had his arm slung around her. She looked pale and physically frail after the weeks in bed recovering from her fall and a coma—events Brock had only learned about today. But there was a glint in her brown eyes.

A fierce light Brock hadn't seen before.

Madeline moved closer to them.

"Can we get you something, Mom?" She gestured toward the kitchen. "A drink? Some tea, maybe?"

Brock leaned forward in the recliner to hear whatever Paige had to say. Was the news true? His stepmother had always been mild-mannered, almost to a fault, given the way she allowed her strong-willed husband's opinions to rule the household. It seemed hard to believe she had masterminded a scheme to assume a new identity as a teenager, moving halfway across the country and marrying a well-known man in Cheyenne without anyone questioning her past.

Then again, the so-called missing Hollywood heiress had never been formally reported as missing. She'd simply stopped appearing in public.

"No thank you, sweetheart. I just wanted you to know." She glanced from Brock's father toward everyone else in the room, sweeping the living room with her gaze. "All of you. It's true, what the tabloids are saying about me." Her voice trembled a little, and she stopped, then tried again. "I didn't use a new name with the intent to deceive anyone. I just...needed a fresh start."

When the room remained quiet, the public relations consultant—Jasmine—looked ready to ask a question. She drew in a breath and opened her mouth, but Carson was seated next to her and he clamped a firm hand on the woman's arm, effectively silencing her.

Donovan hugged Paige closer to his side. "As far as I'm concerned, her name doesn't change the kind of wife and mother she's been. And a news story about the past doesn't alter who she is on the inside." He turned from Paige to stare at the rest of them. "I know everyone else feels the same way."

A chorus of agreement and support echoed around

the room. Maisie darted around her sister to hug their mother.

Paige's eyes were bright as she nodded. "Thank you."

Donovan gently turned her around, guiding her back down the hallway, away from the living area. "Focus on getting well," he told her softly, his words dissolving before they disappeared into the room at the far end of the corridor.

"I can't believe she kept her past a secret our whole lives." Madeline, the oldest of the daughters Brock's father had with his second wife, shook her head in the hallway, looking lost.

Brock knew someone should offer comfort. Words of wisdom. But tonight, with his head throbbing and his thoughts too damn scattered, he couldn't be that guy. The last thing his family needed was to discover he'd lost his memories for at least—as far as he could tell—the last six months. He could recall delivering two fillies to a neighbor with twin girls just after the New Year, but couldn't come up with a memory after that.

Until he woke up with Hannah Ryder staring down at him with concern and secrets in her eyes.

He was pulled out of his thoughts about Hannah when Jasmine tapped a manicured fingernail on the maple dining table to get everyone's attention. "If we're going to get on top of this, we need to issue a statement from the family as quickly as possible."

"Agreed, my dear," Malcolm announced in a weary-sounding voice from his spot beside his girlfriend on one of the sofas. "But as you can see, it's not easy for us to focus on where to go next when we're still reeling with what this means for all of us."

"We could try a diversion tactic until we've come

up with a statement," Jasmine suggested. The woman was apparently a friend of Malcom's grandson, Quinn, and his ballerina wife, Sofia Koslov McNeill. Jasmine had done some PR for the dancer before her marriage to Quinn, helping to boost the woman's profile in the dance world.

That news was, perhaps, fresher in Brock's mind than everyone else's. To him, it felt like the Manhattan branch of the family had been making headlines just last week.

Cody, the older of the twins, rose from his chair at the table and stared out the front window toward the driveway and the darkened fields beyond. "Are you suggesting we manufacture a story to take the spotlight off us?"

"Not manufacture." Jasmine sounded offended. "It has to be a real story, but something big enough to change the narrative. Maybe news about a land deal, or some kind of update about the film?"

Brock wasn't cut out for this kind of thing on a good day. And today had sucked the will—and the memories—right out of him. He needed to get out of the house where all the talk of the blackmail scheme and the film confused him. Figure out how in the hell he was going to combat amnesia.

And coax Hannah Ryder into helping him remember what had happened between them, since that memory promised to be more enticing than any other.

"I can't do this now," he announced to the room at large, regretting that he couldn't be a better family member on a day when his siblings needed him. "My head is throbbing and I can't think straight, so I'm not going to be any help to the cause tonight."

It wouldn't be the first time he'd been a disappointment to his father. The youngest son who flew under the radar was also the one who contributed the least to the ranching operations. Brock's quarter horse program wasn't about raising cattle or increasing herd production.

But it was what he knew best.

Pivoting on his heel, he headed for the exit, already making plans to text Hannah. He'd take a good horse from his father's stable to ride home, unconcerned about the doctor's orders since he was practically born in a saddle. He'd ride past the cabin where Hannah said she was staying since she was practically on the way.

As he was turning the handle, a knock sounded from the other side of the door. He opened it to find a slender brunette in running shorts and a sweatshirt. Her cheeks were pink, her forehead glistening like she'd been sweating. Her eyes were a little bloodshot, like maybe she'd been crying.

"Hey, Brock," she said softly, edging past him into the room.

He had no idea who she was.

But the way Carson charged toward her, concern etched on his features, told Brock it was someone important to the younger of the twins.

"Emma, what's wrong?"

Brock hesitated to leave when everyone else's eyes were glued on the newcomer as Carson wrapped her in his arms.

"It's my mother," she said, glancing around the room at the rest of the family, her gaze finally settling on him. "Brock, you weren't here three days ago when I was sitting with your mother and recognized the picture in her locket—it's of the woman we now know is her mother, Barbara Harris."

Brock knew the locket his stepmother had always

worn. But how the hell could one of Carson's girlfriends identify the face of an actress who hadn't made a film in decades? He nodded, though, unwilling to give away how lost he was, how thoroughly his memories had been stolen by the blow to his head. Although he had to admit, all of this news would be hard to follow even on a normal day.

"I called Mom to talk to her about it since she worked as a maid in the Venturas' home for years." Emma used her long sleeve to swipe at her eyes. "And it turns out Mom is in town. She flew here—to Cheyenne—the day before the second blackmail note was delivered to Paige."

A silence followed. And when no more explanation seemed forthcoming, Maisie stepped closer to Emma.

"I don't understand." Maisie's uncomprehending gaze went from Emma to Carson and back again. "Your mom missed you? She came to see the filming?"

"It's not that." Sniffling, Emma shook her head and straightened. "My mother had an affair with her boss—Emilio Ventura—long ago. She's always been a little obsessed with him, and she's fought manic depressive disorder my whole life," she clarified. "The fact that my mother is here, in Cheyenne, when the demand for money was sent to Paige from this town, makes me very concerned that my mother could be the blackmailer."

Six

As he left his father's house, Brock gave up trying to put the pieces of the blackmail drama together. He wouldn't be any help tonight when he couldn't even identify some of the people in the room.

Maisie made a half-hearted effort to call him back to the house, asking if he was okay or if he needed a ride home. But his father's stable would have a horse that could get him home. The animals raised on-site made the trek between the Black Creek Ranch and the Creek Spill with regularity, and Brock's house was in between, right on the river.

Not to mention, he'd trained most of the quarter horses personally for the past six years. His successful breeding and training program had given him his own domain within the ranching operation, allowing him autonomy despite all the ways the McNeill businesses intersected and overlapped.

Even concussed and suffering amnesia, he understood horses far better than his family.

He saddled a buckskin mare, Aurora, in the closest stall, taking pleasure from the details he remembered about the animal's heritage, facts that came to mind easily. She was five years old, and one of the offspring of the ranch's most prolific sire. Smart and athletic, Aurora was everything Brock enjoyed about the breed.

When he led her outside into the cool summer night, he had only to nudge her in the direction of the path to his house—a finished home now, according to the photos he'd seen in his phone. The last Brock recalled, he had been framing in the walls, so to see the thing finished had been jarring. He was anxious to see it in person, to see if those photos were real.

The mare responded with a brisk pace and soft snort. Brock straightened in the saddle, the pain in his head receding for the first time in hours as the scent of meadow grasses and wildflowers drifted on the night breeze. He could hear the babble of the creek as they neared the shallow water, and some of the tightness in his chest eased.

As they reached the turnoff that would lead to the cabin where he knew Hannah must be staying, Brock leaned back in the saddle, slowing Aurora to a walk. He hadn't texted her, so she wouldn't be expecting him.

But he could ride past to see if her lights were on. He owed her a thank-you at the very least. Their parting had been strained after he'd been blindsided by the news of his stepmother's identity. He hadn't been at his best.

Now, veering away from the water, Brock guided Aurora through a dense thicket. Big box elders gave way to elm trees and then a few scrubby pines before the land flattened and grazing meadows appeared in the moonlight. Lamps glowed from within the cabin and a hurricane lantern flickered on the patio table of the narrow porch.

Anticipation fired through him. The remnants of the day's headache dissipated at the thought of seeing Hannah.

"Hello?" she called out through the dark as he discerned the figure seated in one of the Adirondack chairs. "Who's there?"

He could hear the tension in her voice. Worry.

"It's Brock." He regretted surprising her, and lifted a hand in greeting as Aurora neared the cabin. "I didn't mean to startle you. I'm just on my way home."

To see the house he'd built himself, but for the most part couldn't remember building.

Hannah gave a soft laugh as she rose to her feet and stepped down onto the grass. "I'm not used to hearing big animals heading toward me in the dark."

She stopped short of the horse. Hannah wore a pale, hooded sweatshirt that said I Read Past My Bedtime in bright pink letters. She reached up to stroke the animal's nose as Brock swung down to the ground.

With her face scrubbed clean and her hair pulled back in a low ponytail that rested on her shoulder, she looked relaxed. Maybe ready for bed. His brain ran wild, his thoughts unchecked for a moment before he reined himself in. He stood close to her in the tall grass, the clean scent of her hair close enough for him to breathe in.

He forgot what he'd come here to say. His attention was focused solely on her. Being here felt right. Familiar.

Being with her would feel even better.

She glanced up at him suddenly, gray eyes zeroing in on his. "I wasn't expecting to see you again today."

How come the most ordinary interactions with Brock McNeill felt hotter—sexier—than blatant kisses she'd shared with other men?

Hannah tried to get ahold of her wayward libido by reminding herself why she'd lied to Brock about being with him the night before. She could not afford to be in a relationship with a man whose family had a kinship with her enemy.

It wasn't easy to keep that in mind given how different the two men seemed. But she wasn't in Cheyenne to indulge herself. She was only here to save her sister Hope from falling any further into a dark pit of unhappiness.

Brock sidestepped her, taking the horse's reins and dropping them to the ground.

"I realized I didn't thank you for all you did for me." He was still in the same clothes he'd worn earlier that day at the hospital. He had to be exhausted after the time in the emergency room and the scandal breaking with his family.

"You're welcome. It was no trouble since they canceled shooting to work on the lights." She knew the filming in Cheyenne was going to run over budget and over schedule. Which was just as well since it gave her more time to speak privately with members of the cast to find other victims of Antonio Ventura's predatory behavior. "I don't know how you're still functioning after the day you've had."

Brock lifted a hand to touch the back of his head, muscles flexing in a way that stirred something in the pit of her belly.

"I feel better," he admitted. "Actually, getting out of my father's house and away from the drama helped air out some of the cobwebs in my brain."

A sliver of panic froze her.

"Are you—" Her voice cracked. "I mean, is your memory returning?" What would she say if he asked her why she lied to him about what happened the night before?

A McNeill was a powerful enemy to make. A word in the director's ear could get her fired.

He studied her for a long moment before shaking his head. "I'm struggling to remember anything that's happened after January."

Relieved, she all but sagged onto the porch's wooden stair railing. Still, she couldn't deny a pang of empathy for him. She couldn't imagine losing a whole chunk of your life that way.

"I'm sorry." She hugged her arms around herself; the wind off the mountains was surprisingly cold once the sun went down. "And I'm sure your family couldn't be much help tonight with all the news about your step-mom."

"Are you cold?" he asked, his gaze dipping to her body as she shivered. "There's gas in the fire pit, you know." He pointed to the small stone ring with a slate mantel. "Unless you'd be more comfortable indoors."

Ever since she'd practically dragged him over the threshold into the cabin last night, the place was full of memories starring him. So indoors was not a good idea.

"A fire sounds great," she told him. "But the remote for it might be inside. I didn't read any of the instructions on operating things like that."

Brock was up the stairs and beside the fire pit a moment later. "You can switch it on manually." He reached under the slate mantel and must have found the button because there was a whoosh of orange-and-blue flame from the center of the ring.

Hannah followed him onto the porch, which was just big enough for two chairs, a love seat and the fire pit. There was a ground level patio area where she did yoga in the mornings. The views were incredible.

"This is perfect." She held her hands out to the open flame, warming them. "Thank you."

"No problem." He stood on the opposite side of the fire pit, watching her. "And as for my family not being much help with my memories—you're right. Today, the focus was very much on my stepmother."

"How is she doing?" She wanted to know if the rest of his family had been surprised by the news, or if they'd been well aware of her relationship to the Ventura family.

"I'm honestly not sure how much I'm supposed to say outside the family." He stepped around the fire pit to stand closer to her, the heat and strength of him near enough to touch. "My grandfather brought in a public relations consultant to help us figure out our next move."

"That makes sense." She shivered again, but this time it had nothing to do with the chill in the air and everything to do with his proximity. "The McNeill name is highly recognizable. You'll want to protect the brand."

He shrugged, his gaze moving over her. "It's more of a worry for the resort business than the ranching operations, I would think. And for my part, I can't imagine why anyone looking for a good horse would suddenly decide they shouldn't buy from me because my stepmother is a runaway Hollywood heiress."

"People want to know they're dealing with someone honest. Forthright." She wondered if he really believed his business would be unaffected or if he was trying to look at the bright side. There was no doubt in her mind the scandal would have an impact. "And an association with the Venturas is a dubious distinction. The family might carry industry clout, but they aren't well liked."

"You're right, of course." His lips curved in a humorless smile. "There's bound to be a business impact. I had hoped my head had cleared with some fresh air, but I'm still not thinking straight." He turned more fully toward her. "Can I ask one more favor of you, Hannah?"

Hearing him speak her name tripped pleasantly over her nerve endings. Her throat dried up.

"Sure." She peered up at him, keeping her body facing the fire and not him.

"Maybe it's because we haven't known each other long and we don't have a history. But I find it easier to talk to you than anyone in my family right now."

"You do?" His words shot arrows of guilt into her since they absolutely had a history. She tucked her hands into the pocket of her hoodie, afraid he'd see them shaking.

"Definitely." His blue eyes simmered with the same fire that had scorched her the night before. "It's less pressure to talk to you, and you don't make my head hurt."

"Oh." She knew what was coming and wanted to cut him off, since the less time she spent with him, the better. But how could she tell him that? How could she say that being with him was a constant battle not to touch him? Kiss him? Think about the times he'd touched and kissed her?

"Have dinner with me this week. When you're off, or else after you're done working for the day."

"I. Um—" She tried to think of a compelling reason why she couldn't. But as he reached to graze a touch along her cheek, it was all she could do not to close her eyes and sway into him.

His eyes turned serious. "I know I wouldn't have confided in you about someone blackmailing my family if I didn't trust you. If I didn't want...something more with you."

She straightened, needing to do damage control. Fast.

"I didn't get that impression at all," she protested. "You were just being kind to bring me home last night."

"Hannah." His voice was softly chiding, his knuckle lingering on her cheek in the barest of touches. "Even now, I feel more than that between us. Having amnesia doesn't keep me from knowing I would have been every bit as attracted to you yesterday, too."

How could she argue with that logic? Denying it felt like swimming against a riptide. She didn't have a chance.

"Attracted or not, I'm not sure it's wise." She wanted to follow that up with a compelling argument. She had none she could share with him.

"Don't say yes to dinner with me because it's *wise*. Say yes because you want to get to know me." He leaned closer, his gaze falling to her mouth. "Or because you don't want to go your whole life without kissing a cowboy." For a moment, they breathed the same air. Her eyelids fluttered. "Or hell, say yes because we both need to eat, and I can promise you better food than you'll get from the film's dining services."

He let his hand fall away from her, giving her space to decide.

And how could she refuse? He was right about the attraction, of course. But the main reason she wanted to see him again was to keep an eye on the situation. To know if he recovered his memories. To find out why his stepmother had run from the Ventura household at a young age.

It wasn't about kissing a cowboy, damn it.

Because she already knew exactly how good that felt.

"You make a convincing argument," she told him finally. "I'm done filming most days by seven."

Hannah was still thinking about that impending date late the next morning as she walked the short distance from her cabin to the day's filming location.

She wore a simple sundress and a hat wide enough to keep the freckles at bay in the intense Wyoming sun. Brock had told her he'd message her today once he'd made reservations for dinner. Considering his thoughtfulness, it was too bad her relationship with him was destined for an unhappy end. Most of the guys Hannah had dated in the past were content to go out with a pack of friends rather than make special plans for a one-on-one evening out.

So the fact that Brock wanted to do something nice for her slid right under her defenses. That, coupled with the way he'd put Antonio in his place that first day they'd met, set him apart from most men. In particular, men of wealth and privilege. In her experience, men born with that kind of advantage in life rarely saw past their own comfort.

Witness her father, a prestigious attorney who'd gladly

cut off his daughters from the family fortune when he'd walked out on their mother. Not that Hannah cared for herself. But for Hope's sake? It still made her furious a decade after he'd left. Her father had made mincemeat of his ex-wife's divorce lawyer, his precious money well protected from the family he no longer wanted.

Hannah's phone chimed, and she dug in her bag for it, glad for the distraction from the dark thoughts. She glanced at the caller ID, feeling a charge of anticipation as she wondered if it would be Brock. Her sister's number flashed on the screen instead. Instantly worried, she hurried to answer.

"Hi, Hope." She injected a brightness into her voice she didn't feel before carefully asking, "How are you doing?"

Her sister had moved in with her when she'd turned eighteen, after graduating high school, when their mother announced her plan to go "live her own life" and travel. But Hannah had loved having Hope around. She'd bought them matching rings and told Hope it was them against the world—the Ryder team. Hope attended community college for two years before switching to taking classes at UCLA—classes she'd once been so excited about. Lately, Hannah had to remind her to get out the door to attend them.

"Honestly? I'm not great, Hannah." Hope sounded wound up. More upset than usual. The last few months she'd retreated into days of near-silence, so hearing her voice so animated now put Hannah on alert. "*Winning the West* is all over the news. His face—it's everywhere."

Hannah's brain raced to fill in the blanks. She stopped in the middle of the grassy trail that led to the day's shooting location—a rocky gully where a secret meeting was taking place among three of the film's characters. She still had time before she needed to be in the makeup chair.

"Why? Because of the Eden Harris story?" She guessed it had something to do with the scandal. "I mean, has there been any more news today?"

"I don't know!" Hope spoke in a loud whisper, as if she was trying to be quiet and failing. In the background, shrill pop music blared. She must be at the mall where she had a job in a teen clothing shop. "But all the girls at work keep showing me videos of the ranch where you're shooting because they know you're in the film. And his stupid face is always there."

A new fear crawled up her spine. Tension pulled at her shoulders. Did Brock know about this?

"There's footage of the ranch?" Hannah charged in the direction of the shoot, worried what she might find. "As in, the tabloids are up here now?"

She hadn't checked her media feeds this morning. She'd been too busy enjoying the Zen-like atmosphere of waking up in a country cabin, sipping her coffee in the quiet as she watched the sun come up over the field.

"They keep showing clips of...*him* outside a cowboy bar. Someone asks him if he knew Mrs. McNeill was really Eden Harris when he decided to film in Cheyenne." Hope lowered her voice more as she rushed on, "I don't know why you had to do this, Hannah. I never wanted you to have anything to do with him."

Hannah hated that she was hurting her sister more. But she had to believe she was doing the right thing in the long run.

"Honey, I would have been an extra in this movie to work with him. You know that." She strained to see the

film set in the distance, wondering if she should be looking for drone cameras or photographers in the bushes.
"I'm going to find evidence of the kind of person he is.
Once he's publicly exposed as a predator, he won't be
able to hurt anyone else again."

She thought about texting the wardrobe assistant, Callie, to see if there was any news about paparazzi near
the ranch, but it was hard to see her screen in direct sun.
And if she messaged anyone, maybe it should be Brock.
His family would want to know about this if they weren't
already aware.

Then again, Brock said they'd hired a public relations
manager. So they must know. For that matter, maybe the
McNeills were leveraging the notoriety for business reasons. The thought of Brock having a connection to Antonio Ventura—of possibly profiting from it—made her ill.

"And in the meantime, the man who hurt me is your
boss. Whenever I think about you working for him—"

Hannah couldn't hear the rest.

Because as the filming location came into view, so
did a crowd outside the wardrobe tent. A ring of people
standing and watching something in their midst. Something Hannah couldn't see.

"Hope, I promise I'll be careful." She picked up her
pace, jogging through the grass as the trail flattened out.
"But I really need to go. I'm due on set right now, okay?"

Disconnecting the call, she raced toward the throng
of people—production assistants, wardrobe and makeup
staffers, writers, transportation crew, animal handlers.
Everyone seemed to be gathered around something. A
fight? A member of the media?

But as she skidded to a halt behind the pack, Hannah could hear a man speaking. It was Antonio Ventura.

"—and if that's what it takes to get everyone on this production on the same page, I will do it," he was saying, his voice taking on a vaguely threatening tone. "I've done it on other film sets."

A murmur went through the group and Hannah wondered exactly what he was proposing to get them "on the same page." She sidled closer to Callie and tried to get a better view of the man she despised.

Callie, seeing her, covered one side of her mouth to whisper, "Says he's holding our cell phones hostage if we're not good girls and boys."

The director took his time glaring around at every member of the assembled group. "The added media attention is only a problem if we make it one. I will view anyone who posts updates from this set, or who publicly speculates about the Ventura family, as someone who has no interest in working with me—or this production company—again."

He stormed off toward a production trailer, one of his assistants scrambling to catch up.

He's reaching, Hannah wanted to shout to the younger crewmembers, to let the newbies know that a director didn't have that kind of hold over a production company. Ventura couldn't dictate whom that company hired for future projects. But, selfishly, Hannah appreciated that the unrest on set might result in her overhearing something damning about Antonio sooner rather than later. An unhappy cast and crew would create a better environment for one of Ventura's victims to let her guard down about the man's behavior.

So Hannah said nothing, listening as the crowd broke up. Some people seemed to think it was all grandstanding to get cooperation, but Hannah also heard someone start to recount the reports from one of Antonio's over-seas productions where he did indeed collect the cast's phones, holding on to them for weeks.

As the group thinned out and people began returning to their work, Callie walked with Hannah to the makeup trailer, then held the door for her as they stepped inside the mobile unit.

"So what prompted the tirade?" Hannah asked as she dropped into the makeup chair, settling her bag under the mirrored table in front of her.

They were the only ones in the vintage Airstream. The hair and makeup people must have been lingering to talk after the director's mini-meltdown. Hannah wanted to open her media feeds and catch up on the news from the set since Hope had mentioned a lot of media focus on the film. But sometimes scrolling through a feed sent the message that you didn't want to talk, and Hannah couldn't afford to have people shut her out. She needed confidences if she was ever going to collect damning evidence against Antonio.

"One of the extras posted a photo of Antonio side by side with a photo of Paige McNeill, both of them stand-ing in front of the Creek Spill Ranch welcome sign," Callie explained, reaching to straighten the collar on the shirt that Hannah would be wearing in the day's scene. "The extra added a caption that said, 'Separated at birth?' because they were both wearing jeans and a Stetson."

"Doesn't sound like a big deal to me."

"It shouldn't have been, except that Antonio looks like a sloppy, lewd old man in his photo, with his T-shirt barely covering his gut, while Eden Harris is still as lovely as ever. Since the two of them are close in age, it's my guess Antonio's ego took a hit."

Lewd? The word caught Hannah's attention more than anything else the wardrobe assistant said. Had Callie seen inappropriate behavior from the director? She promised herself that she would circle back to the subject.

"I thought he was angry because there are tabloid reporters in Cheyenne." She debated grabbing her phone now to see what else she could unearth online. Also, she wondered if Brock had messaged her, because he was never far from her thoughts today. "My sister said there's a lot of talk about the filming since the news broke yesterday about Eden Harris."

Callie nodded, dropping onto a bench seat across from Hannah, her long ponytail draping down her arm. "Everyone in Hollywood wants to find out if the Ventura family knew where Eden was all this time since no one ever formally reported her missing. She just sort of disappeared."

Hannah's phone vibrated. She could hear the soft buzz even with the device in her bag. But her attention went to the door of the trailer as one of the production assistants stuck his head in.

"Filming is canceled today, ladies. Security breach at the front gate of the ranch. The McNeill family has recommended we wait a day to film until they get the ranch borders secured."

A second later, the man was gone, no doubt off to spread the news.

Callie clapped her hands together. "Free day!" she shouted, doing a dance on the trailer floor before hopping out the door, too fast for Hannah to stop her or ask about the "lewd" comment. Darn it.

She reached for her bag instead, pulling out the phone to see that a text message had arrived from her date tomorrow.

Security issues mean we can't readily go to a five-star location. I'm importing a five-star chef to my home instead. I'll pick you up tomorrow night at seven thirty.

Hannah read the message twice, her heart pounding. Dinner at Brock's home sounded intimate. Decadent.

She'd have to be very, very careful that she used the time to learn more about him, and not fall further under his seductive spell.

Seven

Brock hadn't wanted to pick up his date with a security detail trailing him. But considering the swarm of paparazzi looking for a way onto McNeill lands since yesterday, he'd finally agreed to have one of the extra guards follow him over to Hannah's cabin. Brock had enough on his mind tonight without running interference with the media if reporters managed to infiltrate the Creek Spill Ranch.

And to the guard's credit, Brock didn't even see anyone else around when he halted in front of the cabin in his pickup truck. Switching off the headlights and the engine, he left the keys on the seat before striding toward the cabin.

Music drifted from the windows, a sweetly haunting aria sung in a foreign language, and not at all what he would have expected from Hannah's playlist. Not that he knew much about her outside the compelling draw between them. Still, he looked forward to learning more about this woman who felt strangely like a calm center in the storm of amnesia, blackmail and scandal.

He'd spent most of the previous day with his neurologist, discussing the results of the CT scan and trying to get answers about his memories. The consultation hadn't given him anything more concrete than he'd learned in the ER, but at least his headache had eased. He'd met with his family again the night before, and the publicist had announced a new family story for redirecting public interest. Malcolm McNeill had proposed to his girlfriend, Rose Hanson, and the pair had revealed a Manhattan wedding planned for the end of the month.

Brock might not remember anything about his grandfather before the last two days, but he had to admit the patriarch of the McNeill clan knew how to put family first. The announcement of the billionaire's late-in-life remarriage had eased some of the intense interest in Paige's Hollywood past.

Now, before Brock could knock on Hannah's door, it opened with a sudden flood of lamplight and a faint hint of orange blossoms. His date appeared on the threshold.

A silky dress swirled around her, strapless and floor length in color blocks of bright purple, fuchsia and pink. A gold lamé belt wrapped the slimmest part of her, while gold shoes peeked out from the pink hem. Her long blond waves were curled in neat coils.

"Brock." Her smile seemed genuine, her tone relieved. "After filming was canceled, I've been worried there would be a rush of photographers if I so much as cracked the door open." Her gaze skittered past him to peer out into the dark. "But there's no one out there?"

"There's a security detail at the tree line." He couldn't peel his attention away from her. "You look beautiful."

"Thank you." Her hands fluttered nervously as she hurried to pick up a remote from the coffee table. Stabbing at it, she silenced the swelling violins of the opera music. "I packed only so much for the trip, but luckily, I had a dress."

She retrieved a small gold clutch and slid her keycard inside before she switched off the wrought iron chandelier in the living area. Brock scanned the room to make sure the place looked secure before they left. Now that the ranch had become a point of interest for the tabloids, he regretted that she was staying in the cabin alone. Vulnerable.

His gaze snagged on the door to the bedroom toward the back. He had a sudden vision of them there, kissing at the threshold of that door, before falling into the bed that awaited—

"...Brock?" Hannah asked, staring at him intently. She worried her lower lip, nibbling one side for a moment before speaking again. "Is everything okay?"

How long had he been standing there, fantasizing about a moment that felt all too real? He shook off the sensation of being caught in a memory that wouldn't come. No doubt he had daydreamed about that scenario when he accompanied Hannah to this cabin before, the way she'd described. His desire for her was sharp, but that didn't mean he would act on it too fast. He looked forward to spending time with her first. Getting to know her.

"Better than okay." He had gone to considerable effort to arrange this evening with her. He refused to make a mess of it before they even set foot in his house. "I've been looking forward to this all day."

Offering her his arm, he guided her out of the cabin and into the summer night. The breeze stirred the silky layers of her dress, blowing it against him as he helped her into the truck, stirring awareness all over again.

Resolutely, he trained his focus on the grassy road that led to his place, needing to stay alert. He saw no one on the way, not even the security guard. His home was more remote than either of his brothers' since he'd chosen a tract of land near the Black Creek between the two main ranches, so perhaps that accounted for the quiet. But his brother Carson had also assured him the security team was top-notch when they messaged earlier in the day. Apparently, Carson had invested in a private security firm before he'd allowed the production company to film up here in the first place. Then, after Carson's girlfriend's shocking announcement the night before about her mother potentially being the blackmailer, Carson had hired even more guards to make sure Emma's mother, Jane Layton, didn't come near McNeill property.

When Brock cleared the final bend before his house, Hannah gasped.

"What's wrong?" He turned to look at her, but she was staring out the front windshield.

"That's your house?" She glanced toward him and raised her eyebrows. "Brock, it's gorgeous."

He wasn't sure that he'd describe it quite that way, but still, her words were flattering. "Thank you. I worked on this place for years, and I'm finding it frustrating that now I can't recall finishing the building."

Parking the truck close to the front entrance so she wouldn't have far to walk, he got out, pocketed the keys and went around to help her from the vehicle.

"You built this?" she asked as she stepped carefully down from the running board onto the flagstones beneath.

He held one of her hands, feeling the softness of her creamy skin, curbing the impulse to stroke his thumb over her palm. Letting her go, he shut the door behind her and stood beside her to stare up at the house.

At almost eight thousand square feet, there was plenty of room. Much of the first level had a river stone facade, the gray rocks blending with the retaining walls and footpaths that led up from the Black Creek. The porch posts on the first level were stone, but the wide porches of the second level were wooden, the two materials blending in a proportion that felt right for a house set against the woods and overlooking a wide creek. Now, with all of the outdoor and landscaping lights on, the house was reflected in the calm water.

"I did most of it. I contracted out the plumbing and electrical. And I had a professional excavator help me with the site's foundation. But the rest was all me." He had, at least, painstakingly preserved the effort in photos. If he never recovered the missing gap in his memories, he had the photo history. "For years, this was my second job after I finished working with the horses."

The scents of smoked pancetta and roasted hen drifted from the kitchen, a reminder that appetizers would be served shortly. Brock led her into the house, explaining a few of the features she asked about on the way, like the beams in the cathedral ceiling of the foyer and the hand-cut logs used as supports in the main archway that led to the kitchen.

They avoided the kitchen, however, since he'd given over the gourmet facility to the chef and her staff for the night. Brock had asked for the meal to be served upstairs on the covered balcony overlooking the Black Creek, a vaulted veranda with an outdoor fireplace already lit to ensure they were comfortable even in the night chill.

"This is incredible." Hannah spun in a slow circle to take in the balcony with its round dining table already set for two. Three white candles burned under a hurricane globe surrounded by sunflowers, roses and orange lilies.

Brock was satisfied that his preparations were to her liking. He only wished he'd hired musicians for the night since he would have liked the opportunity to dance with her. It would have given him a reason to wrap her in his arms.

"I'm sorry we couldn't go out tonight." He hadn't ever met a woman he wanted to romance to this degree. Not that he remembered, anyhow.

His phone hadn't revealed any liaisons in the past six months. He would guess he'd poured all his free time into finishing the house.

Hannah set her gold clutch on an end table by the fireplace. "Who wants to go out when you have this sort of luxury at home?"

"Maybe." Brock strode over to the champagne bucket on a silver stand beside the dining table. "Can I pour you champagne?" He turned the label of the bottle toward him. "The wines are the only elements of the meal I chose tonight. The chef picked everything else."

"In that case, yes." Hannah strode closer, her pink-and-purple gown fluttering around her and brushing against him. "Just a little, though, since I have to work tomorrow."

"I wouldn't be so sure." Brock used a towel to hold the cork as he opened the bottle. "Your director threatened to pack up the whole shoot and return to LA to film on a studio lot if we can't do more to ensure privacy here."

He poured the champagne into two glasses as a waiter entered with a tray of appetizers and discreetly left it on the table. Brock had ordered a tasting menu that would ensure new dishes were brought often, in small portions, since he hadn't been certain of her preferences.

"You've spoken with Antonio?" Hannah asked, her soft fingers grazing his as she accepted a crystal champagne flute. Was that worry he detected in her voice? Perhaps she was concerned about her job, or the quality of the film if the director abandoned the location.

"No, I haven't." Settling the bottle back into the ice, he picked up his glass and led her toward the screened stone hearth where a fire crackled and popped. "Antonio sent a message to my brother Carson, which he shared with the family. The director of *Winning the West* hasn't made a good impression with the McNeills, and we will be glad when he leaves." Brock leaned closer to Hannah, tipping his forehead near hers. "The same can't be said of you."

She glanced up, firelight playing over her delicate features as she gazed into his eyes. He wanted to pluck her glass from her fingers and kiss her. Taste her lips instead of champagne. He gave himself a moment to contemplate that kiss before he continued.

"I'm in no hurry for you to leave, Hannah," he told her, burning to touch her. Instead, he clinked his glass to hers. "Cheers to us, and whatever time we have together."

Two hours later, seated across the table from Brock McNeill in the loveliest outdoor living space she could have imagined, Hannah thought that if she met him now, she would have never mistaken him for a cowboy.

And not just because of the custom-tailored tuxedo that fit him as comfortably as the denim he'd worn the first time she'd seen him. Though she would have to be blind not to notice the way the rich black fabric of the jacket made his eyes even bluer. There was also something about his whole manner tonight that seemed different.

When he'd given her a ride home on his horse that first night, she'd been the aggressor, falling into his arms and kissing him after the ride because the heat had been so intense, and the stress of the shoot had shredded her defenses. Tonight, she couldn't afford to give in to temptation, so she waited. Watched. This time, Brock made the seductive overtures, and he was far more patient. Thoughtful. While she'd simply thrown herself in his arms, Brock tempted her senses with fine foods and wines, tantalized her intellect with insightful discussion about everything from acting to horses, opera to ranches.

He'd been considerate of her comfort and responsive to her smallest request, taking her on an impromptu tour of the grounds between dinner and dessert when she'd asked about the flowering trees she could see thanks to the landscape lighting. Now, pushing aside the final plate of the evening—a personal fruit sampler with one perfect berry of every kind imaginable—Hannah reminded herself she wasn't here to fall for Brock McNeill.

She had accepted his dinner invitation to learn more about his family's connection to the Venturas, and she couldn't leave until she gleaned something that could help her sister.

"So your grandfather is getting married?" she asked, leaning back in her chair while Brock poured them both more sparkling water from the bottle their waiter had left on the table.

"He is." Brock gestured toward the hearth where a blaze still burned bright. "Would you like to sit by the fire?"

"Sure." She brought her water glass with her, setting it on the wrought iron table in front of the love seat. She made herself comfortable in the deep navy cushions, sitting sideways to converse with him better. Or maybe to face him head-on so his allure didn't catch her by surprise. Slipping off her shoes, she tucked her feet under her. "Malcolm's timing must have been a welcome relief for your family. It seems like talk of a McNeill wedding has shifted a little of the tabloid attention away from your stepmother."

"My grandfather did the family a real kindness," Brock agreed, staring into the flames as he took the seat beside her, his broad shoulder almost close enough that she could have tipped her chin forward to lean on him. "His proposal came at an opportune time. But after seeing him with Rose, I believe he would have married her either way."

"You could tell just by looking at them?" she teased.

He took the question seriously, mulling it over for a minute before he nodded. "There was something in the way they looked at each other. Like they would gravitate toward each other even in a crowded room."

"Oh." The idea stole her breath. Especially coming from this man, who drew her toward him in spite of her best efforts. "That's very romantic."

Suddenly too warm, she leaned forward to retrieve

her water, craving a cool drink. Brock's gaze followed her. She could feel it, even if she didn't look his way, focusing instead on the fire.

"I suppose it is," he agreed. "I haven't seen many couples look at each other that way."

"Not even your father and stepmother? They've been together a long time. Or your brothers? I've heard rumors that both Carson and Cody have found the women of their dreams recently."

"You probably know more about my family than I do since I don't remember the last six months." He tipped his head back against the headrest, frustration lacing his voice. "Carson's girlfriend showed up at my father's house the other night and I would have sworn I'd never seen her before."

"I can't imagine how maddening that feels," Hannah admitted, returning her drink to the table. "The only reason I know about your brothers is because of gossip on the set. The McNeill men have been an ongoing source of feminine interest and speculation since I arrived in Cheyenne."

"No one was more surprised than me to learn the twins have settled down." He shifted on the love seat to face her, his knee grazing hers. "And as for my father and stepmother, I always viewed their marriage as one of convenience until I saw them together the other night. My father seemed almost...tender with her. Maybe because of her accident and the coma that she's still recovering from, or maybe he feels bad for her about the scandal."

The warmth of his leg heated her skin right through her dress, the memory of where they'd touched enough to elicit tingly sensations up her thigh. She finally had the conversation directed in a way that might yield useful information about Antonio Ventura, but all she could think about was the awareness pooling inside her. The magnetic draw every time their eyes met.

She had to do better than this. She needed to put Hope first.

"Do you think your father knows why Paige turned her back on her birth family? Or why she left home in the first place? Over twenty years is a long time to stay away."

Hannah had asked herself those questions many times since the scandal broke. Did the McNeill family hide the connection on purpose? Had they even known about it?

Brock shook his head. "I couldn't say. Paige told us she never meant to deceive us. That she just needed a fresh start. And my father supported her, saying her name didn't change who she is on the inside, which I respect."

Hannah searched his eyes, hungry to know more. Perhaps he simply didn't know. Or maybe the amnesia had compromised his ability to remember the details of the scandal in the days leading up to the breaking news. But no matter how the incident had unfolded, she believed him now. She trusted that Brock hadn't known his stepmother was a relation to Antonio Ventura. Trusted that he wasn't helping Ventura hide behind his famous name and Hollywood power.

Brock's sole concern was for his family. And it hurt to think she'd lost out on a chance to have something more with him—to follow this heat where it led for a second time—when he was an honorable man. A simple rancher who also just happened to be a member of one of the wealthiest families in the country.

"Your father sounds like a good man." With an effort, she blinked away the haze of attraction, needing to leave before she did something foolish, like kiss him again. "You're lucky to have grown up with that kind of role model."

"You're not close with your father?"

"Not at all." She shook her head, sitting forward on the love seat and sliding her feet back into her shoes. "He walked out on my mother when we were young. He's always been more interested in his career than his family."

"You said 'we.'" Brock fingered a purple silk ruffle where it rested on the love seat, smoothing his thumb along the fabric. "Do you have siblings?"

"Just one sister. Hope." She regretted that the filming, and her absence from LA, was hurting her sister so much. But she couldn't just pack up and go home when someone on this set might know Antonio's secrets. "She's lived with me in LA for the past two years. I'd do anything in the world for her."

Brock's smile was quick and genuine. Understanding. "I'd slay dragons for my sisters, too. So it kills me to think how much this scandal is turning their world upside down." He shook his head, a sadness making his eyes turn a shade bluer. "The legal battles they'll have to fight to maintain their portion of the family lands and inheritance."

The knowledge of how much they shared in common, despite the surface differences, helped Hannah to better understand why she'd been so drawn to him that first night. She might not have known all those layers of his character, but she had sensed a connection immediately. What would have happened if she'd trusted that instinct? If she hadn't lied to him after he'd awoken with amnesia, and instead admitted that they had started a relationship?

Would things be any different now?

"I'm sorry they will have to fight those battles." She reached for him, unable to stop herself from laying her hand on his knee. "I know how much it hurts when you can't fix things for the people you love most."

She'd only meant to empathize. But as she stared into his eyes in the firelight, she felt the current between them strengthen. Deepen.

Flare hotter.

Tugging her hand away, she straightened before things got even more complicated between them.

"I should go," she announced, not surprised that her voice was a throaty rasp. She'd used all her restraint to prevent herself from touching him more. She didn't have anything left to hide the hunger in her tone. "That is, I have an early call tomorrow."

"Of course." Standing, he extended his hand to her and deftly helped her to her feet. "It's been a pleasure having dinner with you."

Was it her imagination, or did he linger over that word *pleasure* a fraction longer than the others? Memories tumbled through her. Touches. Tastes. Whispers.

She remembered all of it so thoroughly she couldn't imagine how he'd forgotten.

Her throat was so dry she couldn't answer. Settling for a nod, she knew she needed to get outside, away from the romantic firelight and the allure of Brock's undivided attention.

Ten minutes later, as the truck pulled up to her cabin, she all but sprinted out, not waiting for him to help her down.

"Thank you for everything," she called over her shoulder, her whole body still on fire from that briefest of touches back at his place. The night air hadn't done anything to cool things down. "Dinner was lovely. I had a nice time."

Brock was beside her a moment later, his long legs and loafers covering ground faster than she could in her open-toe stilettos.

"If the evening was so lovely and nice, Hannah Ryder, I'm not sure why you're racing away like the hounds of hell are at your heels."

He opened the screen door for her, pinning it with his body while she fumbled for her keycard.

"I'm not sprinting." Although if she'd had her running shoes on, she would have definitely moved faster. "I'm just...not in a good position to take things any further."

"And have I done anything to give you the impression I'm the kind of man who would press the issue?" Even in the dark, his eyes flashed with a hint of anger. Hurt.

She'd offended him without intending to.

"Absolutely not." She backed up a step, leaning on one side of the doorjamb while he bracketed the other side with his broad shoulders and brooding looks. She'd tried hiding her feelings and clearly that hadn't worked out well. There was nothing left but to be honest. "My speed has to do with me trying to outrun my own desires, Brock. Not you."

Some of the tension slid from him. "And if you've already explained that to me, keep in mind, I can't remember. Just like everything else that happened between us that first night—my memory of it is gone."

The scents of meadow grasses and wildflowers wafted across the fields, the breeze catching the silk of her dress. She didn't know what to say, but she couldn't talk about that night anymore. Her conscience wouldn't let her misrepresent the truth more than she already had.

"We didn't discuss it that night." She squeezed the metallic gold clutch harder to keep herself from touching him. "But I'm very involved in my sister's life right now, helping her deal with the fallout of a...traumatic experience. This probably wasn't a good time for me to take a movie role, but I'm committed to getting home as soon as I can."

"My sister is in LA, too." He frowned slightly, looking thoughtful. "Scarlett is frustrated with the family for not protecting her mother more, and I worry about her making major life decisions about her future when she's angry."

Hannah was grateful he understood. That he didn't dig deeper into her reasons for not indulging the attraction between them.

"That gives me an idea," Brock said suddenly, straightening from where he'd been leaning against the doorframe opposite her and stepping closer. "If you end up with more days off in the shooting schedule, let me know. We could fly to the West Coast for the day. Check on our siblings." His eyes glittered with unspoken possibilities. "Share another dinner."

The thought of spending more time with him tantalized her even as she knew he needed to be off-limits that way. Licking her lips, she readied an automatic "no." But then, feeling herself sway on knees weak with want, she wondered how foolish she was being to deny herself the pleasure of his touch when he could wake up tomorrow and remember everything that happened that first night anyhow.

One day Brock McNeill would resent her for lying to him. Deservedly so. It wasn't like he would think any more kindly of her if she refused every kiss until then.

Or was she rationalizing wildly for the chance to be with him again?

"Maybe," she said finally, the word scarcely a whisper between them since they were standing far closer than she'd realized.

Drawn together. *Gravitating* toward each other.

He didn't touch her. And wouldn't, she knew, after how she'd pulled away from him earlier. If she wanted more, she would have to make the next move.

One kiss wouldn't hurt.

She wondered if she'd spoken the thought aloud because his eyes darkened with desire, his gaze moving to her lips. Staying there.

Her heart pounded harder. Faster. Propelling her to take just one taste...

Fingers landing on the bristle of his jaw, she traced the hard edge toward his chin. Swaying closer, she skimmed her hand down the warmth of his neck, curving around the back to where his hair curled against his collar.

And then, she was kissing him. Gently. Sweetly. She nipped and tasted, remembering the feel of his mouth even as the kiss was completely different from that first, no-holds-barred night together. He let her feel and explore, get wrapped up in the taste and textures of their lips brushing. Only when she sighed with pleasure did he give her more. His hand splayed on the base of her spine, a welcome, seductive weight that anchored her against him. Sensations bombarded her, from the warm strength of his chest under his jacket, to the taut muscle of his thigh where it pressed lightly against the inside of her hip.

She clutched at his lapels, straining closer, losing herself in the kiss. His tongue stroked over hers in a way that made her shudder with need. In a way that reminded her how quickly he could take her to the brink, and push her over...

He pulled away then. Slowly. It took her a moment to even register what had happened. Her gaze was fuzzy and unfocused. Her fingers still clenched the silk of his tuxedo as if he was the answer to everything she wanted. Needed. As her senses returned to her, she spied the regret in his eyes that echoed the sentiment tightening in her chest.

With an effort, she disentangled herself from the fabric, easing away from the scent of his aftershave and the taste of his lips. Her skin tingled, and her body hummed with thwarted anticipation.

"I would never press the issue," he reminded her, his fingers lightly combing through her hair before he stepped back, breaking the spell. "But the offer to go to LA is open." He lifted her hand to his mouth and kissed the palm before closing her fingers over the tender place he'd just touched. "Think about it, Hannah."

He settled her forgotten keycard in the door lock and opened it for her before he turned and strode down the steps and back to his truck. Hannah could almost swear she'd forgotten how to breathe until then. Finally, dragging in a gulp of night air, she forced herself to step inside the cabin. Closing the door behind her, she leaned against the barrier for a long moment, knowing she wasn't going to be able to get that kiss out of her mind.

Brock had told her to think about a trip to LA.

Tonight, she'd be lucky if she could think of anything else.

Eight

Gaining access to the Ventura family estate hadn't been as difficult as Scarlett feared.

She'd watched the Beverly Hills home for a day, to acquaint herself with the various entrances and to watch who went in and out of the property. There was a guard at the gate that led to a handful of exclusive homes, but getting past him was the easy part since she'd noticed he didn't ring through to the owners for service deliveries. So she'd bought a box of organic produce and claimed she was delivering it to a house at one end of the street. Sure enough, the guard waved her through the gate, and she went to the Ventura home instead.

There, she only had to wheedle her way past an elderly gardener, who gladly opened another gate for her when he saw her fake delivery. She might have regretted taking advantage of the older man's kindness if she wasn't so thoroughly convinced her mission was just. The Ventura family had done something to alienate Scarlett's mother when Paige—Eden—was just a teen.

Scarlett wasn't leaving until she discovered the truth.

Now, as she lugged two hemp bags full of apples, peaches and Valencia oranges toward the delivery entrance of the expansive French chateau–style home, she wished she had a hand free to text Logan and let him know she'd made it this far. He hadn't wanted her to enter the property alone, but as a rising star in Hollywood, Logan was too well known to sneak in anywhere.

Besides, she didn't want him to compromise his standing with the director of *Winning the West*. Not that he seemed to care what Antonio Ventura thought of him. Ever since the director had held Logan's phone captive on a movie set in the Congo, preventing Logan from messaging Scarlett for weeks, he had no use for the critically acclaimed film guru, even though he was the director of Logan's current movie.

Which, she had to admit, she really liked. She'd been so hurt when she thought Logan had ghosted her. But ever since they'd reconnected, things were looking up. At least, with her relationship. But now her family—her family *name*—was in jeopardy.

Before she could step up to ring the bell on the delivery entrance—which consisted of ornate double doors slightly hidden by a magnolia tree—Scarlett heard a tuneful whistle from the side yard. Curious, she peered through a gap in the boxwood hedge into the European gardens full of paths, statues and fountains. At the far end of the property, a raised gazebo housed a well-dressed older man with his back turned to her.

The gray-haired occupant of the garden pavilion stood

at an easel, a paintbrush in hand as he carefully shaded purple flowers with dark smudges on the canvas. Something about his bearing, or maybe it was the perfectly tailored blue shirt with cuffs perfectly turned up, announced his wealth and status. This was no servant. She'd bet her last dollar that the serene painter in the manicured gardens was the owner of the house.

Emilio Ventura, Antonio's adopted father.

Scarlett's biological grandfather.

Emotions sideswiped her like a rogue wave. Anger and resentment topped the list, total indignation that this man had done nothing to reach out to his daughter in a quarter of a decade.

"Excuse me," she called, marching toward him with a sense of righteous purpose. "Mr. Ventura?"

She was halfway across the central courtyard of the elaborate gardens, a wood nymph fountain blowing water through a shell beside her, when the man stopped painting. He slowly turned toward her.

He didn't seem surprised, or worried. He seemed to silently take her measure before he settled his brush in a clear glass container on the tray in front of the easel. Then, as she continued to charge toward him, he picked up a piece of white linen and wiped his hands on it, taking extra time to clean around his nails.

The action only served to provoke her more. Surely she wasn't related to this fastidious old bon vivant living in an ostentatious mansion, too full of himself to care about anyone else? She strode faster, ready to give him a piece of her mind.

"Do you know who I am?" she asked, arriving in his shaded gazebo at last, only to realize she'd brought her organic grocery bags with her for the confrontation.

She set them down a little too quickly, spilling a few Valencia oranges. They rolled along the cool marble floor, one of them landing right in front of his Italian leather loafer.

He stared down at it in bemusement, his bushy eyebrows lifted in surprise.

"I have a general idea," he answered as he bent to retrieve the orange, inspecting it as he straightened again.

Before she could reply, he peered behind her, giving an angry flick of his wrist, seeming to gesture to someone else. Turning, she saw the security guard from the front gate in a golf cart. He was parked on the lawn, speaking to a young woman dressed in a sharp red business suit, her hair piled on her head in an efficient chignon. The woman apparently knew how to interpret Ventura's wrist flick, and she returned to her conversation with the guard.

Scarlett wasn't sure if Emilio had saved her from being thrown off the grounds, or if he'd merely granted her a window of time to speak before they arrested her for trespassing. Either way, she couldn't afford to waste this opportunity to find out why her mother had moved away from home, changed her name and never gone back.

"You have an *idea*." Scarlett crossed her arms and stared him down. "It strikes me as a sad commentary on your parenting when you only have a general idea of your grandchild. In fact, it makes me question why someone like you should have children in the first place if your only role in their lives is donating genetic material."

He flinched just the smallest bit at those last words. He set the orange on his easel and lifted sad, dark eyes toward her. "Did she say that?"

"Who? Did who say that?" Scarlett still didn't regret the tirade, especially as she couldn't detect the least hint of remorse in his expression.

"Your mother," he ventured, shoving his hands in the pockets of his neatly pressed khaki trousers. "My daughter. Because even though you're taking me to task for not knowing my own grandchild, I certainly see my daughter's face reborn in yours."

There was something kind in the way he said it. Something that, for a moment, made her regret all the times she'd silently wished she looked more like her siblings, who favored the McNeills.

Quickly, she brushed aside any softening of her feelings toward him.

"I can't help but think a man who had treated his daughter with any kindness wouldn't need to guess at her grown child's identity." Scarlett glanced over her shoulder again, wondering if the security guard was on his way over. But the golf cart was nowhere in sight now. "But maybe you plan to have me thrown off the grounds. Is that what you did to my mom all those years ago? Is that why she's never mentioned you? Never visited? Changed her name and hid from you on a Wyoming ranch?"

The older man shook his head, the lines in his face deepening as he frowned. "Never. Eden's mother... Barbara Harris. Have you met her?"

Scarlett shook her head, curious.

"She was a mixed-up girl long before your mother was born," he explained, steepling his fingers together as he walked a slow circle behind the easel. "I loved her deeply, but she wanted no part of a traditional relationship. She was a flower child, I suppose. Full of idealistic dreams that I loved, but she fell into drug use soon after Eden was born. We broke up and I should have taken legal custody of our daughter, but at the time—men didn't do that." He glanced up from his pensive pacing, stopping as if to gauge Scarlett's reaction. "I thought I was doing the right thing to support her decision to live with her mother. I thought she would have extra help. And that worked out okay for a while, until Eden was in middle school and Barbara ran away for months."

Scarlett was drawn in by the family history she never knew, and never even imagined until the scandal broke. She didn't know what to make of her reception, and she still wasn't sure if she was about to be kicked off the property, but she wanted to hear more about her mother's mysterious past.

And as much as she dreaded cutting Emilio any slack, she couldn't deny a strange fascination with watching him as he paced. Seeing him in person and not just in pictures online revealed the likeness to her mother even more. In the way he tilted his head. The turn of a phrase.

"By then, I had married Stella, and I had adopted her son, Antonio. But I told Stella we needed to take Eden in, give her a stable home since her grandmother couldn't watch her all the time. For a few years, it was wonderful having my daughter under my roof. We were a real family." He started pacing again, tipping his chin down to the tips of his fingers. Around them, birds chirped and the fountain babbled musically in the idyllic garden.

Scarlett's stomach knotted, knowing this story didn't have a happy ending. "So what happened?"

"I came home from a long location shoot and Stella said Barbara had returned to take Eden to live with her. I wasn't surprised that it was sudden, or that Eden didn't come back to visit for the first year or so—that's the way Barbara is. I assumed they were traveling. By the time I saw Barbara again, two years after that, she was back to using, worse off than ever, and couldn't tell me anything about Eden."

Scarlett waited for more. When he said nothing, continuing to walk in circles, a fresh surge of frustration simmered.

"And that's it? You figured your daughter was gone so why bother looking for her? It's fine if she never wants to see you again after you—supposedly—did nothing wrong?" It made no sense to her, and she could see in his face that he fully appreciated that it was illogical.

"I did look for her," he protested. "A little. I asked some journalist friends to use their sources." He quit pacing. "But you're right. I always feared she had a reason for leaving."

"Like?" She gestured with her hands, making a speed-it-up motion, tired of him circling the truth the way he was pacing the gazebo. "You've obviously worked hard to give the world the impression you're living in paradise. Is life in Chateau Ventura not all you've painted it to be?"

Emilio heaved a gusty sigh, his gaze moving toward the easel where his canvas rested. The half-finished painting was of green creeping vines and bougainvillea, with the house in the distance.

"Your mother didn't care for Antonio. I wondered if he had... I don't know. Bullied her in some way." Emilio continued to speak, saying something about his wife being defensive of the boy, but Scarlett couldn't focus on what he was saying.

The pieces shifted in her brain, forming a new picture.

Had her mother run from the son, not the father?

And who was keeping Paige McNeill safe from him now that Antonio was shooting a movie in her mother's backyard? Fear for her mother coiled in her belly.

"I have to leave." She withdrew her cell phone from her pocket, dialing Logan's number. "I need to go home."

Grateful to be back at work, Brock stood outside the training yard, watching his top trainer work with a new two-year-old.

The trainer had messaged him about three of the new horses slated as prospects for competition cutting—a sport designed to show a horse's ability to handle cattle. Brock appreciated the guy's input, especially since the evaluation process was far from scientific, even for the most veteran of equestrian judges. The Creek Spill was gaining a reputation for producing winners, with a core group of elite broodmares. Their breeding program had given Brock the financial security to expand their on-site training, something he personally enjoyed.

Here, at the rail watching an afternoon workout, Brock felt almost like himself. He could forget about the amnesia for a few minutes at a time. Pretend things were normal.

He couldn't say the same for Hannah, however. The woman was firmly on his mind every moment, distracting him with thoughts of the kiss they'd shared the night before. She had surprised the hell out of him when she'd wrapped herself around him. Especially after the way she'd tried to run into the house on her own, without so much as a good-night.

My speed has to do with me trying to outrun my own desires, Brock. Not you...

Her words had floated around in his brain all night, giving him red-hot dreams starring her. Them.

He wouldn't press her about another date, let alone a trip to the West Coast with him. But he couldn't deny that he wanted her. It didn't make sense that he hungered for her this way when he still had the feeling that she was hiding something. His amnesia might leave him cloudy on the last six months, but he had a crystal-clear memory of waking up after the head injury and seeing those shadows in her eyes. Hesitation.

Almost as if she were weighing how much to share.

Pulling out his phone, he typed in a few notes about the two-year-old before he forgot what he wanted to say. He had to agree with the trainer on this one. The horse didn't show enough interest in the cow, while the best cutters usually started with a strong reaction—fear or aggression. Either end of the spectrum could be trained well for cutting, but the horses who were more blasé about the cow required more training and might never have the necessary instincts to make a competitive cutting horse.

The notes helped take his mind off his concerns about Hannah. He'd been with a deceptive woman once before. A woman who'd fed him small lies that might have been forgivable in themselves. Like the time she told him that they shared a mutual acquaintance and later he found out his friend had never met her. Or when she said she loved horses, and it became clear she'd never been around the animals in her life. One of his friends had suggested he should be flattered that Clarice had tried so hard to get close to him. But she hadn't been trying to get close to *him*.

She'd simply wanted to be a McNeill.

The truth had been agonizingly clear when he confronted her on the inconsistencies in the things she said. Brock had realized he had no idea who she really was at all since she'd shown him only a fictional side of herself, a made-up facade intended to appeal to him. It unnerved him to think how well that had worked—and what it said about him.

"Brock," a man called to him from the barn.

Turning, he saw his father ambling over, dressed in worn denim and a T-shirt with the ranch logo. Donovan McNeill had taught his kids that hard work and loyalty earned respect. Not a bank account. He walked the walk, too. Because although he'd been born into wealth and privilege, he'd cut himself off from his father after a dispute over land, and had gone on to become a self-made rancher through relentless work and sheer will.

"Everything okay at home?" Brock asked, instantly on alert. He hadn't seen his dad outside the house since the scandal broke. "How's Paige?"

"She's doing better." Donovan's gaze moved to the training rink where the two-year-old was doing his best to follow the rider's commands. The animal would make a good ranch horse, displaying a willingness to work. "How's the training coming?"

It occurred to Brock that his dad probably appreciated the distraction of ranch duties today as much as him.

Briefly, Brock outlined the trainer's concerns. Donovan had never taken much interest in the quarter horse breeding program until it began turning a profit, letting Brock run with the idea. But in the last year—at least, in the time he remembered—his dad had asked more questions. He'd pushed Brock to develop the training side to grow the business even more.

"You're doing well," his father acknowledged after Brock's explanation, words that counted as glowing praise considering the source. "I left Paige with Madeline for a little while so I could touch base with you and your brothers."

"We would have come to the house—"

Donovan waved off his concern. "Of course. But I got the impression Paige needed a break from all the family living room meetings." Squinting into the sun, his father tipped his head back, lifting the brim of his Stetson to feel the breeze. "I think she feels responsible for the recent spate of news stories, even though I told her it's not her fault."

Brock watched the handler release the cow close to the horse again. "Scarlett puts the blame on us for not trying to work with the blackmailer."

"And she has a damn good point." Donovan jammed his hat back on his head and settled a foot on the rail of the training fence. "Did you hear she waltzed right onto the Ventura estate and confronted Paige's father? Asked the old man what he did to scare off her mother?"

"She's lucky he didn't have her arrested."

Donovan laughed. "How could he? She's his family." His expression turned serious again. "Scarlett seems to think it wasn't Paige's father who made her run, but the son. That damned director we have living right under our roof at the Creek Spill."

"Antonio?" Brock tensed. He couldn't remember meeting the guy personally, but the picture Hannah had painted for him about that encounter told him enough. "We need to get that film crew out of here."

"Except that would be another PR nightmare, according to that publicist we hired. She's recommending we allow the filming to continue so we don't attract even more of a media circus." Donovan scowled. "In the meantime, our investigator has added an extra security detail around my house so Paige is protected."

"And what about the blackmailer?" Brock hadn't heard any more about that since the day of his accident when Carson's girlfriend had shared her fears that her unstable mother was behind the whole thing. "Has the investigator looked into that angle?"

"He says he's got multiple people working on it. He doesn't have enough evidence to contact the police for an arrest, but apparently Jane Layton had a lot of access to the Ventura family in her years as their maid."

Brock listened, but his brain was still stuck on Antonio Ventura possibly being the reason his stepmother had left home as a teen. He didn't like the idea of Hannah working for someone like that. Brock wondered if he approached Paige himself and shared his fears for Hannah whether he might have better luck getting his stepmother to share something concrete about her past.

"In the meantime," his father continued, "Maisie said Scarlett is coming home. At least for the duration of the filming since her new boyfriend is an actor in the thing."

"That's good." He didn't hold out hope they could convince his half sister to stick around the ranch afterward, though. "I think we'd all feel better if we could part on better terms with her. At least help her see the family's side of the decision not to negotiate with the blackmailer."

Donovan nodded. "That girl has more grit than anyone I know. I hoped if I kept her on the ranch long enough, she'd find a role for herself. Decide to stay here after all."

"She always wanted to be an actress," Brock pointed out, gesturing to the trainer that he'd seen enough with the two-year-old in the pen. As long as he was here, he might as well view the other animals.

"And I hoped it was a phase." Donovan shrugged, then pounded his fist on the top rail. "But maybe she's going to need that acting career if she's not even a legal McNeill."

Brock noted the set to his father's jaw. The cold anger in his eyes. "Dad, you know we'd never deny the girls their inheritance."

"I'm telling you what the lawyers explained to me. There's no fast way to sort out all the paperwork that details what they're entitled to." His voice had a dry, rough tone, hinting at emotions that Brock almost never saw in him. "Without the McNeill name to protect them, they could lose out on more than just the ranches." He shot Brock a level gaze. "If Malcolm died tomorrow, they'd get nothing from his estate. And I have blamed my father for a lot, but that wouldn't be any fault of his. It's on me for not knowing my marriage wasn't legal."

"How do we fix it?" Brock asked, understanding better now. McNeill Resorts was a global corporation with a net worth that far outstripped the ranches. But even then, it wasn't about the money. It was about the name. Family. Legacy. Future generations.

Because even when Donovan had cut himself off from his father, he'd kept the name, and he'd placed value on it.

"For starters, I've got to marry Paige again." Straightening from the rail, Donovan squared his shoulders. "She has been through too much already to give her just some quickie date with a judge to make us legal. As soon as I can pull the pieces together to make it special, there's going to be a wedding at the Black Creek Ranch."

A wedding.

Brock could tell by the tone of his father's voice that he was counting the hours until he could make it happen. Did that mean tomorrow? The next day?

As his father turned on his heel, Brock guessed that Donovan was on his way to deliver the news to the rest of the family. Or maybe to shop for a new ring. Brock was seeing a more sentimental side of his dad this week, that was for sure.

For his own part, Brock already knew who he was going to ask to be his date. The trip to the West Coast might not be happening with Hannah anytime soon, but he couldn't think of anyone else he'd want at his side when his father said his vows.

Nine

"He invited you to go to a *wedding* with him?" Callie asked Hannah as they stood together in one of the wardrobe trailers.

"Shh." Hannah didn't want the word to get around the set that Paige and Donovan were getting married for a second time. She peered over her shoulder through the open door where she could see an animal handler walking past with one of the horses that specialized in tricks. "It's got to stay between you and me, okay?"

Brock had phoned the night before to ask her if she could be ready within a few hours' notice to attend a secret family wedding, tonight or tomorrow. She had tried to tell herself it would give her a perfect pretext to speak privately with Callie—she could ask to borrow a dress and then try to find out more about why she'd used the word "lewd" to describe Antonio. But instead of coming up with ways to convince Callie to confide in her, Hannah had fallen asleep thinking about how a dance at a wedding reception would put her in Brock's arms again.

As much as she'd like to think the attraction was all just sensual chemistry, she knew better. Every moment spent with Brock McNeill made her like him more. And made her regret the barrier she'd put between them that would ensure he would regret this relationship when his memory returned. She'd done it to keep herself from falling for a man like her father, like the sailor who lashed himself to the mast to keep from following the siren's song. It seemed so smart at the time, but when temptation called...

"Why the secrecy?" Callie asked, glancing up from the rolling rack where she was tucking a lace sleeve back into a garment bag.

"They won't want any media attention." Hannah hoped she hadn't made a mistake trusting her friend. "I don't want to be the one to ruin their wedding after all they've been through."

"Right." Straightening, Callie thumbed through more hangers, looking over the options for Hannah. "I forget this isn't Hollywood where everyone *says* they don't want media attention, when they actually crave it like their next hit." She pulled out a blue lace skirt. "What about this? I brought it by mistake. You could wear it with a silk tank and dress it up."

"Maybe." Hannah could already feel Brock's hands on her waist where the two fabrics might meet. Where a thumb might accidentally brush along bare skin. Shaking off the imaginings, she focused on why she really came to the wardrobe trailer after her time on set. "Callie, I have a question. About... Antonio."

She lowered her voice when she said his name. Then for good measure, she turned and closed the trailer door. They were the only ones inside. Callie stared at her curiously.

"What is it?"

"Do you remember when you told me about the photo someone posted with the 'separated at birth' caption?" At her nod, Hannah pressed on, hoping she hadn't misunderstood the woman's previous comment. "You used the word 'lewd' to describe him."

Callie's face flushed. She looked confused. Betrayed, even. "Did I?" Her hands slid away from the hangers and she folded her arms across her chest. "I'm not sure what you're getting at."

Flustered, Hannah rushed to reassure her. "I'm not getting at anything. And I don't mean to be nosy, I just... I've heard things about him. And I wondered—"

"I haven't heard anything." Callie shook her head, her eyes bright with emotion, her shoulders tense. "And I think you made a mistake about what I said. Everyone is so quick to judge."

"I'm not judging—"

"Hannah, I think you'd better go, okay? I won't tell anyone about the wedding, but this is a conversation I'm not comfortable having." She thrust the blue lace skirt into Hannah's hands and stalked into the trailer's tiny bathroom, locking the door with a *click* behind her.

Did that seem like the response of a woman who didn't know anything about Antonio's behavior? Unsure how to proceed without alienating a potential ally for Hope, Hannah walked toward the closed door. She paused outside, and said softly, "I'm leaving, but I want you to know you can talk to me if you change your mind. I didn't mean to upset you."

When there was no reply, Hannah walked out of the trailer, leaving the lace skirt behind. She didn't want Callie to think she was trying to take advantage of her. Maybe she shouldn't have used the pretense of borrowing a dress as a reason to come here at an off time.

But far from being discouraged about what she'd discovered, Hannah hoped she was on to something. Maybe after Callie had time to think it over, she would decide to confide in Hannah.

Until then, she had a secret wedding to prepare for.

Brock rode home late that night, urging Aurora faster after a long evening working with his brothers to turn an empty barn on the Black Creek Ranch into a wedding venue. The barn they'd cleaned was old and unused, but it was structurally sound with plenty of picturesque appeal. His father didn't want to hire too many outsiders to help prepare for the wedding in an effort to keep the ceremony out of the media, so Brock had pitched in with Carson and Cody to get the space in shape.

Working with his brothers had felt like old times. Especially since the barn dated from the days when the Calderon family had owned the land, before Donovan had married Kara Calderon, Brock's mother. Brock had mixed memories growing up on the Black Creek Ranch, some happy, some—like his mother's death—gut-wrenching. He'd been only three at the time, but his earliest memories were from that day. Flashes of ambulance lights. His father falling to his knees.

But life had gone on at the main house after his mother's death. Paige had joined their lives, becoming a nanny and then, Donovan's new wife. Yet somehow, she'd never really been "Mom." She'd always been quiet. Unassuming. A steady presence in their home while their father charged in and out, his bigger personality the driving force of the McNeills.

It occurred to Brock that while Scarlett favored their mother in looks, she was more like Donovan in personality—someone you noticed immediately. Whereas Madeline, the oldest of the girls, took after Paige, quietly attending to business while running the White Canyon Ranch, a guest ranch where many of the cast members of *Winning the West* were staying.

Guiding Aurora toward home, Brock slowed the mare as he neared Hannah's cabin. He had planned to drop off some things she might need for the wedding earlier, but missed an opportunity when his father asked for help at the barn. He'd had one of the ranch hands deliver the packages instead. Now, it was almost midnight, but the cabin lamps blazed and another opera aria floated on the breeze through an open window. Clearly she was still awake. Besides, the Perseid meteor shower was peaking this week, lighting up the sky with streaking stars.

How could he let her miss it?

Reining in, he dropped down to the ground and then climbed the steps onto the porch. Before he knocked, however, he pulled out his phone to text her so she'd know who was at the door. Through the open window, he could hear her phone chime and, a moment later, a soft laugh.

Then, footsteps.

Anticipation speared straight through him.

When the door opened, Hannah was dressed in a worn purple T-shirt that said But First... Coffee, and a pair of cotton pajama pants in bright blue. Her hair was woven in a messy braid, her face scrubbed clean. With no makeup, she was even prettier. There was nothing to detract from her wise gray eyes and expressive mouth.

"This is getting to be a habit, Cowboy," she drawled, stepping out onto the welcome mat to look over his shoulder. "What will the neighbors say?"

He caught a hint of her shampoo as she stood by him. He battled a fierce urge to lean down and breathe in the scent of her.

"Since there's no one around for almost a mile, I think we're okay." He gestured to his horse. "And Aurora doesn't judge."

"No?" A smile curved her lips. "Then no wonder you chose a career where you're surrounded by horses."

He heard the edge in her voice and wondered if he'd struck a nerve.

"You're in a notoriously competitive field," he said carefully, waving her outside. "And I won't stay long. I only came to show you something out here."

"Outside in the dark?" she asked, her voice full of skepticism.

"Yes, ma'am. Grab a sweater if you want. Or shoes. But you can see it from the deck."

"It's the least I can do, since I owe you a thank-you for the surprise packages you had sent over here today." She leaned to one side, pulling a gray cardigan sweater off a hat rack made of elk antlers by the door. "I was stunned to find a few options for dresses to wear to the wedding."

"It was my pleasure since you were kind enough to be my date on short notice." He tugged the lightweight cashmere from her hands. "Allow me."

He held the shoulders wide so she could slide one arm in, and then the other.

Releasing the collar, he let the fabric fall against her neck. Then, unable to resist, he slipped his hand beneath the braid trapped by the material, tugging it free. Her hair was soft as silk on his skin.

His hand faltered in midair, his brain reeling at how much he wanted to keep on touching her.

"It was very thoughtful of you. Thank you." She edged away quickly, stepping out the door and onto the welcome mat after sliding sandals on her feet. He noticed that her toenails were painted bright pink. "I'm ready."

He took her hand, telling himself it was for practical purposes since he didn't want her to trip in the dark. "Be careful."

Brock wanted to get closer to her. To learn more about her. See if he could unlock the secrets in her eyes.

Failing that, he just wanted to spend time with her. To lose himself in the warmth of her smile. The ease of being with someone who didn't want to talk about blackmail and PR strategies. Hell, he just wanted to enjoy the simple pleasure of stargazing with her.

The opera that was playing ended, giving way to a more haunting melody, the sound growing quieter as he led her to the darker back corner of the deck for the best view.

"Close your eyes." He spoke the words softly, against her hair, his jaw against her temple.

"You're being very mysterious," she accused softly. "I can hardly see in front of me as it is."

"Just trust me." He let go of her hand to cover her eyes with one hand, his arm around her. She felt so right against him, like she belonged there.

But he didn't let himself get distracted by that now. He tipped her head back.

"You can open now." He moved his hand away, staring up into the night sky with her as a streak of light grazed the heavens above their heads.

She gasped with delight, her face full of wonder in the pale glow of the waning moon. "How did you know that would happen?"

"I didn't. That was just good timing." He pulled over a cushioned patio bench for her. "It's the peak of the Perseid meteor shower this week. I thought maybe you'd enjoy one of the benefits of living far from city lights. Our views are usually really good out here."

"That's amazing." Her eyes continued to scan the skies even as she took a seat. "Should I turn off the light inside?"

"I can get it." He jogged around to the front of the house again, reaching inside the front door long enough to flip the main switch before rejoining her.

He dropped onto the bench next to her, tossing aside an extra pillow to make more room for himself. He slid off his hat and set it on the planked floor while the opera ladies sang back and forth on the music still playing inside.

"Look!" Hannah pointed overhead to a streak of green, white and red. "I don't think I've ever seen a shooting star before."

"It's comet rubble, I think. Earth passes through the orbital path of a comet this time of year, so the streaks are bits of cosmic debris hitting the atmosphere."

"'Shooting star' has a more poetic ring to it." She kept her gaze fixed on the sky. "I hope your father and stepmother are watching. It seems like a good omen for the night before their wedding."

"They've got a lock on all things romantic for tomorrow," he assured her. "I just finished clearing out the barn with my brothers, and my sisters were starting to decorate when we left. Madeline showed me a photo of what they're going for and it should look really nice."

"They're decorating now? At almost midnight?" She glanced over at him. "I'm surprised the McNeill family doesn't have a fleet of workers to do things like that for them."

"Dad has always stressed the value of hard work. But even if he wanted to hire out the jobs, his hands are tied this week since he doesn't want to attract any extra attention to the ranch or invite media speculation."

"So this will be a low-key event?"

"Not in the slightest." He spotted the start of another meteor and pointed toward the arc of white light. Here in the shadow of the house with a wide-open view of the night sky, they had the best possible seat for the event. "My father is determined that Paige feel the full love and support of the family tomorrow, so he's doing everything in his power to make it memorable."

"Such as?" Hannah slid off a shoe and tucked one foot under her. Her knee brushed against his thigh and rogue visions swamped him. Passionate visions that he needed to lock down fast.

He dragged in a deep, cooling breath of night air and kept his eyes on the stars.

"I don't want to ruin any of the surprises. But he's having services like the catering truck come through the gates at three in the morning in an effort to elude media interest." Brock had to hand it to the old man. He'd planned carefully.

"Very smart of him." Hannah clutched his knee as

another meteor streaked past in a blue blaze. "The colors are so pretty."

Brock's pulse slugged harder as he began to doubt the wisdom of inviting her out here. He wanted to get to know her better, but it wasn't easy to make friendly chitchat when the attraction rocketed between them hotter than any fiery cosmic debris.

He closed his eyes for a second, trying to stay in the moment and the conversation. Trying to remember he was here to get to know her better, not test the heat of their chemistry.

"I'm happily surprised at the level of effort Dad has made. My stepmother has been the unsung rock of our family for as long as they've been married, and I'm glad he's recognizing that."

Hannah gave a bitter laugh. "Some men go a lifetime without noticing the good people in their lives. My father walked out on Mom, Hope and me the moment he found a woman whose ambitions matched his own."

"I'm sorry you went through that." He plucked up the end of her braid where it sat on her shoulder, testing the ends against his finger. "And even though that was extremely wrong of him, I wonder if it wasn't easier on your mother than if she had stayed another fifteen years with a man who didn't appreciate her enough."

Had Paige stayed with his father only because she felt trapped? Because she was hiding from her real family, using the protection of the McNeill name?

"Maybe it was," Hannah admitted. "But he sure didn't do Hope any favors by writing her off."

"What about you, Hannah?" Brock set down her braid, easing forward on the bench to see her expression now that his eyes were accustomed to the dark. "It had to be equally difficult for you."

"No." She shook her head, vehemence in her voice. "I don't need someone who puts more value on material things than people. But my sister was young enough when he left that I think it made her more...susceptible to the promise of love and acceptance."

"Susceptible?" He wanted to learn more about her, and he'd sure latched on to something tonight, but he couldn't quite identify what it was. Resentment, yes. But Brock felt like he was only getting half the story. "You make love and acceptance sound like an illness."

"It can be when you seek it too desperately because you weren't given enough as a child." Anger tightened her voice. "It makes you a target for people to take advantage of you."

He turned that over for a long moment, thinking through the implications of the little she'd shared. The night sky gave them something to focus on so the silence didn't feel awkward. Finally, he broke the quiet.

"It sounds like Hope has been through a lot." He slid his palm over to where Hannah's rested on the cushion between them. Slipping his fingers between each of hers, he squeezed her hand. "But she obviously has a fierce protector in you, Hannah. You were probably better for her than any inattentive father could have been."

For a long moment, he simply felt her pulse gently drumming in the heel of her hand beneath her thumb. But eventually, she turned her gaze toward him.

"I would gladly trade my own happiness for hers." She spoke with a conviction that made it sound like she'd already made that devil's bargain. "But I'm not sure that it will do her any good."

Brock couldn't add up the pieces of her cryptic confidences. Maybe it was because of the amnesia, and his brain was only working at half speed. Or maybe it was because the attraction thwarted his more noble intentions. But selfishly, he wished he could ease that hurt in her eyes.

"You can't live your life for someone else. Or give away your happiness to save another person's." His free hand found the soft curve of her cheek, his thumb stroking her there. "It doesn't work like that."

Her eyes fluttered as he touched her. Out here, under the natural fireworks of the night sky, it felt like they were all alone on the edge of the world, with no witnesses except the night breeze to hear them.

He caught himself moving toward her. Knew he needed to hold back.

"I haven't given *all* my happiness away," she admitted, opening her eyes wide again, her pupils dilated so that there was only the slimmest gray ring around the edges. "I could still have one taste."

Her gaze dipped to his mouth, torching his restraint.

"One kiss. That's all," he swore...to himself? To her? To the universe?

He didn't know.

Gently, he angled her chin up and captured her lips with his. Heat spiked in his spine, tightening his shoulders and tensing everything else. She melted into him, her lips parting, back arching, molding delectable feminine curves against him.

He untwined their fingers because he needed both hands on her to steady her hips. To still her for a moment. Ensure she didn't end up in his lap. Because if that happened...

"Brock." She breathed his name against his damp mouth as her fingers raked down his back and up again.

She wriggled closer, the heat of her skin warming his palms right through the thick fabric of the pajama bottoms.

Ah, damn.

He hauled her across his thighs, knowing they couldn't take this any further outside under the stars. She straddled him, her knees locked against his waist, the heat of her sex evident right through the denim of his fly.

Things could go off the rails so fast if he wasn't careful.

Especially since he could feel her heart pounding, and the soft moans she made when she kissed him were the sweetest sounds he'd ever heard.

But there was something fragile inside Hannah Ryder. Some secret or some hurt, he didn't know which anymore, that kept her from him. So he was going to honor that "one kiss" vow if it killed him.

And pulling away from her, his breathing more ragged than if he'd run the perimeter of the ranch, he thought it just might.

"I want you," he told her simply, their breathing slowing as they stared at each other in the moonlight. Stars winked behind her, meteors streaking the sky like the world was about to end. "But only when you're sure." He slid her to the bench seat beside him, knowing he needed to leave before he broke the promise he wanted to keep. He pressed a kiss to her temple before standing. "Only when you're ready."

Walking away wasn't easy with her sigh of regret whispering on the wind, even knowing she'd be on his arm tomorrow at the wedding.

Ten

Hannah picked a stray piece of straw from the hem of her silk organza dress. She never would have guessed the first surprise of the wedding day would be arriving at the ceremony in a hay wagon pulled by a big green John Deere.

She'd heard the tractor rumbling closer late in the afternoon when she had been expecting to see Brock. Instead of her date, a boy dressed in a cowboy hat and overalls—boutonniere pinned to the denim strap— knocked on her door and invited her into the wagon. One of the ranch hands had rolled out a carpet for her so she didn't ruin her shoes, and when she'd stepped up into the unlikely conveyance, she'd been greeted by a handful of other guests, including Carson McNeill's girlfriend, the stuntwoman Emma Layton, and Cody's pregnant fiancée, Jillian Ross, the woman who'd been the location scout for *Winning the West*. Jillian, a gorgeous redhead dressed in a bright green-and-yellow tulle dress, explained that the men were helping their father get ready for the wedding, but that Brock had wanted to make sure Hannah had family to keep her company until he could join her at the ceremony.

Now, as the wagon bumped over a ravine close to the Black Creek Ranch, Hannah held on to one of the hay bales strapped to the sides. They were piled high on the exterior of the wagon to help shield wedding guests from long lens cameras and drones since the McNeills were trying to keep the tabloids from ruining their day.

Hannah feared she was going to end up ruining the day for Brock in the end anyhow. She couldn't sleep after he left the night before, regretting that she hadn't come clean with him about what they'd shared that first night together. She couldn't deny that she had feelings for him, a fact pounded home by the way his kiss had dominated her dreams in the fitful hours when she had finally closed her eyes.

She hadn't been honest about their heated first encounter because she'd been consumed with worry about her sister and hatred for Antonio. And when she'd first learned Brock was a McNeill, she'd been floored by the idea that she'd slept with a man related to Antonio Ventura—if only on paper.

Now that she knew Brock better, understood him for the kind of man he was inside, she owed him the truth. After the wedding festivities tonight, she would tell him. He'd been through so much with his family this week it didn't seem fair to ruin his day. She wanted him to celebrate his father's wedding. But her conscience wouldn't let her enjoy another one of those toe-curling kisses without telling him the truth.

And then, it would be over.

So she planned to savor this day as much as she could before she offered her heart up for Brock to break.

"Your dress is beautiful, Hannah," Emma was saying to her. A brunette with wide, dark eyes and delicate features, she wore a simply cut navy sheath. "And you look so familiar to me, I feel like we've met before."

Tensing, Hannah knew her time of reckoning would come with this family. She just hadn't wanted it to be today. At least, not yet.

Hannah forced a smile, reminding herself all the subterfuge had been for a good cause. "Now that you mention it, you look familiar to me, too. I think we worked for the same temp agency last spring."

Emma frowned for a moment, then snapped her fingers. "Yes! I remember. We shared a house cleaning assignment one day in Beverly Hills, didn't we?"

Thankfully, it hadn't been the Ventura house when they'd worked together, which would have been a little too close for comfort.

The tractor downshifted, the engine noise quieting a bit as they slowed their progress. Around them, a few of the other guests took group selfies, posing with wildflowers that one of them had picked on a stop to load more guests.

"We do what we need to in order to make ends meet between jobs," Hannah replied before redirecting the conversation. "How have you enjoyed the stunt work on this film?"

"I've grown really attached to the horses," she admitted, graciously taking the bait. "And I don't know how

I would have gotten through the shoot without Carson, and now, his whole family." She lowered her voice so that only Jillian and Hannah could hear. "I know in my gut now that my mother has been the one behind the blackmail. But we have to wait for the private investigator to have enough evidence before they will—" Emma blinked fast and whispered "—*arrest* her."

Jillian slipped a supportive arm around the woman, quietly murmuring something to her.

"I'm so sorry," Hannah said, meaning every word. She stood up enough to drag her hay bale seat in front of Emma, shielding her from view of the rest of the wagon to hide the other woman's tears. "I had no idea."

Jillian dug in her purse for a tissue and passed it to her friend while focusing on Hannah. "We know Brock has been dealing with a lot, with losing some of his memory. How is he feeling?"

Guilt gnawed at Hannah. She'd been so focused on her own family problems while Brock's had been going through hell this week. "His head doesn't ache anymore, but I know it frustrates him that he can't remember the last several months."

Emma halted in the middle of wiping her eyes. "I don't think he even recognized me when he saw me at Donovan's earlier this week."

Hannah nodded. "I know the dynamics of the scandal have been confusing for him since he doesn't remember everything leading up to it." She bit her lip, wondering if she should ask them the question that Brock couldn't help her with now that he had amnesia. The question that had kept her from telling Brock the truth when he woke up with no memory. "Do you think the

McNeill family knew about Paige's real identity before the scandal broke?"

The wagon rolled to a stop. Violin music played nearby.

Emma shook her head. Jillian blurted, "Cody was blindsided. Completely stunned."

Hannah stood with the other women, unable to enjoy the swell of excitement through the rest of the group as they caught sight of the decorated barn where Donovan and Paige would exchange their vows and host a reception.

She had hidden the truth of that first night from Brock fearing that he could have a loyalty to the Ventura family. She hadn't expected to fall for the rancher in the meantime. She hadn't thought the omission would ever come back to bite her.

As she stepped down onto the lawn outside the barn, glimpsing Brock in his black tuxedo, his blue eyes locking on her, Hannah could already feel the ache of all she was about to lose.

Scarlett felt like an alien on a foreign planet as the wedding music began.

The people filling the barn were familiar enough, of course. She'd grown up on the Black Creek Ranch, and then after college, she'd moved into a remodeled bunkhouse on the property. She'd played hide-and-seek in this barn with her sisters, and she had once rescued a scared kitten from one of the rafters.

But the barn looked nothing like it had back then, when it was full of rusty old farm equipment. With the highest windows opened to let fresh air in, the barn's gray stone walls were a beautiful backdrop to six-foot-tall candelabra spaced every few feet and decorated with cream-colored ribbons and white flowers. The heavy rafters were polished to gleaming, the wood glowing in the reflection of white fairy lights raining down from the ceiling. White tulle was hung tent-like between the beams.

The whole place smelled like lemon wax and roses. The linen-draped tables were decorated with white freesia and snapdragons in clear glass jars filled with bright yellow lemon slices.

And even the people seemed different. Her brother Brock, who normally never left the horse barn, suddenly couldn't take his eyes off the beautiful actress he was with. And their surly father had developed a solicitousness where his wife was concerned, a tender affection that Scarlett hadn't seen in all her twenty-five years.

She squeezed Logan's hand beside her as they took their seats in the front row on the bride's side. Madeline and her boyfriend, Sawyer, sat in the row with them, Maisie was sandwiched between the two couples and decidedly alone.

"I hardly recognize this place," Scarlett whispered to Maisie. "And am I to really believe Dad went to all of this trouble on his own for Mom?"

Maisie poked her with her elbow, more from sisterly habit than anything. A love poke. Scarlett jabbed her in the arm in return. She'd missed her.

"Do you see these bags under my eyes?" Maisie whispered as the wedding music began. "I was up half the night decorating, thank you very much. But yes, it was all Dad's idea."

"Unbelievable. I'm gone for a week and the whole world turns upside down. Suddenly Dad is a romantic?" She was going to have a hard time staying angry with her father after this. She hadn't seen him since her flight had landed late the night before, but her mother had seemed stronger and surprisingly happy when she'd visited with her this afternoon to help her dress.

Scarlett hadn't had the heart to quiz her mother about Antonio Ventura on the day of her second wedding to their father, but she would. Soon.

"Believe me, it's freaking me out," Maisie whispered behind her hand as they stood for the bride's entrance. "I'll be the only cynic in the family at this rate."

All the McNeill relatives in attendance were paired off, too. Ian and Lydia McNeill had made the flight with patriarch Malcolm and his fiancée, Rose. Lydia was pregnant with their first child and positively glowing. Damon and Caroline McNeill were there, too, taking a break from Transparent, the software company Damon headed in Silicon Valley.

"Even Brock is dating again." Scarlett had seen one of Hannah Ryder's films and thought she was talented but didn't know much about her personally. "I asked Logan if he's ever worked with Hannah before, but he said no."

"Brock has amnesia," Maisie reminded her. "I'm worried about him."

"I'll talk to him," Scarlett said before all eyes turned to her mother at the entrance of the barn.

Paige looked beautiful in a slim ivory gown with a lace shrug that covered her shoulders. Her brown hair fell in glossy curls that Scarlett had talked her into. Normally, her mother favored a ponytail, her part a razor-straight line down the center of her head. But Scarlett had begged for curls and a bow, and her mother had agreed that it was "time for some changes."

Behind Scarlett, Logan leaned close to speak into her ear, sending a delicious shiver down her spine just from his nearness.

"Look at your dad," he said.

Scarlett glanced around Maisie's shoulder where she could see her father's face. The naked emotion there caught her off-guard. Love. Tenderness. A shining pride in the woman who walked toward him. Scarlett gulped back a tear at the same time Maisie dug in her handbag for tissues. She passed two over her shoulder.

As the vows began, Scarlett knew she'd been mistaken when she'd accused her father of being unfeeling about her mother's welfare. Of course, she'd been right about her brothers being too protective when they'd sent a private investigator to LA to keep tabs on her. But she was going to forgive them because they were older brothers, and that was their thing.

Besides, she was empathizing a little too well now that she knew someone from her mother's past had hurt her. All her own protective instincts were roaring.

For now, she was going to enjoy the wedding. Afterward, she would talk to her mother about what had happened in Emilio Ventura's home to make Paige a fugitive from her own family. Because Scarlett wasn't interested in simply weathering a scandal and protecting the McNeill name.

She planned to find out who was responsible for hurting her mom. And then hold them accountable.

Hannah stepped outside the barn just as the dancing started, needing a breath of fresh air.

The chamber musicians who had played earlier were packing up their instruments and loading them into the back of a pickup truck nearby. Inside, a country-western band had started to play, bringing the crowd onto a makeshift dance floor in one corner of the barn. The white lights and candelabra made the whole building glow, illuminating patches of the meadow around it through the open windows and doors.

The summer night had brought a cool breeze with it, and Hannah let the wind blow her silk organza dress, the guilty knot of feelings tightening in her belly the longer this night went on.

Behind her, she heard a familiar male voice. "I've been looking forward to a dance all day."

Heat rushed through her, that jolt of reaction Brock could always elicit. With a word. A look. A touch.

She couldn't deny him this dance. Not when the bride and groom were still celebrating inside.

"Me, too," she told him honestly, taking his hand and letting him lead her back inside.

The band had swapped to a sultry slow song, the singer crooning romantic words that amplified all of the things she was feeling. The longing. The hunger. The fear that things wouldn't last. As they reached the dance floor crowded with couples, Brock spun her easily into his arms, a protective hand at her waist, holding her close.

"I'm happy for my father," he confided, nodding toward the bride and groom in the middle of the dance floor.

Donovan McNeill had eyes only for his wife as they swayed together. Paige glowed in his attention, her diamond wedding ring glittering in the reflection of a thousand fairy lights as she rested her hand on her husband's shoulder.

"He pulled off an incredible event on very little notice," she agreed. "And I haven't seen any sign of paparazzi lurking."

"So far, so good." Brock's hand shifted on her waist as he stared down at her, his touch making her breath catch. "You look beautiful tonight."

She felt herself falling for him, her defenses crumbling fast. If only this could be real.

"I owe it to you for sending me the gown." The silk organza hem teased against her calf, the delicate material fluttering around her as they moved.

Pale pink and dotted with tiny flowers, the dress was romantic without being too sweet. The cold shoulder treatment of the sleeves gave it a dose of sexy.

"I'm not talking about the gown," he assured her, leaning closer. "It's all you. Thank you for being my date tonight."

She bit her lip, not sure what to say. She just knew she needed to redirect the conversation before she dug them both in deeper.

"It's a testament to your family that you've come together this way, to celebrate a marriage and focus on the positive after all you've been through."

The slow song came to an end, but Brock didn't let go of her.

"I'm going to try to take a page from Dad's playbook and put the past behind me. Not worry about the memories I've lost. Just enjoy the present with you."

All around them, the couples on the dance floor clapped for the band. Hannah could only think about how thoroughly she'd screwed things up with Brock. Before she could say anything, he whispered in her ear.

"I want to go on a real date with you. Away from the

family and the ranch. Get to know you." He stared into her eyes, even while the singer announced the bride and groom were getting ready to take their leave.

The movement all around them, the rush to share hugs and good wishes with the couple, saved Hannah from having to answer right away.

Brock took her hand and led her toward the doors so they could see off Donovan and Paige. Hannah knew her time with Brock would come to an end once the couple made their exit. She couldn't accept his offer, not when she hadn't been truthful.

And then after she told him, she knew, he wouldn't be asking for another date.

Turning, she faced Brock. He looked far too tempting in his dark tuxedo, his handsome face bathed in moonlight.

She needed to speak fast before she weakened. Inhaling a bracing breath, she blurted, "Once we're finished here, there's something we need to talk about."

Eleven

Half an hour later, back at her cabin for the night, Hannah invited Brock inside so they could talk.

Nerves wound tight, she knew there was no other way to move forward. She needed to tell Brock the truth about that first night they spent together. Even so, it worried her that she wasn't free to tell him everything. Hope's secret was not Hannah's to share, and her sister's emotional health and well-being had to come before everything else.

No matter how much she wanted to unburden herself fully.

"You look so serious." Brock took her hands in his as they stood in the cabin's tiny foyer. "Let's sit and we'll talk."

He pressed the button on the remote that made the gas fireplace blaze to life. The orange flames leaped silently with no logs to crackle or pop. The warm light cast a romantic glow in the living area as Brock tugged her down to sit beside him on the leather sofa.

She shifted to see his face, knowing there was no easy way to say this.

"I haven't been honest with you." She stared down at her hands, her nails free of any polish because of the time period of the film she was shooting. She toyed with the eternity knot ring she wore, a simple sterling silver piece that matched the one she'd given to her sister for her high school graduation.

Even then, Hannah had known they were each other's best support system.

Brock tensed beside her. She didn't have to see him to know. She could feel it. They were so in tune with each other physically. Would she be losing that with her admission? God, she hoped not.

"How so?"

"It's about that first time we met," she answered. "The night you don't remember because of the amnesia. I didn't tell you everything that happened." She glanced up to see him watching her, his expression neutral.

Was he reserving judgment? She wasn't certain.

"What happened?" he asked, his voice remote and lacking its usual warmth. "What did you leave out?"

Her pulse sped faster.

"I made a split-second decision about not sharing the details when you woke up with no memory. It seemed like the right choice then," she said quickly, needing to explain.

"What have you omitted?" he pressed, and she could hear his patience fracturing. There was a tense frustration threaded through the words.

"We were together that night," she blurted, glancing up to see his reaction. "Intimately."

His eyebrows shot up. But other than that, he showed no reaction, saying nothing for the space of three painfully long heartbeats. She held her breath, waiting.

Then his mouth went tight for a moment and she knew. This wasn't going to go well.

"You took advantage of the amnesia to tell me your own version of events." His voice was level, but there was a flash of emotion in his blue eyes. Anger. Frustration.

Both well deserved.

"I did, and I'm not proud of it." She twisted the ring around her finger, again and again. "That night was my fault. I instigated what happened, and we hadn't even—I didn't even know your name at the time." She still couldn't believe it had happened at all. "I never do things like that. It had been a stressful night, and then we shared a horseback ride over here—that part of what I told you was true."

His jaw flexed as he listened. He did not interrupt. Instead, he waited. Shadows from the fire danced across his face.

She pulled in a shaky breath, her emotions all over the place. "The closeness and the touching... I don't know how to describe what it did to me. But the shoot had been so hellish that day, and then when we touched—"

"Why?" he demanded, cutting through her confusion and guilt with one simple question.

"Why did things ignite so fast? I don't know, we just—"

"No. Why was the shoot hellish?" he asked more gently. "Because of the director? Because of the long hours in the hay that day?"

She'd told him those details. Had shared everything right up until he'd taken her back to the cabin.

Her thumb traced the silver loops in the eternity knot. She couldn't share the impotent fury she felt every time she looked at Antonio Ventura, let alone took direction from him. She couldn't confide her sister's pain when Hope wanted more than anything to keep her ordeal private.

It tore Hannah up inside, because the secret hurt her, too. But it was a pain she could never share when Hope's was a thousand times greater.

"Yes," Hannah lied, blinking fast and hating herself. "Ventura is mercurial, and the churlishness of his demands make this business far harder than it has to be."

That much was true. But it certainly didn't give a glimpse of the real torment of her time on location in Cheyenne, the burden of it lightened only by Brock's presence. Her time with him had given her something good to savor in spite of everything ugly around her.

Still, her throat burned, the weight of what she couldn't say weighing down her conscience even as she shared.

"Hannah, look at me." Brock's voice wound around her, his hand sliding over hers in an unexpected touch.

"I didn't tell you about what happened between us because it felt like a second chance for me to...not get so carried away again." Her pulse thrummed faster, nerves knotting with agitation. "I thought if you forgot it, I would, too, and we'd both move on."

"But here we are. Right back where we started that night." His thumb brushed back and forth over her palm.

The tenderness of his touch caught her off guard.

"You should be raging at me for deceiving you all this time." She willed away the flare of heat that came with his caress. "I should have told you the truth."

"Yes. But I can think of a few times in my life that I would have grabbed the chance to rewrite history." The warmth in his voice soothed her soul. "That's forgivable, Hannah."

Not daring to believe her ears, she searched for some sign she may have misunderstood him. But the expression on his face appeared open and honest, his body language open and relaxed.

And hot.

With his bow tie loosened and the top button unfastened on his shirt, he looked enticingly disheveled. His broad shoulders filled out his jacket, the fabric stretching around his biceps as he leaned forward to touch her. His intent was unmistakable.

"Is it truly forgivable?" Her heart skipped a beat.

She hadn't even considered a scenario where Brock would want to pick up where they'd left off. She melted inside a little to think there might still be a way for them to be together.

A future that included a second chance.

"It is. The question I want you to consider is, now that you have a chance to rewrite history, do you still want to forget what we shared ever happened?" He lifted his hand to her face, grazing the back of one knuckle along her jaw. "Or do you want to relive that memory?"

Brock breathed in the scent of her, relishing the way her pupils dilated at his touch. The firelight gave her pale hair a burnished glow, her cheeks even more flushed color.

He could tell she was surprised that he wasn't more upset with her. But he searched inside himself and found only...relief. Now, he knew what she'd been keeping from him. He understood the shadows in her eyes sometimes, the nagging sense that she'd been holding something back.

Hearing what that secret had been, that she'd second-guessed herself after being with him, was a weight off his shoulders. A worry off his mind. That, he could deal with. He could still see a way forward with her. And hell yes, he still wanted her.

"Are you...sure?" She placed a hand over his where he touched her cheek, holding his fingers captive while her eyes tracked his, searching for answers. "That is, yes, I would relive the memory with you. But it's still not fair to you since you don't remember us together."

Her "yes" rang through him, igniting a primal, chest-thumping roar inside. It felt like he'd been waiting for her forever. He'd hardly slept after the dinner at his house. After the meteor shower and the kiss under the stars. She'd invaded his every thought. Dominated his dreams.

"I've imagined it so many times, it's almost real." He tugged her hand to his lips and kissed the backs of her fingers. Lingered on the base of her thumb where he could feel her pulse race. "Besides, how many people get to have a 'first time' all over again?"

She tipped her head to one side, her hair falling away to reveal the vulnerable skin of her neck. More places he wanted to taste her.

"I'm not sure if we can top the *first* first time." Her

fingers walked up his chest, slipping under the tuxedo jacket.

"I love a good challenge." His blood surged hot as he envisioned how things might have happened that night after he'd brought her home. "But tonight is going to have a whole different feel to it since we know each other better now. I've had a lot of time to think about us. To plot the best approach."

He brushed a kiss over the base of her throat and down to her shoulder, sweeping aside the strap of her silky gown for a better taste. She edged closer to him, her knee bumping his, her thigh pressing against him.

Heat seared him. He wrapped her in his arms, dragging her into his lap. She was so soft and fragrant, her hair and her dress tickling and teasing when he wanted to strip everything away and sink inside her.

Already, her fingers were at the fastenings on his shirt. He shrugged out of his jacket for her and realized they'd never pull this off here, on the couch. At least, not the way he wanted.

Lifting her in his arms, he carried her toward the only bedroom in the place. He knew the layout. But there was also something familiar about stepping into the darkened bedroom with her. Almost as if the memory wanted to surface.

For a moment, he chased it. But then, what did it matter compared to the here and now?

Gently, he set her on her feet. She'd kicked off her shoes at some point, her bare toes visible in the moonlight slanting through the blinds. He wanted to see her better, and he reached back to flick the wall switch that worked the fireplace here.

Another action that felt familiar.

"Brock?" Hannah's hand stilled on his chest; his shirt was already half off. "Are you okay?"

He fought off the déjà vu that wasn't real since he didn't remember that first night with her. Instead, he focused on her lips swollen from his kiss. Her dress already sliding off one shoulder where the strap had fallen, a hint of pink lace visible along with the curve of her breast.

Hannah waited, breathing in the scent of Brock's aftershave, a woodsy spice that she knew would make her knees weak for the rest of her days. He seemed on board with being together, but it worried her that his hand had gone to his temple. A pain? It hadn't been that long ago that he took a blow to the head.

"I'm better than okay," he assured her, lifting both her hands and twining his fingers through hers as he kissed his way down her neck. "I'm so damned good I might die from it."

His words vibrated along her neck, sending ribbons of pleasure down her back and making her skin tingle. Her breasts pebbled, the heat between her thighs impossible to ignore.

Just like the first time. Things were getting out of hand so fast she couldn't even keep track of all the ways he made her feel delicious. Feminine. Wanted.

Before she could ask for more, he was unfastening the other strap on her dress, lowering the bodice and feasting on one taut nipple right through the lace bra she wore. Sensation coiled tighter. Hotter. She gripped his shoulders, nails digging in lightly before she caught herself and eased up.

With a growl, he shrugged the rest of the way out of

his shirt, his chest a pure pleasure to see and touch. Her hands roamed all over him, feeling every inch while he unzipped the rest of her dress. When the silk pooled at her feet, she tipped him back on the white duvet, falling on top of him and pinning him to the mattress.

For a moment, he watched her in the firelight, his blue gaze tracking her every move as she kissed her way down his chest to trace the muscles of his abs.

Hannah hadn't expected their new first time together to be even more intense. But it was. Mind-blowingly so. And she intended to savor every second of it.

She worked the clasp of his belt with anxious fingers while he unhooked her bra with a clever flick. She took all new pleasure from the feel of his hot skin against her bare breasts as she slid off his pants. His boxers.

But then, a new light flared in his eyes, his shoulders tensing as sweat rose along his back. He flipped her so that she was beneath him, pinning her there while he kissed her. And kissed her.

When both of their breathing had turned ragged, he pulled himself away long enough to find a condom in a pocket of his jacket. She didn't wait for him to undress her. She eased the lace panties down with a swivel of her hips and a little help from one hand, savoring the way he watched.

Desperately hungry to have him.

He sheathed himself, and she was so incredibly ready. He kneed apart her thighs, positioning himself between them, driving himself...home.

The cry she made was a sound she didn't recognize, a throaty moan of completion when they were only just beginning. She wrapped her legs around him, losing herself in him. In this moment.

In a "first time" that, yes, was even better than the first time.

She stroked her fingers through his hair, whispering in his ear how much she liked every single thing he did to her, asking for more, giving him everything in return.

The sensations heightened even when she thought they couldn't possibly go higher. Her heels dug into his hips, her arms wrapping around him to hold him close. When he reached between them to stroke the juncture of her thighs, right where she needed him most, she went utterly still. A riot of sensation crashed through her, waves of pleasure coursing so hard she could only close her eyes and hold on.

Before she could even think how to give him that incredible sensual gift in return, he found his own peak. His thighs tensed, his shoulders and arms going rigid with the same bliss that had rolled over her.

She kissed his neck and chest, clinging to him. Lost with him.

She hadn't imagined he would possibly give her a second chance after the secret she'd kept from him, but the real possibility of more with him tantalized her now. Defenses nonexistent, she let herself feel all the delicious aftermath of being with him. The secret, joyful hope that this could be...everything.

When he rolled to her side, taking her with him to lie next to him, she tucked into his chest as if they'd been sleeping together for a lifetime. The rightness of the moment surrounding her, she savored the first sense of total well-being since the night her sister came home in tears.

The memory struck a painful note, but she pushed it to the side, promising herself she was going to find a way to avenge Hope. If anything, she felt stronger than ever in the shelter of Brock's arms.

Surely Hope would understand how much Brock meant to Hannah, and give her blessing to share the last of the secret Hannah had kept from him.

She was everything he ever wanted.

Even in his dreams, Brock relived the night with Hannah. The haze of slumber and sensation drew him deeper in, immersing him in her with an intensity that made him loath to wake up...

He lifted her in his arms, skimming off the scrap of blue lace around her hips before he pulled her down to the white duvet with him.

She made soft, sexy sounds of approval in his ear as she speared her fingers into his hair and drew him down to kiss her. Shadows flickered across the bed beside them in the firelight, the need for her—for this— ratcheting higher.

He'd never bedded a woman so fast. Never imagined a night like this where desire smoked away reason and sensual hunger roared with predatory demand. But Hannah was right there with him, her hands shifting lower to smooth down his chest, back up his arms. All the while she urged him faster, whispering soft commands to touch her. Taste her.

He couldn't get enough of her...

Waking with a start, Brock glanced down to see Hannah asleep by him, her blond hair covering her shoulder like a blanket. He eased aside the strands to stare down at her in sleep, the remnants of his dream still clinging to the edges of his memory.

Their night together had been incredible. But as his

gaze snagged on her pink lace panties on the end of the
bed, he thought back to his dream. He'd been so sure
they were blue.

He could picture them perfectly. Bright, peacock blue.
Even her bra had been blue.

Not pink.

Head aching, a rush of images assailed him. Of a
horseback ride with Hannah. She was wearing a dark T-
shirt, a black ball cap and a pair of leggings that helped
him to feel every nuance of her curves when they'd been
on the horse.

It wasn't a dream. It was reality. A memory.

He remembered.

The realization was so welcome, such a relief, he
nearly woke her up to share the good news. Except
that, with his memory came a sucker punch that landed
squarely in his chest.

He'd gone to see her on set the morning after their
first time, specifically to ask her about her guarded reaction to learning his name. He recalled vividly that Hannah had been upset to learn he was a McNeill. Why?

He'd asked her point-blank.

She hadn't been honest with him then. And she sure
as hell hadn't told him the whole truth now. As much as
he wanted it not to matter—it did.

Shifting away from her, he needed to get to the bottom of it. Before he could wake her, however, his cell
phone vibrated on the nightstand. Lifting it, he saw a
text from his oldest brother, Cody.

The words on the screen couldn't have shocked him
more. The private investigator the family had hired
wanted to talk to Hannah.

Twelve

"Hannah." Brock heard the ice in his voice but was powerless to fix it. Soften it. The realizations about Hannah were too damning. "We need to get dressed."

Already stepping out of bed, he had no choice but to slide on his tuxedo pants and shirt from the wedding.

"What's going on?" she asked sleepily, sitting up in bed, the sheet clutched to her.

"Two things." He buttoned the tuxedo shirt with impatient fingers, needing to get outside into the fresh air. Clear his head. "First, Cody asked us to come to the Black Creek Ranch main house. There have been some developments in the blackmail case, and apparently the private investigator has asked to speak to you."

He watched as she came fully awake, her face draining of color. "Me?"

"Yes." He grabbed his shoes and headed for the door. "And in other news, I've got my memory back."

He didn't wait to hear her reaction or her explanations. He couldn't process what was happening or why she was doing this to him, drawing him back into her life when she had purposely tried to distance herself from him after he'd gotten amnesia. Right now, all he could think about was getting to his brother's house fast and finally getting to the bottom of the scandal, the blackmail and—most painful of all to him personally—Hannah Ryder's deceit.

An hour later, the whole family had gathered in Cody's great room. It had cathedral ceilings and a stone fireplace that went up to the second floor, the room's tall windows letting the morning sun in on three sides.

Brock stood at the window while his brothers spoke in low voices with Dax, the private investigator who'd taken over the legwork on the blackmail investigation for the family. Hannah had attached herself to Emma and Jillian as soon as they'd arrived, which was just as well since Brock couldn't think of a single thing to say to her until he knew what was going on with the investigation.

She still hadn't been honest with him. Even after the performance she'd given the night before—the insistence that she had come clean with him. Why had she even bothered when she was still withholding information?

She'd pulled on black leggings and a long gray T-shirt and tucked her hair in a ponytail before they'd left. She was sharing a cushioned ottoman with Emma near the fireplace. Madeline and Maisie put out some of the food they'd planned to serve at today's post-wedding breakfast for out-of-towners—pastries and sweet rolls—along with coffee and fruit. Not that Brock was hungry. But the scent of cinnamon and dark roast hung in the air from the kitchen island that lined one side of the great room. His father helped himself to a plate while they waited for Scarlett and Logan, the last to arrive. As the pair walked in the door, Dax—an Ironman competitor who used his digital forensics background in his work as an investigator—strode to the middle of the room.

"Thank you all for coming." The guy looked like he hadn't slept. There were shadows under his eyes, and his gray T-shirt and jeans were both wrinkled. "To bring you up to speed, the police arrested Emma's mother, Jane Layton, last night for trespassing on the Black Creek Ranch property."

Brock turned to look at Carson's girlfriend where the stuntwoman sat beside Hannah. Hannah squeezed Emma's hand while Carson stood behind her, his hands on her shoulders. Judging by her calm expression, Emma already knew about her mother's arrest. And now that Brock's memory had returned, he recalled meeting her, as well as her announcement that she feared her mother was the blackmailer. He had no idea why she believed that, however. He'd left his father's house early that night, unable to make sense of anything with his amnesia.

The investigator flipped pages in a notepad, his eyes scanning the small pages as he continued. "Jane is being held in custody as a person of interest in the blackmail case, and I'm close to having some additional evidence to share with police. But before I delve into that, Paige and Donovan have asked me to reveal a few things about Paige's past to help orient you."

Behind Dax, Cody was ushering his pregnant girlfriend into a chair at the kitchen counter and sliding a plate of fruit in front of her.

Seeing his brothers both so damned happy and in love only underscored the hole burning in Brock's chest this morning.

"Eden Harris voluntarily left home at age seventeen with the help of her stepmother, Stella Ventura." Dax nodded at Paige before turning back to the rest of the family. "Stella covered for her absence by assuring Eden's father, Emilio, that she'd left with her mother, Barbara. Stella also helped Eden disappear by putting her in touch with someone who gave her new identification papers and Social Security number so that she could become Paige Samara."

Brock was glad to learn of the logistics. He'd wondered how it was possible for a seventeen-year-old heiress to vanish, but clearly, his stepmother had help. His gaze drifted to Hannah, wondering if any of this was a surprise to her, or if she'd already known. Resentment simmered at the thought she may have used him to get close to his family.

Cody spoke up from his place near Jillian. "Paige has asked that we respect her privacy about why she left, and we're going to do that. Dad's lawyers are already working with a government agency to help her avoid any legal trouble since she used the false name and Social Security number under duress. But we thought it was important that we all understand who helped her to leave, and who was aware of her new identity, since that narrowed the field of possible blackmailers."

Close to where he stood, Brock noticed Scarlett's thinly veiled impatience. She shuffled from one foot to another and looked ready to speak until Logan King slid an arm around her waist. She seemed to settle down then, tucking close while the investigator took over the story.

Dax paced in front of the fireplace, his leather loafers creaking softly in the quiet as he tugged a pencil out from the wire ring of his notebook. "No one knew about Eden's new identity but Stella and, Stella realized afterward, her maid Jane Layton, who had overheard some of what transpired the day Eden left home."

Brock's focus shifted to Hannah in time to see her bite her lip. Did she know something? But just then, Emma squared her shoulders and sat forward on the ottoman.

"My mother has battled bipolar disorder since I was very young," Emma explained. "I've always known she had an affair with Emilio Ventura, Paige's father, but I wasn't aware until recently that she tried to tell Mr. Ventura that I was his daughter. That's definitely not the case, by the way. I bear a strong resemblance to my father, who passed away a long time ago. But I think my mother might have tried to taunt Mrs. Ventura with the affair and with the idea that I could be Emilio's biological child."

Behind Emma, Carson shook his head. "None of that gives Jane a motive for blackmailing the McNeills, though." He cast a thoughtful glance over toward Paige. "Unless she thought Paige would pay to keep her secret quiet?"

Paige appeared unruffled. Relaxed even. Brock wondered if having her secret finally out had given her a new sense of peace. Certainly, she seemed happier than he could ever remember seeing her.

She finally weighed into the discussion. "Carson, I'll tell you what I already explained to Dax. I have no memory of Jane, either by sight or even by name. You have to remember, I was only a teen at the time, and I didn't grow up in my father's house. I simply stayed there for a few years when my mother was unwell."

"I met him, Mom," Scarlett blurted, straightening from her spot beside her actor boyfriend. "Your father, that is. And for what it's worth, I think he really misses you."

The two of them stared at one another, a silent conversation going on between them that Brock didn't begin to understand. Frustration built inside him; his shoulders pulled tight as he ground his teeth. He was tired of waiting for answers.

"So where does that leave us? Is Jane the blackmailer or not?" He was being abrupt, maybe, but his family had been dealing with too much these last weeks. Hell, *he'd* been dealing with too much trying to recover from amnesia while his family publicly fell apart at the seams. "And what does Hannah have to do with any of it?"

He heard her quick intake of breath, even from the other side of the room. No doubt he was still far too in tune with her, too aware of her every move. Breaking that bond was going to hurt, but it would be critical to moving forward.

Dax gave him a level look, a hint of displeasure on his face. Perhaps Brock had upset the guy's flow. Or maybe he'd wanted to speak to Hannah privately. But whatever it was, Dax recovered quickly enough.

"Much of what we have to tie Jane to the blackmail scheme is circumstantial, but it will be stronger once we eliminate any other possible connections between *Winning the West* and the Ventura family." Dax pointed to Scarlett's boyfriend with the chewed end of his yellow pencil. "Logan King has already spoken with me at length about his experiences with Antonio Ventura, and he has a firm alibi to clear him. The only other person with access to both the Venturas and the McNeills, as well as an interest in the movie, is Hannah Ryder."

All eyes turned toward her.

For a moment, Hannah wondered if the investigator would have tried questioning her in front of the whole group if Brock hadn't practically encouraged him to do just that. Not that it mattered. Helping her sister had somehow connected her to a blackmail investigation, and she couldn't impede a criminal case because of Hope's need for privacy.

She just wished she didn't have to speak about it in front of the whole family.

It hurt even more knowing that she was in this position because a man she'd trusted with her heart didn't trust her at all. But if she allowed herself to think about that now, she wouldn't be able to keep her composure through the questions. She was keeping herself together now by only sheer force of will.

"I can explain." Hannah stood, nervous energy making her want to pace. Or fidget. Her acting training wouldn't allow her to give in to that impulse. She understood the nuances of body language. "I was actively researching the Ventura family two months ago, and I briefly worked with a temp agency cleaning their home. I saw photos of Eden Harris and her mother in Emilio Ventura's study, and Jane Layton made an unusual remark about them that helped me link Eden with Mrs. McNeill."

"Why would you research the Ventura family?" Brock asked tightly. "You never mentioned that last night."

Hannah heard the disdain in his voice. Brock thought

she was deceitful. A liar. And that hurt after what they'd shared.

Swallowing back the pain, she focused on the investigator instead. "I can explain why I did that, but since my story involves someone else, someone who wouldn't want her name mentioned, I would ask that you let me share the rest of it privately."

She waited for Dax's reply, prepared to answer his questions to the best of her ability. Maybe it would even be a relief to share with someone. The stress of what Hope had gone through had eaten away at both of them this year.

When the investigator nodded his approval, Brock crossed his arms over his chest.

"How convenient."

His cold words froze her feet to the hardwood floor, preventing her from following Dax into the dining area.

Mute with hurt and an anger of her own, she stared him down in front of his family. Willing her jaw to unclench, she said, "Excuse me?"

"You don't think I deserve to know what else you've been hiding from me?"

Before she could answer, Paige McNeill stood. "Brock, please. Has it ever occurred to you she might need to protect someone?"

Gratitude filled Hannah's chest, a soothing balm, even if it would never fully ease the hurt of Brock's mistrust. Blinking away the sudden threat of tears, Hannah looked over at Paige. Really looked at her.

And something in the set of the older woman's chin, the tone of her voice, even the wringing of her hands, made Hannah think of her sister. It was a flash. An instinct. But in that moment, she knew without question why Eden Harris had run from the Ventura home. Why Eden had become Paige Samara McNeill and never looked back.

She'd been hurt once, too. By the same bastard who had hurt Hope.

"Thank you, Mrs. McNeill," Hannah murmured, hurrying past them to follow the PI into the dining room on the other side of the huge foyer. At the threshold, she paused, her heart thumping. She glanced back at the room full of Brock's family. And at Brock himself.

He stared out the front window, his expression inscrutable. He hadn't followed her, giving her the space that his stepmother had wanted him to. Hannah understood she'd hurt him. That in protecting her sister, she'd done deep damage to her fledgling relationship with someone she really cared for.

And maybe she'd done all she could to protect Hope now. She'd protected her sister's privacy as much as she could, even when it cost her a chance at something that could have been...so much more. Later, she would call Hope and ask for her forgiveness. Her understanding. But now, Hannah called back to the man she'd given her heart to, offering him the answers he craved. Already knowing it was too late for them.

"Brock?" She watched as his head came up. Their gazes locked, and his detached expression killed her a little inside. The hurt of what they'd lost left her breathless as she called back to him, "You're welcome to join us."

Maybe a better man would have simply trusted her, taking it on faith that her secrets were her own and didn't have any bearing on their relationship.

But Brock had been burned before. Not just by his ex-girlfriend, but by Hannah herself. Just yesterday she'd admitted she'd been lying to him. How was he supposed to take today's revelation that there were even more holes in her story? That she had some kind of connection to the Ventura family that she'd never mentioned.

So hell yes, Brock followed Hannah into the dining room, taking a seat near her as she began talking to the PI.

The story that came out made him half wish he'd never heard it. Not because the truth implicated Hannah. Far from it. His stepmother had understood the subtext of all that Hannah hadn't said, and as Hannah spelled out Antonio Ventura's crimes against her younger sister, the shattering facts made Brock fear what his stepmother had gone through living in the same household as Antonio.

It became all too clear that Antonio's sister—related only through adoption—had probably been his first sexual assault victim. And over twenty-five years later, the bastard was still getting away with taking advantage of young women who didn't have the resources or support system to take on a powerful man.

His first instinct, before Hannah had even finished giving her account, was to rally his brothers and inflict as much damage on Ventura as possible. But he knew that wasn't the way to stop a serial predator. Furthermore, he'd implied a level of discretion and respect for Hope Ryder's privacy by even setting foot in the room with Hannah as she spoke to the PI.

Now, like Hannah before him, he carried the weight of an ugly truth that wasn't his to share. But he would do everything in his power to leverage his resources and influence in a way that would help convince women to come forward. Perhaps even starting with his step-mother.

But first? He needed to find a way to talk to Hannah. To make some kind of amends for his lack of trust. Judging by the way she fled the dining room as soon as the private investigator assured her he had enough information, Brock didn't think she was going to give him that chance willingly.

Damn it.

He stood up fast, following her out into the living area. His father pointed wordlessly to the front door. And, out the huge windows, Brock could see her blond ponytail bouncing as she hurried away from the house with determined steps.

He needed to follow her. To apologize for not having faith in her. But first, he needed his whole family to understand one thing.

"Carson." Brock slid out of his dress loafers from the wedding, and grabbed a pair of boots by the door, not much caring who they belonged to. "I know you signed a contract with that movie production company. And it's fine if the movie films here, but not as long as Antonio Ventura is attached to the project. If he remains the director, we're going to shut the whole thing down, whatever the cost."

Donovan nodded tersely from his spot on the couch beside Paige, his arm tightening around his wife. "I will pay for the lawyers. Hell, I'll finance a whole army of them if that's what it takes."

Brock wondered how much his father knew about the director of *Winning the West*. He guessed Donovan didn't know the full story either, or Antonio would have met with a mysterious hunting accident a week ago.

"Thanks, Dad." He spared a quick glance at Paige, and a spear of guilt cleaved him in half for all the time she'd spent leading a quiet life, out of the spotlight, when she'd been an heiress in her own right. She'd been in hiding from a monster for too long, and it was going to end now.

He stepped over to the couch long enough to lean down and press a kiss to his stepmother's cheek. "You were right about Hannah. I love you, Mom."

Then, turning on the heel of his borrowed boots, he headed out the door, determined to find Hannah—and find a way to make things right between them.

Thirteen

Hannah had ridden over to the Black Creek Ranch with Brock, so she had no choice but to walk back to her cabin.

Not that she minded. She welcomed the fresh air after the intense family meeting with the investigator and then, the more private discussion with Dax while Brock listened. Telling Hope's story had taken a lot out of her, but she was glad to have shared the truth. Now, she planned to pack her things and fly home as soon as possible.

Her sister didn't want her here anyhow, and she was worried about leaving Hope alone for much longer. If quitting the film ruined her career in acting, she truly didn't care. She would rather go broke fighting a legal battle to break her contract than spend another day taking orders from her sister's molester. Being in Wyoming this week had given her a taste for the life she'd rather be living anyhow. One that involved midnight stargazing and walks in the country. Horseback rides.

Her heart ached at the thought of that. She knew she'd never have a ride quite like the one she'd had with Brock.

"Hannah, wait."

The voice behind her was unexpected. And feminine.

Not that she planned to see Brock before she left, but she certainly hadn't cultivated personal ties with anyone else in his family.

Hannah shielded her eyes to see Brock's youngest sister, Scarlett, hurrying toward her. They had spoken briefly at the wedding the day before, just enough for Hannah to learn that Scarlett was excited about her move to Los Angeles and starting her own career in acting. Hannah had invited the younger woman to stay in touch after the filming ended in case she needed any advice. They'd do a lunch date.

And while the offer had been heartfelt, Hannah didn't think she could make small talk with her heart breaking. As Scarlett reached her side, Hannah turned to keep walking.

"I'm sorry, Scarlett, but I need to get back home." She stared down at the worn tire tracks she was following, grass encroaching on both sides. Cicadas made a high-pitched buzz while the sun beat down. "This morning has left me wrung out. Empty."

"My brother was out of line back there." Scarlett doubled her pace in order to keep time with Hannah's determined march.

"He's entitled to his opinion." She blinked at the burning in her eyes. Beneath her feet, the grass got blurry and she cursed herself for crying over something she couldn't change.

"Not when it's so wrongheaded." Scarlett took her hand and gripped it tight, forcing Hannah to stop unless she wanted to drag Brock's sister with her. "Men aren't always on our wavelength. At least, my brothers aren't. Brock can tell you the kind of mood a horse is in the moment he walks in the barn. But a woman? Not so much."

Hannah laughed. It was a watery yelp without much humor, but she appreciated Scarlett's attempt to defuse the tension. "He's great, actually. I screwed up by trying to hide things from him."

"I get it." Scarlett dug in her bag for a tissue and passed it to her. "And my mom obviously understood what was going on back there, too, which scares me."

"I think she ran away from home because of him."

"Antonio," Scarlett clarified. "His father even admitted to me that he's always worried his adopted son was a 'bully' and that's why Eden never returned home."

"I'd call him far worse than a bully, but I really can't share any more—" There was a vibration under her feet that surprised her. Then a horse and rider came into view from around a bend.

Brock sat tall in the saddle on Aurora's back, his tuxedo shirt open at the neck, the sleeves rolled up to his forearms, his black dress trousers tucked into dark leather boots. Her thoughts, and her gaze, stayed glued to him.

"Hannah." Scarlett squeezed her hand to get her attention. "I just wanted you to know that I'll talk to my mother. She's not a scared seventeen-year-old anymore. She's a woman of considerable power if she'll step up and own it. And I feel sure she will."

Hannah tore her eyes away from Brock. "What are you saying?"

Scarlett gave her a level look. She had a feminine flair in her dress, and an almost girlish beauty with her curls and wide blue eyes. But there was an absolute certainty about her, a grit and pride that only a fool would mistake.

"I'm saying Paige McNeill is an heiress two times over, and her word will carry weight in the court of public opinion. If we can get her to condemn Antonio, it's going to be vindication for whoever you're trying to protect."

Hannah thought about what she was saying. If Paige spoke out against Antonio, shared her own story, it could be career-ending for the director. Hope would see some justice served even if she never brought charges.

But maybe, if she saw others speak out against him, she would, too.

In her peripheral vision, Hannah saw Brock dismount the horse and begin walking their way.

"That would be...amazing," Hannah admitted, nerves jangling at the thought of talking to Brock. "Thank you."

It would make her trip to Cheyenne well worth it if she accomplished what she'd set out to—to let the world know that Antonio Ventura was a sorry excuse for a human being who did not deserve his vaunted place in the film industry.

Scarlett gave her an encouraging smile before backing up a step. "I'm going to start my campaign with Mom right now."

Brock's sister stalked off in the direction she'd come from, toward the ranch house that was now out of sight. That left Hannah very much alone with the man who'd condemned her in front of his whole family.

"I'm leaving," she told him, stuffing the tissue that

Scarlett had given her into the pocket of the drapey, gray yoga shirt she'd thrown on this morning with her leggings. "I think that will be best for both of us."

She had fresh clothes on while Brock wore his recycled tuxedo shirt and pants, yet he still managed to look like a brooding lord out of a Jane Austen novel.

"That won't be good for me at all, Hannah, and I'm sorry that I've put you in a position where you feel like that would be best for you."

He sounded so sincere. And maybe he was. But it didn't change the things that had happened between them. It didn't mean he would ever trust her.

She dragged the toe of her running shoe through the grass, thinking she was going to miss the wide-open spaces here. The never-ending blue sky. She wished Hope could have seen it.

"In the end, we had different loyalties. My family had to come first for me. They—she—always will." She felt teary again and she needed to keep walking. Keep moving. "I'm in a hurry to get back now that I've made the decision. Do you mind if we continue walking?"

Brock whistled for the horse and the mare followed at an easy pace, nosing in the grass now and then.

"I know I overreacted today," he told her as they strode deeper into the wooded area along the creek. "Everything has been so intense this week. Ever since we met, I've had a scandal hanging over my head, and a blackmailer to catch. Then, the amnesia made it ten times harder to be any help to my family when they needed me most. So when my memory came back this morning and it still felt like you'd left things out, I didn't handle it well."

"You're protective of your family. I'm protective of

mine. It put us at odds today." And that broke her heart as she thought of what could have been between them if things had been different.

"It wouldn't always." He snapped a dead branch from a nearby tree and tossed it deeper into the woods, away from the trail. "That is, it doesn't have to."

She weighed the words as she allowed them to sink in, wondering if she was understanding him correctly, unable to squelch a flash of hope. Hope was scary, too, because she wanted to be a part of his life, to have more of those horseback rides and nights under the stars with him.

"I don't know what you mean." She picked up her speed, wishing she could outrun the hurt of losing him.

"I admire that you put your family first, even at the cost of you and me." He bent sideways to pick a tall Indian paintbrush, never slowing his step. "But how many times in a life does something like this come up? How often would family put us on opposite sides?"

Hannah shook her head. "Maybe never. But what does it matter when we've already broken this fragile thing we were building? When you've already shown me how quick you are to not believe me? You threw me under the bus back there, Brock."

"Like an idiot," he agreed, his boots following the worn path of one tire track while she remained on the other, a strip of high grass between them. "But just so you understand, I was thinking of my family, too. I assumed you were an enemy to the McNeills when the investigator wanted to ask you about the blackmail scheme. I didn't believe that for long. And if I'd had more time to think about it, I would have known you'd never hurt my family."

She thought about that, trying to see things from his perspective. Wondering where all of this was leading.

"So you want to call a truce? Shake hands before I leave and part on amiable terms?" She stopped walking, needing answers. "Please tell me what you hoped to accomplish by following me out here, Brock, because— in spite of what you think—I have no love for secrets. I'd prefer we speak plainly. Put our cards on the table."

Behind them, Aurora stopped to nuzzle through some grass. Hannah watched her because it was easier than looking at Brock, with his dark whiskers shadowing his jaw. She had too many memories of last night every time their eyes met.

"You want it plainly," he said. "Here it is."

She felt the soft brush of flower petals against her cheek as he encouraged her gaze. When she turned to see him, he tucked the stalk of Indian paintbrush in her pocket.

"I let one bad relationship color the way that I saw you, Hannah, and I'm sorry." He stepped closer as they faced off across the tall grass. "I pride myself on never making the same mistake twice, though, so if you could ever find it in your heart to forgive me and give me another chance, I promise I'd never hurt you that way again."

A bird chirped an optimistic song overhead, urging her to take a chance. To feel hope, and maybe even happiness.

The pull was so damn strong. Brock looked at her like she was the only woman in the world who mattered to him. The temptation to believe him, believe in the two of them together, was heady stuff.

"Let's suppose for a second that I did that. I said,

okay, we'll try again." Her chest filled with too many feelings just saying the words aloud. Talking to him about this was like lifting the lid on Pandora's box and she was afraid she'd never be able to leave once the conversation started. She shook her head, willing her voice to stay strong. "What would that even look like? Hope lives in Los Angeles and she needs me there. You're a successful rancher with livestock and family who need you here. I just don't see a way to try."

And even as she said it, she found herself hoping he had the answer to make it all work. She couldn't deny that she wanted him in her life.

Brock lifted her hands, taking one in each of his. "Those are logistics. We can work around those. And if it came down to you and Hope wanting to be on the West Coast, I will gladly find a way to be there with you. The quarter horse program won't end if I leave the ranch."

"You would do that for me?" She thought about it for a moment, trying to picture that.

"Without a second thought."

"I never really thought about moving Hope here, though. She might actually be open to a fresh start."

The months of therapy hadn't helped. Maybe a move would give her sister a chance to heal.

"We don't need to decide today. I can fly back and forth until you're sure. But, Hannah, I promise, we could make it work." He squeezed her hands gently in his. "Maybe you could start by calling your sister. See if she wants to visit Cheyenne, just as soon as we get that bastard Ventura off McNeill lands forever."

"I'd like that. And I think Hope would, too." Hannah wanted to close her eyes and hold that vision tight. Hope here with her, finding peace in this beautiful land while she grew strong again. Except if Hannah closed her eyes, then she wouldn't be looking up into the eyes of the man she loved, and she wanted to keep that vision, too.

"Like I said, those are things we can figure out as we go. What matters is if we want to—that is, if *you* want to—try. I already know how badly I want to." He kissed the back of one hand. Then the other. "I'm in love with you, Hannah."

His words shot through her confusion with the precision of Cupid's arrow. The intensity in his blue eyes made her breathless.

"I'm in love with you, too," she admitted, shaking her head, the worries sliding away in light of that one simple fact. "That's why this all was hurting so much."

Relinquishing her hands, Brock wrapped his arms around her and pulled her against him. The tightness in her chest eased, giving away to the warmth of a happiness so full and sweet she thought she might overflow with it.

"I don't want to ever hurt you again," he promised, kissing her hair, her forehead and then, tilting her chin up, her lips. "I'll do whatever it takes to make you happy, and to help keep your sister safe."

She smiled against him, her teeth nudging his as a happy laugh bubbled up. "I trust you to keep that promise."

She wound her arms around his neck, pressing herself fully to him, giving herself over to the kiss.

They lost themselves in it, mouths moving together, until they were both breathless, the promise of a future together stoking passion higher inside her. She gripped his shirt, certain of what she wanted.

A forever with Brock McNeill.

He eased away slowly, tipping his forehead to hers.

"So we are in agreement." He stroked her shoulders, warming her all over with one simple touch.

"Perfectly. I'm going to call Hope just as soon as we get home." She wanted to phone Scarlett, too. She had the feeling Brock's sister was going to be an amazing champion for Hope's cause. "Maybe we can go on horseback?"

Her gaze slid to Aurora, remembering that first night with Brock.

His wicked chuckle told her that he remembered every delicious detail, too.

Epilogue

Nine months later

Hannah's bags were packed. She finished zipping one of the designer suitcases that Brock had given her for Christmas, her brain full of lists and preparations for her first week away from Hope since her sister had moved to Cheyenne with her last fall.

"Are you sure you have everything?" Hope asked from her seat at Hannah's dressing table, where she'd plopped herself with her tablet to oversee the packing. Hope had been working on a screenplay for the past two months, her thirst for writing returning in what her therapist called a good sign of her emotional recovery. "That doesn't look like enough luggage for a Hollywood movie premiere and a vacation in wine country. You're living the McNeill lifestyle now, Hannah. You deserve some extra luxuries," she teased.

Hannah looked into her sister's eyes, grateful every day she saw the spark of happiness flaming brighter and brighter there. Of course, Hannah had a lot to be grateful for lately. Antonio Ventura was facing prison on harassment and molestation charges. To date, over fifty women—including Hannah's friend Callie—had come forward to add their voices to the case after Brock's stepmother had shared her story with the police.

Hope hadn't wanted to share hers publicly yet, and the therapist said they needed to respect her journey. Hope told Hannah she felt vindicated enough that he was behind bars, and she seemed to be thriving in Cheyenne, taking a part-time job exercising horses at the Creek Spill while she completed college classes online. She'd talked about returning to campus next fall, but for now, she had her own suite in Brock and Hannah's home.

"I just don't have the diva instinct, I guess." Hannah had found a joy in the simpler rhythm of the days on the ranch, developing a special affinity for the cowboy boots that had been Brock's "housewarming" present for her when she agreed to move in.

Like Hope, she found plenty to keep her busy helping out with Brock's quarter horses, especially keeping the website updated with photos of the animals in training, and tracking each animal's progress for interested buyers. Brock had said those stories had led to more and better sales for the ranch, so she was contributing. But like her sister, she was contemplating a second act. For Hannah, it might be in producing. She had a strong interest in bringing female-driven stories to the big screen, and it was a job that would give her flexibility, too. Something she'd need for the family she and Brock had talked about.

Hope shut off the screen on her tablet and set it on

the dressing table, folding one foot underneath her. "It's funny that you—a former Hollywood actress—moved to Cheyenne and forgot how to be a diva. While Scarlett—a rancher's daughter—moved to Hollywood and has made a name for herself as the Diva Cowgirl."

Hope was referencing Scarlett's popular social media account that had attracted followers around the globe. Scarlett and Logan King were still a hot item, and Scarlett's date nights always made great photo ops. If Brock wanted to know what his youngest sister was up to, he asked Hope, who could show him up-to-the-minute photos from Scarlett's account.

But there was far more to the Diva Cowgirl than great clothes and glitter makeup. Scarlett had been instrumental in Antonio Ventura's downfall, leading the charge against him in the media. Hannah loved her dearly.

"Diva or not, you'll notice she still comes home most weekends," Hannah reminded her, wanting to plant it in Hope's head that she could return to Cheyenne as often as she liked if she decided to move back to Los Angeles.

"That's mostly because of Charlotte," Hope added, sniffing one of Hannah's perfume bottles. "She's gaga over Cody and Jillian's new baby girl."

Their child was a double blessing since Jillian was a breast cancer survivor who had thought she'd never have children. Mother and baby were both thriving, and shortly after Charlotte had been born, Emma and Carson announced they were expecting, too. Emma had been glowing with happiness when they'd revealed the news over a Sunday dinner with most of the Cheyenne branch of the McNeill family.

Sadly, Emma's mother had turned out to be Paige's blackmailer, but Jane Layton had been found unfit to stand trial and, according to Emma, seemed more at peace now that she was receiving additional care for previously undiagnosed mental health issues.

"Of course she's thrilled. We're all excited for the baby," Hannah agreed just as Brock stepped into her bedroom.

"Who's having a baby?" Brock asked, dressed in a blue suit and white shirt with no tie, more handsome than any Hollywood leading actor, in her opinion.

But then, this was the man who made her heart beat faster with just a look. Like the one he was giving her now. The one that said they shared a secret. Hannah felt warm all over and was grateful when Hope answered for her.

"We're talking about your brother's new baby. Charlotte is too adorable for words, and I think I'll go visit her if you two can ever get out the door to catch your flight." Hope hopped to her feet, heading for Hannah's luggage. "Want me to carry a bag down?"

Laughing, Brock strode past her, gently taking the bag from her hands. "Not a chance. One of the stable workers is going to load the car for me and drive us to the airfield."

"Really?" Hope looked interested and headed for the door. "I hope it's Chad. He's the cutest." She was already hurrying down the hall to look out the front window.

"Are you ready, Hannah, my love?" Brock asked, taking both her hands in his and helping her to her feet. "Are you prepared to go see the premiere of *Winning the West*?"

The production company had done extensive reshooting of the film after Antonio was fired as the director. Hannah had to admire that they hadn't wanted their name—or the film—tainted by association, so she'd stuck it out and reshot her scenes with the new director.

"Now that I'm officially proud to have my name attached to it, yes." She stood in front of him, letting her body graze his, tempting them both with what they would share tonight. "Mostly, I'm looking forward to having you all to myself for a few days."

"How am I going to keep my hands off you in the car ride to the airstrip?" he whispered in her ear, releasing her hand so he could splay one of his along her back.

"Not to mention on the plane." She eased back a step, her arms looped around his neck. "Maybe I'd better behave."

"The plane won't be a problem," Brock assured her. "Didn't I mention we're taking my grandfather's private jet?"

The McNeill patriarch continued to be generous to his Wyoming relatives, flying them all to his spring wedding to Rose Hanson. Hannah had never attended a more romantic ceremony than the union of the dapper octogenarian to the feisty former Harlem torch singer. They were a perfect match.

Hannah smiled, toying with the hair at the nape of his neck. "You didn't say one word about a private jet, Brock McNeill, or I would have remembered."

"It's the first of many surprises I've got planned for you this week," he assured her, his gaze dropping to her lips before he slanted his mouth over hers and kissed her with slow, heart-melting thoroughness.

She would have forgotten about the trip if he had kept going. He still did that to her.

"Do you want to see another one of the surprises?" he asked.

Intrigued, she angled away from him to see his expression. His blue eyes were full of warmth. Love.

He'd kept his promise to make her happy, that's for sure.

"Okay," she said. "Yes."

He reached into his jacket pocket and withdrew a small, velvet box.

Her heart did a backflip. Her gaze was glued to this unexpected gift.

"I think we've really covered the logistics of being together," he told her, his voice serious. Sincere.

"Me, too." Breathless, she remembered that conversation with him nine months ago when she'd first trusted him with her heart.

"These months with you have been the happiest of my life, Hannah. I can't imagine spending another minute without you, knowing how much I want to be with you forever. How much I want to have a family with you." He dropped to one knee in front of her and opened the box as he took her left hand. "Will you make me the happiest man ever and marry me?"

She wasn't sure if the tears in her eyes were making the round diamond look like a huge, glowing crystal ball, or if it was simply that magnificent. But it seemed to emit a light all its own, sparkling with promise in a simple platinum band.

There wasn't a single doubt in her mind.

"Brock, you've made my dreams come true." She wrapped her arms around him again, dragging him to his feet so they could hold each other. She laughed and cried and kissed him all at the same time. "Yes, I can't wait to marry you."

She felt the sigh of relief rocking through him as he

hauled her to his chest. His heart beat fast, too, letting her know just how important this was to him. Their love was a deep, incredible gift. They held each other close for a long moment.

From outside the bedroom, Hannah heard a car horn and her sister shout that their ride was here. Hannah didn't move, though. Not yet. She kissed Brock again with all the love in her heart, knowing their story together was only beginning.

* * * * *

COMING SOON!

We really hope you enjoyed reading this book. If you're looking for more romance, be sure to head to the shops when new books are available on

Thursday
6th September

To see which titles are coming soon, please visit
millsandboon.co.uk

LET'S TALK

Romance

For exclusive extracts, competitions
and special offers, find us online:

 facebook.com/millsandboon

@millsandboonuk

@millsandboon

Or get in touch on 0844 844 1351*

For all the latest titles coming soon, visit
millsandboon.co.uk/nextmonth

*Calls cost 7p per minute plus your phone company's price per minute access charge